WHILE
GALILEO
PREYS

Look for Joshua Corin's next novel

BEFORE CAIN STRIKES

available April 2011
from MIRA Books

Joshua Corin

WHILE
GALILEO
PREYS

MIRA®

MIRA®

Recycling programs
for this product may
not exist in your area.

ISBN-13: 978-0-7783-2811-7

WHILE GALILEO PREYS

Copyright © 2010 by Joshua Corin.

All rights reserved. Except for use in any review, the reproduction or
utilization of this work in whole or in part in any form by any electronic,
mechanical or other means, now known or hereafter invented, including
xerography, photocopying and recording, or in any information storage or
retrieval system, is forbidden without the written permission of the publisher,
MIRA Books, 225 Duncan Mill Road, Don Mills, Ontario M3B 3K9, Canada.

This is a work of fiction. Names, characters, places and incidents are
either the product of the author's imagination or are used fictitiously, and
any resemblance to actual persons, living or dead, business establishments,
events or locales is entirely coincidental.

For questions and comments about the quality of this book please contact us
at Customer_eCare@Harlequin.ca.

MIRA and the Star Colophon are trademarks used under license and registered
in Australia, New Zealand, Philippines, United States Patent and Trademark
Office and in other countries.

www.MIRABooks.com

Printed in U.S.A.

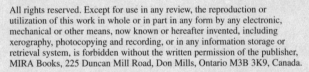

To my nephew Benji
(for when he is much, much older)

1

The bum wore pink. A prom dress, really. Torso to kneecaps swathed in bubble-gum taffeta. His spidery limbs, black with grime and hair, jutted out in wrong angles. The bum was facedown in the basin of a puddle in the middle of MLK Drive, and lay undiscovered until 3:16 a.m.

Andre Banks (age twenty-eight) and his pug Moira (age three) were out for a stroll. Andre was walking off his insomnia. His parents were coming to visit and that never ever boded well. Andre and Moira normally kept only to Lincoln Street, the dimly-lit cul-de-sac in which they lived, but the young man had a lot more anxiety than usual to walk off. Moira made sure to baptize every hydrant on their path, and was christening her eleventh when Andre spotted the bum in the road.

Even in Atlanta, January meant freezing temperatures. The city's homeless did not nap out in the middle of MLK Drive in January, certainly not in brand-new prom dresses. The bum was almost perfectly centered inside the milky oval of a nearby streetlight's humming glow. Andre stared through the fog of his breath at the man in the road and then Moira, finished with her ritual, saw him too, and barked.

Prodded by his loud little dog, Andre left the sidewalk and approached the facedown man. He didn't bother checking for traffic because A. It was 3:16 in the morning. B. This stretch of MLK Drive was cordoned at either end by wooden barricades due to (unapparent) DOT construction.

Moira skittered a few feet ahead of him, tensing at her leash, impatient to reach the mysterious pink shape. She barked again, and hopped up, giddy. The shape didn't budge. As they entered the circle of electric-powered light, Andre wondered what circumstances led the bum to end up here, (and dressed like that!). Had the man once been successful? Did he have a family? Had his family kicked him out? Maybe the prom dress was his daughter's and she was dead and wearing it helped the man remember her. Maybe the bum was a transvestite, and that's why his family had kicked him out. The sins of a stubborn family, mused Andre, never forgetting that his own parents, bastions of disappointment, would be landing at Hartsfield-Jackson in ten hours and—

Moira pounced on top of the bum's taffeta back and licked at his neck.

"Hey!" Andre tugged on the leather leash. "Bad dog."

With a petulant whine, Moira fought back. She lapped again at the bum's neck, savoring the salt mine she'd discovered. Andre yanked his pug off the man, and then realized the bum in the road hadn't reacted, hadn't even groaned, hadn't even *breathed*.

"Fuck," Andre concluded, and at 3:18 a.m. (according to his cell phone) he dialed the police.

They didn't arrive for twenty minutes. This cordoned-off stretch of MLK Drive was not popular. The strip malls and chain stores which populated MLK down by the Georgia Dome tapered off west of Techwood, and Andre's neighborhood was far, far west of Techwood. The grass in the local park, fifty feet from the bum's corpse, was rusted, as if neglect had soured it to old metal. One hundred feet away, bordering the park, loomed a three-story mortar slab called Hosea Williams Elementary School. Its windows were shingled with iron bars. Andre taught physical education at Hosea Williams. His parents didn't approve of the job, and they certainly didn't approve of the area. No one did.

Since the police didn't arrive for twenty minutes, Andre finished walking his dog. He knew he'd have time, and Moira was restless. He led her down the block, past the Atlanta Food Shop (boarded shut) and the redbrick Holy Life Baptist Church (gated shut). But by then Andre heard the siren. He reached the dead body around the same time the squad car circumvented the construction barricade.

Two cops emerged, eau de French fries. They clicked off their siren but left on their red-and-blues to sweep and bounce in careful rhythm over the block. To Moira, essentially color-blind, the lights were meaningless, but to Andre, the colored lights painted his neighborhood at 3:40 a.m. into a party-hearty discotheque. That just reminded him of his age, and his misbegotten teenage years, and how much his life had changed in so short a—

"You called it in?" asked Officer Appleby, arms crossed. He was the black one. Officer Harper, the white one, knelt beside the body. The cops who served this neighborhood always showed up in this demographic: one black, one white. In fact, some of Andre's more clever students referred to them not as *pigs* but *zebras*. Yo, zebras on patrol today, watch out.

"I was taking my dog for a walk," said Andre. He exhaled warmth onto his hands and rubbed them together. Even though he wore a fleece coat over his sweats, winter was still winter. "We just found him lying there."

Officer Appleby frowned, uncrossed his arms, and crossed them again. His stomach was bothering him. "Did you know the deceased?"

"No, sir."

Down by the corpse, Officer Harper did a rudimentary investigation of the bum's hairy, muddy limbs for frostbite. In a few minutes they'd call it in and the case would belong to the detectives and medical examiner but until then, if he was careful, if he didn't disturb the body or the scene, he could do some actual police work. Let Appleby chat up the witness, predictable waste of time that would be. In the meantime, Harper would work the case. Find a clue. Share it with the cavalry when they arrived and when his name came up for promotion, they'd remember him for this and he'd be free of this beat patrol graveyard shift bullshit forever.

Moira nudged against his ass with her nose. Harper scowled down at the pug. God, he hated dogs. They slobbered and chewed up nearly anything of value. They constantly needed attention. The county taxed you for their tags, the pet store taxed you for their food, the vet taxed you for their shots. Dogs. God.

Moira nudged again against his ass and Harper slapped her away. He glanced over at his partner and the witness. Neither of them had noticed his violent outburst. Good. The last thing he needed was yet another pissed-off civilian lodging a valueless complaint.

Andre felt Moira rub up against his sneakers. Out of habit he reached down and scruffed her behind her ears. She probably wanted to go home. It was almost 4:00 a.m. She would have no trouble sleeping.

"Now, Mr. Banks, are you usually out this late?" Appleby coughed into his fist, shifted his weight from his right foot to his left. "You and your dog?"

"Insomnia," replied Andre.

Appleby offered a sympathetic nod. The witness didn't seem too disturbed by the dead body, but this was Atlanta. This was MLK Drive. Death had long ago put up residence here. Appleby had worked this beat for ten years. If every person in this neighborhood was gathered together, the stories they could tell. After all, as an officer of the law, he only dealt with what was reported. What went unreported—those were the crimes that gave him nightmares.

"Well, Mr. Banks, we'll need to get an official statement, but it probably doesn't have to be—"

The glass bulbs atop the police cruiser exploded in a crescendo of noise. All four of them—Andre, Moira, Appleby, and Harper—glanced at the ground, now covered in shards, then at the roof of the car, then at each other. Moira cocked her head in thought.

"Someone must've thrown a baseball or something," said Appleby.

Harper had his gun out. "Show yourselves, you little pricks!"

With the discotheque lights gone, the only illumination left was the milky oval of the streetlight, and that enabled them to see each other, but not whoever had shattered the glass. Harper cocked his gun, and Appleby reached for his. They relied on their ears to detect the vandal, but could only hear their own heartbeats in the cold night air.

Then Harper didn't even hear that, because a bullet passed through his brainpan and he was dead. He collapsed like a stringless marionette, not three feet from the body of the bum.

Appleby opened his mouth to speak, scream, something, but a second bullet took care of that, and he joined his partner on the gray pavement. The blood from their wounds dripped out of their bodies and co-mingled, like holding hands.

A minute passed.

Andre didn't move.

Moira trotted over to Appleby's body and poked at his cheek with one of her front paws. She looked back at her master and whimpered.

Slowly, Andre took a step toward the squad car. He

would be safe inside the squad car. They were bullet-proof, right?

"Moira," he whispered. "Come here, girl."

She followed him as he inched away from the carnage. The car was twenty feet away. Presumably, the doors were unlocked. He would get inside and radio for help and he'd be safe. He and Moira would be okay.

Fifteen feet away, they reached the pool of glass. Moira skirted around it. She and Andre were almost out of the arc of the streetlight. Ten feet away, and Andre decided that going slow made no sense—he wasn't walking a tightrope. He took a deep breath (as he taught his students to do at Hosea Williams) and prepared to sprint.

The third bullet dropped him before he had a chance.

And the fourth bullet took care of the dog.

Clouds shifted. The streetlight hummed. At 4:25 a.m., the squad car's radio squawked to life. Dispatch wanted a 10-4 on their whereabouts, over. By 4:40 a.m., Dispatch got antsy and sent out Pennington and O'Daye to investigate. Pennington and O'Daye arrived at five to six. Dawn was just a commercial break away.

Pennington got out first, while O'Daye shifted the car into Park. They both saw the car, then the bodies. O'Daye called it in, tried to remain calm, but her voice trembled like a plucked string.

"Dispatch, this is Baker-82. We're at the scene. We have four bodies, repeat four bodies. Officers Harper and Appleby are down. Request immediate backup. Over."

Gabe Pennington scanned the area with his hazel eyes. His prescription lenses fogged up from the cold, and with frustration and panic he lifted a gloved hand and wiped them clean. No doubt about it—that was Roy Appleby. Ever since his divorce, Pennington had played poker at the bastard's house every Saturday night. Appleby was a lousy poker player but he loved the game. Pennington hated the game, but craved the companionship. He was living out of a motel room off I75. It was Appleby who'd reached out to him. Now the man was leaking blood on MLK Drive. Damn it.

"Copy Baker-82," Dispatch responded with the same authority as always, "Backup is on the way. Dispatch out."

Officer O'Daye stared through the windshield. "Maybe they're still alive."

Pennington glanced down at her, then back at the bodies in the milky oval. Indeed, his first instinct had been to rush out to them and check for pulses. Perform CPR. But they didn't know the scope of the scenario, and until you knew the scope of the scenario, you played it safe. Safe may not have worked for his marriage, but it had kept him clean of serious injury for fourteen years on the force. O'Daye was young. She would learn.

As he rejoined her in the car, Melissa O'Daye checked the time on her wristwatch. 6:00 a.m. Soon the block would be awake. Parents would be walking their kids, all bundled up in their woolies, across the street to Hosea Williams. The corner boys would be out soon too, and the early-bird alcoholics. None of them had to see this. No one should have to see this. She shouldn't have had to see this. She should've been in bed. She didn't need the overtime. What was she trying to—

The dog moaned.

O'Daye and Pennington popped to attention.

The little dog was half in the light and half out. They'd just assumed she wasn't breathing, just like the others, but she moaned again, breathy, tenuous.

"Christ Jesus," O'Daye muttered.

She opened her door.

"Wait." Pennington held up a hand. "There's nothing you can do."

"Nothing I can…? That dog's alive!"

"Are you a vet? No. So sit tight. Backup will be here momentarily."

"We can't just—"

"It's not cowardice," he explained. "It's procedure."

She closed her door.

They waited.

The dog, Moira, age three, wept. She was dying and she knew it and just wanted to pull herself to a dark and quiet place, away from her master. But she couldn't move. All she could do was fill the January air with her requiem sobs.

When backup arrived, they showed in droves. Three squad cars and two additional unmarked vehicles pulled up to the crime scene. Officers were down—their brothers and sisters in blue were damn sure going to avenge their deaths. Their sirens crashed through the neighborhood like an aural hurricane. Parents and children sat up in their beds and pondered the end of the world. Some peered out their windows. Some bolted shut their doors. Even the sun peeked out over the skyscrapers to catch a glimpse of the ruckus.

Lead officer on scene was Deputy Chief Perry Roman. He was division commander over Zone 4. Appleby and Harper were his men. He climbed out of his beige station wagon, left his microsuede unbuttoned (and his paint-spattered Police Academy sweatshirt exposed), and quickly assigned roles:

"O'Daye and Pennington, tape off the area and assist in crowd control. Halloway and Cruise, Jaymon and DeWright, canvass the area. Williams, Kayless, Ogleby, take statements, someone must've seen something. Detectives, homicides don't get plainer than this. You know what to do."

Officer O'Daye wanted to check on the dog. She couldn't hear her keening anymore—there was too much chatter now in the air—but she needed to know if the dog was still alive. It's not that she had dogs of her own…she didn't have any pets at all. She lived alone in her apartment. Is that why she worked the overtime? And now she was pining away for an animal (and not for any of the four human beings!). Foolish. She shuffled her neuroses to the niches of her mind, just as her therapist had taught her to do. When Pennington (who *was* a coward—everyone knew it) grabbed a thick roll of yellow tape from the trunk of their cruiser, she didn't go for the dog. She went for the tape, and helped her cowardly older partner zip up the perimeter.

The deputy chief remained on the sidewalk, hands

on his hips, and surveyed. Eleven cops working the scene—it would be so easy to contaminate evidence. The last thing any of them needed at this hour, for these fallen soldiers, was an example of negligence (or worse, incompetence) the shooter's defense attorney could attack in court. And Perry Roman had no doubt they would catch the shooter. The morning shift came on in two hours. By 9:00 a.m. every street corner in southwest Atlanta would have a shield working the case. Two of their own were dead. Roman made a note to himself to warn his men, when they found the shooter, not to mortally wound the motherfucker. This was going to be a clean, by-the-book operation. The dead deserved nothing less (even if Harper was a lazy prick).

Perry fixed his gaze on the two homicide detectives. Not his most perceptive team, but they'd suffice, at least for two hours. Some administrators, he knew, would see this tragedy as a chance to piggyback to a promotion. Perry Roman just wanted to get the job done. Perry Roman was a churchgoing man, went every Sunday with his wife and three kids. If the good Lord saw fit to reward him with a promotion, so be it. In the meantime, he'd just be the best man he could be.

He felt the rising sun tickle the back of his head. The milky oval on the pavement was fading away like a dream. Perry stared past the violence to the unkempt park on the north side of the street, and to the elementary school on the other side of the park.

The sniper, on the roof of the elementary school, stared past the violence to Perry Roman. The dawn provided adequate illumination for all sorts of misbehavior. He tracked his rifle to the two gesticulating detectives; to the old cop with the yellow tape and his young female sidekick, the one who kept looking at the dog. He adjusted his scope for the day's new brightness and fingered his gentle trigger. Yep. All sorts of misbehavior.

2

Fourteen dead in Atlanta, GA.

Esme clicked away from the *New York Times* and typed in the URL for the *Atlanta Journal-Constitution*. The story took up most of the front page. She read every article.

Fourteen dead. Fifteen, if you counted the dog.

The names began to become familiar. Perry Roman, the deputy chief. Appleby and Harper. Andre Banks, the bystander who first found the vagrant on the street, called it in at 3:18 a.m. Good man. Some would've just minded their own business. Had Andre Banks minded his own business, though, today's newspaper headlines would have been very different.

The articles didn't give the vagrant's name. Police probably were still working on an ID. Hoping beyond hope that someone in the local soup kitchens would recognize his absence. Hoping the man had a criminal record so his fingerprints would match those on file. Esme knew the drill. Oh, yes, she knew it.

She surfed to the home page for the Associated Press and read their version. Then Reuters. Then *USA Today.*

The vagrant had been the bait; this much was certain. He had been placed there in a bright ridiculous outfit in a well-lit, controlled area specifically to attract prey. The DOT roadblocks were fake; the killer had put those up to control his trap, keep out automobile traffic. Half of this Esme read in the reports; the other half she easily deduced. Surely the task force assigned to the case had made the same deductions. Her hand drifted to her landline. She still knew people at the Bureau. One simple call wouldn't hurt....

No. No. She was not going to turn into one of *them,* one of those retirement ghosts with so much free time they come back to haunt their ex-workplace and harass their former colleagues. Unlike most retirement ghosts, Esme was not in her late sixties but her late thirties, but still. No.

She put down the phone and went into the kitchen to make a sandwich. She slipped two slices of whole wheat bread into the toaster and set it to dark. While the bread crisped, she sliced up a tomato and a cucumber, broke off some leaves of iceberg lettuce, and took out a jar of low-fat mayonnaise. The jar was almost empty. She made a mental note to stop at the grocery store on the way back from picking up Sophie from Oyster Bay Elementary.

Esme Stuart, this is your life.

She deliberately kept away from her computer for the next hour and instead spent the time with an Elvis Costello biography. She put on her disc of *My Aim is True* for verisimilitude. No, not her disc. This one was

Rafe's. Hers was in a used CD store in D.C. When Esme and Rafe moved in together, their musical collections were so identical that they'd had to get rid of the many duplicates. Her mind wandered away from the biography. Had someone bought her old CD? What was that person like? Was it an impulse buy or had they been searching desperately for the album? Had they heard about what had happened in Atlanta?

Which brought her mind back to that.

She shut her biography and shuffled off to the bathroom. *"Alison..."* begged Elvis, *"I know this world is killing you..."* She clicked on the light and eyeballed her reflection. What was wrong with her? It's not like this was the first murder she'd read about since she quit seven years ago. Was it the body count? Was it the fact the victims were law enforcement? She rolled her eyes. Talk about a wicked subconscious. Read about a sniper attack and put on an album called *My Aim is True.*

She tucked a strand of chestnut-colored hair behind an ear. Her ears were not small and dainty. When she was younger, when she was Sophie's age, she insisted her hair remain long. But her ears always found a way to poke through. By the time she reached her twenties, she just gave up and cut her hair to her shoulders. It added years to her life, but when she was in her twenties and starting out at the Bureau, looking older was an asset. She believed it meant she'd be taken more seriously.

Christ, she had been so naive.

Esme washed her hands, padded back into the living

room, and on principle switched the CD to something less substantial. *Bananarama's Greatest Hits?* Perfect. She pushed Play, stared a moment too long at her computer (what new developments had occurred in the case?), and fell back onto the couch. Her hand absently reached for one of the Sudoku books strewn across the glass table. Esme opened it to her bookmark—a cheap black pen—and pondered a puzzle tantalizingly labeled Crazy Hard.

The clutter on the glass table provided Esme with her only comfortable chaos in the whole room. Rafe made sure the rest of their two-story Colonial was organized and spotless. He wasn't a neat freak per se; he had guests over all the time from the university and, like Esme had at the Bureau with her short hair, wanted to give a positive impression. Esme didn't mind keeping house (she recognized the value of appearances) as long as she had a nook in each room to herself. Anyway, Sudoku books were easily straightened.

The Bananarama CD ended. It took her five more minutes to complete her puzzle, then she put on her olive green parka and got ready to pick her daughter up. She reminded herself again about the mayonnaise, slipped her mittens on, and entered the cold, cold garage. Outside the windchill had to be below zero Fahrenheit, and last night's frozen rain had doubtless left patches of black ice on every side street. Welcome to the north shore of Long Island, December to March.

Esme clicked on her Prius's satellite radio. She loved to be surrounded by music. Music, language—anything creative, really. It charged her up like ephemeral photosynthesis. Without music, without the spoken word, she might as well remain in bed. Tom Piper once suggested she suffered from depression. But she'd just told him she was quitting the Bureau, so perhaps context had influenced his expert analysis.

Tom. Lanky-limbed Tom and his '78 chrome Harley. Surely he was being kept in the loop about the sniper. Surely they had him (and his Harley) down in Atlanta right now. Walking the scene, sketching out what made this particular madman tick, deciphering his message. And this series of murders in particular…

Bait, trap, fourteen homicides. Patience. This madman wouldn't want his intent to be misinterpreted.

Had he left a note?

Esme and Tom still traded Christmas cards, birthday cards…calling him to confirm her suspicions wouldn't completely be out of the blue….

No, Esme. That's not your life anymore. And besides, Tom Piper's a big boy, more than capable of catching the bad guys himself. You're a soccer mom now, Esme. Live with your decision.

She backed her crimson Prius out of the driveway. Around her, every snow-capped home glowed with young money. Her and Rafe's black-trimmed white Colonial was no different. Good Americans lived in these here parts. Still wide-eyed enough to be Democrats and believe that the world made sense. Most days now, cloistered in the insulation of Oyster Bay, Long Island, Esme believed it too.

Her radio segued from the Public Enemy Ltd. anger anthem "Rise" to Elvis Costello's menacing "Riot Act."

Elvis again. Must be something in the air. Esme turned left onto Main Street. Oyster Bay Elementary was just a few blocks. In warmer weather, they walked. Mothers and their children along the sidewalk like a parade. Today the sidewalk was empty, with only a parade of phantoms walking the line. A wicked breeze rolled in from the ocean, five miles to the north. Somehow the wind always got by those multi-acre mansions that guarded the beachfront.

Not that Esme lived in a hovel. Not since she'd met Rafe.

She pulled in front of the school. Usually she had to fight with the other parents for parking but she was ten minutes early. All to avoid her computer and the information it transmitted. Of course, she could easily switch to a news station on her radio….

Mercifully, at that moment, she spotted one of her neighbors committing a class A misdemeanor. Amy Lieb, she of the smallest multi-acre mansion in Oyster Bay (and mother of a doe-eyed daughter named Felicity who was in Sophie's grade), was hammering a KEL-LERMAN FOR PRESIDENT placard into the school's grassy courtyard. Either the school's security guards didn't know the latest electioneering statutes (unlikely) or they didn't care (more likely). The Liebs' money carried a lot more heft than some simple law.

"Hey, Amy," said Esme, gooey with innocence. "Whatcha doing?"

Amy Lieb, ever chipper, squinted over and waved. She and Esme had a cordial relationship. Since both of their husbands worked in the sociology department at the college, they often attended the same book clubs, mingled at the same soirees, etc. Essentially, the Liebs were the Stuarts with a fifteen-year head start. Their daughter Felicity was their youngest of four. Their oldest, Trevor, boarded at Kent School in western Connecticut where he excelled in trigonometry and tennis.

Amy Lieb wore her long black hair bound in a white bow, as if it were a gift to the world. Her diaphanous outfits always kept her figure a mystery, and today's flowing faux-mink coat was no exception. She smiled at Esme, and into the sun, as the younger woman approached.

"Primary election's coming up," said Amy. "Got to get out the word!"

Esme smiled back. "Yeah, but, you know, seven-year-olds can't vote."

"Their parents can!"

Esme looked around. The aforementioned parents were beginning to pull up in their station wagons and SUVs. She leaned into Amy and, as kindly as she could, whispered: "Look, you can't put that here. It's municipal property."

Amy blinked at her.

"It's called electioneering. It's against the law."

Amy glanced down at her sign, not harming anyone, then back at Esme. "Why?"

"It implies the school is supporting Governor Kellerman."

"Well, he's the best man for the job, don't you think?"

Esme felt her good cheer beginning to waver. It

appeared Amy's convictions were as rooted as her placard. Great.

"Relax, Esme. And besides, who's getting hurt?" The other parents were beginning to congregate. "Oh, speaking of, did you hear what happened down in Atlanta?"

That night, after putting Sophie to bed, after Rafe left to attend an evening lecture by a visiting socio-linguist, Esme finally called Tom Piper. She didn't expect him to answer, and mentally prepared the message she was going to leave on his voice mail. However—

"This is Tom."

Esme brought a mug of green tea with her to the computer desk. Although they'd exchanged holiday cards, they hadn't actually spoken to each other for, what, four years? Four years. A whole election term, she mused. The Amy Lieb incident was still fresh on her brain. She felt like a swimmer returning to the sea after a long absence. After almost drowning. God, did he still resent her for quitting? Maybe calling him was a mistake—

"Hello? Is anybody there?"

Shit. What was she, twelve years old?

"Hi, Tom," she exhaled.

Silence.

Esme hugged her knees.

Then, finally: "Hello, Esmeralda."

His Kentucky baritone engulfed her. Esmeralda. Not her full name, but always what he called her. As if she had somersaulted out of Quasimodo's bell tower and into the bowels of Quantico. Tom Piper. The mentor she never deserved.

"So…" said Esme, quashing her insecurities, "how's the weather?"

"In Atlanta, you mean?"

"For example."

"I had a feeling you'd call."

Esme couldn't help but smile. Of course he had a feeling. His instincts bordered on psychic. When she started seeing Rafe, when she would come into work after a night of lovemaking that left scratch marks, she always made sure to avoid Tom until at least 10:00 a.m., lest he somehow zero in on her less-than-virginal proclivities. What he thought of her meant the world. But what did he think of his Esmeralda now?

"It's bad," he said. "We've got maybe six people down here who think they're in charge, and that's not counting the mayor, the governor, and the president of the United States, all of whom have weighed in."

"So the bureaucrats have their tantrums and meanwhile, the adults skulk back into the shadows and actually work the case. Maybe some of the adults even make sure the bureaucrats keep fighting so they don't suddenly interfere."

"You make it sound so Machiavellian."

She chuckled. "Hey, if the ends justify the means…"

"It's bad, though. The case."

Esme let go of her knees and reclined into her chair. "Can you talk about it?" She sipped her hot tea.

Tom didn't reply.

Damn it. She'd gone too far. Fuck. Best to back-pedal, and fast…

"Tom, I'm sorry. I know you can't…I probably shouldn't have called. But anyway, so…how are you? How's Ruth?"

"My sister is still gardening. We even built a little greenhouse for her out back so she doesn't have to worry about squirrels messing with her daffodils."

"That's nice. You built it together?"

"And it took practically a whole month. Neither Ruth nor I are what anyone would call 'mechanically inclined.' "

"I know." Esme felt the tension ease out of her shoulders. "I remember that one time your engine wouldn't start. I can still see you standing there with the hood open in the parking garage. You just stared and stared at that engine block like it was a murder suspect you could make blink."

Tom chuckled. "We all have our faults and foibles."

"And some of us even have jumper cables."

"Ha-ha."

Esme smiled, stared out the window. Snowflakes tumbled in the moonlight. It was probably balmy down in Hotlanta. She'd been there once, in August. Humidity was a living breathing organism in the South, and Atlantans had no nearby body of water for respite. No wonder their crime stats spiked in the summertime. The heat cooked people's brains.

But this was January, and fourteen people were dead.

"Are you still there?" he asked.

She held her palm to her forehead and sighed. "I'm sorry, Tom, it's just…I read about what happened last night and…it's been almost seven years since I left the Bureau. There have been other high-profile murders. But this one has just…crawled under my skin…and I don't know why."

"You don't?" He sounded surprised. "How do you think I knew you'd call?"

"What do you mean?"

"The homeless man. As soon as I learned about him, how the killer used him as bait, I knew this case was going to stick to you like a bad dream. *I* almost called *you*."

"The homeless man? Why would he…?"

"Because of your parents, Esme."

Oh.

Esme shrank down in her seat to a little girl.

Her parents.

Who'd lived on and off welfare all their life. Who falsified addresses to get their daughter into the best public schools. Who pushed her every day to rise above their situation and, when she did, when she got that scholarship letter to George Washington University, when she said goodbye to them and went off to start her freshman year…

There was a shelter in the south side, Coleman House. Lead paint on the walls but walls were better than the open air in December in Boston. Eighteen-year-old Esme came home from her first semester in D.C. full of stories but home was no longer there. Coleman House was there, yes, but her parents had

gone. All they had left her was two blue ink words—
her mother's careful cursive—on a piece of yellow
paper.

BE FREE, it said. BE FREE.

She spent the entire two weeks searching the city for
her mom and dad but they didn't want to be found, and
when you didn't want to be found in the cross-streets
of Boston, you might as well have been vapor.

She almost didn't go back to school, but her friends
urged her. They insisted it's what her parents would
have wanted. Still, every break she returned to Coleman
House, and the Congress Ave. YMCA, and searched
every shelter and underpass in the whole city for her
family. Until the day she got into Quantico, when she
decided to never go back.

Rafe didn't know.

Almost all of her friends didn't know.

Tom knew only because he knew everything.

"The man's name was Merle Inman," said Tom. "He
grew up in Macon, moved to Atlanta in his twenties to
be an architect, fell into drugs…every story's the same
story. He was forty-two years old. We're going to
release his information tomorrow, but, well, there it
is."

Esme realized she was crying, and wiped her
cheeks. "Thanks."

"The guy who did this—he's something else. Using
people as clay pigeons. Fancies himself a gamesman.
Thinks he can beat the house. Nobody beats the house.
Not my house."

"Go get that fucker," she said.

"Yes, ma'am."

After she hung up, she remembered her musings about whether or not the killer had left a note. But it just didn't seem as important to her anymore. Maybe what she'd really needed was to talk with Tom. Mentor, profiler, friend, therapist. That she couldn't have connected the relevance of the case herself—forget about God, it was the human mind that worked in mysterious ways.

Esme prepared a bath. Rafe wouldn't be home for another hour. Sophie was fast asleep in her bed, perhaps dreaming of the man made out of balloons. That had been a recurring dream of hers for a few days now. The man made out of balloons. All different colors. And tomorrow morning she'd saddle up to the table and declare, "I dreamt about the balloon man again." Apparently it was a happy dream.

Her daughter was having happy dreams. Esme lowered herself into the hot, hot bathwater. Life was good, wasn't it? She thought again about Amy Lieb. This was the high drama in her life now. Hundreds of miles away, Tom Piper was searching for a madman. She hoped he caught him. She hoped Rafe returned home soon. She clicked on her bath stereo (Joy Division this time, "Love Will Tear Us Apart"), shut her eyes, and allowed her mind to finally, finally, exhale.

3

On February 11, someone lit the Amarillo aquarium on fire.

In the days that followed the conflagration, security tapes confirmed police suspicions of arson. FBI investigators went frame by frame over footage of the night janitor, a new hire named Emmett Poole, mopping up the third floor, twenty minutes before the fire began on that floor.

It was Tom Piper who figured it out.

"That's lighter fluid," he said. He pointed at the freeze-frame of the mop bucket, then at the broad-shouldered back of Emmett Poole. Upon further review, they couldn't find any footage of the janitor's face, none at all. Employees described him as nondescript. He'd only been on the job about a week. He'd answered an ad in the paper. His references had checked out. The authorities gathered to raid the address he'd listed. But it was a church. Emmett Poole, like the aquarium he'd ignited, had gone up in a puff of ash.

Tom Piper and his task force weren't in Amarillo, though, because of the arson.

He was there because of what had happened shortly thereafter.

Station 13 had responded to the blaze at 9:55 p.m. Most of the crew had been watching the Democratic debate between Jefferson Traynor and Bob Kellerman. Up in his home state of Ohio, Kellerman was a volunteer fireman, so the boys in the firehouse (thorough Texas Republicans one and all) were rooting for one of their own. They watched the debate up in the bunk room on a soot-smeared fifty-two-inch LCD they'd rescued back in September from the toasty remains of a Best Buy. Then the call went out, and the TV went off, and the men grumbled into their gear.

On the way to the aquarium, Lou Hopper declared, "Kellerman kicked his ass." Lou Hopper was the shift's resident pontificator. Every workplace in America sported (at least) one. The self-educated expert. The know-it-all. The bar in *Cheers* had Cliff Clavin. Station 13 had Lou Hopper. He even had a gray mustache like Clavin, although not a wisp of hair on top. He claimed it had been singed off in a fire; somehow the flames had slipped their hot tongues underneath his helmet and licked off his hair.

Three other firefighters crowded the back of the engine with Lou. The chief sat up front with Bobby Vega, who always drove the truck.

It didn't take them long to reach the aquarium from their home base off of Third Avenue. Amarillo was a city of daylight and most businesses closed shop by six o'clock, so the chief didn't bother to activate the engine's blaring siren. The few still on the road at 10:00 p.m. either knew enough to get out of the way or deserved to get run over. The three boys in the back, though—they had a tradition to uphold: feline-faced Roscoe Coffey popped a well-worn cassette into a boom box (acquired in 1989 from the toasty remains of a Conn's—which the aforementioned doomed Best Buy had replaced) and pressed Play. As they neared the aquarium, a crown of streaming smoke rising from its brick skull, Johnny Cash and his mariachi horns warbled to life.

"I fell into a burning ring of fire…"

Never let it be said Station 13 lacked a dark, dark sense of humor.

Bobby Vega navigated the engine up North Hughes toward the aquarium. His family had settled in Amarillo when he was three years old. Everyone had assumed they were originally from Mexico, so that's what they'd claimed. Coming from Mexico meant fewer questions than coming from Colombia. They had left Colombia in the middle of a drought and the year after they came to Amarillo, the city suffered its longest dry spell in one hundred years. Even today, water conservation remained a major concern; the fire department had been chastised on more than one occasion for their "extravagant use of water."

The same moronic bigwigs who had chastised the fire department for their extravagant use of water later funded a three-story aquarium in the heart of a parched city. Bobby's parents, who still attributed Amarillo's

meteorological bad luck to their arrival, read the news
and laughed. Bobby didn't laugh. He never found the
government's foolish behavior all that charming. Fools
endangered. Fools led to an alarm at the firehouse and
his brave friends risking their lives.

Bobby Vega was an angry young man, true, but
driving the rig helped him vent. There was something
about controlling that wide wheel and guiding his
brothers to their destination which sated his fury. The
usual tightness in his jaw went away. He kept the
engine on a straight line toward the aquarium and
enjoyed these few minutes of solace, not even minding
that asinine country song on the tape deck.

"I fell down, down, down, but the flames went
higher…"

For Tom Piper and his task force, reviewing the
events leading up to the second massacre, much of the
information about Station 13 and its actions on
February 11 was circumstantial at best (and anecdotal
at worst). They had no definitive proof the six men
took North Hughes to the aquarium, or even that
Johnny Cash had accompanied them on their trip. All
Tom Piper had to go on was what he later learned about
the men's habits. He assumed what they did that night
on the way to that fire was what they did every night
they went out on a job. He interviewed Station 13's
other firefighters, many of whom had served at one
time or another with the boys on the night shift. He
interviewed their families. He put together a composite.

It was like figuring out the universe from a handful
of photographs.

Amarillo had one firehouse. Some decades back, a forgotten politician had labeled it Station 13, because Amarillo was in the Thirteenth Congressional District and the constituents should be reminded. Lucky #13. At their first charity football game vs. the local police force, way back in the early '80s, when the firefighters had marched out onto the field at Amarillo High, rather than having individual numbers stenciled on the backs of their jerseys they had each borne the same two red digits: one and three. The crowd ate it up.

The chief had been on that inaugural team. 1982 had been his rookie year, so the vets kept him on the bench for most of the game. He knew it wasn't a comment on his playing ability; after all, every grown man in West Texas knew how to throw a football. He just didn't have the seniority, and in public service (even on the football field), seniority trumped everything. The chief accepted that.

They finally put him in for the last quarter. He took his position as a tailback (he lacked the size for anything else) and readied for the snap. The play called for him and the fullback (#13) to fake left while the QB (#13) readied a forward pass to the wide receiver (#13), who would charge right, hopefully receive the pass, rush forty-six yards for the touchdown, and bring the game out of its 21-21 deadlock. The cops, impatient at being on the defense, blitzed the line. So instead of charging right, the firefighters' wide receiver got trampled.

The chief saw panic in the QB's eyes. Hell, the *crowd* saw panic in the QB's eyes. If he didn't get rid of the ball in the next five seconds, he'd meet a fate worse than his receiver. So the chief, as he interpreted it, had two options: use his small body to run interference and get pummeled or attempt a charge through the mass of blue uglies and pray for a pass reception.

The chief charged. His minimal size helped him shuttle through a needle's eye of a hole. He rushed past the line of scrimmage and glanced back. Had the QB noticed? Would the ball come his way?

Yes.

In his last moments before getting walloped, the QB tossed off the ball. It didn't spiral so much as wobble…but it was wobbling in the right direction. The chief outstretched his arms. He was wide open. The defense was all up field. Thousands watched from the stands. The chief's young wife, Marcy, watched from the stands. If he completed this play, he'd become legend. If he dropped the ball, or tripped, or if half a dozen other common errors occurred in the next ten seconds, he'd be jeered forevermore.

The chief ruminated every day about the game. He ruminated about it now, as they passed Amarillo High on the left. The aquarium was within view, but the chief glanced over at the high school stadium. That's where he really wanted to be. That's where he'd caught that wobbling pigskin and sprinted forty-six yards to score the winning touchdown. Him. The little rookie.

The chief loved firefighting and had numerous accolades and recommendations but when he died, he knew what would appear in the first paragraph of his obituary.

"That's why everyone called him Catch," Jed Danvers told Tom Piper. Danvers had been a rookie, too, during that game (for the other side). Now he was lieutenant governor of the state. Jed and Tom were sipping coffee on the fifth floor of Baptist St. Anthony's on Wallace Boulevard, not far from the crime scene. For security reasons, they'd made sure to get Catch a room here all by himself. Two Texas Rangers were posted outside his door.

Catch's head was double-wrapped in gauze. His eyes were shut. Tubes were glued every which way to his arms and face. He still hadn't awakened, and thus was unaware he was the sole survivor and only witness to what had happened.

Station 13 had arrived in front of the glass-and-brick structure at 10:09 p.m. Plumes of gray-white smoke tunneled from the roof into the sky, but so far the fire appeared contained. The aquarium didn't have many windows—like most museums (and casinos), the architectural objective was one of timelessness, and this meant blocking the outside world. However, there were a few narrow panels along the stairwell. The panels appeared intact.

Daniel McIvey and his son Brian were the first out of the engine, followed by Roscoe Coffey and, lastly, Lou Hopper. Daniel and Brian looked like a project in time-lapse photography; same moppy red hair, same ruddy fat cheeks, only the father was a little taller, a little heavier, had a few more lines on his brow. Like twins they spoke in shorthand.

"Do you want to…?" asked Daniel.

"Yeah," Brian replied. "I'll get the thing. I'll meet you where you'll be."

Brian hustled together two Halligan pickaxes out of the truck while Daniel met up with the chief, who was interrogating the aquarium's security guard.

"…was just doing my job!" wept the guard. Big man named Cole. Six foot six. 300 pounds. Bawled. "I smelled the smoke and checked the monitors and that's when I called you! I swear!"

The chief nodded, feigning sympathy, and then asked the most important question of all: "Is there anyone left in the building?"

"The night janitor…name's Emmett Poole…I didn't abandon him! But I think he's still on the third floor…"

Daniel and Brian were the designated rescue team. Brian handed his father one of the Halligans and they rushed into the building. They knew the layout of the aquarium. They went here every summer. Family outing. Daniel and his wife Margie. Brian and his wife Emilia. Brian and Emilia's twins.

Roscoe and Lou grabbed a pair of extinguishers and ran in after them. Soon they were in the lead, and heading up the stairwell. Roscoe illuminated their path with a flashlight. By the time they reached the second floor, the yellow emergency lighting kicked in. By the time they reached the third floor and smelled the smoke, they knew they'd arrived.

Brian touched the door.

"We got a cooker," he said.

Roscoe and Lou readied their extinguishers. All four

men were swathed in fire retardant bunker gear, but still—fire was fire. Prometheus stole it out of heaven and it's been pissed ever since.

Outside, Bobby Vega sat by the radio. If the chief gave the word, he'd call the boys left at the station to get the ladder truck. They always always always left at least two men at the station. Reinforcements were the saviors in any war. The two boys back at Station 13 had changed the station on the fifty-two-inch LCD from the boring debate and were now watching something more relevant: a WWE title bout. Not that they were lounging; relaxation wouldn't be an option until their brothers returned from the battlefield.

Cole, the aquarium's gigantic night watchman, leaned against the fire truck and wiped wet salt from his eyes. He'd taken this job as a low-stress alternative. His life coach told him his chi couldn't deal with anxiety. His life coach told him fish were supposed to bring good luck. The next day, Cole saw the job opening at the aquarium.

He steadied his breath with a yoga exercise. What had he done so wrong in a past life that his karma would be so toxic? Had he been a serial killer? Cole blew his nose on his sleeve.

Back inside the aquarium, Roscoe and Lou were foaming the third floor, to little effect. Although the fire appeared localized to knee level and lower, residual smoke clogged all visibility.

"Mr. Poole!" called Daniel.

"Mr. Poole!" called Brian.

The third floor was arranged like a glassy labyrinth.

The four firefighters crouched their way through the maze. They had no idea where the point of ignition was and they saw no sign of Emmett Poole. Lou offered his usual uninformed hypothesis.

Then one of the exhibits exploded.

Its water (and exotic fish) spilt onto the conflagration. Instead of being extinguished, though, the fire tracked the water back to its source and filled the exhibit orange-green.

This was a chemical fire. Class B.

"Shit," said Roscoe.

The four men quickly backed out of the third floor. They needed different equipment. Roscoe radioed the chief with their status. No response. The old man was probably dealing with the cops, the press, who knows what. Roscoe took the lead and the firefighters hustled down the stairwell to the lobby.

Daniel and Brian thought about their previous trip to the aquarium. The twins adored the seahorses. What floor had the seahorses been on? Please. Not the third.

Lou Hopper thought about his knees. He needed to lose weight. Running up and down these stairs was taking its toll.

Roscoe thought about nothing at all. He operated purely on instinct and muscle memory. Otherwise he probably would have been concerned that the chief *still* hadn't replied on the radio.

The four men ran out of the lobby into the open air and went down like ducks in a gallery. Roscoe, Lou, Daniel, Brian. Pop—pop—pop—pop. The bullets easily pierced their helmets, muscles, and, yes, cartilage.

Bobby Vega sat hunched over his beloved steering wheel. His blood puddled on the dash.

Cole the giant lay sprawled on the pavement.

The chief, full name Harold Lymon, nicknamed "Catch," had tried to push Cole out of the way of the gunfire, then had run to save Bobby when the bullets found him. Catch, though, had been an object in motion. Hard to stop. Just as in 1982. The bullet grazed his left temple and left him bleeding and, mercifully, unconscious. He never saw Roscoe, Lou, Daniel, and Brian go down.

And two days later, Catch was still unconscious. He'd lost a lot of blood at the scene. Meanwhile, the third story of the aquarium collapsed into the second story. Thousands of sea animals were dead. The local paper actually listed the different species. Some of the national outlets had arrived. Connections were already being made between this attack and the one in Atlanta. The bastard had assassinated twenty people now and left a trail as cold as the Long Island Sound.

And he was just getting started.

4

"Haaaaaaaaaaaaaaaaaaaappy Vaaaaaaaaaaaaaaaaaaalentine's Daaaaaaaaaaaaaaaaaaaaaaaaaaaaaay!"

Sophie hopped into her parents' king-size bed. It was 6:03 a.m.

Esme groaned. Forced open her eyelids. Her daughter stared back, her blue eyes (identical to Rafe's, who was still asleep) full of energy.

"I made breakfast!" Sophie declared and ran out, presumably to the kitchen.

Esme groaned again. 6:03 a.m. Love was never ever easy.

But that didn't mean she had to suffer alone.

Esme slapped her husband on the ass. Twice. Hard. Finally, he stirred. Glanced over at her as if she'd stolen his baby blanket.

"Our daughter made breakfast," said Esme.

Rafe's blue-eyed gaze (far from identical at this moment to his daughter in that they conveyed No Energy Whatsoever) shifted from Esme to the clock on her nightstand, then back to Esme.

"Do I know you people?" he muttered.

She poked him playfully in his paunch.

"I love you, too," she replied. "Now let's get to the kitchen before Sophie burns it down, okay?"

Esme's concerns proved unwarranted. Sophie had made cereal. And by made, she had poured her favorite brand (Count Chocula) into two bowls and soaked the bowls in milk. She had even provided napkins, forks, and spoons. She would have provided knives too, but she was forbidden to open the knife drawer.

As Esme and Rafe shuffled into the kitchen, their daughter was already at the table, placing folded sheets of red construction paper on their wicker seats. She wore her red-and-white Cupid pajamas, with its little hearts and arrows and diapered cherubs. Red clothes always made her chestnut hair appear auburn, as if she had on a hat of autumn leaves.

"Do you want orange juice or grapefruit juice?" Sophie asked.

"Huhwhahuh," Rafe replied.

"Grapefruit juice," said Esme. "I'll get it."

Soon they were all three enjoying their breakfast. Esme and Rafe's cereal had gotten soggy, but soggy chocolate was still chocolate. The construction paper Sophie had left on their seats were Valentine's Day cards, lovingly Crayola'd. She drew Rafe with his glasses on and with his beard trimmed. Neither applied to Rafe at the moment. Crayola Esme had small ears. Sophie knew how sensitive her mother was about her ears.

"Come here," said Esme, and hugged her daughter close.

Rafe finished his cereal first. His breakfast was normally comprised of a stale doughnut and a cup of instant coffee, both procured from the social sciences department faculty lounge, so this was a huge improvement. True, he continued to act half-asleep—mumbling answers, exaggerating every yawn—but in actuality Rafe was having a wonderful time. He absently ruffled through his thinning black hair and wondered how he could make this moment last the rest of his life…or at least until the end of the semester.

Ah, the work of the day beckoned. Rafe lumbered into the shower while Esme remained in the kitchen and helped Sophie finish filling out the Valentine's Day cards for her classmates.

"But, Mom…I don't want to give one to Thad Crotty…he's gross."

"What makes him gross?"

"He smells like the garbage disposal."

"We shouldn't judge people, Sophie. Everyone is unique and different. Like a snowflake."

They sealed tiny candy message-hearts into each of the miniature red envelopes—one for each of her classmates and one for Mrs. Leacy. Sophie deliberated extensively which message-hearts went to which classmates. By the time Rafe had rejoined them in the kitchen, dried off and spectacled and in full professor-mode, Esme and Sophie were only half done.

"Better hurry up, kiddo," said Rafe.

He was Sophie's morning chauffeur. They usually left the house at 7:15. Esme hustled their daughter into her bedroom and helped her select The Perfect Outfit for Valentine's Day.

Meanwhile, Rafe contributed to Team Sophie by finishing up the cards. Before departing for her bedroom, Sophie gave him strict instructions. As he attempted to follow them, he also attempted to recollect his elementary school valentines. He couldn't even recall the names of his instructors. He would be forty years old this July. This fact, unfortunately, he never seemed to forget.

Esme joined him back at the table.

"Sophie's brushing her hair," she said. "She wants privacy."

"Well, sure."

They kissed. Briefly—but briefly then lasted a minute. Two minutes. Hands touched cheeks. Mussed hair. Three minutes.

"Happy Valentine's Day," whispered Rafe.

"Happy Valentine's Day," whispered Esme.

Sophie marched into the kitchen. "I'm ready!"

At 10:00 a.m., Esme texted their babysitter, Chelsea, reminding the slightly scatterbrained but quite responsible teenager to come by the house no later than six o'clock. Rafe and Esme had strict dinner reservations at 6:30 p.m. at Il Forno.

As soon as Esme returned her cell phone to the counter, it buzzed. Was that Chelsea already, sneaking a text message back to her from some high school classroom? Esme checked the screen.

Tom Piper.

Her phone buzzed again.

Like most Americans, she had read about the attacks in Amarillo. The 24-hour news channels were still filled, three days later, with footage and interviews and expert opinions, not the mention rampant speculation. Was this attack related to the one in Atlanta? Was there a serial killer on the loose? It made for compulsive TV.

Except for Esme. After her initial obsession about the Atlanta shootings, after Tom Piper had deconstructed her obsession into simple displacement, her interest in the story quickly faded. One might even say she became just as obsessively uninterested. Instead, Esme concentrated her days on her Sudoku puzzles, her books (she'd moved on from the Elvis Costello biography to a schmaltzy novel her reading club had selected), and her ever-surprising daughter. She'd even started paying attention to the presidential elections. It was unavoidable, really. Amy Lieb was roping all of Oyster Bay into her campaign for Bob Kellerman and now that it looked like he'd be the nominee, her efforts (in her mind) had ascended to Great Importance. To not be involved would be un-American. So Esme found herself volunteering on weekends with the other housewives at Oyster Bay's KELLERMAN FOR PRESIDENT campaign headquarters (i.e. Amy's mini-mansion). She licked envelopes, cut decals and traded gossip with everyone else.

Bzzzzzzzzzz!

Tom Piper, calling to snatch her from the jaws of mediocrity.

Bzzzzzzzzzz!

"Let it go to voice mail," she muttered. She was content, damn it.

Bzzzzzzzzzz!

There were men and women at the Bureau far more in the loop than thirty-eight-year-old Esme Stuart from Oyster Bay, Long Island. Tom had no right to call her, really. The responsible thing for him to do would be to go to his own people. Yes, *she'd* called *him* last month, but as Tom himself had pointed out, that had been a moment of temporary lunacy. She was retired now. She was a housewife.

Bzzzzzzzzzz!

"Just go to voice mail!" she growled. How many times did it have to ring before—

It stopped. Finally. She felt her shoulders slacken, and ambled to the stereo and pondered a distraction. Joy Division? Too morose for right now. Pavement? Too loud.

The Kinks. Ideal for any mood and setting. She popped in the CD. Bless you, Ray Davies.

And her phone buzzed again.

"Jesus, what the hell?"

She stomped back to the counter and checked the screen. It was just a note from her voice mail. One new message.

One new message.

Damn it, Tom.

It was Valentine's Day, for fuck's sake.

Esme slipped her phone into the utensils drawer (out of sight, out of mind) and lay down on the sofa with her water-damaged paperback. "Lola" strummed in the background. She thought about lighting some peppermint incense, decided against it, and forced herself into the book.

Six people had died in Amarillo…

No. No. People die every day. Read the book.

Fourteen in Atlanta, six in Amarillo. Someone had to speak for those victims.

And they would. Why her? She had done her bit for king and country, hadn't she?

More would die. This sniper had a purpose.

He *must* have left a note.

Esme closed her novel.

"Fuck," she concluded.

She dialed down the volume on her stereo, went in the kitchen, and retrieved her phone. Didn't bother listening to Tom's message. Just dialed him direct.

"This is Tom."

"Hi, Tom."

"I just called you."

"I was in the shower."

"Mmm-hmm."

"How are you?"

"Busy."

"I can imagine."

"I know you can. That's why I called."

"For my imagination?"

"Have you been following the case?"

"I've actually been a little busy."

"Oh?"

"I'm campaigning for Bob Kellerman."

"Mmm-hmm."

"I've become very civic."

"Mmm-hmm."

"How can I help you, Tom?"

"You don't seem as enthusiastic as you were before."

"What can I say? Love fades."

"He's going to kill again."

Esme closed her eyes, then opened them.

"I'm sure you and your team are more than capable of stopping him. Our tax dollars at work, right?"

"He left a note in Atlanta."

The cell phone trembled in her hand. No—it was her hand that was trembling.

"What did the note say?"

"I thought you weren't interested."

"What did the note say, Tom?"

"He left it in a shoe box. We found the shoe box on the roof of the school. It was just lying there. We also found the spent shells from his rifle. Sixteen shells."

Sixteen shells. Fifteen dead in Atlanta, including the dog, plus the squad car's red-and-blues, which were the first target. Sixteen shells. The sniper hadn't missed, not once.

"We opened the shoe box and found the note."

"What did the note say?"

"I just scanned it and e-mailed it to you. Call me back after you've read it."

Click.

Esme introduced the phone to her middle finger, then clomped to her computer and turned it on. The Kinks segued into "Waterloo Sunset," one of the sweetest rock and rolls songs ever recorded. Esme didn't notice.

Windows took two minutes to boot up.

Fuck you, Bill Gates. Esme plopped down in her seat and clicked on her e-mail client. Another thirty seconds for *that* to boot up. Fuck you, fuck you, fuck you.

And what did it matter if she read the note, anyway? Why was she making such a big deal out of this? She could read it, give Tom her two cents over the phone, and be done with it. What was the big deal?

Finally. Three new messages. One from Amy Lieb, one from Hallmark (Rafe must have opened one of the e-cards she'd sent him), and one from TPiper@fbi.gov.

Esme double-clicked on the message. The note the sniper had left in Atlanta loaded in the body of the e-mail:

IF THERE WAS STILL A GOD, HE WOULD HAVE STOPPED ME.

—GALILEO

Esme felt her adrenaline turn to ice. This was not the rambling, incoherent manifesto she expected. In her time at the Bureau, she had encountered more than her share of rambling, incoherent manifestos. But this— this was just a direct statement. Yes, he chose a colorful moniker like so many of the other lunatics, but what insight could she possibly...

He had to have left another note in Amarillo.

Bzzzzzzzzzz!

She rushed to the phone.

"What was in the second shoe box?" she asked.

"What shoe box?" Rafe replied.

Esme swallowed hard. She suddenly felt like she'd been caught with her hand in the cookie jar. "What shoe box?" she echoed innocently.

"You said something about a shoe box."

"What's up?"

"I just read your Hallmark card. The one you sent me online."

Esme tapped her fingers on the countertop. "Did you like it?"

"It made me laugh."

"Good."

"I'll see you tonight at six. Wear something slinky."

"How risqué."

"Love you."

Rafe hung up.

Esme sat down on the floor. Why did she feel so guilty? When she got pregnant, they'd agreed her life-style—shuttling about the country working on violent crimes—was not conducive to raising a family. She'd made a pact with Rafe to leave the Bureau and move to Long Island. Gloria Steinem might not have approved, but Esme savored the time she got to spend with her daughter while the other mothers had to hire nannies or ship their children to day care. Surely a few phone calls with her old boss wasn't a betrayal of her family. It wasn't as if Tom was asking her to fly down to Amarillo….

But he would.

She knew it even before she'd answered the phone. Whatever he was dealing with was too much for him to handle. There was only so much help one could offer from Oyster Bay, Long Island. Elect a president— perhaps. Catch a sniper—you've got to be kidding. No, to really help, she'd have to walk the crime scene and examine the evidence. Not scanned images of the note, but the note itself. What paper had he used? What typeface? What kind of shoe box was it? What was the pattern the shell casings made when they left his rifle and landed on the rooftop asphalt? Any of these could be clues to locating the guy, but they couldn't be judged from a thousand miles away. If she walked the crime scene and examined the evidence…who knows?

All modesty aside, she had been very, very good at her job. Where others saw randomness, she recognized patterns, and patterns always led back to the perpetrator. Tom Piper could read anybody, even over the phone line. She read patterns. They were, so to speak, life's intelligent design. She just filled in the blanks (thus her affinity for Sudoku puzzles). Even the entropy of madness, given the proper data, could be divined. Effect always followed cause. All actions carried context.

She knew there had to have been a second shoe box, one in Amarillo. It fit the pattern. And if she only knew what was inside it…

She stared at her cell phone. Tom was waiting for her call.

He was counting on her.

But so were Rafe and Sophie.

5

Six deaths meant six separate funerals, but Amarillo, like Atlanta, held one memorial service to honor them all. There was much debate over where the service should be held. The Amarillo metropolitan area boasted over 1,000 churches, and almost all of them jockeyed for the opportunity to host the service. Mayor Deidre Lumley, however, insisted the memorial service remain non-denominational (although many of Amarillo's more prominent clergymen were assured seats on the dais).

The memorial service in Atlanta had been held at the 4,500-seat Fox Theatre and every seat had been filled. Amarillo had Dick Bivins Stadium, which seated 15,000, but Mayor Lumley A) didn't want to associate tragedy with sports, and B) didn't expect 15,000 people to show up. All those empty seats would look very bad on national TV. After much deliberation, many pots of coffee, and a quid pro quo from the editor-in-chief of the local newspaper, Mayor Lumley and her staff decided upon the Globe-News Center. It was relatively new, seated over 1,000 quite comfortably, and was very media-friendly (as it was named, after the local newspaper, the *Amarillo Globe-News*).

By the time Tom Piper arrived at the Center, about an hour before the service was scheduled to begin, there already were 5,000 people milling in the parking lot. Law enforcement did their best to conduct the traffic, but sheer numbers forced new arrivals to turn back; park their cars three, four, five miles away, and walk. Children and elders were dropped off, and with a half hour to go the crowd had surpassed 6,000.

Some carried candles. Some carried billboards with the names of the fallen handwritten on them in Magic Marker. All carried grief—in their hearts, in their eyes. Their community had been attacked. A demon had singled them out. Six of their heroes had died trying to protect them. And there was no closure—the demon was still at large.

He might even be one of the 6,000 here at the service.

Tom Piper surveyed the men and women. Despite what he considered frankly outlandish claims about his ability to decipher minds, he knew the probability of his detecting an irregularity, especially in a mass of people this enormous, was astronomically low. Detection was the justification he'd offered his team (while they remained behind and worked the evidence—what little of it there was) for his attendance here today, but this was bullshit.

The truth was far simpler and quainter: He was here out of a sense of duty.

He secured his helmet and protective leggings to his Harley, adjusted the feeling of his baggy black leather coat on his slim shoulders, and joined the throng. Tom wanted to maintain his anonymity here, in this vigil, but that was the easy road. Twenty people were dead. He hadn't yet earned the easy road.

He displayed his badge.

The questions came almost immediately:

"Do you have any leads?" "Who could have done this?" "What are you doing to keep this from happening again?" "How did you let this happen at all?"

The questions pelted him, pricked at him. He felt every one. The sight of his badge, though, forced everyone, friendly or not, to let him pass. He silently made his way to the red sandstone building, showed his badge to the cops at the gate, and entered.

Inside the auditorium, Tom identified the four distinct cliques. The family members, mostly culled from Amarillo's lower middle class, wore black polyester. They all knew each other, and chatted freely amongst themselves. Tom picked out the genetic resemblances— these giants over here must be kin to Cole the night watchman, those fair-skinned redhead variations over there must belong to Daniel and Brian McIvey. Among the firefighters in attendance, the genetics varied wildly, but as a group they were easily distinguished by their Class A's, the black-and-gold uniform each wore in honor of their fallen brethren. The third pocket of attendees, smaller than the first two, was the politicians. Here were the $2,000 suits and the once-a-week haircuts. Tom recognized the state's congressmen and senators.

The fourth, final, least significant clique was the press. They sat in the rear, set up their cameras. Here was the widest variety of humanity. They carried on their faces bleary evidence of two-hour naps in tiny motel rooms, and their clothes looked shopworn. Some attended funerals for a living. It was part of their job.

Tom took a seat in the back, with the press. After all, he identified most with the press. He too, it seemed, attended funerals for a living.

The service was scheduled to begin in five minutes.

Six large black-and-white photographs hung like flags from a pipe above the stage, as if to remind the attendees the reason they were here. As if anyone needed reminding. Underneath the photographs were eight black chairs and a miked podium. Tom wondered if Mayor Lumley and the other seven distinguished guests (which included Catch's pal Lt. Governor Jed Danvers) were milling in the green room, eating cubes of cheese.

Tom fixated on the photographs.

Cole Kingman.

Bobby Vega.

Lou Hopper.

Daniel McIvey.

Brian McIvey.

Roscoe Coffey.

Names forever added to his memory. Names, like the fourteen in Atlanta, forever associated to a madman with a gun.

And Esme still hadn't called him back.

He'd sent her the e-mail around 10:00 a.m. EST. It

was almost 12:30 p.m. now in Amarillo, which meant it was almost 1:30 p.m. in Oyster Bay. She hadn't e-mailed him back—he had his BlackBerry set to notify him when he received new messages at his work account. What was she doing? Surely she wanted to help out…right?

Perhaps the seven years had changed her more than he'd expected. Perhaps he didn't know her anymore at all.

And yet *she'd* called *him*…

The speakers took the stage. Gradually, the attendees settled, and sat. Mayor Lumley approached the podium. The shoulder pads in her dark blue pantsuit made her look like a transvestite.

"Good afternoon," she began…and then Tom tuned her out. He'd met the woman the previous night at city hall, and she'd seemed to possess the trait of being both ignorant and condescending at the same time. It was a trait most commonly found in politicians and actor-activists, and there actually was a psychological term for it. The Dunning-Kruger effect: the dumber you are, the smarter you think you are. Tom's father, a lawman in Jasper, Kentucky, had a better phrase to describe them: "arrogant fuckwits." As in: "there's that arrogant fuckwit on TV again, vomiting at the mouth."

Tom pursed his lips in a small grin.

"Special Agent Piper," whispered the young Asian woman to his left, "what's so funny?"

She was an itty-bitty thing, with spiky faux-black hair. Twenty-two years old, if that. Her dark V-neck cardigan went down to her knees. Her right nostril was pierced. Who is she, thought Tom, and how does she know my name?

As if psychic, she held out her hand. "Lilly Toro. *San Francisco Chronicle*." She had the body of a child but the croak of a chain-smoking octogenarian.

Tom shook her hand, didn't notice nicotine on her fingertip. "You're a long way from home, Ms. Toro."

"So are you, Special Agent Piper."

They spoke in hushed tones, so as not to disturb those around them, who were apparently enraptured in the mayor's oratory.

"I sat next to you on purpose," she said.

"Are you asking me out on a date, Ms. Toro?"

"Not unless you're hiding a vagina." Her breath smelled of spearmint and menthol. "And call me Lilly."

"Why did you sit next to me?"

A pasty gentleman to Tom's right stopped jotting notes onto his steno pad and gave them an accusatory look.

"Sorry, Roger," said Lilly.

"Sorry, Roger," echoed Tom.

Up on stage, Mayor Lumley wrapped up her remarks and turned the helm over to Pastor Manny Jessup. Both Roscoe Coffey and Bobby Vega had been congregants at his church. He stepped up to the podium, took a deep, steadying breath, and spoke.

The service lasted another hour. By the time it was over, much of the mighty crowd outside had dispersed. Plastic cups and candy wrappers were strewn across the parking lot, as if the fair had just left town.

Tom made his way to his Harley.

"Special Agent Piper…"

Lilly Toro, more than a foot shorter, hustled to catch up.

"I'm in a bit of a hurry, I'm afraid, Ms. Toro…"

"Lilly."

"Lilly." He fastened his protective leggings over his slacks, lest he crash his motorcycle, shatter his bones, and accidentally bleed on his clothes. "I don't mean to be rude, but I gave my statement yesterday at the press conference."

"Okay."

Tom offered her a sympathetic shrug and mounted his bike. The engine started with a tiger's roar. He petted it. Good boy.

"I was just wondering," she yelled over the roar, "I was just wondering why you haven't disclosed anything about the shoe boxes!"

Tom sighed. He *hated* press leaks.

"I don't suppose you're going to tell me who your informant is?"

"No," replied Lilly. "But thanks for confirming his story. Or her story. Maybe their story…"

"You don't really want to know why I haven't disclosed that information, because you already know why I haven't disclosed that information. You understand the principle of withholding key evidence because you're doing the same thing now with me."

She lit up a Marlboro, blew smoke away from his face, and grinned.

"Okay, so now, Ms. Toro, I guess I'm going to ask you what your price is for your discretion. What is it your newspaper wants to keep any mention of shoe boxes off the front page?"

"An exclusive."

"Mmm-hmm."

"Not an exclusive on the whole case. I know you can't give me an exclusive on the whole case. I want to report about your team."

"Me."

"'What's it like, firsthand, to track down a serial killer?' I want to be embedded."

"Uh-huh. That's very much not going to happen."

He revved the Harley.

"You know," she yelled, "once we print the story, you're not going to have any leverage to tell the difference between the fake leads and the real ones! I imagine that'll make your team's lives a lot more complicated!"

He gritted his teeth. Before she even said it, he knew she was right. By keeping some elements of the crime a secret, his team could sift out the crazies and the wannabes. Once those elements became public, his task force would have no easy way of confirming or denying the validity of any call they received. Their time and resources would be wasted while the real killer remained at large.

He *really* hated press leaks.

He killed the engine. Again.

"Let me give you my number," Tom mumbled.

"Don't worry," Lilly replied. "I've already got it."

"Of course you do." When he discovered which cop/flunky/politician was slipping information to the press… "Goodbye, Ms. Toro."

"Special Agent Piper, please. Call me Lilly. After all, we're going to be seeing a lot of each other."

On his way to the hospital, Tom grabbed a bite to eat at Whataburger. He ate out in the restaurant's parking lot. Eating outside, come rain or shine, was one of his private pleasures. The quality of the food itself rarely mattered—right now he was at a fast food joint, for Christ's sake—but the combination of environment and nourishment offered Tom his few fleeting moments of peace.

As it turned out, by midafternoon the day had become unseasonably warm, and Tom, atop his bike, gratefully shrugged off his heavy leather coat. The breeze tickled at his neck. Although the sun remained hidden behind gray clouds, it was most assuredly up there, somewhere. Trying. One couldn't help but admire the effort.

Esme still hadn't called.

Tom was tempted to phone her back, but refrained. If she didn't want to get involved, she didn't want to get involved. He had to respect that. He *didn't* respect it—just as he hadn't seven years ago—but he had to at least pretend. Pushing only created distance.

She would be such an asset on this case. There were so many variables, so many questions unanswered. This was a killer who thought outside the box, and Tom knew his capture would only be achieved by a detective who thought outside the box. And Esme flourished outside the box. So what in the hell was she doing in cookie-cutter Long Island…?

Tom washed down the last of his burger with a swig of tangy lemonade and tossed his refuse in a nearby bin. Across the street was a superstore which specialized in hats. Sometimes Amarillo reminded him of his childhood back in Jasper. Only Jasper wasn't as flat. Nothing was as flat as the Texas Panhandle. The landscape was populated, as it were, with forests of shrubs that rarely rose above Tom's ankle. The rest was desert, and went on for infinity.

Tom motored up Wallace Boulevard to Baptist St. Anthony's. Chief Harold Lymon, nicknamed "Catch," was situated on the fifth floor. Since no one from the hospital had left Tom a message, he assumed the man was still, sixty-five hours after being shot, unconscious. The doctors had insisted that Catch's condition wasn't critical, that he had been extraordinarily lucky, that his brain functions appeared normal and he could awaken at any moment. However, that likelihood decreased with each passing hour. Catch—and what he might have seen at the aquarium—was their best hope—their only hope—in identifying the sniper who called himself Galileo.

So imagine Tom's relief when he received a text message, just as he pulled into the hospital lot. CATCH AWAKE, it read. It was from Darcy Parr, the youngest member of his task force. She'd drawn the morgue assignment, and since the morgue was situated in Baptist St. Anthony's, it made sense she'd be the first to learn any status change in Catch's condition.

Three minutes and thirty seconds after reading the text, Tom had locked up his motorcycle, secured his gear, and was riding the hospital elevator up to floor five. Darcy met him at the nurses' station.

"The doctors are in with him right now," she said. "They said he may be too weak to talk, but I convinced them to give us five minutes as soon as they're done."

Darcy was Tom's little blond-haired puppy dog—hyperactive, always eager to please, sidling up beside him. She was twenty-six years old. Her youthful energy sometimes drove Tom insane. Today it helped stretch his lips into a cheek-to-cheek grin.

Two different Texas Rangers were stationed outside Room 526. The door was closed. As soon as Catch had arrived at the hospital, the Texas Rangers had stepped up and volunteered their time. Everyone wanted to help. Well, except Esme Stuart.

The Rangers—two tin-starred linebackers topped with cream-colored cowboy hats—stood at attention on either side of the door. Tom offered them a salute. Darcy followed close behind.

"How long have they been in there?" he asked.

"About fifteen, sir," replied Sgt. Conwell.

"Catch called out to us, sir," added Sgt. Baynes. "He knew where he was. He knew what had happened."

Tom's grin filled his whole face. He paced the hall, eager to chat with his star witness.

"How was the service?" Darcy asked.

"It was nice. Very respectful."

He glanced at Room 526's closed door. Any minute now.

"Has his family been notified?" Tom asked her.

"As far as I know," Darcy replied. "I'm sure they'll

be here soon. I'm sure they'll want to talk with him, too."

"Well, then, they've just got to wait in line."

Any second now…

"He's had a lot of visitors, sir," said Sgt. Baynes. "We only let immediate family in to see him. And the lieutenant governor." Perhaps he was just trying to occupy the silence. Perhaps he was crowing his achievements. Tom didn't care.

"Thank you, Sergeant."

"There was one reporter who tried to see him a few minutes ago," Baynes added. "Rude little bastard. Even tried to take a picture of Catch with his camera phone. We got rid of the scamp right quick."

"Thank you, Sergeant."

Any second now…

The rude little bastard Sgt. Baynes was referring to was now on floor four of the hospital, in the men's room. Underneath the sink was a briefcase, secured there with duct tape. He peeled the tape away and hefted the briefcase into his arms. It was not light.

Back on the fifth floor, the door finally opened. Four doctors filed out.

"Two minutes," the eldest doctor warned. "He's still weak."

Tom nodded eagerly and, with Darcy in tow, entered Room 526.

Room 426, in the primary care ward, was occupied by two patients. One was off having tests. The other, a rotund fellow with red mullet named Curly McCue, was watching *Jerry Springer* on the TV fastened to the wall.

The rude little bastard entered Room 426 and wedged the door shut with a small piece of wood from his pocket.

"Hi there," said Curly, happy to have a visitor, "can I help you?"

"My name is Special Agent Tom Piper," Tom said, one story up. Although the room's blinds were drawn (safety precaution), the fire chief's hazel eyes seemed to glow with daylight and vitality.

"I saw him," he told the agents. His voice was raspy. He took a sip of water from a paper cup the doctors must have given him. "He was on the roof of a building across the street."

Tom kept his ever-bourgeoning excitement in check. This was a man who had almost died, whose team of firefighters had been murdered. "Did you get a good look at him, Chief?"

Catch nodded.

Back in Room 426, the rude little bastard was assembling his M107. From barrel to stock, it was twenty-nine inches long and weighed almost twenty-nine pounds. A certain symmetry, that. It could accurately fire .50 caliber rounds at a distance of 6,561 feet, or over one mile. His target today, though, was only twenty feet away. Vertically. Galileo double-checked the snapshot he'd taken on his cell phone to verify the corresponding location in the room of his prey.

Curly McCue didn't budge. His bed was soaked with urine. On TV, two scantily-clad pregnant women were wrestling. Curly McCue tried to recall the words to the Lord's Prayer.

Tom leaned into the bed. Catch's parched voice made his words difficult to understand. Darcy mimicked her boss and stood at the other side of the bed and also leaned.

Catch swallowed down another gulp of water. Smiled at the agents. And then his heart splashed Valentine's Day blood against the ceiling of the room, across Tom and Darcy's faces, and the world.

Tom and Darcy recoiled from the bed. Catch's face still displayed that patient smile, frozen now in time and spattered scarlet. The plastic cup was squeezed in his left fist. Water trickled down the side of his hand and dripdropped against the tiled floor below. Blood soon joined.

The Rangers burst into the room, pistols at the ready.

"Seal the exits!" Tom demanded. "Go!"

BAM! Catch's body jumped again. The assassin had taken a second shot, just to be sure. The bullet angled off a rib and nabbed Tom in his left shoulder.

"Stay here," he ordered Darcy, who was leaning against the wall. Possibly in shock. "Keep everyone outside the room." In case the shooter fired again.

Darcy nodded, catching her breath. She was wiping Catch's blood from her nostrils and irises when she noticed Tom's wound. With his right hand he unsheathed his Glock from its shoulder-holster and dashed out to the nearest stairwell to intercept the sniper. He took the steps three at a time, emerged on the fourth floor, and didn't have to worry about getting lost—he just followed the sounds of the screaming.

The wound in his left shoulder screamed in unison. He knew it wasn't just a flesh wound. The bullet was lodged inside his muscle. Blood soaked his inoperable left arm. Tom, left-handed, did his best to ignore the pain and briskly walked to the nurses' station.

The nurses were on the floor—uninjured, but seeking shelter. The screams came from the patients on the ward. Hospital security wasn't there—the Rangers had undoubtedly commandeered them to help man the exits.

The door to Room 426 was wide open.

Chunks of ceiling panel crumbled on to Curly McCue's bed. Curly had a single gunshot wound to the forehead, close range. His eyes were closed. He had known what was coming.

The sniper was gone.

"Which way?" Tom barked at the nearest orderly.

"I…"

"WHICH WAY?"

But no one replied. They either didn't know—or were too afraid to say. Tom approached the nurses' station and dialed security.

"Did you get him?" he asked. But he already knew what the answer would be.

6

For their Valentine's date, Rafe bought his wife a wrist corsage. He spent most of his office hours in line at the florist's down the block from the university. Apparently every married man in Long Island was both a romantic and a procrastinator.

"A kelly green carnation," he requested. That's what she'd had in her wedding bouquet, so he knew he was on safe ground. He didn't want to screw anything up, not today, not for Esme. The florist secured the delicate flower, still dappled with water droplets, in its plastic container.

He stored it in the fridge in the faculty lounge. He made sure to stick on a Post-it with his name on it, and hoped that would be enough to dissuade thieves (although he knew in academia no property—especially intellectual—was ever sacred). Fortunately, the corsage remained undisturbed, and by 5:30 p.m. he was carrying it (and a valise heavy with student papers) to his Saab.

It was a long walk. Rafe was out of breath by the

time he reached his car. The arctic weather didn't help; he could feel his ears and bare hands ache with each blast of wind. How peculiar, he thought, that both extreme heat and extreme cold turned bare skin red. He surmised it had something to do with blood. But Rafe Stuart was an associate professor in cultural sociology. He dissected demographics and memes. Anatomy was two quads away, in an oblong, curvaceous building shaped roughly (and somewhat appropriately) like the starship *Enterprise*.

Rafe tossed his valise in the trunk but very, very gently placed the corsage on the passenger seat. He was a little nervous. Big romantic evenings were not his forte. He much preferred a quiet night at home where he wasn't under pressure to be Casanova. He loved his wife dearly, desperately, but loathed the typical dinner-and-a-movie rituals that society demanded, especially on days like this. Romance, he always had believed, should be a private affair. But today was Valentine's Day, and so a corsage (for charm) and Il Forno (for pasta by candlelight). All for Esme. Anything for Esme.

Stuck in traffic on the way home, Rafe adjusted his rearview mirror to verify his necktie's knot. He'd changed into a suit before leaving campus but hadn't felt confident about his knot. Sure enough, it canted to the left. As soon as he exited the expressway, as soon as he reached his first red light, he tried to fix it. Loosen—straighten—tighten. Nope, try again. Drive another mile. Next red light. Loosen—straighten—tighten. Close, but still a bit askew, no? Drive another half-mile. He'd reached downtown Oyster Bay.

Sophie's school was to his left. He braked at a red light by the school and gave the knot one last go. Loosen—straighten—tighten. Some of his colleagues in social sciences wore ties year round. How could they breathe?

He angled his Saab into his subdivision. While questions like why one's skin turned red were well beyond his field of knowledge, the matters of appearances and social perception were very much in his reach and grasp. Although he rarely wore a tie to work, he always wore a long-sleeved, iron-pressed, button-down shirt, even in the summer. Neutral colors, nothing flashy or flamboyant. Respect had to be earned, and man was the most superficial of God's beasts. When they first met, Esme would have been happy attending a cocktail party in a T-shirt and jeans. He'd shown her the error of her ways.

Butterflies zipped around inside him. Did what was left of his black hair look adequately flat? Were his eyeglasses clear of specks? He shuffled out of his Saab and headed to the front door. He adjusted his tie knot one last time and rang the doorbell to his own house. Their teenage sitter greeted him with a mouthful of braces.

"Hello, Mr. Stuart. You look very nice tonight."

"Thank you, Chelsea," he replied. He didn't want to come in. That wasn't what he'd planned. Esme would meet him at the door. It would be like a prom date. That's what he'd planned. That's what would have been romantic. He was sure of it. But instead here was their brace-faced babysitter—

"Daddy!"

Sophie rushed from her homework to the doorway

and slapped her arms around her father's belly (well, as much of it as she could circumnavigate) in a snug embrace.

"Hi, sweetness." He kissed her scalp. She gleamed up at him with blue eyes. For a moment, he forgot about his plans, his tie, Valentine's Day, brace-faced Chelsea, the corsage he'd left in the car, the papers he needed to grade, the chill of the wind, the tilt of the earth's axis, every-thing. Rafe's little girl could induce amnesia, yes, she could. But ah, only temporarily. "Where's Mommy?"

On cue, Mommy strolled down the stairs. She wore a form-fitting evening dress, red for the occasion. It brought out the freckles on her nose. For the second time in two minutes, Rafe's mind went ecstatically blank.

Esme, responding to the awed expression on his face, shyly tucked a loose strand of hair behind an ear. Even after eight years, he still found her beautiful. She took his hand, they bid good-night to Sophie and her sitter, and walked out into the night.

They arrived late at the restaurant, but after a minimum of fuss the cheery maître d' led them to their table. Il Forno rested on a cliff and overlooked the dark blue Long Island Sound. Esme and Rafe took their seats by the window and stared out through the glass at the undulating waves.

Her right wrist sported the green carnation. She'd almost sat on it when she'd opened the car door, back in their driveway, but a last-minute warning from Rafe averted disaster. Rafe hurried to her side of the car and placed the corsage on his wife's wrist.

Esme grinned. Was anyone more adorable than her husband? She kissed him full on the lips and whispered into his ear, "Thank you."

Their tuxedoed waiter introduced himself—but needn't have, as he was one of Rafe's Meme Seminar students.

"Great to see you, Professor!" Nate said. "I didn't know you came here!"

Rafe maintained his friendly smile. Had he known any of his students would be here, no, he wouldn't have come. If romance couldn't be a private affair, it at least could and should be shielded from his college girls and boys. While students were often cavalier in class about their personal lives, an instructor's personal life was sacrosanct.

Once Tuxedo Nate took their drink orders and left, Rafe leaned in to his wife and casually inquired if she'd prefer to go somewhere else. But Esme laughed it off. "Because of our waiter? I think it's funny. Why—is he failing your class? Are you worried he's going to poison your food?"

Rafe winced. This was not the evening he had planned. But at least Esme had loved the corsage. And hopefully the food would be good. He gave the rest of the restaurant a cursory scan. No other students, either waiting on table or on dates with their significant others. Good. Il Forno was a little out of their price range, anyway.

Nate arrived with their merlot. He poured each their glass and left them the bottle in its decanter.

"Are we ready to order?" he asked.

They were. They did. He left.

"So," Rafe inquired, savoring his wine, "what did you do today?"

"Not much. Did some laundry. Finished that crappy novel I had to read."

"Sounds like a peaceful day."

"Oh, and Tom Piper called."

Rafe gently steadied his wineglass back on the table. "To wish you a Happy Valentine's Day?"

Esme sighed. "Rafe…"

His azure gaze fixated on the waves in the moonlight. They followed the dark water as it lapped against the shore, then back into the void.

"He just wanted to talk to me, you know, about what's been going on down in Atlanta and Amarillo. Get my take on it."

"Did he get it? Your take, that is."

His eyes shifted from the ocean to his wife. Sometimes she could make him forget about the world, true. But sometimes she could make every memory caged in his brain explode at once into searing clarity…

"I didn't call him back," she replied, and clasped his thick hands in hers. "My responsibilities are here now. Aren't they?"

Romance should be a private affair? Fuck that. Rafe reached over and in the presence of the entire restaurant (including Tuxedo Nate) kissed his wife full on the mouth.

When they got home, Chelsea was sprawled across their divan, gabbing on her cell and noshing on carrot sticks. She said her regretful goodbyes to whoever was on the other line (her boyfriend, probably—today *was* Valentine's Day) and hopped to her feet.

"Sophie's asleep," she said.

Esme nodded. Sleep was not a bad idea. She'd consumed more than her share of the merlot and was feeling its hypnotic tingle all through her body—but especially in her legs. She leaned against the kitchen counter, aiming for nonchalance and achieving full-out drunken goofiness.

If Chelsea noticed, she didn't say anything. She seemed too intent anyway on the greenbacks Rafe was counting out from his wallet. Not a bad salary for carrot stick noshing and divan sprawling. Rafe offered to drive her home, but she lived only a few blocks away.

And she just wants more alone time with her boyfriend, mused Esme. Oh, to be young and in love. Although being in love in your late thirties wasn't so bad either…

Esme's lips stretched into a loopy grin. She wandered toward her daughter's bedroom and peeked inside. Sophie slept curled up like a corn chip. Her small fists had her pink comforter pulled up to her chin. Esme knew she used to sleep like that, when she was younger. She would wake up with her bed sheet wrapped around her body like a protective cocoon. But Sophie had many cocoons protecting her. Esme suddenly felt the urge to embrace her daughter, but relented. Better to let her sleep, she decided. Sleep, dream and grow.

Esme strolled back into the living room. Chelsea was

gone, and Rafe was returning the carrot sticks to the fridge.

"I'm just going to check my e-mail for a minute," said Esme. She hoped he caught her subtext: *and then we'll retire to the bedroom for some appropriate Valentine's Day sex games.* But if he noticed, he didn't say anything. Instead, he was sniffing the milk for freshness.

She sat down at her desk. It was time to reply to Tom's e-mail. As the computer booted up, she went over in her mind how she would phrase her rejection. Above all, she needed to remain compassionate but firm. Of course she recognized how horrible his situation was. Of course she would help if she could—but she couldn't. Her heart went out to all those victims' families…but her heart then was obliged to come back here, to her home.

As she waited for the e-mail software to load, she occupied her mild ADD by also opening her Web browser. What was happening in the world today? Her browser went to its MSNBC home page and she scanned the headlines. Earthquake in Pakistan, rally for Governor Kellerman in his home state of Ohio, Congress reinvestigating farm subsidies in Nebraska and Wyoming…

Her eyes then found the story about the shooting at the hospital.

In the kitchen, Rafe had poured himself a glass of milk. His chicken marinara had been a bit too spicy and he was hoping a cold glass would soothe his indigestion. Or perhaps, he pondered with amusement, indigestion was just symptomatic of the warm glow he had felt ever since the restaurant.

And then his wife said, "Fuck," and began to fumble through her purse. She took out her cell phone and began dialing.

"Who are you calling?" he asked calmly. The kitchen clock read 8:26 p.m. Not terribly late. Maybe she was calling Amy Lieb. After all, they both were in that silly book club and—

"Tom," she said. "It's me."

That's right. She hadn't called him back yet. Rafe tried not to eavesdrop, but his better angels were asleep on the job. Make sure you let him down easy, babe. We don't need to piss off the federal government.

Esme was fiddling with her computer. "No, I just read the story. I was out with Rafe."

Rafe sipped his milk. Good girl. Name-drop the husband.

Wait—just read *what* story?

"I'm checking the flights now," she said. "The earliest I can take is a 6:05 a.m. flight out of LaGuardia. I'll have to change planes in Dallas, but I should get into Amarillo at 11:45 a.m."

Rafe placed the glass of milk in the sink. "Esme."

She didn't look at her husband, but instead put up her hand to shush him. "No, Tom. I'll pay for it. The Bureau can reimburse me."

"Esme."

Rafe marched into the living room.

This time she looked at him.

"Tom, I'm going to have to call you back. Okay. Talk to you soon."

She hung up.

Rafe stared at her. Then:

"Esme, what the hell was that?"

"Rafe, listen, there's been another shooting. At the hospital in Texas. The fire chief, the one who survived the thing at the aquarium—the sniper walked right into the hospital and shot him."

"So—"

"He shot Tom, too."

Rafe could swear there were tears in her eyes. He threw up his hands in exasperation. "Tom has a very important and dangerous job. People in dangerous jobs get hurt. It happens."

"Don't talk to me like I'm a—"

"Then don't act like one! Your going down there isn't going to make him heal any faster, Esme." He cocked his head, studied his wife for a moment. "But that's not why you're going down there, is it?"

She stood up. "Listen…"

"How long?"

"What?"

"How long do you plan on being away? A week? A month? Sometimes it takes the FBI years to catch these guys. Are you going to be gone a year, Esme? I need to know so when our daughter asks, I can tell her."

"That isn't fair." She balled her hands into fists. "I fly down there and—what? What do you expect is going to happen? I'm going to rejoin the fucking Bureau? I'll be there as an extra pair of eyes. I'll be there to put in my two cents—which shouldn't take very long—and then I'll be on the next plane back home. I promise."

"What about Sophie? Who's going to pick her up after school?"

"We can let Sophie stay after school with the Kleins or the McKinleys. It's not a big deal. I'll call Holly McKinley right now to make sure."

She started dialing.

Rafe wanted to smack the phone out of her hand. A part of him even wanted to smack *her*—and that's what gave him pause. He would not be the villain here. He was not the one who…

But being stubborn would accomplish nothing. Correction: being stubborn would just carve out an abyss between them which would widen and deepen with time. Sophie would notice. Their neighbors would notice. He was a sociology professor. Inflexible societies eventually snapped like twigs. Was he so implacable? Was he willing to risk so much?

"Three days."

She stopped dialing. Looked over at him. "What?"

"You can have three days. Anything more than that and you're not just putting in your two cents. Anything more than that and you're on the task force. And then your responsibilities will be even more divided than they already are. You're there three days and you're a consultant. You're there any longer and they'll start counting on you. I'm pretty sure I'm right."

She shook her head. No, he wasn't wrong.

"But just so we're clear," she added, "you don't get to ever—ever—give me an ultimatum like that. You don't think I'm torn up over this? You made your point and you're right. Three days it is. But that's *my* choice."

7

On the evening of February 14, whilst young lovers kissed and old lovers spooned, Darcy Parr went looking for drugs. Claritin, Zyrtec—any antihistamine would do. Finding a drugstore still open in Amarillo after 10:00 p.m., however, was proving to be a chore, and so she ended trolling the luminescent tiles of Walmart.

Also, it provided her with an excuse to leave the hotel. Not that she was getting stir-crazy. But Tom Piper was two rooms down, and his vicinity reminded her of this afternoon.

She blamed herself.

The hospital had been her responsibility. Her primary assignment had been to coordinate with the M.E.'s office, and the M.E.'s office was at Baptist St. Anthony's. That the fire chief was also under her jurisdiction went without saying. No one else from the task force was stationed at the hospital. No one else was even close. The sniper infiltrated the place on her watch. Their witness died on her watch. His blood was on her hands.

And face…and hair…

No. She had gotten all of it off in the shower. Right? Yes.

She found the nearest mirror—glued to an endcap for sunglasses—and double-checked. Yes. No more blood. Pores clean. Blond hair pulled back in a ponytail. She looked like a coed in a sorority, not someone who'd just…

Shake it off, Darcy. Get your allergy medicine. Maybe send an e-mail to Pastor Joe when you return to the hotel. He never slept, and he always knew exactly what to say. Pastor Joe ran her parish church back in Virginia. Much of the congregation consisted of spooks, spies and Bureau instructors. It had been Darcy's home church growing up. These were the people she knew. A career in the FBI had pretty much been predestined. It was these connections which enabled her to join Tom Piper's esteemed task force.

She found the pharmacy aisles near the racks of get-well cards. How appropriate. It didn't take her long to stock her basket with antihistamines. She even tossed a box of Sudafed in there, just in case.

It's not that Amarillo contained an unusually high pollen count or that February was a particularly bad month for allergens. That's why she hadn't brought any medication with her on the trip from Virginia. But her symptoms, as she well knew, had nothing to do with the environment. They were induced by stress, and she'd suffered their effects since early childhood. Nobody said being an overachiever was easy.

And then there was the matter of Esme Stuart.

Darcy pressed down on her swollen sinuses, sniffled and coughed. Esme Stuart had left the Bureau long before Darcy Parr left the Academy, but her legend resounded up and down every wall at Quantico. She had been Tom Piper's prodigy, and now she was coming back. It's not that Darcy was jealous. It was silly to be jealous of someone so far out of your league. But Darcy was the newest member of the task force, the youngest, the greenest, and if Esme Stuart were to come back for good, if her return proved permanent…well, it didn't take a Vegas bookie to foretell whose place on the team was most vulnerable.

Adding what happened today at the hospital to that little fact and Darcy was fortunate her stress hadn't flared into the full-blown anxiety attack. The irony, of course, was that she could do the job. She had been at the top of her class at the Academy, and not because the instructors had offered a local girl special treatment. The reality had been exactly the opposite, but Darcy had persevered and now she was here in Amarillo, on her first case as a member of the most elite task force in the entire FBI. Her first case. And possibly her last.

She detoured to the Hallmark greetings. A get-well card for Tom wasn't totally out of line. It was thoughtful. After all, her boss had been shot. And he wouldn't very well tell her to pack her bags after she gave him a get-well card, would he? Would he?

"Miss, are you all right?"

Darcy glanced to her left. A sandy-haired man in his forties stood there, a kind smile on his face. He wore ranchers' gloves, and held out a handkerchief in one of his gloved hands.

"I'm fine. It's just allergies." She chuckled a bit to herself. "I know that's what people say when…but, really, I'm fine."

He pocketed the handkerchief in his weather-beaten jean jacket and added, with a chuckle of his own, "Valentine's Day takes its toll on us all."

Darcy nodded. With all that had happened, she'd completely forgotten today was a holiday. Not that she had a sweetheart back in Virginia. A social life was, well, low on her list of priorities. If she got lonely, she had relatives she could visit in almost every county in Virginia. She wouldn't be like Esme Stuart. Her commitment to the FBI would be permanent. Surely Tom recognized that about her.

"But I see you're not even looking for Valentine's Day cards, are you? How foolish of me to jump to that conclusion. But that's what I do. Look before I leap. That's me. But someone you know is ill." He offered a look of sympathy. "That's why I'm here too, actually."

"Oh?"

The sandy-haired man shrugged humbly. "It's unfortunate, really. The ways things happen in this life. We do what we do and meanwhile people get hurt, every day, and that's just the way the universe works."

"I don't know if it's as bleak as all that," replied Darcy. She noticed the man wore a shoulder-holster. What was that tucked inside, a Beretta? Normally she'd be concerned, but this was Texas. The Second Amend-

ment was as beloved here as any of the Ten Commandments. "God only gives us what we can handle."

He mumbled something in response, probably in
agreement, then looked around the aisle. He suddenly
seemed weighed down with despair.

"Who are you getting your card for?" she asked
him.

"It's not someone I know very well. But sometimes
the message is really more important to the messenger
than to anyone else. You know?"

Darcy reflected on her own semi-selfish reasons for
card-shopping. "Yeah," she said, and felt a bit ashamed.

"The unfortunate part of it is—her condition's
terminal and she doesn't even know it. I mean, all of
us are dying in increments, but…"

"That's terrible."

He nodded sadly. "It is."

He picked out one of his cards and, with impressive
dexterity considering the thickness of his gloves, was
able to take a pen out of one of his jacket's many inside
pockets and scrawl a message on its inside. All the
while his eyes appeared moist. Not from allergies.
Darcy wanted to give the man a hug.

"Ah, well," he sighed.

He returned the pen to its pocket, took out his
silenced Beretta, and with it shot Darcy twice in the
forehead. He placed the get-well card (a Shoebox
Greeting) on her chest and strolled away.

It was Lilly Toro who picked the parking garage for
the clandestine meet, not out of any affection for

Woodward and Bernstein but because it was, at this late hour, so reliably vacant. She perched on the hood of her VW Beetle and smoked her fifteenth Marlboro of the day.

Spending Valentine's Day outside of her hometown blew.

Her informant showed up an hour late, but he was a cop, so his tardiness was not entirely unexpected. As soon as his metallic gold Crown Victoria whipped into view, she flicked the nub of her cigarette into outer space and took out her notebook. The guy didn't like to be tape-recorded. Few snitches did.

He parked across the painted lines. He didn't leave his car. He motioned for her to join him inside.

With a sigh, Lilly hopped off her VW and wandered to the passenger side of his Crown Vic. So this was how it was going to be.

The cop's name was Ray Milton. He'd served on the Amarillo Police Department for eleven years. He worked in Property/Evidence and had known two of the slain firefighters personally. He bummed a Marlboro off her an hour before the memorial service.

Five minutes into the conversation, he was bitching about how the feds had stolen the case. Ten minutes into their conversation, they'd agreed to a quid pro quo: Ray would supply her with the leverage she needed to infiltrate the task force (namely, the bit about the shoe boxes). In return, once on the inside, she would funnel back to him updates on the case's status. If the Amarillo P.D. was going to be benched, it at least was going to get to watch the game.

And so, upon learning from a very gabby receptionist in city hall about Esme Stuart's impending arrival (11:45 a.m. tomorrow morning), Lilly phoned Ray. She zipped her VW to the meeting spot she designated, the abandoned parking garage, and so, here they were, at 11:45 p.m., in Ray's twenty-year-old metallic gold Crown Victoria.

Which smelled like cinnamon.

This confused Lilly to no end. She'd expected the familiar tang of slow sweet death she inhaled every time she lit up, but no. Cinnamon. Then she noticed the red cardboard leaf dangling from Ray's rearview mirror. Ah. Cinnamon. The man probably had kids and didn't want to reek up the car pool on the way to Little League. Had he mentioned kids? After the memorial service, Lilly had done a background check on her informant just to verify his details, badge number, etc. One could never be too careful. But the data she'd accumulated had made no mention of kids. Whatever.

"So what's your big news?" he asked.

His brown eyes bulged with eagerness.

Down boy, she mused.

"Yeah, I see you hustled right over here," she replied. Waiting an hour in the middle of February in a nowhere-to-go-nothing-to-do city had been less than fun. "If you got here any faster, we could've had breakfast."

"Sorry. Had an errand to run. Didn't expect you to call so soon."

"What can I say, Ray? I missed your sweet Texas charm."

He scowled, charmingly.

She held up her hands. "Okay, okay. Jeez. So here's the scoop—your pals at the FBI have got a ringer flying in from New York."

"A ringer?"

"Her name's Esmeralda Stuart. And you should've seen Special Agent Piper when he told his crew the news. It was like he was talking about the Second Coming. Apparently she's some kind of savant. I don't know."

Lilly was lying. She did know. As soon as Tom Piper had made the announcement, she'd beelined for her Hello Kitty laptop and gleaned as much information on Esme Stuart as was available. But Ray Milton didn't need to know that. Ray Milton needed to know what she decided he needed to know. Give a man a fish and he'll eat for a day; teach a man to fish and baby, that boy won't need you no more.

Ray studied his steering wheel for a moment. Then: "When is she arriving?"

"Tomorrow morning."

"Thank you." He smiled at her. His teeth were eggshell white. He must spray them or something—no smoker has teeth like that. "Maybe the FBI knows what they're doing after all."

"Nobody knows what they're doing, Ray. That's what makes it all so much fun."

She saluted the middle-aged cop and exited the cinnamon cloud of his vehicle. She felt him watch her go. She couldn't blame him. When she wore the right outfit, her curves could cause whiplash in the most modest of spectators. So what if she liked women? That didn't mean she couldn't appreciate being ogled now and again by the lesser of the species…

Sigh.

Spending Valentine's Day outside of her hometown really blew.

Lilly meandered her way back to Motel 6. She hoped some of her friends would be online to distract her. She wrote her best journalism when she was distracted, and she didn't want to squander this opportunity. Her articles on the task force had the potential to be front page, above the fold. The public loved to peek behind the curtain and see the wizard at play, and this time there was the sexy bonus of a serial killer. If she played to her strengths and created the rock-solid reportage she knew she could produce, these articles would follow her portfolio until the day she died, when some other journalist would mention them at the top of her obit.

Her sixteenth (but not last) Marlboro of the day accompanied her on the short walk from the parking lot to her room. She passed a vending machine on her way, considered buying a bag of pork rinds, but continued on her way. The only thing worse than being stuck in Texas would be getting fat in Texas. It's not that she was biased against the entire state. Austin, for example, was a wonderfully progressive city, and she had some friends who swore that the arts scene in Houston was thriving. However, most of the folk she had met, at least here in Amarillo, had been of Ray Milton's ilk: a Bible in one hand and a shotgun in the other. Her lifestyle—hell, her very appearance (when she wore all her piercings and left her tattoos uncovered)—was diametrically opposed to everything these people held dear. She knew it. To them, she was the demon spawn. Worse yet, she was *California*. Not everyone here felt this way, of course, but the majority did, and in America, the majority ruled.

Whatever.

Back in her motel room, Lilly returned her Hello Kitty laptop from hibernation mode, instant-messaged with some friends for an hour, and wrote 500 words for her piece. Her editor Ben Blackman at the *Chronicle* wanted pages? He was going to get them.

She didn't include anything which compromised the task force's capability. She was a responsible journalist...and had only landed her plum source very recently. Still, as an exposé on one of this nation's top crime-fighting units, her story had the potential to sizzle. It had colorful personalities. It had turf wars among different branches of government. It even had a hateful villain. Forget about Pulitzer—this could be her ticket to network television.

Lilly Toro nodded off around 1:00 a.m.; still in her black boots, stockings, the whole nine yards.

At 4:43 a.m., she awoke. Looked around, befuddled. Why the hell am I awake at—

BAM! BAM! BAM!

Someone was at the door.

BAM! BAM! BAM!

Someone not very happy.

Lilly padded over to the peephole.

BAM! BAM! BAM! BAM! BAM!

"I'm coming."

She peered through the peephole. Who the fuck would be banging on her door at 4:43 a.m.?

Lo and behold: it was Special Agent Tom Piper.

Even more confused, Lilly took a moment to straighten her hair, and then she pulled open the door.

"Special Agent Piper. What a semi-pleasant surprise."

He stared at her for a full thirty seconds. Thirty seconds of nothing but his eyes on hers. He was trying to peer into her soul. She could feel it. She was terrified of what he wouldn't find.

After thirty seconds, he reached some kind of conclusion. "Okay," he said.

Then she noticed the blood on his palms.

What the hell?

He noticed her noticing.

"It's Darcy Parr's," he said. "He shot her a few hours ago at Walmart."

Darcy Parr was dead? Jesus Christ. Wait—Walmart? Where had she seen…?

"The license plate of the guy you met tonight? It's registered to a Pablo Marx out of Lubbock. Pablo Marx—"

"Wait…"

"Pablo Marx was reported missing ten days ago."

"How do you know I—"

"How do you think?"

Lilly shouldn't have been surprised, but she was. Of course they would tail her. They knew she had an informant. Of course they would want to find out his identity.

"His name is Ray Milton," she told him. "He's a cop with the Amarillo Police Department."

"Ms. Toro, all due respect, but I guarantee you the man you've been speaking to is neither named Ray Milton nor he has ever, ever, worked with the Amarillo P.D. We're going to need you to come with us. Right now."

Lilly nodded, reached for her coat. Her mind was spinning (and the lateness of the hour didn't help).

"Am I going to look at mug shots?" she asked.

"No, Ms. Toro. You're going to help us trap the son of a bitch."

8

Esme had three days to solve the case.

She solved it in nine hours.

While the rest of the task force was prepping Lilly Toro for the sting operation, Esme sequestered herself in a conference room, set her iPod to random selection, and through careful analysis of the case files and aggressive prodding of the FBI computer database, was able to deduce not only Galileo's next likely target, but also his endgame.

This is how she did it:

Tom met her at the airport. The new lines on his long face weren't just from age. It was obvious he hadn't slept. Nevertheless, he put in the effort to smile.

"Esmeralda," he said. "You look good."

"So do you," she lied. His left arm hung useless in a mauve sling. Oh, Tom.

They hugged, two old friends, and waited beside the baggage carousel for Esme's two Louis Vuitton suitcases to emerge. Outside the bright Texas sun foretold a day luminescent with possibilities.

"Do you have any new photos of Sophie?" asked Tom. "She has to be, what, in grad school by now, right?"

Esme smirked. "Practically. Don't worry, I've got a whole bunch of pictures in my digital camera. I'll show them to you later."

"Great."

"How's your family? Is your cousin still married to what's-her-name with the Komodo dragon?"

"They've added a second pet to the household."

"A unicorn?"

"A sea otter."

"Oh, God."

"It lives in their swimming pool in the backyard."

"Of course it does."

Her baggage arrived, intact and unblemished.

As they lugged it outside, Esme wondered how it all would fit on his Harley. To her surprise, a black sedan pulled to the curb and its trunk popped open. Behind the wheel sat 242 pounds of Norm Petrosky.

"The prodigal returns," he said. Norm was one of the task force's expert profilers.

Tom took the passenger seat and Esme sat in back. It felt odd to Esme, being chauffeured like that, but times had changed…

"How was your flight?" asked Norm.

"It didn't crash."

"Oh, well. Maybe next time."

They accelerated onto the highway. Esme had never been to Amarillo. It looked modest, wholesome, which made what had happened here all the more insidious. Tom filled Esme in on Darcy Parr's murder.

"You would have liked her," he said. "She reminded me of you at her age."

Then I probably wouldn't have liked her, decided Esme.

By the time they pulled up to city hall, the perfect blue sky had faded to a tin hue. Esme followed the men into the building. By way of explanation, Tom told her that Mayor Lumley had *insisted* the task force operate out of city hall rather than out of the police department, as was customary in a city without its own federal field office.

"She wants our successes to be associated solely with her," said Tom. "She sees this tragedy as her ticket to the state house."

"If our killer knew he was responsible for that," added Norm, "he'd turn himself in today."

Their offices were limited to the second floor. They had an entire bullpen and its adjoining four offices to themselves. According to the signage, this area was regularly used by the Community Relations Office. The Community Relations Office workers had been displaced somewhere else. Perhaps to the police department.

Tom led Esme into the conference room. On the large cherrywood table—all the furniture in the entire building being made of 33-year-old cherry—were stacks and stacks of crime scene reports, lab analyses, evidentiary samples, etc. Almost the entire surface of the table was covered.

"Do you need anything? Juice? Danish?"

Esme shook her head.

"I'm glad you're here," he said.

He closed the door.

She started with the shoe boxes. They were bright orange. The police had conscientiously stuffed each in a plastic bag. She picked up the one labeled Atlanta, placed it on her lap, and carefully removed its contents. Inside the box was the note Tom had e-mailed:

IF THERE WAS STILL A GOD, HE WOULD HAVE STOPPED ME.

—GALILEO

The paper was standard twenty-pound bond, the kind you'd find at any office supply store. No foolscap, no insignia. The typeface was standard too: Courier New. The list of possible suspects narrowed down to anyone who had access to a PC and a printer.

Great.

It was the contents of the note that were revelatory. Esme already had several nascent theories, but she needed more data. She put the first shoe box aside and grabbed the second one. This was the unknown. With anxious anticipation, she un-bagged the orange box and opened its lid.

Inside was a flash drive.

"Tom!" she called. "I need a computer!"

In the bullpen, the FBI task force was working what few leads they had. Norm was updating the psych profile, adding the latest murders to his mix of educated conjecture and professional supposition. Daryl Hewes handled logistics; thanks to his wizardry at obfuscation, the task force always covered its ass both fiscally and legally. Anna and Hector Jackson (no relation) were reviewing for the sixth time the videotape from Wal-mart. Others were at the police station with Lilly Toro, getting her fitted for a bulletproof vest.

Tom was on the phone with Darcy Parr's mother.

"Your daughter, Mrs. Parr, was a tremendous young woman." He gazed out the tinted window. Amarillo city hall overlooked an oblong fountain. Right now the water appeared clear, and even from the second floor Tom could peer through its surface to its ceramic base, which was dotted with pennies. "I'm so sorry for your loss."

Tom felt someone's shadow on the back of his neck. He turned to look. It was Esme. She offered his shoulder a sympathetic squeeze. He nodded. She walked over to Daryl.

"One minute," he said. He typed up another clause on his laptop, perused it, deleted it, then gazed up at Esme through thick black glasses. "I'm just working on your per diem forms and your liability documents. You would think we'd have basic boilerplate language I could adjust to suit these circumstances but it seems the suits continue to lack any semblance of foresight." He scratched at his curly blond pouf, retyped the clause he deleted, and gazed back up at Esme. "Was there something you needed in the interim?"

It took Daryl five minutes to work his magic and find Esme a laptop of her own, five more to link it into their network. She didn't ask where he'd acquired the computer. She didn't want to know. She just thanked him, signed his per diem and the liability documents, and then kindly asked him to close the door on his way out.

Then she plugged in the sniper's flash drive. It contained one file. A movie. Two minutes and twenty-four seconds long.

She pressed Play.

First: a black screen. Underneath it: a scratching noise, the sound of a needle tracking across an old record. Esme upped the volume on the laptop.

White letters slowly bloomed to life out of the black backdrop:

> The men the American people admire most extravagantly are the most daring liars; the men they detest most violently are those who try to tell them the truth. A Galileo could no more be elected President of the United States than he could be elected Pope of Rome. Both posts are reserved for men favored by God with an extraordinary genius for swathing the bitter facts of life in bandages of soft illusion.
>
> —H. L. Mencken

Then, just as slowly, the letters faded back into the darkness. The scratching noise ceased. For a few seconds, silence, then:

Smash cut to MLK Drive. 3:00 a.m. Under a streetlight stand Andre Banks and the two cops, Appleby and Harper. All from the vantage point of the roof of the elementary school.

Suddenly there's music.

Kate Smith, booming "God Bless America." Esme jumped a bit, startled by the loud sound.

Kate's Smith's voice soars as—

Harper goes down.

Appleby goes down.

Andre Banks, panicking, tries for shelter behind the squad car.

The music continues.

Andre Banks goes down.

Smash cut now to an hour later. The local cops are swarming the scene. Pennington, O'Daye. Perry Roman. All ten of them familiar faces now, from the news reports, from what's about to happen.

The first victim is Perry Roman. He drops down like a bag of cement.

The detectives search for their attacker, but it's all in vain. They've already been snared, and marked for slaughter. One by one they collapse.

Officer O'Daye is the last one standing. She is struggling to pull her partner's body out of the line of fire. She's the last to die.

The music suddenly halts.

Cut to black.

Esme didn't realize she was crying until the soundtrack stopped, and she heard sobs, and knew they were her own.

Around midday, Esme took a break from her work to call her neighbor Holly McKinley. Surely Holly had remembered to pick Sophie up from school, right? Esme flipped photographs of the Amarillo crime scene upside down and waited through one, two, three rings before Holly picked up.

"Well, if it isn't my favorite crime-fighter," chirped

Holly, probably between swigs of Evian. "How is life down in the Lone Star State?"

"It's okay. How's the weather up there? I heard it was supposed to snow."

They small-talked for a few minutes more, and finally Esme asked to speak with her daughter.

Holly hesitated.

"Oh…she can't come to the phone right now…"

Esme swallowed hard. "Why's that?" Her mind became flooded with images of Sophie stranded on the steps of the schoolhouse, Sophie in tears, Sophie all alone.

"Well, Esme, I'll be honest. She's covered in green paint."

"Beg pardon?"

"Oh, don't worry. It's just finger-paint. She's making you a card. Turns out I had finger-paint and construction paper in the closet from when Merideth was her age and, well, there you go. Don't worry. I'm making sure she's not eating any of the paint."

"Holly, can you put her on speakerphone?"

"Speakerphone? What a novel idea. No wonder you're such a VIP! One second."

While Esme waited, there was a knock on the conference room door. It was Tom.

"I have the updated psych profile," he said. "Thought you'd want to take a peek."

"Sure. But just a peek. I'm underage."

"Who's underage?" warbled Holly from thousands of miles away. "Esme, you're not doing anything worth gossiping about, are you?"

Tom went to exit but Esme signaled for him to stay.

"Holly, am I on speakerphone?"

"Hi, Mommy," replied Sophie.

Esme's face lit up. "Hi, baby! I hear you've been making me a card."

"I was drawing the state of Texas in green paint."

"Why green?"

"Because it's your favorite color."

So precious. She spotted Tom, still in the doorway. "I miss you, baby. You know that, right?"

"Sure, Mommy," Sophie replied. She sounded so casual. "What are we having for dinner?"

"That's up to your father." Esme got an idea. "Tell him I said you should have macaroni and cheese."

"But he hates macaroni and cheese."

Yep. Rafe hated its creamy taste, its gooey texture, and, most of all, its cheesy aroma, which lingered for days. This would show him. Act like an ass? Deal with mac and cheese.

Esme told Sophie how much she loved her and kissed the air, pretending it was her. Then she hung up.

"Macaroni and cheese, huh?" Tom's face was aglow with bemusement. "I think I ate that every day one summer. When I was six."

They sat down at the table. Esme reviewed the profile Norm had typed up. It didn't take long.

"The card should be back soon from the lab," said Tom. He was referring to the Shoebox greeting which Galileo had left on Darcy's body. Esme had already reviewed the missive scrawled inside: Don't stare into the barrel of a gun.

"Fingerprints?"

Tom shook his head. "Not likely." The killer was too cautious.

"Handwriting analysis?"

"Well, the way he dots his i's proves he was abused by his mother."

"Really?"

"No."

Esme examined the crime scene photos. "He's an atheist on a crusade. The irony alone just kills me."

"Mmm-hmm."

"He's angry at people of faith, but he's not targeting pastors and priests. He's targeting civil servants. He blames religion on the public authority. He's just starting with cops and firefighters. Jesus, Tom, it's an election year. That's not happenstance. We need to alert the campaigns."

"If all goes well tonight," replied Tom, "we won't need to."

9

Lilly Toro wanted to vomit. She rolled down the driver's window of her VW. The fresh air didn't help. She was in the parking garage. It smelled of oil and frustration. Her one consolation was that she wasn't alone. Dozens of cops and G-men were concealed on every rooftop within a two-mile radius, all armed, all watching her back. One FBI agent was literally watching her back: Tom Piper was hidden on the floor of the VW's backseat, his six-foot-plus frame contorted like a curlicue. The fact that Lilly wasn't the only uncomfortable soul here provided her with a modicum of solace. But she still wanted to vomit.

She was a journalist, damn it. She wasn't meant to be part of the story. Yes, she wanted to be embedded with the task force, but in a few minutes a mass murderer would be appearing in this parking garage and his focus would be on her. The flak jacket underneath her sweater did little to allay her concerns. After all, the fucker had a tendency to shoot people in the head.

Lilly was wrong, though, about Tom's discomfort.

Discomfort didn't even begin to describe the amount of pain he was in, most of it radiating from his left shoulder. He didn't have to be here. Another agent could have easily taken his place in the car. This was his operation. Procedure dictated he remain at a distance so as to best oversee and coordinate. But Darcy Parr was dead. She had been his responsibility. If he had to suffer a bit to help catch her killer, so be it.

Which led Tom back to Esme.

She was back at city hall. When Tom last checked in on her, before heading out, she was sitting on the floor amongst teetering towers of paperwork. As her hyperactive IQ absorbed every datum of information, her lips moved along with the words of whatever British rock song was emanating from her iPod. Every so often she'd tuck some of her chestnut-brown hair behind an ear. Did she realize how adorable she was? Did her husband? It's not that Tom didn't like Rafe. It's just…

Well, no. It was that. Tom didn't like Rafe.

Not out of jealousy, mind you. Tom's affection for Esme went well beyond romantic. She was the daughter he never had. Like any good father, he simply wanted what was best for his daughter. Rafe Stuart was not that. How could Tom respect a man who took a shining star and covered it with a tarp?

"We're coming up on nine o'clock," announced Norm over the radio. Since Tom had relegated himself to being Lilly's body man for this particular op, he'd given Norm the reins. Right now Norm was crowded into an unmarked van with the chief of police and a cadre of his finest officers. They had tiny cameras planted all across the city block, and they all fed into the twelve monitors in the van.

Meanwhile, Norm was chowing down on a bean burrito. To his mind, nothing beat genuine Tex-Mex cuisine. When he was buried, he wanted to be buried near Corpus Christi, so his eventual decay would fertilize the corn crops used to create such crisp and succulent tortillas. What a righteous spin on "you are what you eat," eh?

"Okay, girls and boys." Norm washed down the last bite of his burrito with a mouthful of Coke. "It's nine o'clock. All points, check in."

All points checked in.

And waited.

And waited.

Daryl Hewes, who didn't handle idleness very well, used the time to calculate his taxes. In his head. He was situated on the roof of the Santa Fe Building, one of the city's oldest skyscrapers, with two of Amarillo's finest. One of the cops held a pair of binoculars. The other peered through the scope of his rifle.

Daryl Hewes didn't handle idleness well, but there was an even more primal motivation for his mental distractions. Since he'd met her months earlier, the accountant had been carrying a small torch for Ms. Darcy Parr. He could float off at the very sight of her blond locks, the very sound of her down-home Virginia accent. And now the girl was dead, and now his chest felt like razor blades. He would never float off again.

"I hope he tries something," said the cop with the rifle. "I'd love to put a .45 right between the fucker's eyes. That's what you get for pulling this shit in Texas."

"Yep," agreed the other cop. "A .45 to the forehead would do it. Or we could just feed him one of your wife's brownies."

"Don't you be assaulting my wife."

"She delivered the first blow. I think I spent the whole evening on the can. Eventually I just asked Dorleen to bring me my pillow."

"If my wife's brownies were so rotten, how come you ate half the container?"

"'Cause the container tasted better than the brownies!"

"At least my wife bakes. Dorleen wouldn't know a stuffed ham if it sat on her lap and said hello."

"I don't know. Why don't you sit on her lap and we'll find out?"

"Gentlemen," chimed in Norm over the radio, "as amusing as your discussion is, try to keep it off channel. Okay?"

"Sorry, boss," the cops replied.

Norm and the boys in the van had a good chuckle. It helped lighten the mood. Because their man was now twenty-five minutes late for the meet, and that was far from good.

"Should we go?" Lilly asked Tom.

"No."

"I think we should go."

"It's not up to you."

"I'm the one behind the wheel. What's to stop me

from turning the key, gunning the gas, and heading off into the sunset?"

"Well, for one," replied Tom, flexing his shoulder, "the sun set four hours ago."

"Bite me."

"Ms. Toro, we've got seven sharpshooters trained on your location. You move this vehicle even an inch and you're going to need to get a new set of tires."

"Are you threatening me?"

"I'm threatening your car."

"Why do you need me here, anyway? I called him. I set everything up. He pulls into the garage and you take him down. Why do you need me here?"

"Verisimilitude, Ms. Toro."

Nine twenty-five became 9:30. Tom began to feel uneasy. Tardiness was one thing, but thirty minutes?

"I wasn't really going to drive off. I'm not a coward."

Tom glanced up at her. "I never said you were."

She opened her window and lit up a cigarette.

"That's why I wanted to write this story, you know. I know I come across as a Grade-A bitch but I admire what you do. You bring down the bad guys. We take you for granted."

"We're not in it for the accolades, Ms. Toro."

"Modesty gets you a modest-sized office and lets you live a modest-sized life. You bring down the bad guys. Tell me that doesn't tickle your ego just a little."

"Is this an interview?"

"How else are we going to pass the time? The guy's always late."

A warning bell sounded in Tom's head. "He is?"

"Man, you're the ones who had all that surveillance on me. Don't you people talk to each other?"

"How late is he usually?"

"Like forty-five minutes. Really pisses me off, but what can you do, right? Rule number one—don't alienate your scumbag informant. Anyway, that's why God invented menthols…"

Lilly said a few more things, but Tom was no longer listening. His mind whirred. Forty-five minutes late? Galileo was a control freak. If he was late, it was by choice. If he was late, it was because…

It was because he used the time to scope the vicinity.

But from where?

Every building in a two-mile radius had been quietly emptied of all personnel, including custodial staff. Every rooftop was occupied by at least one police officer, and everyone had checked in.

Damn it.

They'd spooked him. He'd gone to wherever he usually went, and had either seen the evacuation or a uniform on a roof. He wasn't going to show.

So where was he going to go? The Rangers had set up roadblocks at all points in and out of the city. He may not have been trapped in the parking garage, but he was still trapped in Amarillo. Where was he going to go?

And why had he killed Darcy Parr? The two men posted outside the hospital room were much better witnesses than she. They'd actually seen him, in his faux beard, with his cell phone. If he was concerned about identification, he would have gone after them. But he went after her. Yes, their encounter at Walmart was a co-incidence, but wasn't it a tremendous risk for a control freak like him to kill in such an uncontrolled environment? Couldn't he have at least waited until the parking lot?

No, he couldn't have waited. Esme had said it herself. He was a man on a crusade. And the task force stood in his warpath. That's why he'd positioned Lilly to be his mole. He wanted to know about them, so he could take them out. But the task force was all here downtown, augmented by the Amarillo P.D. To try something here would be suicide.

Wait.

No.

Tom realized, and his face blanched bone-white. The entire task force wasn't here. One of them was still at city hall, unarmed and unawares.

Oh, God.

Esme.

After concluding that all Atlanta, GA, and Amarillo, TX had in common were their vowels, Esme reviewed the shoe boxes and rewatched the video. It didn't take much critical analysis to see that this guy had a serious beef with religion. Both Atlanta and Amarillo were Bible Belt cities. Was that the link? If so, why target the police and firemen rather than the ministers and preachers?

She then reviewed the photographs of the crime scenes themselves. Was there a connection in the street addresses or in the architecture? No, but it was too early in the investigation to rule anything out, no matter how obscure or arcane.

However, it was never too early for David Bowie. She dialed up *Aladdin Sane* and let her little gray cells kick into high gear. Deductive reasoning could be taught, and was, but her ability to think outside the box was a gift. The problems arose whenever Esme had to force herself to think inside the box. But she had been conditioning herself for years now to direct the train of her thoughts along more logical rails. She had dulled her edges. She had made herself less special.

What if her normalizing efforts were permanent? What if she couldn't do this anymore? What if her gift, like an ignored dog, had just gone away for good? Was Rafe correct? Did she even belong here? As the bombast of Bowie's "Drive-In Saturday" flooded her ears, she gazed at all the evidence arrayed before her in the conference room, and nothing happened. No ah-ha. No lightbulb. No oblique realization. Nothing.

She wasn't Sherlock Holmes, not anymore. She was Amy Lieb.

Esme rubbed at her eyes. Was it true? Had living in Stepford lobotomized her? Was she now no different from Amy Lieb? She reflected on Amy, so enthusiastic about her bake sales and her position as treasurer for the Oyster Bay Elementary PTA and her gung-ho campaign for Bob Kellerman, even going so far as to hammer placards in front of the schoolyard. Silly Amy, so eager to do good that she was willing to violate the separation of—

Esme frowned. She was about to mentally accuse

her neighbor of violating the separation of church and state, but proselytizing for a certain presidential candidate on school property—while illegal (and a little foolish, given that ten-year-olds couldn't vote)—was hardly the same thing as proselytizing for a certain religion. The Democratic Party wasn't quite the same thing as the Catholic Church, now was it? So why had her mind veered in that direction?

The unsub, "Galileo," was anti-religion (church) and only targeted public servants (state). Was it because the line between the two was so blurry in the South? Was that it? If Galileo was that fixated, then why not go after the state congressmen who enforced God-centered government? Hell, why stop there? Why not just go after the president of the United States? Well, for one, the president of the United States was about to end his eight years and be replaced…

With Amy Lieb still on her mind, Esme typed a few words into a Google search, and felt her heart smile. What did Atlanta and Amarillo have in common? They both had recently hosted speeches given on separate occasions by one of the men running for president, Bob Kellerman. Her heart's smile stretched ventricle-to-ventricle when she read the name of the one organization which had sponsored both of his appearances: the Unity for a Better Tomorrow.

According to their own Web site, the Unity for a Better Tomorrow was a not-for-profit organization out of Omaha, Nebraska, started in 1971 by Donald and Roberta Chappell. They claimed to have over eleven million subscribers nationwide. Esme had never heard of them, but, then again, that wasn't really the company she kept back on Long Island.

The Unity for a Better Tomorrow wasn't strictly Christian. It said so on their home page so it must be true. So what if all of the good family values they promoted happened to coincide with the teachings of Jesus Christ? That just proved once again how universal and valid those teachings were, didn't it?

The Unity for a Better Tomorrow had a comprehensive presence on the Web. One of its pages was entitled Contemporary American Saints and listed 242 faith-based congressmen and governors and the churches they attended with their families every Sunday. Next to each name was an Add to Cart button, which brought you to a billing page, so you could donate to these fine citizens' individual reelection campaigns. Likewise, on the much more comprehensive Contemporary American Sinners page, was a list of 116 elected public officials who were "antagonists to faith." Next to these names was the official's telephone number and home address, presumably so you could call them up and/or write them a letter to ask why they were such evil, evil people.

"Faith is patriotic." This, from Donald Chappell, on the Unity's home page. "It was for our God-given rights that we declared independence in 1776. It is on a Bible, that Great Book of Truth, that we swear in open court to tell the truth, so help us God. It is affirmed in our Pledge of Allegiance. It is written on our currency. We are one nation under God. That is what makes us indivisible.

"And yet this very core of our Americanism is under attack. Intellectuals seek to strip our country of our laws. They seek to replace our core values with wantonness, anarchy and secularism. These are the same mistakes which doomed the Romans. These are the same mistakes which doomed the Soviets. Do not, do not, *do not* let these misguided elitists doom our great nation.

"'With malice toward none, with charity for all, with firmness in the right as God gives us to see the right, let us strive on to finish the work we are in.' These are the words of perhaps the greatest American to ever live, Abraham Lincoln. With them, he roused our nation from a dark calamity. As we face another, even darker calamity, let Lincoln's words rouse your faith in your country, and help us protect the blessed soul of the United States of America."

Esme spent an hour on the Web site. She found no mention of "abortion," no mention of "capital punishment" or "prayer in schools" or any of the typical hot-button issues. The Unity for a Better Tomorrow was undoubtedly passionate, but in such a carefully vague way so as to avoid radicalism.

And so left-wing Democrats like Bob Kellerman could with a clear conscience attend the Unity's sponsored events, such as a charity football game held in November of last year at the Georgia Dome (not far from MLK Drive), and a benefit one month later at the Amarillo Aquarium. The Unity's promotion of non-specific family values allowed Governor Kellerman to accept donations from their eleven million subscribers, appear on their list of Contemporary American Saints, and not upset his liberal base.

Well, it had upset someone, and he had a gun.

The Unity for a Better Tomorrow had co-sponsored several other events in the Kellerman campaign, one in Santa Fe, one in Kansas City, and one in Nashville, Tennessee. These would almost definitely be the sniper's next targets.

Esme had him.

With a grin on her lips, she tugged out her iPod earbuds and rifled through her pocketbook for her phone. It was almost 10:00 p.m. She had expected Tom to call by now—

But her phone was dead. Ah. Well, it stood to reason. She hadn't recharged it since leaving Long Island. She had been too busy with other things, like solving a multi-state murder spree. What foolish priorities.

She sifted through the clutter of papers against the wall until she found an outlet, and she plugged in her phone. The display lit up, as did the icon for voice mail. She dialed the requisite number and listened:

"You have…three…new messages.

"Message one…received at…6:11 p.m.

"Esme, hi." It was Rafe. "I…I'm sure you saw my name and are screening my call. I…I don't blame you. I think back on the way I behaved last night…the way I acted…Esme, I'm so sorry. Just…just please call me back. I miss you terribly."

Esme sighed. Oh, Rafe. Truth be told, she missed him, too. She could do without his now-and-again spates of self-righteousness, but his intentions were pure. He was only possessive because he cared so much. He never laid a hand on her in anger (and if he ever did, she would jujitsu him into instant regret) and, unlike her parents, he was reliable. He wasn't going to abandon her, not ever.

She listened to the message again. Had he been crying? She wanted to take him in her arms and hold him close to her breast. Everything was going to be all right. She had solved the case. Soon she would be home with Rafe and Sophie. Spring break was just around the corner. They would go on a vacation. Rafe had an uncle and aunt who lived outside of Glasgow. Sophie would adore Scotland.

"Next message…received at…9:04 p.m.…."

This had to be Tom.

"Hello, Esme!"

Nope. It was Amy Lieb. Couldn't that busybody leave her in peace for a day? For a single day?

"Today was the Get Out the Vote assembly at the high school. It just wasn't the same without you here! Your spunky attitude is simply vital to this campaign!"

Esme groaned, and pulled herself into a chair, which caused her to groan even louder. Sitting on the floor for hours on end was not something her thirtysomething body seemed to enjoy.

"Anyway, Esme, I'm calling because who did I run into at the assembly but an old pal from Wellesley who now writes for *Newsday* and I told her all about you and guess who she wants to interview for this Sunday's edition? You you you! She's especially interested in how you made the transition from working for Uncle

Sam to a Long Island housewife like the rest of us! She's big on transitions. I did mention to her how integral a part of the Kellerman campaign here in Oyster Bay you are, so make sure you name-drop us, okay? I hope you have a pen ready. Here's her digits."

Esme reached down for her pen, which she'd left on the carpet floor, and thus narrowly dodged the .50 caliber bullet which entered through the conference room's open doorway and careened with hot purpose toward her skull.

It left a fist-sized gorge in the drywall behind her.

Esme dropped her phone and slipped off her chair. Doing so, she matched gazes with steely-eyed Galileo, who stood twenty feet away in the dimly-lit bullpen, and she watched helplessly as he took aim for a second mortal shot.

10

Esme scrambled to the conference room door and slammed it shut just as the sniper again fired his M107. BAM! The bullet drilled through the door. It missed her face by centimeters; her cheek was sprayed with sawdust. Through the eyeball-sized bullet hole in the door, she spied the sandy-haired man slowly advance toward the room.

Think! She locked the door and searched the room for something defensive, a weapon, anything. But her options were limited to paper. Reams and reams of paper, all of which pointed to the conclusion the man outside the door wouldn't be deterred for long by a simple lock.

He was here to kill her.

Esme grabbed the conference room table, put all of her weight into her back, and pulled with every ounce of strength inside her body. It inched slowly across the carpet. She would have to drag this massive mahogany table five feet for it to function as a viable barricade at the door. There was no way she'd be able to do that in time. Galileo was already kicking at the door from the other side.

Think, Esme! You were an FBI agent, for Christ's sake! She once again scoped the room for possibilities. No windows, one door (which shook as the 175+ lbs. of psychosis pounded against it). Undoubtedly the only reason he didn't just shoot off the lock was fear of a bullet shard ricocheting off the metal and back at him. The laws of physics bought Esme perhaps two minutes.

So she went up. She climbed atop the table and punched up one of the ceiling tiles. People did this in movies all the time. Rectangular panels made of cheap cardboard would support her weight. Wouldn't they?

She had no time to second-guess. Without a moment to spare, Esme hoisted herself up into the ceiling. Muscles she hadn't used since high school gym shouted at her to cease and desist, but still she pulled. She weighed, on a good day, 116 lbs. She moderated her breathing and ignored the beads of sweat sliding from her forehead down her eyelids. Lift! Lift!

To her left, the door frame cracked.

Lift!

She managed to get one leg over the wooden plank, then used the plank itself to provide support for her to swing the rest of her body into the ceiling crawl-space. She considered placing the tile back to cover her tracks, but decided against it. Stealth right now was secondary to speed.

The crawlspace was at most two feet high, so "crawlspace" was a bit of a misnomer. Esme slithered from tile to tile through a fog of noxious white dust.

From down below she heard the conference room door smack against its jamb. She had no idea where she was in relation to that, but hoped her slithering across old pinewood and thin cardboard was as loud and creaky to the sniper as it was to—

BAM!

A bullet passed between her legs.

She slithered faster than she thought possible. She had no sense of direction and even less a sense of balance, but none of that mattered. Her lizard brain transmitted only one thought: *move.*

Physics, however, which had been such a pal minutes earlier, chose that moment to switch teams, and mere feet into her mad slithering dash across the crawlspace Esme crashed through a cardboard panel and fell twelve feet down and onto a cherrywood chair in the bullpen. It was Daryl Hewes's cherrywood chair, and it shattered underneath the weight of her fall.

Something was on her abdomen, pressing against its right side.

Had a piece of the ceiling fallen down with her? She lifted her head a few inches off the floor to see what was causing this strange sensation and beheld a three-inch shard of wood, wet and jagged, protruding from her right abdomen at a thirty-degree angle.

Tears of pain tracked lines down Esme's dust-coated cheeks. Through a blurry mist, she could make out the shape of a man approaching her. In his hands was a short rifle. Her eyelids fluttered and shut. It was too taxing to keep them open. She felt the hot tip of the gun barrel press against her scalp. He wasn't taking any chances. He wasn't going to miss.

She retreated in her mind to her happy place. She retreated in her mind to the first time she met Tom Piper.

This was before the existence of the task force. Tom was just a decorated field agent, and he and his partner, the irascible Bobby Fink, were on the tail of a loony-tune from Cape Cod who had a habit of kidnapping tourists, bathing them in chum, and tossing them into Buzzards Bay for the sharks to gobble up. Local, county and state officials were quarreling over jurisdiction, so the FBI came in to clean up the mess. But on a boat in Buzzards Bay is not where Esme met Tom. Nor was it at the crime lab in Boston, where intrepid technicians were piecing the McGonquin family together from the stomach contents of a well-fed blue shark. Esme met Tom one week later at Quantico. The Buzzards Bay Butcher had eleven victims to his tally. Tom was outside Assistant Director Trumbull's office at Quantico waiting to meet with some profilers. Esme was outside AD Trumbull's office waiting to get fired.

Propped up on Daryl's desk in the middle of the bullpen, impaled on a sliver of old wood, her breathing ragged, her eyes shut—this was how Esme was going to die. But no bullet, not yet, so her mind flitted from AD Trumbull's office to the delivery room at LIJ in New Hyde Park, Long Island, seven years ago.

Rafe stood beside her. Rafe held her hand. She had been in labor for eight hours. Rafe hadn't sat down, not even for a moment, and he hadn't let go of her hand, not once.

"I love you," he told her. He wore a beige Oxford shirt. He had come here from work. The sides of his shirt were soiled with perspiration. "I love you too," she replied. Then the pain came again, her billionth contraction of the day, and she let out a throaty moan, and Rafe squeezed her hand, and their OBGYN spoke and she looked down at him, through a haze of dope and fatigue, and he was smiling, the doctor was smiling, what shiny white teeth he had, and he was standing up from a crouch and there was something in his hands, and Esme thought: oh, it's a loaf of bread—but that was silly because why would the doctor bring a loaf of bread in the delivery room…maybe it was for her husband, Rafe had to be hungry, but wait, no, no, it wasn't a loaf of bread at all, because bread didn't cry, oh, Sophie—

Esme opened her eyes, and was confused. Where was the OBGYN? Where was Rafe? Then the daggers of pain resumed their attack, and with them came the reality of the moment: she was in Amarillo, TX. She was in city hall. She was lying on the remains of Daryl's computer and she was dead….

Except she wasn't dead. She hadn't been shot. She couldn't move her head but she could shift her eyes, and her eyes took in the room and the sniper wasn't there. Where had he gone? Why hadn't he shot her? Had he left her for dead? No, that didn't make sense. That didn't fit his methodology. She'd watched him approach her. He intended to kill. He had pressed the barrel of his gun to her scalp. Why hadn't he pulled the trigger? Why—

But Esme's mind switched off before she could ask any more reasonable questions.

After Tom aborted the sting, it took the task force and the police fourteen minutes to converge on city hall. Fourteen minutes. Anything could happen in fourteen minutes. And Esme still wasn't answering her cell phone.

Tom was out of the Mini-Coop before Lilly turned off its engine. He raced up the stone steps. Most everyone else was still coming down from rooftops, but the team in the surveillance van—including the chief of police and Norm Petrosky—met Tom at the front door.

Although city hall closed to the public at six o'clock, an armed guard manned the vestibule 24/7. As Tom and the others marched in, the guard—a forty-three-year-old cowboy named Lyle Costas—stood up from his chair. He recognized the chief of police.

"What's wrong?" he asked. "Is it the mayor?"

The chief recognized him too. "Lyle, has anyone been here in the last hour or so?"

"Just that FBI agent on Two. And Officer Milton."

Tom's blood froze. "Officer Milton?"

"Sure. He signed in and everything. I even wrote down his badge number."

As Lyle reached for his clipboard, Tom raced past his desk and toward the marble stairs. He instinctively reached for his gun with his left hand—but his sling held fast and in the confusion almost lost balance on the third step. By then Norm had caught up. His pistol was already drawn. Together, Tom and Norm ascended to the second floor.

Their offices were down the south corridor. Low wattage lighting poured out from the bullpen's open door. Slowly, the FBI agents approached.

Twenty feet.

Fifteen feet.

Ten feet.

Tom wore boots. Norm wore hard-soled shoes. It wasn't easy for either of them to tread unheard across the hallway's ceramic tiles. They made the effort. They were professionals. One of their own was in danger.

Five feet.

I'm going in first, indicated Tom. He held his .45 in his off-hand.

Norm shook his head. *Don't be an idiot,* he mouthed.

They didn't have time to argue. Tom acquiesced.

Norm took the fore. He led with his gun. Tom followed. They could almost peer into the bullpen.

All was quiet.

What if Esme was dead? Try as he might, Tom couldn't banish the nightmarish possibility from his mind. He had put her in harm's way before. He put all of his team in harm's way. It was part of the job. They knew the risks when they joined the FBI. But Esme had left. Esme had gone and become a civilian. He had knowingly, willingly, and selfishly endangered the life of an innocent woman, of a close friend, and for what? He swallowed deep.

Norm turned the corner, and stepped into the room.

"Shit," he said.

Panicking, Tom joined him in the bullpen. Norm was standing beside Esme's body. She lay sprawled across Daryl's chair. The wound in her right side had begun to drip to the floor. A thinner line of blood tracked down the side of her lips.

Norm had his fingers on her jugular.

Despite it all, Tom did his job. His gaze swept across the room for any sign of the killer.

"She's got a pulse," said Norm.

Tom headed toward the conference room. It looked like the door had been forced open. Was he deliberately avoiding the sight of Esme, so frail and helpless, so broken? Perhaps he was. He stepped into the conference room, saw the bullet hole in the wall and the ceiling panel out of place. It didn't take long to piece together the narrative.

But the villain was gone.

Where had he gone? He couldn't have made it out the front. How many entrances and exits did this building have?

Norm was on the radio. He was calling for an ambulance for Esme. Once he was finished, Tom got on and ordered everyone to sweep the building. Their quarry had to be *somewhere*. As the Amarillo Police Department swarmed into city hall, Tom considered joining them. It would be yet another excuse not to be near Esme…

No. Enough was enough. Be a man.

He walked toward her body. Her chestnut-brown hair was scattered across her forehead and cheeks. Tom tucked a few loose strands behind one of her ears.

"She has a strong pulse," said Norm.

Tom nodded. He held her hand.

The EMTs soon came. Carefully, they secured her head in a brace, strapped her into a gurney, and rolled her into the corridor. Tom shadowed them the entire way, and accompanied them into the elevator. Not a word was spoken.

In the vestibule, Tom was stopped by the chief of police.

"There's a window open," he said, "in a reception room on the first floor. Looks like that's how he got out."

"Mmm-hmm."

"He left this." The police chief showed Tom a shoe box. Inside the shoe box was Ray Milton's badge.

The EMTs were halfway to the ambulance. Tom had to hurry if he wanted to catch up.

"Where are you going?" the police chief asked. "You need to stay here."

The cop was right. Tom's responsibilities were here. This was now a crime scene, and he the lead investigator. To leave now would be negligent. There was nothing he could do for Esme.

But Tom put Norm in charge and left anyway.

He reached the ambulance just as the medics were about to shut the doors. They knew who he was. They let him in.

Esme remained unconscious.

Unconscious was good, decided Tom. That meant she wasn't aware of any pain. Maybe she was even dreaming. Again he held her hand. She was like a daughter to him, and she was unconscious.

His mind retreated into memory, to the first time they met.

He was back at AD Trumbull's office at Quantico to enlist help in profiling the Buzzards Bays Butcher. He smiled at the young woman listening to her Discman and waiting in the Trumbull's sparse anteroom, and he took a seat. He had the red case file on his lap. According to the secretary, Trumbull was on the phone with the deputy director. It was more than likely.

The young woman removed her headphones.

"So," she said, "you're Tom Piper."

"I am."

"And you're here about the Buzzards Bay Butcher."

"Yes."

"Me, too."

Tom frowned. "Do I know you?"

She held out her hand. "Esme Shepherd. GS-10."

GS-10 was the lowest pay grade for a Bureau agent to have. This woman was either a recent graduate or a tremendous fool.

"Special Agent Shepherd, I'm curious. In what way are you connected to the case?"

"I read the file."

Again, Tom frowned. "I don't understand."

"You sent a copy here by courier for the assistant director to peruse."

"Mmm-hmm…"

"Well…I read it."

"Is your name on the case?"

"No, sir."

"Then how did you get a copy?"

"You sent it by courier for—"

"How did you get to read it?"

"I intercepted the copy."

Tom was no longer on the fence re: recent graduate/absolute fool. "Why did you do that?"

The young woman shrugged. "I wanted to help. It's not like it's the first case file I've read."

"It's just the first time you got caught."

Trumbull's secretary hung up her phone. The assistant director could see them now. Both of them.

They rose from the chairs.

"Looks like he wants an audience for my beheading," said Esme.

"You know what you did was wrong, don't you?"

"I don't know, sir. I think that depends on whether or not I've solved your case."

"You think you found something in the file?"

"Yes, sir. I do."

"I see."

The assistant director's office was sparse. On the wall was the requisite photograph of the president of the United States, along with a framed Jasper Johns print. His bookshelves were packed with never-read tomes and his window afforded a grand, unappreciated view of rural Virginia. Trumbull stood up when they entered. He was a handsome man, with the hairline of a twenty-year-old, the physique of a thirty-year-old, and the gravitas of a forty-year-old. He grinned warmly at Tom. He did not even acknowledge Esme, not even with a glare.

"Before we begin, Tom, I wanted to bring this young

woman to your attention. It seems she's been eaves-dropping on your cases."

"Cases?" Tom raised an eyebrow. Plural?

"You get the good ones," she murmured.

"Mmm-hmm."

"I wanted you to be here for this, Tom, because her brand of malfeasance is not tolerated here. I wanted you to be here for this because her crime victimized you, and you deserve to bear witness to her—"

"Beheading," said Tom.

Trumbull smirked. "Call it what you will. Given the nature of her actions, I wanted to hear your input on what course of justice we should pursue."

Tom paused. For her crimes, Esme could be facing ten years in prison.

He turned to her. Suddenly she looked so small, appropriate as her fate now fit in his hands.

"What do you think you found in the case file?" he asked her.

And so Esme told him: she believed the Buzzards Bay Butcher was a Red Sox fan.

Each of the victims, she explained, had a soiled Yankees T-shirt or sweatshirt or ball cap in their luggage. Soiled, because they had already worn it on their trip, worn it outside, worn it within view of someone so psychotically appalled to seeing Boston's rival team on display so close to Boston itself that he reacted.

"Have someone go undercover," she said. "Have them wear a Bucky Dent jersey. Have them walk around Buzzards Bay. Our guy won't go after them that day, but maybe the next. And then you'll have him."

Trumbull rolled his eyes.

Tom didn't.

Her theory may have been flimsy (it was the very crossroads of coincidence and conjecture), but what if she was correct?

He asked Trumbull for a week to test it out. What was one more week, if Esme's fate was really in his hands? Reluctantly, the assistant director agreed. Tom called up Bobby Fink and informed him of the plan. Bobby bought a Yankees jacket (not the easiest thing to find in Massachusetts) and spent the rest of the day wandering the shops in Buzzards Bay.

The killer made his move the next day, outside of a clambake on the beach. He was tackled to the ground by four officers. Bobby read him his rights. He and Bobby got the credit for nabbing the Buzzards Bay Butcher, and their capital with the Bureau soared. Tom spent his on Esme. He had the charges on her dropped, and a few months later when the deputy director created the task force and put Tom in charge, Esme Shepherd was his first recruit (on her guarantee that she would never—ever—bend the rules again…at least not without his permission first).

And now they were in Amarillo, so many years later, and Esme lay unconscious in an ambulance, on the way to Baptist St. Anthony's in Amarillo, Texas. Somewhere out there, her assailant roamed free. He was targeting them now, and he showed no signs of giving up, or getting caught.

11

Never before in her life had Lilly Toro so desperately wanted to be home. And not her apartment, either, but her childhood home, her parents' home, a walk-up in Oakland which perpetually reeked of boiled cabbage and/or cheddar cheese. She hadn't seen her parents in a while. They didn't approve of her lifestyle. As far as she knew, they didn't even look for her byline anymore in the *Chronicle*. But she so desperately wanted to run into their arms right now, maybe share a bowl of soup, sit with them on the sofa and watch a western on their old TV. Instead, she was here, in a small musty room in the Amarillo P.D., a thousand miles away.

They had taken her cell phone. They had taken her wristwatch.

"Am I under arrest?" Lilly had asked the two FBI agents. Their names were Hector and Anna Jackson (no relation).

"This is just a precaution," Anna Jackson explained. "In case he comes after you."

Then they left.

Lilly had no idea how much time had passed. Maybe hours. The walls lacked a clock. The walls lacked everything except gray paint. The same paint covered the door. The door was locked. She had tried it. She had also pounded the door with her fists and kicked the door with her feet.

In one of the corners of the ceiling, a small video camera recorded it all. Lilly gave her viewers the finger and sat back down in her chair. More time passed. She craved a cigarette. She craved answers. She craved home.

The door opened. It was Jackson & Jackson.

"I want a lawyer," said Lilly.

Hector Jackson and Anna Jackson exchanged a look. They appeared amused.

Lilly wasn't.

"I'm an American citizen," she said.

"So am I," replied Hector Jackson.

"Me, too," replied Anna Jackson. She had a file in her hand. She placed it on the table.

"What's that?"

"Your FBI file."

"I have an FBI file?"

The agents once again exchanged looks. "You do now."

Lilly stared at the file for a minute, then rose to her feet. "If I'm not under arrest, then—"

"Sit down."

"Fuck you." She headed for the door. It was locked. "Open it."

The agents stood up, and walked toward her. Lilly

stepped out of the way. With a buzz, the door unlocked. Hector opened it, and exited. Anna followed him out. Before Lilly could do the same, Anna pulled the door shut.

"Damn it!" howled Lilly. She kicked again at the door.

They'd left the file on the table.

They wanted her to see it. Why?

She approached the table.

No. She wouldn't give them the satisfaction.

She turned her back on the table, arms crossed. Fuck 'em.

More time passed. Maybe hours.

Lilly pulled a chair into the corner and sat facing the wall. They wanted to play games with her? She could out-stubborn a donkey. She could out-stubborn her *mother*, and her mother had a reputation in the Bay Area for her stubbornness. Her mother refused to upgrade from vinyl records. Her mother refused to acknowledge the existence of the Internet. Her mother voted Republican.

More time passed.

Lilly got tired. And hungry. And bored.

She glanced back at the table. The file was thick. It would make a nice pillow. And if she "accidentally" peeked inside while adjusting it, well, these things happened....

Lilly "accidentally" peeked inside.

The cover page was a drawing, a copy of the sketch taken from her description of Ray Milton. Maybe it was the light, or maybe it was the police artist's rendition, but the face on the paper looked like, well, Robert Redford. Redford circa 1972. Redford circa *Jeremiah Johnson,* one of the better westerns in her father's VHS collection.

Lilly turned the page.

It was blank.

She flipped to another page. Also blank.

She rifled through the file. Blank, blank, blank, blank, blank.

"What the…?"

The door opened. A middle-aged cop strolled in, bald save for the black sideburns that tracked down the sides of his face.

"Hi," he said, and held out his hand. "I'm Ray Milton."

Lilly let go of the file. Hundreds of pages of empty paper fluttered to the hard gray floor.

Officer Milton gazed down with sadness at the mess. Then his steely eyes once again found Lilly.

"I was at the memorial service," he said. "When I got home, I noticed my badge was missing. I didn't report it. That was my mistake, and I'll be duly punished. Everyone's mighty upset right now, and we're going to take the fall."

Lilly wiped her moist forehead. Was it getting warmer in here? "I didn't do anything wrong."

"I know."

He bent down, which took some effort, and began to clean up the papers. After a moment, Lilly helped him.

"Nobody intends to screw up," he said. "I've got a

clean record. I'm a good cop. I got injured a while back—stupid thing, really—so now I spend most of my days behind a desk. But there's lot of important stuff that needs to get done in-house. I like my job."

They planted the blank paper on the desk. Officer Milton evened out the pile, and slid it back into its manila folder.

"My badge went missing and I should've reported it. That's what they call hubris. But for the life of me I can't figure out why he chose me to steal from. There were hundreds of cops at the service. Why choose me? For that matter, why choose you? There were hundreds of reporters there too. You and me—we're in the same boat, Miss Toro."

Officer Milton sat down and let out a long sigh. Lilly sat down near him.

He picked up the sketch, let out a brief chuckle, then put it down.

"It was ego," she said, finally.

"What was?"

"When he approached me," Lilly continued, "when out of everyone in the crowd I suddenly became the one with the inside information…I figured he liked the way I looked. And suddenly I was in! I was embedded with Tom Piper on a hunt for a serial killer! I did check, by the way. I called the station to check his bona fides. I gave them your badge ID. 'Yes, ma'am, Ray Milton is an officer here. Would you like us to transfer you to his desk?' I didn't do anything wrong."

"Neither did I," Ray Milton said, "and yet here we are."

"What are they going to do to you?"

The cop shrugged. "Whatever it is, I'll accept it. My family? They'll accept it. You got a family?"

"Yeah."

"Are you close with them?"

Lilly paused. "No."

"That's a shame. I don't know what I'd do without my family. But different strokes for different folks, I guess, right?"

Lilly nodded, looked away.

"The fact is, Miss Toro, they can't charge us with a crime. We didn't break any laws. Being stupid ain't illegal. I let my guard down. But they can make us sweat. Leave a blank file to tease you with. Mess with your head. And I just know come April I'm going to be audited."

"It's not fair." This time, her words came quieter. "I didn't do anything wrong." The conviction in her voice was as empty now as, well, as a blank sheet of paper.

Officer Milton pushed himself to his feet. Once more, he held out his hand.

"Anyway, I just wanted to introduce myself."

This time she shook it. The policeman cocked his head goodbye, and left.

Time passed.

Lester Stuart prided himself on being a one-suitcase type of guy, so when he got the call from his son Rafe, he unearthed Old Blue from the closet, set her on his queen-size, spun the three-digit combination (7-2-7— his and Eunice's anniversary), and tugged her open.

Old Blue's hinges needed oil, and her inner cloth lining had a bit of mildew, but otherwise, she was shipshape. Not bad for a thirty-four-year-old piece of luggage ordered from a Sears catalog.

It's not that Lester couldn't afford a new model. A lifetime of hard work in the vending machine business had made him a wealthy man. And it's not that he was miserly with his funds. He just loathed waste. Why buy a new suitcase/car/house when his current one worked just fine?

He started with his socks and briefs. They always went in the suitcase first. They were foundation garments, after all, so they should form the foundation here. There was the right way to do a thing and the wrong way to do a thing and only fools (like his daughter-in-law Esme) chose the wrong way.

When he heard what had happened to her in Amarillo, he wasn't surprised. The girl was a loose cannon. He'd said as much to Rafe, many times, scotch in hand. "It's because she doesn't have any parents," he'd opine. "She's rudderless, so she goes where the wind takes her, even if it's smack dab into a storm." But the boy married her anyway. At least Rafe had had the sense (with some financial prodding from the old man) to move his family to Long Island. But a leopard doesn't change its spots, and Esme remained a loose cannon and now she was in critical care in Texas and Rafe was flying down to be with her, and Lester, as always, was doing what needed doing. That meant packing up Old Blue for an indefinite stay at their house in Oyster Bay. Sophie needed baby-sitting, and he was just the grandfather for the job.

After his socks and briefs, the next layer Lester added was pants. Lester was a fan of jeans. They were durable, reliable and matched just about everything. He folded two faded pairs of Levi's on top of his underwear. The third he would wear on the trip. On top of his jeans went two button-down plaid shirts. Next came his toiletries, which he stuffed into a sealable freezer bag; his mud-dappled Nikes; and his heart medication, which he placed next to the bag of toiletries. Lastly: a very old paperback of *Leaves of Grass,* inscribed by Eunice. It was the first gift she ever bought for him, and no matter the destination, it always had a place in Old Blue, right at the top.

The suitcase shut without effort. Lester was ready to go.

He'd already asked his neighbor Gus Francis to collect his mail while he was gone. Gus, who was a retired army colonel, lost his wife around the same time Lester lost Eunice. Every weeknight, they shared a pint in Gus's kitchen. Weekends belonged to family.

Lester secured Old Blue in the trunk of his Cadillac, started up its engine (still ticking at almost 190,000 miles), and commenced his three-hour road adventure through the wintry southeast corridor of New York State. His musical accompaniment on the journey, via CD player, was Bob Dylan. A love of twentieth-century music—the only quality he shared with that flibbertigibbet daughter-in-law of his.

In fact, she first met his son through one of her many acts of careless spontaneity. They retold the story of their first date at their wedding, and how the reception hall had laughed and cheered! Eunice laughed and cheered! Lester played along with the rest. It would have been ungentlemanly to scowl during his son's wedding toast.

"It's all because," said Rafe, "of a personal ad."

The groom proceeded to reach into the left pocket of his tuxedo jacket and remove the ad, clipped and laminated. The wedding guests listened on in rapt attention. Esme, seated beside him at the head table, blushed.

"SWF," he read. "Twenty-eight, in search of intelligent life in the universe. Partial to earthlings. Bonus points for spontaneity, creativity and equal-mindedness. Must enjoy traveling!"

He smiled down at his new bride and slipped the ad back into his pocket.

"Except I'm not the one who responded to the ad. I was neck-deep in my dissertation at GW. Those last six months, I don't think I even glanced at a newspaper. Fortunately, I had a roommate."

Rafe pointed to Table 1. Donnie Washington, former roommate and current best man, stood up (and up and up—he clocked in at six-nine) and took a bow.

"You still owe me!" called Donnie. "I'm still single!"

The crowd laughed. Donnie sat back down.

Rafe continued:

"Donnie responded to the ad. Left a message. Two days later, he and our travel-loving SWF scheduled a date. They agreed to meet that Saturday at a coffeehouse on K Street called the Lemon Yellow. The night before, Donnie ordered takeout. I got chicken and broccoli. He got the shrimp and pork chow mein. And food poisoning."

Lester surveyed the crowd. His son had them on the edge of their seats. Apparently all that experience in the lecture hall made him quite the orator. Lester admired his boy's technique—even if he objected to the speech's loathsome content.

"Donnie didn't have the girl's number. You see, when you put a personal ad in the paper, the contact information is for a switchboard at the newspaper. It helps to guard a person's privacy. Donnie and the SWF had exchanged anonymous messages. He had no way of contacting her directly to postpone the date, but he was in no condition to be more than three feet from a toilet at all times. So he asked me to go in his stead, explain the situation to the mystery woman, and reschedule their date. And I went."

Rafe looked down at Esme, and clasped her hand in his.

"When I left the apartment that night, I was nervous. You got to understand—by this time I was living and breathing my dissertation. Just the act of driving to anywhere but campus was a big change. I chalked my anxiety up to that. But maybe I knew. Maybe some part of my subconscious was aware of how important the next couple hours were going to be. I showed up at the Lemon Yellow at a quarter to nine…and there she was."

Was it romantic? Sure. So was *Romeo and Juliet,* and that ended splendidly, eh? Lester sipped down his champagne. Since Esme didn't have a family, Eunice had convinced him to foot the bill for this soirée. Talk about adding insult to injury!

"She said in her message to Donnie that he'd be

able to recognize her when he arrived because she'd be wearing her FBI Academy sweatshirt. What she didn't say was how beautiful she was. I walked into the Lemon Yellow and she was sitting on one of those funky old sofas you get at a yard sale—that's the kind of place this was. She was sitting on one of those funky old sofas and she was listening to music on her CD player. I sat down beside her and asked her what she was listening to. And what was it? The Sex Pistols! The official band of love at first sight."

Laughter, laughter from the crowd.

"I told her about Donnie. I said how much he wished he could be there right now, although, I added, he hated punk music. But he was a sweet guy, blah blah blah, and I gave her Donnie's phone number. Now that concluded my responsibilities, right? I mean, I had a monster dissertation waiting for me back home. I didn't have time to hang out in a funky café, much less buy an adorable girl a coffee. But common sense left the building, ladies and gentlemen, the moment I laid eyes on her."

The crowd aww-ed and cooed.

Lester swilled down some more champagne. His common sense left the building. At least he admitted it.

"We got to talking. Not about anything in particular. She told me her name was Esme and she worked for the FBI. We talked and talked. I refilled her coffee. Around midnight, Donnie called me on my cell, wanting to know what had happened. I let it go to voice mail. Sorry, buddy."

Donnie lifted a glass in toast.

"Our conversation continued. That funky sofa was very comfortable. Anyway, suddenly it's 3:00 a.m. and management is kicking us out. 3:00 a.m.! Well, we stepped out into the night air, but it was obvious neither of us was tired. I asked her if she wanted to take a ride, just ride around. She said yes."

"Must enjoy traveling!" quipped Esme.

The wedding crowd laughed.

"We must have hit every street in the D.C. metro area. No route. No destination. Just the two of us and the city and the Sex Pistols on my CD player. I'd occasionally steal a glance at her. She'd occasionally steal a glance at me. Finally I asked her the one question that had been burning on mind. 'What's an amazing girl like you needing a personal ad in the *Washington Post?*' Her answer? 'I'm looking for someone I can take to weddings.' And here we are!"

Everyone cheered. Someone stood, and then the rest followed. Finally, reluctantly, Lester joined them in the ovation.

Rafe and Esme locked hands and kissed.

At Table 8 were her colleagues from the FBI, including that hippie boss of hers who rode that loud motorcycle. They appeared so happy for her. How happy would they be when she told them she was quitting? Lester allowed himself to savor the pleasure of superior knowledge. He and Rafe had co-signed the papers for the house in Oyster Bay. Suburbia would tame that daughter-in-law of his.

Lester took the exit off the expressway. The Bob

Dylan CD had already cycled four times, and was now about to begin track one yet again. "Like a Rolling Stone." That's her theme song, mused Lester. He followed the route to their idyllic subdivision. They had been married seven years. Seven years, and still she'd managed to wiggle out of the cocoon he had created and gotten herself fucked up halfway across the country.

Lester wasn't heartless. He felt immense pity—for his granddaughter. It might be days, even weeks before Rafe would return. Perhaps this was a blessing in disguise. Weeks afforded Lester plenty of time to spend with beloved Sophie, plenty of time to illuminate her about the truth, about the dangers of irresponsibility, about her mother.

12

"I'm not dead?"

The doctor frowned. "Would you like to be?"

Esme tried to sit up, failed. What little strength she had quickly dwindled. It was an Olympian effort just to keep her eyelids open.

Her hospital room was small, and the shades were drawn. A heart monitor beeped to her right. Beside it stood a pole, and on the pole hung two bags: one half-full with a clear liquid, perhaps morphine, and the other half-empty with a red liquid that could only be blood. Both trafficked intravenously into her right arm via thin tubes.

She smelled antiseptic and body odor.

"Are you in any pain?" the doctor asked.

Esme focused on him. Small dark man, big white coat. His nametag read DR. ACHMED AZIZ.

"Can you feel this?" He tickled the bottom of her left foot. His fingertips were soft, like the hands of a child. He gauged her reaction, and then tickled the bottom of her right foot. Her lips involuntarily pulled into a grin. Esme was, after all, ticklish.

"Mrs. Stuart," he said, "you are very lucky."

"Why can't I sit up?"

"You are in a rigid brace which limits your upper body movement. Sitting up right now could very well pop your staples and then we'd have a big old mess, wouldn't we?"

Esme blinked. "Staples?"

"To sew you up, Mrs. Stuart. From your surgery."

"Surgery?"

Dr. Aziz leaned toward her. "Mrs. Stuart, do you know what year it is?"

"Yes," she answered, and told him.

"And who is the president of the United States?"

She told him that too.

"And what is the last thing you remember before waking up here?"

Esme frowned. The last thing? She had been at her desk in Oyster Bay—no, that wasn't right. She boarded a plane. She was in Texas. She was in Amarillo. There was a sniper on the loose. She was helping the FBI catch him. She was helping Tom.

"Where's Tom?"

"Mrs. Stuart, I need you to tell me what the last thing you remember is."

Memories continued to shuttle through her brain. The shoe boxes. The video. The Unity for a Better Tomorrow. She had been in the conference room at city hall. She had solved the case. She was going to call Tom and tell him what she'd discovered. There were voice messages on her phone. Rafe had apologized to her. Then there was a gunshot. Galileo! She evaded him, though. She had climbed into the ceiling. But it had collapsed beneath her and she fell and the sniper came toward her and he pressed the barrel of his gun to her scalp and…

"Mrs. Stuart?" He raised an eyebrow. "What is it?"

"I wasn't shot," she said.

"Shot?" Dr. Aziz replied. "No."

She focused on the doctor's calm brown eyes. "I need to speak with Special Agent Tom Piper."

"Mrs. Stuart, do you know why you are in the hospital?"

"I fell."

"Yes. You did. And a piece of wood pierced your right kidney. When you arrived here, you'd lost several pints of blood. You almost died, Mrs. Stuart."

No. That was impossible.

"We were able to transfuse your blood loss, but your kidney suffered irreparable damage. We had to perform an emergency nephrectomy."

"An emergency…?"

"We had to remove your kidney."

"Wow."

"You'll be in a brace for a few days to keep your movement limited. We'll also need to keep careful watch on your remaining kidney to make sure it's up to the task of doing the job of two. This isn't like an urban legend where you wake up in a bathtub of ice and can go to work the next day. However…"

"However?"

"Your electrolytes and your blood pressure look very decent. Provided you stop trying to sit up every five seconds, and you promise not to fall out of any more ceilings, you should be able to make a full recovery in four to six weeks. There may be some permanent stiffness, but…here, let me get you a tissue, Mrs. Stuart. You're crying."

Shortly after the doctor left, the painkillers lulled Esme asleep. When she woke up again, it was nighttime. Her shades were still drawn, but while before some sunlight had managed to squeeze through, now there was nothing but a moon-bone shadow.

"Esme?"

Her eyes darted from the window to the left side of her bed. Someone stood there, in the darkness. It took her vision a moment to adjust.

"Rafe?"

His face split into a joyous smile. "It's me, jellybean. I'm here."

She felt his large paws wrap around her left hand, and echoed his smile with one of her own. She looked past him. Was Sophie here too?

"Who are you looking for, baby?" His voice grew an edge. "I am here."

"Who…" Esme swallowed. Her throat was dry. "Who's watching Sophie?"

Rafe relaxed. Whatever unnerved him had passed. "My father's babysitting her. He just dropped everything and drove down. So I could be here with you."

Esme rasped, "Thank you."

"Do you want some water? Nurse, can you get my wife some water? Nurse?"

One of the duty nurses entered and kindly showed

Rafe where the sink was (hidden in plain sight), and where the cups were (sneakily located beside the sink). In minutes, Esme was wetting her whistle with sweet cold Texas *agua*.

Rafe took a seat.

"I'm staying at the Holiday Inn across the street," he said. "It's kind of neat. The architecture is faux adobe. From a sociological standpoint, this is an interesting city."

Esme smiled at him. She was too tired to speak.

"I wanted to get you something from the gift shop, but I couldn't make up my mind. They had carnations, but not green ones, and I know you like the green ones. I don't know why, but I came this close to buying you a teddy bear. Maybe I'll get one for Sophie."

Esme nodded.

"So—" he looked at the tiled floor "—did you listen to my voice mail?"

"Yes."

"I meant every word. I'm so sorry, Esme. I had my head up my ass. We both know it's not the first time that's happened. I just…didn't want anything to happen to you…" His gaze lifted up, and matched hers. "And I'm not going to say 'I told you so.' I'm not blaming you for what happened. What's done is done."

Esme forced a grin. She didn't believe his altruism, not one bit—but it was considerate of Rafe to at least pretend, wasn't it?

"So, are you in much pain?"

She shook her head.

"That's good. The doctor thinks you'll be jogging

again in no time. I tried to pin down how long, but he refused to stick to a specific answer. Not that it matters. If he said six weeks, you'd be up and about in four. That's just who you are."

Esme responded with a shrug.

"There's a restaurant in the lobby of the Holiday Inn. I took a look at the menu before I came here. Their special is a seventy-two-ounce steak. A seventy-two-ounce steak! Apparently, if you can finish the whole thing without dying of an infarction, you get your name on a board. A seventy-two-ounce steak. Can you imagine? Speaking of steak, you must be hungry. Want me to get the nurse to bring you some food?"

Esme replied, but her voice was too weak from exhaustion, and her diction too slurred from the painkillers. Rafe got up from his chair and bowed close to his wife's lips.

"What was that?" he asked. "What is it you want?"

She inhaled a breath, then repeated her request:

"Tom," she said. "I need to speak with Tom."

While Tom was meeting with the mayor, a bird shat on his Harley. He exited city hall and found the white goo on his leather seat. He slogged back to city hall to retrieve soap and paper towels, so it was in the first-floor men's room that he got the call. Esme was awake.

But first he had a stop to make at the police station.

Among this case's many, many perturbing questions, the most recent was this: why had the killer gone to city hall? He had no way of knowing anyone would be there. In fact, he would have been under the assumption that the entire task force was staking out the parking garage. And if he hadn't gone to city hall to add to his tally, what then had been his goal?

Tom biked in silence to the police station. Muddy clouds milled overhead. There would be rain, soon. His Harley's engine hummed against his chaps. Some thought him frivolous, having his motorcycle flown with him wherever he went. Tom pitied them, for they obviously never knew true love.

He parked it in the station lot, secured his gear, and moseyed in through the back door and down two flights of stairs to the sub-basement, and the crime lab. Much of their equipment from the bullpen had been moved here overnight for forensic analysis. Daryl, hands wrapped in latex gloves, was fiddling with one of their laptops.

"Talk to me," said Tom.

"This is Esme's laptop, the one she was using in the conference room." Daryl glanced back at him. "Except she wasn't the last person to use it."

Tom's heart jumped an inch. He took a seat. "Explain."

"Every other computer in the bullpen had been switched off around 8:00 p.m. I scanned their BIOS to be sure. Esme's was never switched off."

"She was using it when we left."

"Yes, she was. And I have a complete history of every key she typed and every Web site she viewed through our network. Now what's surprising is what happened to this machine at 9:58 p.m."

"What happened?"

Daryl brought up a window on the laptop and pointed at a series of algorithms. "Do you see it?"

"Yes, I see it. What is it I'm seeing?"

"At 9:58 p.m., someone inserted an unknown external device in this USB port. I'm thinking it was a portable hard drive."

"Why would…?"

"At 9:59 p.m., the user accessed the network. At 10:01 p.m., they found what they were looking for and downloaded it onto their portable hard drive."

"Daryl, what were they looking for? What did Galileo go to city hall to get?"

"That's the thing. I don't know."

"But…"

The tech brought up another window. This one Tom recognized. It displayed a Windows error message.

"He fucked up the OS," Daryl explained. "It's not a complicated virus, and can be easily cured."

"By reinstalling Windows."

"And reformatting the hard drive."

Tom rubbed at his temples. "Were you able to lift any fingerprints, anything off the keyboard?"

"We got some hair. It fits the description Lilly gave us. Short. Blond."

"That's great," he replied. "Now we can—"

"It's from a wig, Tom."

Tom sighed. Of course it was. Back to square one.

No. That wasn't quite true. There was still Esme.

"I'll be back in a little while," Tom said, and went for the exit. Minutes later he was on the road to the hospital, and then hurrying up the stairs (past the policemen he had stationed *everywhere*—there would be no repeat of what happened to the fire chief) to Baptist

St. Anthony's second floor. Being back here cramped pangs of déjà vu throughout his left shoulder, yet another mark left by the sniper. His heart, however, was surfeit with hope, that his dear friend was all right, and that she had once again come through for him and cracked the case.

Rafe intercepted him in the corridor.

At first Tom didn't recognize him. Since last they'd seen each other, Rafe had lost his hair and gained a belly. Such were the metamorphoses of time.

Rafe recognized Tom immediately.

"Well," he said. "I was about to call you up."

"The doctor beat you to it," Tom replied. "He told me she's awake. That she's going to make a full recovery."

"She's something else."

"Yes. She is."

Tom took a step forward, but Rafe nonchalantly blocked him.

"Where were you?" he asked.

Tom raised an eyebrow. "What do you mean?"

"When Esme fell. I'm not asking why you didn't catch her. I'm just curious where you were."

"We were trying to arrest the man who's been responsible for all this—"

"Right. Yes. Did you? Arrest him, I mean?"

"Not yet. That's why I need to speak with Esme."

"I see. To apologize."

Tom looked past Rafe. Esme's room was only a few yards away. It would be so easy, even with only one good arm, to shove this fat man aside and proceed.

Match Rafe's pigheadedness with some of Tom's own, Kentucky style. But Tom held back. The last thing Esme needed right now was her husband sporting a black eye. "Look, Rafe, you must know it was never my intention for Esme to be in harm's way. I feel as bad about the whole thing as anyone."

"I'm pretty sure she feels worse."

He again tried to move forward, but again Rafe blocked his path.

Tom didn't have time for this.

"So, tell me, Special Agent Piper. Tell me what you're going to do to make it up to us."

"Make it up to you?"

"I don't mean financially. I'm sure you made her sign all sorts of waivers of liability. It's not like our government to take responsibility, if you know what I mean. So that's why I'm asking you. You, Tom Piper. What are you going to do to atone for dragging my wife down here and letting her almost get killed?"

Rafe's voice quavered with emotion, and his eyes were wet with anger.

"Look…" said Tom, but at that moment the dam burst inside Rafe and he took a swing, a fat roundhouse aimed straight at his opponent's face. Tom anticipated it, though, and easily slid away. Before Rafe could bring another fist to bear, Tom booted him in the groin, not too hard…but not too soft either. Rafe fell to his knees, gasping.

"You always did have a temper," muttered Tom, and he passed him onward to Esme's room. On his way, he motioned to one of the nurses and indicated poor Rafe, still on his knees. As she ran to Rafe's rescue, Tom stepped into Esme's room, and shut the door.

She was staring at him.

"I heard you," she croaked.

Tom grimaced. "I was afraid you might have."

"Did you hit him?"

"No."

"Can you do it now?"

Tom smiled, and approached her. She looked so small there on the hospital bed.

"He means well," said Tom.

Esme nodded. She knew.

Tom placed a hand on her shoulder. "I'm sorry, Esmeralda."

She attempted to shrug, but her brace only allowed her to nudge her chin. "I'm not a child. I knew the risks."

"Mmm-hmm."

Esme pointed at the cup of water. Gingerly, Tom irrigated her palate.

"I got a good look at him," Esme rasped. "Lilly's description is solid. He is medium height. Blond hair. He—"

Tom shook his head. "It's a wig."

"It's a nice wig." Esme took another swallow. "He knew about the sting?"

"Yes."

"He's smart."

"Yes."

"I'm smarter."

And a grin spread across her parched lips.

Tom sat down.

"It's about the election," she explained. "There's a group called the Unity for a Better Tomorrow. They're a Christian organization. They've sponsored events for Kellerman. Their first event was in Atlanta last November. Guess where the second event was?"

"And the religious angle ties back to the Mencken quote in the videotape. Galileo's a zealot."

"Most psychopaths are." She took another gulp of water. "The next event was in Santa Fe, right after Christmas. That's where our guy's going next."

"What a coincidence," replied Tom. "That's where I'm going next too."

Esme nodded.

Silence passed between them. Silence, and history. Then:

"He could have killed me, Tom."

"I know. You're very lucky."

"No." She took a breath. "He had his gun to my head. He could have killed me. He could have pulled the trigger. But he didn't. Why?"

"I don't know. But I'll be seeing him soon. I'll be sure to ask him for you, okay?"

She nodded weakly. The past few minutes had been quite an exertion, and all her energy was now drained away.

Tom knew it was time to go. He kissed her forehead.

"I am so sorry," he whispered.

Esme muttered something in response.

"What?" He leaned in close. "I didn't hear you."

But she had fallen asleep.

13

Meteorology in San Francisco was a mug's game. No amount of technology or science could predict what warm, cold, dry, wet, windy, calm weather would occur from moment to moment, seasons be damned. And in the City by the Bay, it was possible to be warm, cold, dry, wet, windy, and calm at the same time.

On today, the first of March, the weather gods brewed up something fierce. It began with a fog, as most everything here did. Residents woke up to white soup. Folks wielded flashlights to find their morning paper. Lilly Toro used her Bic lighter, and carried her copy of the *San Francisco Chronicle* back to her ex-girlfriend Penny's kitchen table. Penny was already gone. She worked the morning shift at a twenty-four-hour sex shop over in Chinatown. Usually Lilly would be gone too, either on assignment or at least on her way to Mission Street, but as of two days ago she was on suspension, pending review.

"The problem," explained her editor, "is that your ambition superseded your common sense. You're very gifted, Lilly, but extraordinarily callow, and the fact is you compromised the security of a federal investigation."

Had her informant been the real deal, none of this would have happened. She would have written a great story and, instead of a reprimand, she'd be getting a raise. She'd have been barraged with offers, instead of crashing at her ex's split-level. Had her informant been the real deal, had he been a cop, the data she'd given him on the task force wouldn't have come back to bite her at all. At worst, the inside scoop would have leveraged a better working environment between the feds and the local P.D.

Was she ambitious? Sure. But this was America. Since when was ambition a crime in America? Was she callow, naive? Lilly sat down at the kitchen table, lit up a Marlboro and exhaled plumes. Who wasn't a fool, in this day and age?

To wit, she read the paper.

By the time she got to the business section, the sky outside had blackened like dried blood and the first rumbles of thunder echoed throughout the city. Lilly had to turn on the kitchen light, lest the words on the page fall into shadow. She was on her third cigarette now. The mug she was using for an ashtray was filling up nicely.

She could have read the paper on her Hello Kitty laptop. SFGate.com was one of the oldest and most comprehensive Web sites of any newspaper in the country. In fact, her first job at the company had been to maintain some of its Internet content. This led to blogging, which led to offline reporting, which led to, which led to, which led to, etc.

Rain now, pelting. Thunderstorms were so percussive.

Lilly moved on to sports. The Giants were readying for their first exhibition game. They were playing the Dodgers. How funny it was that two New York franchises, two rivals, ended up out west in the same state. Lilly's love of the game came from her father. The man loved his westerns and he loved his baseball. What an apple-pie American.

She hadn't spoken to them since she'd returned. They had called her. They had read about her ordeal. They left her messages, asking if she was all right, if there was anything they could do. But it was too little, too late. The day she came out of the closet, when she was only fifteen years old, they had practically kicked her to the curb. And now they wanted to be nurturing?

Outside, a cat meowed. Someone must have left her out in the rain. Poor thing. Lilly considered heading out into the storm to find the animal. She knew Penny had tuna in the cupboard.

She turned to the metro section.

She could have read the paper on her laptop, yes, but there was something textural about newsprint. She liked the fact that it got all over her fingertips. There was a symbolism there. Or maybe she was, in her own way, just as much a traditionalist as her old man.

Outside, again, the cat meowed.

She was about to snub her cigarette and rescue the poor kitty when an item in the Metro section caught her eye. Presidential candidate Bob Kellerman was scheduled to speak today at Sproul Plaza, UC-Berkeley's historic rally point. Undoubtedly the *Chronicle* had its soporific political reporters covering the event. But were any of them high school buds with Deedee Rimes, esteemed sergeant with the Berkeley campus police?

Lilly scrambled for her cell phone.

Deedee was not pleased. "You got to be fucking kidding me, L."

"D, you owe me…"

"Don't even go there."

"In eleventh grade—"

"Don't do it, L."

"If I hadn't written that essay for you—"

"Oh, sweet Jesus."

"D, you know I'm right."

"Of course I know you're right. You remind me about it every fucking time we get a beer. You tell the bartender. 'My friend Deedee's going to buy me a drink. Let me share with you why.' "

Lilly sucked on her Marlboro and sighed fumes. "I'm in a bad way, D. My luck's been for shit. I need this."

Silence on the other line. Then:

"This makes us even, L. You even mention the eleventh grade again, and I'll knock you on your ass so hard your ancestors'll need crutches. Got it?"

Lilly got it, and hopped in the shower. What she knew about politics could fit on a napkin, but a back-stage exclusive with a national figure was sparkly from all angles. All she had to do was poke him or his staff with the right question—the kind of wild inquiry the sleepyheads in political journalism would never dream of asking—and she could leverage whatever quote she received back into the good graces of her lord and master, the *San Francisco Chronicle*.

It was an old trick, really. Public figures are armored against most anything relevant the press can throw at them, so you blindside them with an allegation so preposterous they just have to take the bait. Then you've got them. But what to ask?

Lilly didn't kid herself. This wasn't the noble approach. This was the recourse of desperation. Speaking of, once dressed she grabbed a tin of tuna from the cupboard and carried it out with her to the front porch. In the time she'd spent in the shower and getting ready, the rain had tapered off to an ugly drizzle. The cat, a white tabby sodden with mud, was curled up underneath an awning.

"Good kitty," she said, and headed for her precious pink VW Beetle, parked beside the mailbox. She'd found the old car on Craigslist, of all places. It always took a minute to start, but once it got going, it purred like, well, like a good kitty.

Berkeley was a three-cigarette drive. As she neared the campus, the traffic became predictably dense. Fortunately, her Beetle could travel nicely in the narrow breakdown lane, and Lilly skipped ahead of the honking throng and up to the south gate. She snagged her press ID from the glove compartment and dangled it for the guards. They directed her to a nearby parking lot.

UC-Berkeley's massive campus was oriented around

Sather Tower, a 300+ foot clock-and-bell obelisk col-loquially referred to as The Campanile. As she locked her car, she couldn't help but stare at the mighty stone finger. Her mind immediately flashed to Charles Whitman, the boy who in 1966 mounted the administration building at the University of Texas at Austin, a rifle in his arms, and proceeded to target forty-five people.

The Campanile would make the perfect staging ground for her sniper.

She reached in her purse for another cigarette. Her tiny hands were trembling now. Get a grip, she chastised herself. Amarillo was old news. Today was about your future! By now her hands and feet were tingling, and inside her rib cage her heart was galloping.

She was experiencing an anxiety attack, her fourteenth since she'd returned to San Francisco. Her doctor had prescribed Xanax, but she'd just sold them to a buddy for some easy cash. Now, as her lungs squeezed and squeezed like angry fists, as the dizziness came, and the nausea, she just wanted to climb back into her Beetle and drive to her buddy's apartment and snatch back those pills and down the whole vial. The first time she had suffered an anxiety attack, she thought she was dying. Because that's what it felt like. And even though she knew she wasn't dying, that her onslaught of symptoms was completely psychosomatic, that she was actually okay, even though she knew these things—it didn't make one lick of difference. Perception was exploitative, perception was everything, and who knew that better than Lilly Toro.

Lilly closed her eyes and took account of her organs,

one by one. Chill out, she demanded. She shuttled her imagination to a pleasant memory: her first adult kiss, behind a church on Martin Blvd. The ways that kiss had made her feel were ironically quite similar to now—the racing heart, the tingling limbs—but all saturated with such warmth and security. Lilly let that wink of sunshine suffice her panic, override it. Good conquers evil, she insisted. And her symptoms began to subside. Yes. Yes.

She opened her eyes, checked her reflection in her Beetle's side mirror. Her black hair was matted to her sweaty forehead. She fixed it, took a final, steadying breath and marched on to Sproul Plaza, carefully avoiding any glimpse of the looming bell tower in the distance.

Okay. Back to more important matters. What to ask Bob Kellerman? As she approached the masses gathered on the quad, she started narrowing her choices. She could go kinky ("Is it true you enjoy paddling?") or she could go criminal ("Is it true you enjoy gambling?"). Both were sensationalistic. Both would amount to a denial, but by then she'd have her foot in the door.

Bob Kellerman denies allegations of gambling.

It was tabloid journalism, to be sure, but the balance in news between ethics and entertainment had been tipped long ago to favor the latter. That was what had been so attractive about her task force story. She maneuvered through the crowd of undergrads. The storm clouds had dissipated and a sunny drunken glow poured out over the field. And there was Deedee near the dais on the stairs. The candidate and his handlers were probably still inside, prepping their talking points. Lilly shoved toward her old pal.

"Hey, D, how about a kiss?" Lilly's bravado was just that—one didn't recover from an anxiety attack in twenty minutes. But bravado was expected, so bravado was provided.

"What have you got now, L, thirty-one piercings?"

"One for every flavor, babe."

"You can go backstage," said Deedee, "*after* the speech. You'll have maybe thirty seconds."

"That's all I need."

"I know. I've heard."

Lilly rolled her eyes and scanned the crowd for a good place to stand. The audience was diverse, but she expected nothing less from a Berkeley crowd. Still, her fellow Goths had to be somewhere, usually in the shade…and there they were. Lilly joined them under a poplar tree.

The president of the college, Nancy Holland, approached the podium. It was time.

"Ladies and gentlemen," she began, and Lilly tuned out the rest. She wasn't here to listen to Nancy Holland. She wasn't even here to listen to Bob Kellerman. She was here to snare a quote.

A pasty-faced teenager to her right offered her a clove cigarette. She gladly accepted. She felt like a kid again.

Finally, Bob Kellerman took the stage. The audience sang out in symphonic applause. Lilly couldn't help but be swept up in the adoration. She couldn't see what was so special about the man but the crowd ate him up.

He was a good-looking man, not movie-star handsome but the physiognomy of a Norman Rockwell character, one who loved to watch his first-born son hit a home run in Little League. Another apple-pie American. His hair and eyes were the same shade of chestnut brown, and the maple-colored tie he wore underlined their earthiness. He had a curious scar across the middle of his left eyebrow, almost indistinguishable and yet impossible to ignore. Did it stem from a childhood accident? One of the few facts Lilly recalled about the man was that he was a volunteer fireman. Perhaps the scar came from that. Perhaps there wasn't a scar at all, and some genius in makeup had penciled it in to make Kellerman appear more rugged.

He spoke for forty-five minutes. Much of the time he seemed to be extemporizing off the top of his head, but Lilly was certain it was an oratory trick. The thesis of his speech was conservation, always a safe topic in enviro-conscious Northern California. He referenced Berkeley's activist past and encouraged everyone to vote for change and…Lilly tuned him out. Politics wasn't her thing. She used the time he spoke to come up with her Outrageous Question. By the time he wrapped up, she'd chosen.

According to Deedee, the candidate was going to retreat into Sproul Hall where he would reconnoiter with his entourage, and then they would exit out the Telegraph Avenue door to a rope line. According to Deedee, the best time for her thirty seconds would be in Sproul Hall, and she had to climb over (and under) co-eds to get there. Fortunately, Lilly's small size and big attitude made crowd-climbing none too difficult, and she met up with Deedee at the top of the stairs.

"Thirty seconds," Deedee reminded her.

Lilly nodded and entered the building and there he was, the man of the hour, surrounded by a cadre of Important People whom Lilly neither knew nor cared about.

"Governor Kellerman!" she called out, inflecting her voice with even more hoarseness than usual—all the better to grab his attention. And grab his attention it did. He glanced over at her, curiosity in his eyes, and then his human pit-bull bodyguard stomped between them.

"No press," the bodyguard growled.

"Just one question?" She angled her tiny head to the side and again caught Kellerman's gaze. She flashed him an innocent grin. "Please?"

"Sure," the governor replied. He probably thought she was an undergrad. She weaved past the bodyguard and approached Kellerman. He was taller than she expected, and that kind fatherly air he projected on stage intensified in person. This was a man you wanted to hug after a hard day's work.

"What's your question?" he asked.

But Lilly had nothing to say. She suddenly didn't want to ambush this obviously good man. She suddenly didn't want to be there at all.

"I…"

"Yes?"

A few of the Important People now stared at her, waiting.

"Your…" She'd never felt so ashamed in her life.

Not for her inability to speak but for the horrible words she'd come so close to saying. "It…"

One of the Important People whispered in the governor's ear. He nodded and held out his hand.

"I'm afraid I have to go," he said. "It's been a pleasure meeting you, Ms. Toro."

She shook his hand and they went out the south gate and Lilly remained in the lobby of Sproul Hall, utterly flustered. He'd called her Ms. Toro. How had he known her name? Oh, the press pass around her neck. Right. Yes. The press pass. She fanned a hand—the hand he shook—in front of her face.

But wait! Maybe if she asked him something relevant, something substantive…

She rushed out the south doors. The governor was already halfway down the rope line, signing auto- graphs. When someone would hand him a gift, which happened every fifth or sixth person, he warmly but mechanically passed it back to one of his handlers, who was carrying a large bag for that very purpose. Photographers were capturing the candidate in all his user-friendly charm. Lilly recognized a few of them from the *Chronicle*.

Then she saw Galileo, wearing a 49ers cap, nearly blended in the crowd.

Governor Kellerman was about to shake his hand.

"No!" she cried, but the crowd was much louder than even she could yell, especially when her hyperven- tilating returned. Because anxiety attacks aren't tamed so easily, and hers returned with reinforcements. The sight of the killer, her "Ray Milton," reignited her tingling, her nausea, her palpitations. The world spun off its axis. She wasn't going to faint. She was going to implode.

Through blurred vision she watched as he reached into the pocket of his red raincoat for a gun. No—wait. Not a gun. A short white envelope. He slid the envelope into Kellerman's outstretched hand…and Lilly could stand still no longer. Kellerman wasn't going to be shot, not today, thank fucking Christ, and so she ran, ran from the noise, the crowd, the air, ran away, pushed through the door and back into Sproul and toward the nearest restroom and into the first cubicle and she locked the door and fell to her knees and dry-heaved into the still water, which shimmered with each empty breath.

The killer was here. Why? He hadn't pulled the trigger. He hadn't even taken out his gun. He'd handed Kellerman a goddamn *envelope.* No, that was good. Stop analyzing. Control your breathing or you're going to pass out on a toilet in Berkeley. Wouldn't be the first time, but still. Think about that first kiss, that first kiss, that first—

What if he saw her? What if he had spotted her up there, on the steps, by the door? She had seen him. It stood to reason that he could have seen her. He could even have followed her here into this isolated restroom…

No. That's the anxiety talking. He hadn't seen her. His attention had been fixed on Kellerman. She was okay. Well, no, she wasn't, she was far from okay, her brain had initiated a code-red for her heart, lungs, stomach and limbs, but it would pass. Eventually.

And pass it did. Three hours later. By then, her legs were painfully cramped from crouching and her head swam with oxygen overload. She pulled herself to her feet and exited the stall. Sproul Hall had returned to its regularly scheduled programming of undergrads, junk food and laughter. Lilly walked outside into the sun, and the tranquil blue sky. It was hard to believe this day had begun with rain and lightning. But so much had changed since she'd woken up. She wondered about the cat on the porch.

She wondered who she should call.

Her gut instinct was to phone her boss at the *Chronicle*. She had spotted a serial killer at a rally in Berkeley. If ever there was news, this was it, and it would certainly be an exclusive. She could parlay this tidbit into a suspension of her suspension. It was a far more palatable and dignified pathway than the gambit of the Outrageous Question. And in this instance, her goings-on in Amarillo, her face-to-face with Galileo, added credibility rather than subtracted it. The irony was delicious.

Or she could call Tom Piper. She could alert him to what she saw. His task force needed to know this information, didn't they? Although she was positive that if she did call Tom and relay what she'd witnessed, he would demand she not tell anyone else, especially the *Chronicle*.

So which would it be? The lady or the tiger? The paper or the feds?

She took out her phone, made her decision and dialed the number.

14

Esme awoke to an empty house. Once again her pain-killers had caused her to oversleep and miss breakfast. Sophie was long gone by now, and so was Rafe. Even Lester appeared to be gone, probably off on one of his errands. What the old man did with his time was a mystery.

What Esme did with her time was obsess about Galileo.

She had already filled up the margins of her Sudoku books with her theories and hypotheses. She even included the conjectures made by all those pop psychologists which CNN and MSNBC and Fox seemed to stock in endless supply. But no matter how much mileage she gained from their hypotheses ("Galileo is lashing out at authority figures because he was abused as a child," "Galileo uses a sniper rifle because he is afraid of confrontation," etc.), it all, for her, came back to one unaddressed, unanswered question: why had she been spared?

She turned on the TV and caught up on the latest

non-news the networks had to report, but she couldn't stomach any punditry right now. With considerable effort, she roused herself from the sofa—a long-taloned finger jabbed at the small of her back. Oh, God. But this was typical now, with every morning, and she reflexively reached for the amber vial of Percocet on the coffee table. She already had a half-empty glass of water next to it, ready to help chase down the 325mg white pills. Two of those little guys and the jabbing finger of death would go far, far away…for at least six to seven hours.

Ah, the easy road.

So little was easy these days, why not take advantage? The doctor wouldn't have prescribed them if he didn't think they were necessary. Esme was a big fan of progress. If modern medicine could make pain optional, so be it. She held the pills in one hand and the glass of water in another…

The front door opened, and Lester stomped indoors. The old man wore hiking boots, jeans, and a plaid shirt—every day that Esme had known him. All he needed was an ax slung over his shoulder and a pet blue ox by his side.

"Morning," he said. "Just get up? Sophie tried to wake you up earlier to say hi, but I guess you must've been having a nice dream."

Esme put down the glass and pills. The talon poked and poked at her back. So be it. "Good morning, Lester."

He wandered into the kitchen. "It's almost noon, so I'm going to fix myself a sandwich. Want me to make you some flapjacks or something?"

"I'm fine. Thank you."

"Well, if you want to go back to sleep, you can. Your therapist's appointment's not 'til four. I gassed up the Caddie while I was out. Wouldn't believe how much more expensive it is down here on the Island."

"Uh-huh."

"If you're running low on pills, we can refill your prescription while we're out."

She watched him slap some ham between two slices of wheat bread. He lathered on some mustard too. Her stomach keened, but she suppressed it. She was not going to share a meal with her father-in-law, not if she could help it.

Her cell phone sat on the coffee table, next to the pills and water. She unhooked it from its recharger and checked for messages.

Tom still hadn't called her back.

Well, she reasoned, he probably was busy. For all she knew, he was in a hotbox right now with Galileo, interrogating a full confession out of the madman. Tom could do it. It had been good to see him again, to work with him, albeit briefly. It had felt so right, and now everything felt so wrong.

From the kitchen came a belch, which meant Lester had finished his sandwich. How considerate of him to announce his satisfaction after every meal. Sophie sure got a kick out of it.

Sophie.

It was the thought of her daughter that got Esme, finally, to her feet. She baby-stepped to the bathroom, contemplated emptying the pills down the toilet, decided that was a tad too dramatic and instead just tossed the vial into the trash.

"If you need me," called Lester, "I'll be in my room."

She listened to him clomp down the hall and waited until she heard the door to the guest bedroom shut before she baby-stepped back out into the living room, and slowly, very slowly, made her way to the kitchen. It was just part of the process, as her therapist reminded her. She had to retrain her muscles, and these things took time. Perhaps weeks. Perhaps months. Perhaps longer.

She spent the first few minutes in the kitchen searching for her strawberry Nutri-Grain breakfast bars. One of Lester's habits, one of many, was rearranging the contents of the pantry. Esme finally found her box buried behind the chunky peanut butter. She took out two bars, poured herself a glass of orange juice, and ate standing up. Sitting in a chair apparently put too much pressure on her back. She couldn't remember the last time she'd just sat without excruciating pain. This made operating her PC nigh impossible. It sat unused on her desk, growing a hat of dust.

Fuck it.

She limped over to her computer and depressed its sunken On button. The motor hummed to life. In a few minutes, she would be able to escape the confines of her invalidity and soar (or at least surf). And she'd also be able to learn what the blogosphere was speculating about Galileo. Any clues—no matter how half-baked—fed her obsession. The Windows welcome screen appeared and she leaned down to sit in her chair—

every neuron along her right side exploded at once. Her entire body flooded with pain, drowned in it. She missed the seat entirely and landed on the carpet and arched back as far as her brace would allow, mouth open in a silent scream. She couldn't move, couldn't shift her body into a better position, couldn't imagine a better position, couldn't imagine anything but the complete and total searing which engulfed her.

She stayed there on the carpet, twisted up, for minutes. She became aware of her fingertips on the carpet and concentrated on that tactile sensation. Her legs slowly kicked, as if she were climbing a ladder. She reminded herself to breathe. It was just like giving birth, except without the birth and with all the pain. The world came into focus. The computer screen came into focus. All the little icons on her desktop came into focus. They were so close, yet so far away.

Biting down on her lower lip, she used the chair to pull herself up. That seemed to enrage her neurons even more, if possible. But she mustered every ounce of positive energy left in the niches of her being to make her way across the ocean of her living room and to her bathroom. With great concentration, she managed to bend her knees, reach into the wastepaper basket, and rescue her vial of pills. The glass of water was still on the coffee table, miles and miles away. She didn't need it. She emptied four pills into her palm and swallowed them dry. She placed the vial next to the bathroom sink, closed the door for privacy, and laid herself down on the cold tile floor. Oh, those angry neurons relaxed at the touch of the cold tiles, and soon the Percocet took effect and they simply fell asleep. And so did she.

This was not the first time Esme had suffered a major injury. When she was five years old, she'd shattered three bones in her left hand. She had no recollection of this, but her parents had held on to the little plaster cast—which was signed by everyone at the shelter they were staying at the time—and when she turned eleven and broke a collarbone falling off the jungle gym at school, her parents stayed with her all night in the hospital and brought the little plaster cast with them and showed it to her—and to anyone within eyesight—and regaled her with stories of her childhood and their childhood until she'd forgotten about the pain in her collarbone, and then until she fell asleep.

When she was sixteen, she broke the same collarbone when she fell down a flight of stairs. In her defense, the stairs had just been waxed and the custodian had forgotten to put out a sign. Again she found herself laid up in the hospital, and again her parents brought out the little hand cast from when she was five. They held the cast to her teenage hand and marveled at the size difference.

Then she turned eighteen and went off to college and her parents disappeared, and with them went the little plaster cast. So it's no wonder that as she lay on the bathroom floor of her house in Long Island, as she lay still in a hazy stupor after a brief drug-induced nap, her mind went back to that cast. Not a day passed when Esme didn't think about her parents, but she hadn't

thought about that little cast in years. She could visu-
alize it now, though, and the dozens of illegible
messages scrawled across it in black ink and blue ink
and red ink by her parents' friends (though none by her
friends—for at five years old she'd had no friends to
speak of—she'd been too shy). She imagined the
messages to be tattoos, and the cast to be an old skin
she had slinked out of by the time she was six. How she
longed to slide back into that skin now…

But self-pity was pointless. She wiped at her eyes,
trying to scrub away the blurry Percocet haze. What she
needed was to get out of this house. No overexertions.
Everything in moderation. Baby steps. The sooner she
recovered, the sooner she could put all this behind her.
The sooner her father-in-law could hightail it back
upstate. The sooner she could really get back on the case.

But first, she had to get off the floor.

Easier said than done. Her muscles were jelly, and
jelly didn't respond well to motivation. She slapped her
thighs to wake them up. They replied with a sheepish
smirk and went back to ignoring their mistress.

"Damn it," she mumbled. Even her words sounded
cloudy. Could words evaporate? As she pondered this
thought, her eyelids started to flutter and shut. Maybe a
few more winks of slumber wouldn't hurt. She could be
proactive tomorrow. There was no law that said she had
to—

Stop. Don't be a lazy twit. Think of Sophie. Think
of Rafe. Get your narcoleptic ass in gear. Open those
eyes. Open them. Good. Now reach for the sink and
pull yourself up. Pull yourself—okay, maybe reach for

the doorknob instead. Baby steps. Good. Now pull. Pull. Lift with your arms, stupid, not your back. Good.

Now for some positive reinforcement.

She teetered out of the bathroom and past the couch—which looked so soft and welcoming—and made her way to the desk. The computer monitor displayed the old school screensaver she'd downloaded a few months ago: dozens of toaster ovens, winged, flying from left to right. She reached for the top of her CPU, where her iPod was synched to her computer. She hadn't listened to it since Amarillo. The TV commentators had provided soundtrack enough.

She fished the earbuds out and tucked each into an ear. Her thumb scrolled through the player's many albums. Whatever music she selected had to be upbeat. No Joy Division, no Smiths. Baby steps.

ABBA. "Waterloo."

Perfect on so many levels.

She pressed Play, and let the Swedes' goofy, over-dubbed, three-minute pop masterpiece saturate and awaken every fiber inside her. She let each muscle group yawn and smile. Time to get back in the game, folks. The clock by the computer read 12:56 p.m. Perfect. The mail usually arrived by now.

Overexertion had recently landed her supine and in pain—so she patiently inched toward the front door. Her feet were bare, her pajamas were sweat-stained, her bandage made her look like she'd been gored by a Pamplona bull, but what did it matter? So what if any of her neighbors saw her? They all knew what had happened down in Amarillo. The entire country knew what had happened in Amarillo. In the first few weeks, the media had tried to make a story of it, but then some Hollywood starlet was caught *in flagrante delicto* with a quarterback for UCLA and that was a much, much juicier steak to chew.

"Waterloo" segued into "Take a Chance on Me"—a song even more vibrant and sunny—and Esme wanted to pet her iPod. Good boy. Instead, she opened the front door. It was a cool, cloudy day, perfect for a nap…but no matter. The mail waited. One foot and then the other…

The front steps were made of cement. Cold cement. Esme felt a shiver travel up her spine, which meant her neurons were beginning to reawaken. Terrific. She left the front door open and padded down the steps to her grassy lawn. The blades tickled with each step. She tried to walk in beat with ABBA but their tempo was too fast, and her tempo was too restricted. So be it.

The mailbox was fifteen feet away. Esme focused on every step. The late winter breeze fluttered through her cotton pajamas. She should have put on a coat. No matter. The mail waited. One foot and then the other…

Maybe Rafe was right.

Wait—where did that come from? Maybe Rafe was right? Right about what? Esme paused in her journey, and her subconscious realization crystallized into substance. Rafe had chastened and chastised her about Amarillo. He had been a brute. But if anyone was entitled to crow "I told you so," it was him, and he hadn't. Not to her, at least.

Maybe he was right all along. Maybe she shouldn't have gone to Amarillo. Maybe her place was here, and now, and the universe was punishing her for not letting go of the past. After all, it was when she'd gone to the computer, when her curiosity had propelled her to act beyond her limits, that she'd fallen. The universe was telling her something and she needed to listen.

And besides, Esme concluded, it was obvious her margin-crammed theories about Galileo were flawed. Perhaps the killer just liked cities that began with the letter *A*. It was as solid (and silly) an hypothesis, wasn't it? No wonder Tom wasn't returning her calls. Best to shrug it all off. Take that weight and let it tumbleweed away. She didn't need it anymore. She recommenced her journey, as the cascading pianos of "Dancing Queen" washed her clean.

Despite the cool temperature outside, by the time she reached the mailbox her forehead was beaded with sweat. It didn't matter. It was time for her reward. She hinged the squeaky lid, reached inside, and found…

…one letter. That was it. One stinking letter. Better be a good one. Better be from Ed McMahon announcing she's just won…but no. It was from Amy Lieb. It was an invitation to a party she was having next month, a fundraiser for her idol, Bob Kellerman. Esme weighed her likelihood of attendance: somewhere between a snowball's chance in hell and when pigs would…

Wait.

She read the invitation again, searching the fine print, and there it was, right at the bottom: "co-sponsored by the League of Women Voters, the Daughters of the American Revolution, the Democratic Party of Long Island, and the Unity for a Better Tomorrow."

Just like Atlanta and Amarillo.

She pushed through her pain and trekked back to the house. She hoped her phone had fully charged, because she had a lot of calls to make.

15

"So," said Tom, "what do we know?"

"Not a lot," replied Norm. He was navigating the wide streets of downtown Omaha, Nebraska, in their rental, a white Geo minivan. According to the dashboard GPS-navigation, they were five minutes (and two left turns) away from their destination.

"Let's go through the list."

"It's not really a list."

The rest of the task force was in Santa Fe, working with the New Mexico state police in setting up a dragnet for the at-large sniper. It all tied back to Esme's insight linking the crime scenes to rallies held by the Unity for a Better Tomorrow, which was headquartered in…Omaha, Nebraska. It had taken Tom the better part of two weeks to arrange a meeting with Donald Chappell, the Unity's co-founder and erstwhile spiritual leader. Apparently, they were not fond of federal inquiries.

In the meantime, he was dodging calls from Esme. It's not that he felt threatened by Rafe or believed those accusations of selfish disregard had been accurate…but still…in the realm of the conscious, and the conscience, especially Tom's, sometimes possibility outweighed probability.

"I'll start with the facts," said Norm.

"Good place as any."

"He's a trained sharpshooter. Where did he acquire his training? Is he ex-army? We don't know. According to ballistics, he uses an M107. Organizations which employ the M107 include the NYPD, the U.S. Coast Guard, and IRA. So what we're looking for is a seafaring Irish ex-cop."

"Funny," replied Tom.

"His victims have almost all been civil servants, which implies anger toward the government. This is reinforced by the video he left for us at the second crime scene. Speaking of the crime scenes, we know he infiltrated each of them by posing as a janitor. We have videotape footage of him from the aquarium, and we know he gained access to the rooftop of that school in Atlanta by posing as a janitor there. But here's where we hit a roadblock."

"Go ahead."

"Now I trust Esme as much as anyone when it comes to this sort of thing, but this whole Unity for a Better Tomorrow connection—I mean, I'm here because you asked me to join you but if the key really is this organization or the Kellerman campaign or whatever, why isn't he targeting them?"

Tom shrugged. "It's a valid point."

"Instead he runs into Darcy at Walmart and shoots

her then and there. However, he confronts Esme at city hall but lets her live. Why?"

Tom stared out the window at the passing Midwestern architecture and remained silent.

"Fact of the matter is—we're in the dark here, Tom. Maybe the Unity is connected. Maybe Santa Fe is his next target. But how do you expect to confirm any of that? What are you going to ask Donald Chappell?"

They pulled into a two-story parking garage exclusive to the midrise skyscraper which housed the Unity for a Better Tomorrow and parked their Geo minivan between a Cadillac and a Lexus. From here they crossed through a causeway to the main lobby of the building, where they beheld a sunny-faced blonde standing beside a metal detector.

"Good afternoon and welcome! How may I help you today?"

"We have an appointment to speak with Mr. Chappell," replied Tom, reaching into his black leather coat for his badge. "Special Agent Tom Piper."

"Of course!" Her teeth were cartoon-perfect. "One moment, please."

While the blonde typed their information into her computer, Tom and Norm took stock of their surroundings. The lobby was awash in rich reds and yellows and browns. Even the large tasteful artwork on the walls had been painted to match these soothing earth tones. Tom observed the painting behind the counter. It depicted a young and spry Andrew Jackson, thwarting the British at the Battle of New Orleans. He glanced around at the other paintings. Each showcased an episode of American heroism—Lewis & Clark on the untamed frontier, Thomas Edison tinkering with a lightbulb, Martin Luther King in front of the Lincoln Memorial. Nowhere in the lobby was a cross. Nowhere was a Bible.

"All right," said the blonde. "I've confirmed your authorization for Floor 21."

In order to reach the elevator bank, they had to pass through a metal detector. Norm went first, and wasn't at all surprised it sounded a brief alarm.

"Sir, I'm afraid you're going to have to temporarily relinquish your firearm."

"Yeah, that's not going to happen."

"I'm afraid it is, sir, or you won't be permitted upstairs."

Before Norm could retort, Tom unholstered his pistol and motioned for his colleague to do the same. They handed their guns to the blonde, who collected them in a plastic basket.

"Thank you so much. They will be right here when you're through."

Tom and Norm ambled through the warm space to one of the gold-plated elevators. There were no buttons on the elevator wall. The automated doors closed as soon as they were inside, and their slow ascent, undoubtedly activated from the desk in the lobby, began. Gershwin's jazzy "Rhapsody in Blue" rang from its speakers and accompanied them on their vertical climb. Norm hummed along with the orchestral tune. The elevator finally came to a gentle halt, and its golden doors opened up to the twenty-first floor…

…and to a four-year-old boy in an astronaut costume, staring up at them from his abbreviated height.

Tom and Norm stared right back at him.

"Hi," he whispered shyly.

"Hello," replied Tom.

The twenty-first floor was a labyrinth of reds, browns and yellows. Seven different arteries wandered off from the elevator bank. Fortunately, a tall sallow-faced man in pinstripes soon appeared out of one of them.

"Right this way, gentlemen," he said. "Mr. Chappell will see you now."

The boy sucked on his left thumb.

"Joey," said the man, "aren't you supposed to be in the toy room?"

The boy mutely nodded, and ran down one of the other corridors.

"Mr. Chappell's grandson," the man explained. "Someday, God willing, all this will be his."

Tom and Norm exchanged a glance, then followed the man back down the wide hallway from which he came.

"Would either of you care for a beverage?"

"A Heineken?" asked Norm.

The man glanced at him, confused.

"Kidding," Norm added.

The man nodded. The hallway was lined with beautiful cedar doors. They stopped at the one labeled Chappell.

"If you need anything at all, my name is Paul. Like the apostle."

Paul opened the door, and the two FBI agents entered the office of Donald Chappell. Compared to the rest of the complex, his office was surprisingly small, even intimate. Donald Chappell, a white-haired, broad-shouldered octogenarian, sat behind an architect's easel. He was oil-painting the Omaha skyline, visible from his picture window.

"Have a seat," he said. His deep voice, hardly touched by age, resonated off the close walls. That was why Chappell chose to have his office so small, Tom surmised.

They sat down in the room's only unoccupied chairs, a pair of hundred-year-old high-backed jobs with plush crimson seats and hand-carved legs and arms. Norm did his best to keep his weight off the wood. The chair probably cost a year's worth of his salary.

"I admire the FBI," said Chappell. He continued to paint. "Your greatest failures are flaunted and your biggest successes remain confidential. And still you persevere. I would imagine you're under a great deal of heat right now, Tom, given the debacle in Texas. Your superiors must have you on a short leash."

Norm shifted in his seat, but Tom remained unfazed. "I'm glad you brought up the case. That allows us to get to the point."

"By the by, Bob is not the only candidate we have held rallies for. We've also invested a great deal of time and effort in the vice president's campaign on behalf of the Republican Party. The Unity for a Better Tomorrow is both nondenominational and nonpartisan."

"Except our guy isn't targeting the rallies you held for the vice president," Norm replied.

"That's assuming your conjecture is accurate. As you can imagine, we at the Unity for a Better Tomorrow would prefer you to be wrong. For us to be connected in any way to this monster is sickening."

"It's possible he's already sent you a message…"

"I doubt it. As soon as you contacted me, I had my people sift through our mail. We receive our share of negativity—all causes do—but there's been nothing unusual. Otherwise we would have already contacted you."

Tom's cell phone buzzed. He let it go to voice mail. "Could we have our people sift through your mail?"

Chappell finally looked up from his easel and over at the two gentlemen. His eyes were hazel, and rheumy. "I'm afraid that's not possible. It's all been destroyed. We believe it best not to keep hate around."

The man was lying. Tom was certain of it.

This was the real reason he wanted to meet the man in person. He hadn't expected to learn anything from Chappell's answers. Men like Chappell rarely spoke in substance, except to their inner circle.

Chappell returned to his painting. "Hatred is antithetical to all religions, and yet society remains muddled with those who reject the principles that set us above the other species—empathy, honesty, and selflessness."

"You need religion to make you a good person?"

"It reinforces, Tom. It protects us against temptation. Surely as a member of law enforcement you can agree that if something is a proven deterrent to sin, it deserves exaltation. Religion steered our forefathers to break free from the yoke of tyranny and pursue our 'God-given' rights. In God we trust, Tom."

"How about any former employees," asked Norm. "Maybe somebody you fired or someone who quit…"

This brought a smile to Donald Chappell's face. "We've never fired anyone. Not since we first opened our doors in the early '70s."

"You've never…"

"Every one of our employees goes through a careful vetting process. I'm certain the FBI does the same."

"Well, sure, but that doesn't mean none of our agents have ever been fired…"

"Well—" Chappell shrugged "—I guess my vetting process is more thorough."

Norm, exasperated, glanced over at Tom, who replied: "Thank you for your time," and rose. So did Norm.

Tom waited until they were back in the relative privacy of their rented Geo before sharing his suspicions.

"I hear you, but our hands are tied," Norm said. "You really think any judge is going to grant us a warrant with what we have to investigate these people? In an election year?"

Tom grunted. Norm was correct. And what he'd omitted was the pressure bearing down on them from the assistant director's office. As Chappell had noted, their failures were public—and the AD was quickly losing patience with Tom and his task force's recent public failures.

Tom then remembered the cell phone call he'd

ignored during the meeting, and checked his call history.

"What?" asked Norm, noticing Tom's curious grin. "Who called?"

Tom showed him. It was Lilly Toro.

Lilly shared with Tom Piper everything she saw at the rally. She described the envelope to the best of her ability. She even told him about her panic attack. She knew it wasn't especially relevant—but once she started talking, one piece led to another. She wasn't usually so loquacious. Maybe she still had some leftover anxiety in her tongue. Or maybe she simply needed to talk.

By the time their conversation had ended, it was midafternoon, and that meant traffic. Lilly lit up the last Marlboro in her pack, started up the engine of her pink Beetle, and joined the slow-moving mob on the westbound freeway across the Bay Bridge.

As expected, Tom had ordered her not to divvy what she knew to anyone else, especially her (ex?) coworkers at the paper. Ah, well. Lilly had resigned herself to that option when she made the call. Why did she choose the FBI over the *Chronicle?* Perhaps it had something to do with—

Fuck. She was being followed.

She glanced again in the rearview. Fifteen feet behind her was a blue Ford sedan. She was certain it had been there when she'd pulled out of the lot at Berkeley, but had thought nothing of it. Berkeley was a busy campus. But here she was, almost at San Francisco, and…

No. She was being silly. It was practically rush hour. Did she think she was the only person who lived in San Francisco? The driver of the blue sedan probably was a professor. More than likely, he lived in Pacific Heights with his wife and 2.5 children. He may have even been at the rally. Big deal. Chill, girl.

Just to be safe, just to put her doubts at rest, she adjusted the mirror to get a gander at the driver. She was part of a five-mile-per-hour trickle moving across the eight-mile-long Bay Bridge, and the sun was to the fore, not the aft, so it was easy to get a good look at the guy behind her without any hindrance of speed or glare. So it was that she saw Galileo, unobtrusively, behind the wheel of the blue Ford sedan.

And he waved at her.

Lilly sank down a few inches in her seat and gripped her wheel as if it was her only friend in the world. She perused her options, few as they were. The Bay Bridge was notable for having exit ramps at its midpoint, which led to Yerba Buena and Treasure Islands respectively. She wasn't far from the ramps. Maybe if she left the bridge for one of the islands…he would follow her and she would then be stranded on an island with a mass murderer. Bad idea.

So she had to stay on the bridge and follow it through to the West Bay and San Francisco. Locals got lost all the time on San Francisco's hilly, labyrinthine streets. And Galileo wasn't a local—as far as she knew. If he was foolish enough to pursue her into Chinatown, labyrinth to end all labyrinths, she could lose him. She knew she could. She just had to keep her head down.

This was a man who could grow impatient and just shoot her from the seat of his car. She just had to keep her head down…and make some phone calls.

First call: Tom Piper.

It went to voice mail.

"Tom," she rasped, so craving a cigarette, "it's Lilly again. I'm on the Bay Bridge in San Francisco and he's right behind me. He's going to try to kill me, Tom, but I think I can lose him in Chinatown. In the meantime, be a dear and call every goddamn agent you have and rally them to me right fucking now. I'm driving a pink VW Beetle. He's behind some piece of shit blue Ford four-door. License plate number…uh…" She popped up for a peek. "JG3-94Q. I am in danger. Call me back."

Next call: 911.

"911," intoned an Asian-inflected operator, "please state the nature of your emergency."

Lilly reiterated her situation to the operator. Accordingly, "patrol cars would be dispatched to her area as soon as possible" and she was "to remain calm." How was she supposed to remain calm? How was anyone supposed to remain calm in an emergency? It was natural to go crazy. Evolution had programmed the human body with a biological imperative to survive, and adrenaline played its part in that process. Her panic attacks—and she noticed she wasn't having one right now—were as much an overreaction, as much a wrong reaction, as "remaining calm" would be.

The traffic stream had finally poured her across the Bay. The first exit was the one she needed—Fremont

Street. She didn't bother with her blinker. No reason to give Galileo advance notice, right? Fremont Street emptied out into the city's financial district, mecca of high-rises and corporate logos. Lilly passed the head-quarters of VISA and The Gap. She remained hunched in her seat—not that difficult given her tiny frame—and chanced another glimpse at the rearview. Galileo remained fifteen feet behind her, steady as a stone.

She took Pine and then north to Kearny, and the neighborhood began its transformation from California chic to Mandarin peasantry. Tiled awnings stretched out over entrances. Cubical buildings became pagodas, and signage—so commonly horizontal—now hung ver-tical, to better suit the ancient language being conveyed.

The major thoroughfare in Chinatown was Grant Avenue, so Lilly made sure instead to take one of the slender side streets. So many of these were dead ends, but Lilly knew the area well and avoided getting trapped. Galileo was still on her tail, but the overall for-eignness of the area had to be frustrating him, and his chunky blue Ford barely squeezed between the brick buildings in a narrow lane like Ross Alley.

Take that, motherfucker…

Lilly felt her grip ease up a bit on her wheel. She was actually going to win. She, Lilly Toro, was going to defeat the big bad wolf. Strangely, she suddenly thought about her parents, and not with malice. They would be proud of her. They, who loathed her lifestyle, who had kicked her to the curb at age sixteen, would be bragging about her victory to their neighbors.

When she saw the police substation coming up on

the right, her nascent joy blossomed into unbridled bliss. She was home free. She had made it. She pounded on her horn, which got the attention of the three or four cops hanging out on the station's front steps, and then she pulled alongside the curb.

"Can we help you?" one of them asked.

"Yes, I…" Lilly looked back to point at the Ford— but it was gone.

"Ma'am?"

"I was being followed," she said with a grin, "but I guess I lost him."

As the cops glanced back down the street at the complete absence of a threat, Lilly shifted into Park and got out of her car. Her legs felt rubbery from tension, but alive. Alive! Her cell phone rang. It was probably Tom Piper, finally calling her back. Late again. She put the phone to her ear.

"Yo," she said.

"Thank you for standing still," answered Galileo, and from 2,000 feet away he tugged the trigger of his rifle and ended Lilly's life.

16

"Fear," said Rafe, "and desire."

He wrote the words in large black ink on the dry erase board, and some of the more dutiful freshmen in the lecture hall jotted them down. Rafe took a moment to smirk at this—would they forget those two words if they didn't copy them down? Then again, these were college students. With their away-from-home-for-the-first-time overindulgence of alcohol, drugs and sleep deprivation, who knew what condition their recently matured brains were in?

He continued his talk.

"It's the dialectic of human psychology. When we say that people 'push our buttons,' there are only two buttons and these are they. And as societies can be said to have a collective psychology, we can too list them on this paradigm. To wit—the Roman Republic falls closer to Fear, yes? The xenophobia of the early Romans allowed them not only to be on guard for the elephants of Hannibal but also informed the way they absorbed nearby cultural memes and without exception colored them decidedly Roman. The psycho-sociology of the Roman Empire, interestingly but not surprisingly, is another story altogether."

He paused again, to allow the note-takers (few and far between as they were) to catch up. Rafe knew that the effectiveness of using historical examples to explain sociological concepts was waning with each passing year, but in his heart of hearts he was a history buff and couldn't resist the efficacy these comparisons provided, at least to the astute in the room. Catering to mediocrity was not his style.

His mind drifted to his old father, now ensconced in their guest bedroom with his dumbbells and his magazines, and to his wife, for all intents and purposes an invalid on the living room divan. Much like the Romans of old, his life of late had shifted quite dramatically along the Fear-Desire paradigm.

A student raised her hand.

"Yes?"

"How do you spell 'Hannibal'?"

When Amy Lieb laughed, which she did with inordinate frequency, she sounded very much like a panting dog. Oftentimes when Amy had launched into one of these laughing fits, Esme felt the need to take a step back, lest she be splashed with hot air and germs. So even though she was on the phone, even though she was in her home and Amy was miles away, ensconced in hers, as soon as that breathy canine laughter began, Esme instinctively moved away from her phone receiver.

"I'm sorry," Amy said finally, once her breathing had simmered down, "it's just that, well, you can't be serious."

"I am very serious. At the very least, Amy, you need to remove the Unity for a Better Tomorrow from the fundraiser's list of sponsors."

"Because—and let me make sure I understand you—because this serial killer specifically targets cities where—"

"Yes."

"Esme, honey, have you eaten today?"

Esme blinked. "What?"

"Let me bring over a casserole. I'll have Lupe whip something up. She's a wonder with noodles. How do you feel about scrod?"

Esme clenched her teeth. She was lying on the sofa, ice packs numbing both sides of her slowly-mending abdominal wound. She still felt pain, though, because no amount of ice or Tylenol or even Percocet could combat the anguish of talking to a fucking wall.

"Amy, listen. Even if you think I'm wrong, even if it's inconvenient, wouldn't you rather err on the side of caution? Galileo is still out there."

"Oh, honey, I know he is. Do you have a pen handy? I used to see this shrink, Dr. Fleishman, back when I had that episode with my gardener, and he worked miracles for my post-traumatic stress. He's board certified."

Esme did have a pen handy, and she was doodling an unflattering caricature of Amy Lieb on the back of one of her Sudoku books. How could anyone be so willfully naive? Was the stereotype accurate? Was enough exposure to suburban life the equivalent of a lobotomy?

"Anyway, I hate to cut and run, but the caterer's on the other line. Don't ever try and order lobster bisque in April. Ta!"

Ta.

Before moving to the next person on her list—the mayor—Esme needed a few minutes to calm down. It wouldn't do to vent her frustration with Amy Lieb at Mayor Connors. She knew the mayor a little, more from social functions at the college than anything else. He was a cleavage-watcher, but he also seemed to have the best interests of the community at heart. She would appeal to his sense of duty—but first, she needed to tranquilize herself with some TV. And if only Tom Piper would return any of her messages, she wouldn't be feeling like she was fighting this battle alone.

She clicked on the remote and watched Fox's talking heads gab about oil and about a minute later read along the bottom of the screen, embedded in the nonstop crawl of succinct ledes, these words: *Journalist involved in Galileo case found dead near home.*

For Tom Piper, the optimal dialectic wasn't Fear-Desire but Win-Lose, and he knew exactly where this case fit on that paradigm. But that didn't stop AD Trumbull, with whom he was on a conference call along with several other higher-ups, from reminding him.

"It's disgraceful," said Trumbull, and then coughed

for a minute. It was an open secret that the old man had lung cancer, but if a career employee for the United States government wanted to die in his office, so be it. Everyone on the conference call patiently waited for Trumbull's bronchial attack to subside. Tom used the time to rub his tired eyes. He was in a secure room behind closed doors at Eppley Airfield, the historic airport which served the greater Omaha metropolitan area. Most rooms of this nature—where questionable passengers were detained—had chipped paint on the walls and creaky furniture. This room had recently been repainted—eggshell white, of all colors—and the wooden chair on which he sat couldn't have been more comfortable. It was simple pleasures like these that Tom had to embrace right now, because they were all he had. His own phone buzzed from inside his luggage. Someone was calling him. Whoever it was had to be better conversation than this. Tom was tempted to press mute on the room phone and take the personal call, but then Trumbull cleared his throat and carried on with his tongue-lashing:

"Explain to me how it is that you diverted manpower to Santa Fe and our guy shows up in San Francisco. Was San Francisco even on your radar, Tom?"

"With all due respect, sir, I asked for surveillance on Lilly Toro. I believed she might be at risk, and my request was denied."

"I read your request," piped in another assistant director. "You had twenty-two names on that list. How are we supposed to prioritize when you give us twenty-two names?"

"I'm sorry, sir." Tom stared at the bright wall. "I wasn't aware there was a limit on the number of people the Bureau is supposed to protect."

"There is a limit on the number of resources the Bureau has at its disposal, as you well know. And when those resources are squandered in the middle of New Mexico—"

"We have credible evidence that Santa Fe is on Galileo's list. What happened in San Francisco doesn't—"

"And how long is *that* list, Special Agent Piper? Twenty-two names?"

Tom sighed.

"I've also looked at this so-called 'credible evidence' and it is awful flimsy, Piper. "

"Except what happened today, sir, confirmed the connection between Galileo and the Kellerman campaign, which was the lynchpin of Esme Stuart's hypothesis. It stands to reason—"

"The Kellerman campaign is off-limits, Piper."

"Beg pardon?"

"They don't want federal intrusion on their day-to-day operations. They seem to think we're beholden to the vice president since he used to be Bureau director and that we'd report everything back to him. That's their paranoia, not mine."

"Sir, paranoia's not really a defense against obstruction of justice."

"It's an election year, Piper."

"It's always an election year," Tom replied.

"We need to tread carefully, especially given your— our—recent performance. We need to reassure the public that contrary to popular belief our heads are not up our asses. We're going to have ourselves a press conference, gentlemen. The people want someone to blame for this clusterfuck, and since we can't seem to get the son of a bitch who's actually responsible, whether he's in San Francisco or Santa Fe or Timbuktu, we're going to have to throw one of our own to the lions."

Tom knew this was coming, but it still hurt to hear.

Trumbull's hoary voice hammered in the nail: "That means you, Tom. You and your team are going to take the fall here. I'd apologize, but with the body count this perpetrator is accruing, which includes police officers and firefighters not to mention one of our own, I'm not sure if the media crucifixion you're about to suffer is entirely undeserved."

The SWAT team descended on the car. They wore ceramic body armor over bulletproof vests. Thick black helmets protected their skulls. As they were well aware, Galileo was partial to head shots. Each member of the 12-man squad carried an assault rifle in his hands and had a pistol strapped to his left leg.

It was a beat cop named Mary Chu who had found the blue Ford sedan—license plate JG3-94Q—parked in an alleyway in the urban Mission District. This was miles outside the canvass area, but nevertheless, the vehicle matched the description. Mary had maintained her distance, called it in, and waited inside a nearby bodega. The SWAT van had showed up twenty minutes later, at exactly 6:16 p.m. Lilly Toro and the three cops on the stairs of the substation had been dead for almost ninety minutes.

As the SWAT team slowly approached the Ford, Mary Chu watched from the grocery store. The bodega's owner stood beside her, sipping from a hot cup of Mexican coffee. Both were thinking the same thought: this could be a trap. Hadn't Galileo lured his victims in Atlanta and Amarillo much the same way these twelve men and women now were being lured to this abandoned car? Mary knew their body armor was bullet-resistant. She knew these were the city's finest. Nevertheless, she took a step back from the bodega window and into the shadow of a shelf.

The car sat in a dark alley. The falling sun's fiery light failed to provide the slightest illumination. The SWAT team activated their helmet lights. Twelve beams of bright blue shot forward, and passed across the Ford like a kaleidoscope of long fingers.·

It was a stolen Ford. Its owner, a Mrs. Harriet Rehoboth of Oakland, had reported it missing yesterday. She'd gone into her neighborhood Safeway to spend her social security check on some groceries and when she returned to the parking lot, her shopping cart stuffed with oranges and lamb chops and two-for-one bottles of Pert, her Ford was gone. Mrs. Rehoboth was upset, but she was also confused. The parking lot was dotted with Saabs and Jaguars and Mercedes. Why would anyone steal her crappy eighteen-year-old blue Ford? Who would do such a thing?

The police now had their answer. The SWAT team advanced on her car, every step measured, every breath modulated. They had spotters on the lookout for Galileo, but he was a crafty bastard, and could be anywhere. Like Mary Chu, most of the officers on the scene were assuming the worst—that this was another one of Galileo's bait-and-hooks. But what was the alternative? Leave the car alone? They had a job to do, and none of them joined SWAT for the stylish uniforms.

They approached in a modified phalanx formation. It was the most defensive stance they could take. This was why Sgt. Tyler Murphy, who was at the fore of the column, was the first to spot the shoe box on the passenger seat. To better facilitate matters, the window to the passenger seat was already down. Galileo wanted the shoe box to be seen. Murphy reported his discovery to Captain Rodriguez. Rodriguez ordered the SWAT team to retreat, and sent in the bomb dogs.

Mary Chu nibbled on her lower lip.

Three German shepherds were escorted into the alley and sniffed the car for several minutes. The K-9s were specially trained at detecting explosives. All it took was a bark, and the bomb squad, on the standby, would march in. But the dogs didn't bark. They didn't even growl. The car was safe.

Rodriguez himself took out the shoe box and looked inside.

"What the hell?"

Someone had to claim the body. It wouldn't be released until an autopsy was performed—standard operating procedure for a homicide—but claiming the body at least set into motion the other requisite task—

finding a mortician, etc.—which accompanied death. As the police were busy tracking Galileo, the coroner's assistant, a fidgety man named Chiles, took it upon himself to locate the next of kin. He took out the deceased's cell phone, found the number, traced the number to an address, and hopped into his SUV. Due to the manhunt, many streets were cordoned off, making evening traffic a bitch, but Chiles managed to get to his destination by 7:00 p.m. His stomach growled for sushi. Dinner would have to wait. Someone had to claim the body.

The deceased's next of kin lived on the sixth floor of a walk-up in Oakland. Chiles, ever impatient, took the stairs two at a time. By the time he reached the apartment door, 6F, his hamstrings were displeased. He located the doorbell and pressed it.

A middle-aged Asian woman answered the door. She wore a flower print dress. From her apartment came the smell of boiled cabbage. Once again, Chiles had to ignore his appetite. Someone had to claim the body.

He took out a photograph from a pocket of his windbreaker. She looked at the photograph and then nodded. Her face became wet. Chiles informed her that she would have to come with him to the morgue. She nodded again, and got her coat. On her way out, she left a note for her husband. He was working late.

On the way down, they took the stairs one at a time.

Because return journeys are always quicker, they arrived at the morgue shortly before 7:30. The rain clouds from that morning had come back, and provided a steady drizzle to their walk from the parking lot to the deliberately featureless building which housed the M.E.'s office. As the M.E. herself often put it, death needn't advertise.

Next to the meat locker was a small quiet room set aside especially for purposes like this visit. The body was already on the table, and covered with a clean white sheet. They used an industrial-strength bleach to get the sheets that white. Appearances were important.

Chiles made sure the woman was ready and then he folded back the top of the sheet to the body's bare shoulders. Its eyes were open, and dark. A hole the size of a thumbtack dotted its forehead, which appeared to the woman, herself a devout Buddhist, to resemble a Hindu *tilak*. She reached out her hand to touch the hole, then stopped. Her fingertips instead grazed the body's right cheek. The flesh was cold. A slab of beef from the grocery store felt exactly the same. There were other, tinier holes, in its earlobes and nostrils and lips, but the jewelry that ornamented those parts was gone. The woman's fingertips touched those lips too. They were spongy.

Chiles handed her a clipboard (pen attached) with some forms to sign. The woman read the top form. The first question asked what her relation was to the deceased. "Mother," she said aloud, softly. "I'm her mother."

Instead of flying to Santa Fe, which would have been a quick jaunt from Omaha, Tom and Norm were instead rerouted to D.C. By the time they touched down at Dulles, it was after midnight. Half the cabin was asleep. Norm was asleep. Tom was not.

He reviewed the past four weeks. What could he have done differently? What could anyone have done differently? Bringing in Esme was a solid idea. The theory she came up with fit so well. But what if her instincts had dulled over the years? What if his had too? He knew he was getting older, slower. He knew it every morning he pulled himself out of bed. He knew it every time the joints in his legs reminded him that rain was coming.

Two FBI agents met Tom and Norm at the gate. They identified themselves as Agent Dwyer and Agent Casey, waited a few minutes for their baggage to arrive, became impatient, and escorted the senior agents into the back seat of a new model Crown Victoria. Its windows were tinted.

"Someone will take care of your luggage," explained one of them. "You'll get it back."

Tom and Norm took their seats and exchanged a glance.

"Look," said Tom, "I know you think this pick-them-up-at-the-airport bit is all meant to be intimidating, but it's almost 1:00 a.m. and my colleague and I just want to get to sleep."

Agent Dwyer had the wheel. Agent Casey, in the passenger seat, turned around.

"We've been instructed to take you and Special Agent Petrosky to a nearby safe house."

"A safe house?" This roused Norm from his half sleep. "Why?"

This time it was Casey's turn to exchange glances with *his* associate. Dwyer nodded permission. Casey reached into his valise and handed both Tom and Norm a sheet of paper. On it were the names, social security numbers, and addresses of everyone on the task force.

"A few hours ago, police found a shoe box in a car in San Francisco. We're almost certain the car was left there by Galileo."

"That doesn't explain why we're—"

"What was found in the shoe box, sir," said Agent Casey, "was this list. The other members of your task force are being gathered as we speak. Please sit back."

Tom took out his cell phone. Enough was enough—he needed to speak with Esme. If anyone could make sense of this, it was her. Would she be mad at him for dodging her calls? She had every right to be. Bringing her down to Amarillo had been sanctimonious, and avoiding her ever since had been every bit as—

Agent Casey's meaty hand suddenly snatched the phone from his grasp.

"No calls. Bureau policy."

Tom seethed. "Mmm-hmm."

"It's about a forty-minute drive to our destination, sir." Casey showed some teeth. "We'll wake you when we arrive."

Tom didn't sleep, and, this time, neither did Norm.

The bar closed at 2:00 a.m. Rafe splashed down his last glass of scotch, paid his tab, and strolled out to his car. His friends—fellow professors, mostly—had left long ago for their spouses and their beds. How fortunate for them.

The bartender, locking up, asked him if he was okay to drive.

"I'm not drunk," replied Rafe.

He wasn't drunk, but was a little buzzed. He started up his car without a problem and, reluctantly, headed home.

It's not that he was avoiding his home. It's just…

He switched on WCBS-AM to distract him from his thoughts. The on-air reporter was recalling the latest March Madness highlights. Rafe had watched the last few minutes of the Syracuse game at the bar.

He didn't need to hear the news, and turned off the radio. Like everyone else in the country, he'd watched the reports from San Francisco on the TV. Galileo had struck again. His tally now neared thirty. A press conference with the FBI was scheduled for 11:00 a.m. Rafe hoped they raked Tom Piper over the coals. The irresponsible bastard had almost gotten his Esme murdered, and for what? They weren't any closer to finding the sniper. If Tom Piper could be crucified over this, well, maybe Rafe's day-to-day existence wouldn't be quite as miserable.

Rafe had been paraphrasing Freud in his freshman lecture with his "fear-desire" dialectic. He knew exactly where he fell on that line. His life had become overwhelmed with desire, desire for change, desire to turn back the clock and return life to the way it was on February 14. But the best he could do was stay out late, drink his beer and scotch, and make believe.

He pulled into his driveway. The garage door always seemed so much louder when everyone was asleep. Could machines be spiteful or was that a characteristic solely reserved for people? He quietly got out of his car and entered his home.

The TV was on in the living room. Esme must have fallen asleep without turning it off. Again. Rafe found the remote control on the coffee table and clicked it off. His wife lay beside him on the couch, most of her body wrapped in a multicolored afghan. She said she couldn't sleep in the bed. Her right side was still bandaged, wrapping from the small of her back to her belly button, and she said the mattress aggravated her soreness.

Even when she slept, her face was clenched in pain.

Rafe was halfway to the stairs when she called out his name.

"Hi," he said. "I thought you were asleep."

"What time is it?" she yawned.

"It's late. Go back to sleep."

They stared at each other through abject darkness, their faces painted with shadows.

"Lilly Toro died."

"I saw. Did you know her?"

"Kellerman's coming to Oyster Bay."

"It's all the buzz at the college," Rafe replied. "It's heartening to see some of the undergrads showing some enthusiasm for a change."

His drooping eyelids betrayed his own enthusiasm, but those faithful shadows fortunately concealed his tipsy exhaustion from his wife.

"No, you don't understand." She tried to sit up, despite the obvious pain that entailed. "Kellerman is linked to Galileo. We're practically inviting a serial killer to our home. For Christ's sake, he was a janitor at an elementary school in Atlanta! Sophie… God…"

He took a step forward, out of the safety of the shadows and toward the woman on the couch. She needed comforting. He reached for her hands. "Esme, our daughter's not in danger. We're not in danger. Maybe you should discuss this with your therapist. I'm sure—"

"How can you be willing to take that chance?" Esme slapped his hands away. "Don't you care?"

"You're asking me if I care? Honey, I'm not the one who turned my back on my family and went gallivanting off to Texas. I think the last thing you have the right to accuse me of at this moment is where my priorities are."

"Which is why you spent tonight at a bar, instead of home with your—"

Rafe held up his hands and walked away. He was done with this conversation. But first, he made sure to stop in on Sophie. His little angel. How dare Esme accuse him of not caring? When she was pregnant, he had had his doubts about his abilities as a father. He knew he could provide financially, but what about emotionally? So many men seemed to instinctually know how to do the right thing for their children— would he? And when he saw her in the delivery room, all 7 lbs. 8 oz., when he saw his eyes staring back at him from that tiny perfect face, all doubt vanished from his core, and he suddenly knew that he would die for this being, who was only one minute old, he would *die* for her. How dare Esme accuse him of not caring. As he carefully, quietly, shut Sophie's door and passed down the hall into his own room, he was glad, maybe for the first time in his marriage, that he wouldn't be sharing his bed with his wife.

17

After removing Tom Piper and his task force from the case, the Powers That Be unilaterally rejected Esme's theory and shifted their manpower from Santa Fe to San Francisco. By March 14 the Bay Area was teeming with federal agents. Someone must have seen something useful, even if the FBI had to question, as AD Trumbull had so tritely put it, "every Chin in Chinatown." The FBI had abandoned Santa Fe for San Francisco, and that was a shame because Galileo had abandoned San Francisco for Santa Fe, and on March 18 he struck.

Andy Longtree, superintendent of the Santa Fe Public Schools, had the not-so-intelligent idea of holding the spring faculty development (mandatory attendance) on the morning after St. Patrick's Day. While the city's students got the day off, the city's teachers had to rouse themselves out of their hangovers and down to Peralta High School's auditorium. As they filed in, some gazed bleary-eyed at the banners on the gym's walls, boasting the achievements of SFHS's mighty Demons. They staggered down the aisles and sat in the soft red seats, coffee in hand, profanity in check.

Andy Longtree stood by the doors, welcoming by name those he recognized, waving at those he didn't. Peralta High School was the gem in his crown, the city's first new high school in thirty years and built on his prodding and under his watch. Santa Fe was not a wealthy city by any means, but its increasingly diverse population required increasingly more space, and their children deserved an education. Sacrifices were made, teacher raises were put on hold, donations from questionable sources were accepted, animosities rose to epic levels, but Peralta High School was built, damn it, and it was mighty fine. Sometimes, late at night, he fantasized that, after his death, the city would rename Peralta High School after him. Right now it was named after a Spanish governor from the seventeenth century. Andrew Longtree High School—now that had a much better ring to it, didn't it?

Andy knew his faculty had spent the previous night drinking, but he didn't drink, so he didn't care. March 18 fell squarely in the middle of the second half of the school year, and therefore made for an excellent date for their state-mandated faculty development. If anyone wanted to complain, he was more than happy to listen. It wouldn't change his mind, but he was astute enough to know that an administrator with the illusion of flexibility was much easier to swallow than one with no outward flexibility at all.

Nine o'clock inched closer and closer, so Andy

began his stroll to the stage. In the enclosed lighting booth to the rear of the auditorium, two students readied the lighting cues. Since the computer did most of the work, it really was a one-student job, but Gwen didn't want to be lonely, so she asked her friend Ric to tag along. They both sat on stools. A long keyboard operated the computer, which displayed a series of numbers on a small square screen. These numbers indicated levels of light. Gwen joined the AV club so she could get out of phys ed. Ric tagged along with her so he could get laid. Both the dimness and the isolation of the lighting booth were in his favor. Now if only he could convince Gwen to take their relationship to the next step.

The superintendent took the stage. The house lights lowered, and then so did the audience chatter. All very Pavlovian, thought Andy. He had been a psych major in college, oh, so many moons ago. It was the love of a woman that sent him through grad school for his education degree. Marlene's family didn't abide "headshrinkers" but they were fond of teachers, being that they all taught at the city schools, and Andy was fond of Marlene, so he did his additional two years at the University of New Mexico, got a posting at Santa Fe High School, and much to his surprise found he liked it.

Marlene ran off to Seattle with a stockbroker. Andy still ate Sunday dinner with her family. He dated occasionally, but never found anyone to replace Marlene. No one ever could. He worked his way up from science teacher to department chair, let the city pay him to get a Ph.D., and was principal of SFHS by the time he was forty. It was Marlene's family, tenured and well-connected as they were, who got him anointed superintendent. Marlene still lived in Seattle. She was divorced, had two kids and ran a Starbucks. They exchanged Christmas cards.

Andy stepped up to the lectern. It always felt like the first day of school when he began one of these events. He surveyed the crowd of 200-plus public school teachers. Because the lights were on him and not them, he couldn't make out any of the faces. All the better—most of them were probably scowling.

He began:

"Good morning, ladies and gentlemen. I'd like to take this opportunity to…"

Back in the lighting booth, Gwen was setting up the film. According to the schedule she had been given, in fifteen minutes the superintendent would leave the stage. That was her cue to lower the movie screen and start the projector.

"So," whispered Ric, "what do you want to do for fifteen minutes?"

Gwen slid a chunky textbook out of her bookbag. "Can you help me with my econ homework?"

Ric helped her with her econ homework. He was a nice guy. He should have known better than to expect paradise. Nice guys were admired for their sympathetic smiles and for their cry-worthy shoulders. Any body part lower than the shoulders never even registered with members of the opposite sex.

Back onstage, Andy Longtree had entered the difficult middle portion of his address. This was where he deviated from the pleasantries and dealt out the hard truths. Yes, curricula would continue to be tailored (in other words: lowered) to meet federal guidelines. No, there wouldn't be any new hires. Yes, average classroom sizes would remain at thirty-five students. No, there wouldn't be any new desks. He seeded his conclusion with the obligatory optimism:

"One of the first settlers of this great land, William Bradford, once said that 'all great and honorable actions are accompanied with great difficulties.' You are the settlers of the future and your students' minds are your fields. Plant well. Plant integrity. Plant ambition. Plant knowledge. Raise a good crop, ladies and gentlemen, and the harvest will feed the world. This is your mandate. This is your gift. Thank you."

The applause was halfhearted, but Andy didn't mind. He wasn't saying anything the good ones didn't already know and the bad ones didn't already ignore. *C'est la vie.*

"And now, ladies and gentlemen, for the next item on our agenda. Due to recent events in Albuquerque which will remain un-discussed, the state has required all public school instructors to watch a twenty-minute video on sexual harassment."

Groan, moan, hiss.

"After the video, there will be a short recess, and then we will commence with our 11:00 a.m. sessions, as detailed in your packets."

Andy strolled to the wings of the stage. In the lighting booth, Gwen flicked a switch and a large white movie screen whirred down, almost touching the lectern the superintendent had been using moments ago. She dimmed the rest of the lights, pressed a button, and the projector beamed "Sexual Harassment and You" above the heads of the crowd, through the dust of the auditorium, and onto the large white screen.

A pair of plastic windows peeked out from the lighting booth to the auditorium. One of them was closed, but one was still open. Ric used this opportunity to shut the open window. Now he and Gwen had total privacy. The lights were as low as they were going to get. Only one door led into or out of the booth and it was closed. A video about sex (sort of) was flickering in the background. If this was not the perfect setting for romance, he didn't know what was.

"Gwen," he said, "why don't we take a break from econ?"

She looked up at him. Her eyes were hazel. Ric dreamt about those eyes. He once wrote a poem about those eyes.

"A break?" she asked, and he leaned forward and—

The only door that led into the booth opened, and a middle-aged man rolled in with a plastic trash bin.

"Oh, sorry," he muttered, "I didn't realize anyone was in here."

"It's okay," replied Gwen. "Don't mind us."

He offered them a short, shy smile, and went about his duties.

Gwen glanced back at Ric.

"What were we talking about again?"

Ric shifted on his stool. He couldn't do this with the

custodian in the room! He glared over at the gray man and watched him reach into the gray bin. The man's eyes flitted up and met Ric's. There was sadness in the man's eyes. Ric immediately felt sorry for him, but then the man removed his hands from the bin and they held a shoe box and Ric wondered why he had a shoe box in his bin, wasn't that funny, and the man placed the shoe box next to the sound system, gently, the way one lays an injured bird back in its nest.

"What's in the shoe box?" asked Ric.

Gwen, whose attention had wandered back to her econ textbook, looked to see what Ric was talking about, and was just in time to see the custodian reach back into his bin for his next surprise.

With respectful care, Galileo laid the teenagers' bodies side by side on the floor, and then he perched up on one of the stools. He slid open one of the plastic windows and spied out on the oblivious crowd. His rifle was loaded. He was ready.

On the screen, a fat man in a brown blazer was flirting with a young woman. The young woman was dressed in a conservative pantsuit. They were twenty feet tall, which made their bad acting and stilted dialogue loom large. A few of the teachers, those who were actually paying attention, snickered at the silliness. The vast majority of the audience, though, was ignoring the visual antics and was using the time—and ambient light provided by the movie—to grade papers. There was no shame in this; after all, it wasn't like they were playing hooky. They were using school time to do schoolwork.

As in any group, there were cliques. The largest classification was by school. Santa Fe had twenty elementary schools, four middle schools, and three high schools. In these large pockets were further subdivisions by race, gender and even style. The preppies hung out with the preppies. The hippies hung out with the hippies. The newbies congregated away from the veterans. The history teachers kept to themselves, and the science teachers kept to themselves. And, as in any group, there were the outsiders, who kept to themselves because they were left to themselves. They either dressed different or looked different or smelled different…it was an old story and it didn't just change when one graduated from one side of the desk to the other. Naturally, these outsiders filled the seats along the walls of the auditorium, a protective aisle demarcating them from the rest of humanity. They were unseen, even amongst themselves.

Their deaths went as unnoticed as their lives. That's why they were the first targets. When Joffrey Davis, a forty-year-old physics instructor with bad dandruff in his receding hair, suddenly slumped over, no one thought twice about it. When Linda Perelman, a twenty-two-year-old substitute teacher whose terminal shyness only went into remission when she was around little children, when her gradebook slid out of her hands and slapped against the auditorium floor, when she subsequently *joined* it on the floor, no one even cared. The few who saw her on the floor chalked it up to that weird new teacher deciding to take a nap. It was the morning after St. Patrick's Day.

Although how could anyone sleep with a movie this loud? Andy Longtree, still standing in the wings, concluded that the incompetent A/V students must have set the volume too high, and he exited through the side door to confront them in the lighting booth. It was Galileo, of course, who had raised the volume. Eventually his actions would be discovered—that was part of his plan too—but he wanted to delay that inevitability for as long as he could.

That turned out to be twenty more seconds. Sanjay Patel, a middle school art teacher, was Victim #9. Patty Rice taught at the same middle school as Sanjay and thus sat near him—in her case, in front of him—and suddenly noticed that the back of her neck was moist. She ran her fingers across it and in the shimmering glow provided by the film she could tell the moisture was dark, and that it was blood. She turned around in her seat and found herself face-to-face with the top of Sanjay's scalp. Blood snaked out from his forehead to the floor in one thin, steady drip.

Patty screamed, and then her brains shuttled out the back of her head, but enough people nearby had heard her screams before they were abbreviated and therefore saw her get shot and that was the ball game. More screams now in the darkened theater, the sound passing from person to person like contagion. Some stood and ran. Others crashed to the floor to hide. Others still froze in their seats.

They were ducks in a shooting gallery, and they fell one by one. Keith Henshaw pushed a pregnant colleague aside only to get a bullet between the eyes.

Ingrid Yolen tried to push Keith Henshaw out of harm's way, but when he died his large bulk fell to her, and in keeping his body from toppling undignified to the ground, she was stuck in place long enough to fall into the crosshairs herself. Department chairs rounded up the teachers in their employ and directed them to the exits in the rear. In crises, those accustomed to lead did what was most familiar.

Nancy Pasternak, who worked here at Peralta High, saw the congestion at the rear of the auditorium, and decided to be smart. She knew that the rear exits were not the only way out. There also were the doors off stage left. She ran against the flow of the crowd and climbed on to the stage to make her rapid departure. Up there on the stage, in front of the movie screen, she made the perfect target, and Galileo took her down easily, and decided to call it a day. Expediently, he turned around to leave—just as the door to the lighting booth opened.

During Andy Longtree's stroll here from backstage, as he readied himself to abrade the volume-happy A/V crew, he had heard the screams. He had no idea what was going on, but suspected to find something amiss in here, not necessarily two students dead and a janitor with a rifle, but he was prepared for anything. He always was prepared for anything. So when the janitor raised his gun and took aim, Andy grabbed a nearby wrench and threw it at the gunman. It clattered against Galileo's right hand, and the rifle rolled out to the floor. He glared at the superintendent. Andy's hands balled into fists. The fight was on.

But it didn't last long. Andy threw the first punch, and Galileo ably dodged out of the way. He used his opponent's momentum against him, and shoved him into the lighting board. Before Andy could turn around, Galileo was sending jabs to his lower back, knuckles aimed squarely at the superintendent's kidneys. Andy's hands found Gwen's econ textbook, left open on the table, and gripped it for dear life. With all the strength and fierceness he could muster, he spun around with the textbook. Luck was on his side. He walloped Galileo in the nose.

The gunman began to bleed.

Andy readied a second blow, but Galileo just reached down to his ankle, removed the Beretta he'd used to kill Darcy Parr, and shoved its barrel against his rival's chin.

That's not fair, thought Andy, and then he didn't think at all.

Galileo holstered his pistol and picked up his rifle. His right hand throbbed and his nose was oozing plasma. It was time to go. He tossed the rifle back into the garbage bin and rolled it toward the door.

By now, almost everyone had made their way to the parking lot. The police were on their way. Some cried. Some searched for friends and acquaintances. Where was Nancy Pasternak? Had anyone seen Nancy Pasternak? Some just stared back at the school, horror-stricken.

Actually, a few of the missing were still alive. They remained in the auditorium, hiding on the slate floor. They weren't cowards. Cowardice was shameful. What shame could there be in surviving?

Eventually, fear became replaced by speculation, and the mood of the crowd in the parking lot shifted. Was this the same killer who had struck in Atlanta and Amarillo? What was he doing here? What was it he wanted?

Squad cars from the Santa Fe police howled into sight, followed by a series of ambulances. The cops wore bulletproof vests. So did some of the paramedics. A barricade was set up along the front steps, and the teachers were corralled further away from the building.

Next came the media, the TV newsmen in their labeled vans and the paper reporters in indiscriminate Chevrolets. Camera shots were set up. Tape recorders were activated. It was time to make the story a story.

The paramedics dealt with the small injuries first, the cuts and bruises sustained in the mass exodus. One woman who had tripped had the pinky of her left hand trampled. Another received an inadvertent elbow to his throat and was having trouble breathing. The paramedics dealt with the small injuries first, while the police entered the building and began to count the dead.

Among those interviewed by the reporters, though not on camera, was one of the school's janitors, who had been injured, though not seriously. The reporter offered him a handkerchief for his bloody nose.

"Thank you," replied the janitor. "You're too kind."

Policemen began to file out of the school. There were pale faces. One of the sergeants walked to his squad car, took a deep breath of air, and radioed a requisition request to HQ. They were in need of eighteen body bags.

18

"It's so good to see you," Esme lied, and wrapped her arms in a very loose embrace around Pamela Gould, the FBI bureau chief for Long Island. She had her long bottle-blond hair bound in a bun, and the makeup on her face made her dark skin appear almost purplish. Purplish seemed appropriate, though, as Pamela Gould's office smelled vaguely of blueberries.

Esme maneuvered herself into a copious wicker chair and Pamela perched her considerable weight on the corner of her glass desk. "Can I get you something to drink? An espresso perhaps? A cup of chai tea?"

"Oh, I can't have caffeine," replied Esme, although Pamela knew that, was well-informed about her injury, and probably had offered the caffeinated beverages *because* of her kidney. Such was Special Agent Pamela Gould, bitch-queen of the FBI. "I'd love a bottle of water."

"I'm sorry. We're all out of that."

Sure they were.

Pamela Gould's bookcase was arrayed with a

myriad of seafaring paraphernalia, including an antique nautical clock. Another clock, on the opposite wall, indicated the date (March 18) and the local times in Washington (1:46 p.m.), Los Angeles (10:46 a.m.), Moscow (9:46 p.m.), Paris (7:46 p.m.), and London (6:46 p.m.). Esme had wanted to drive here alone, but a few days ago her temperature had, for a brief period, climbed to almost 103 Fahrenheit, so just to be on the safe side she still needed Lester to chauffeur. Fevers were not wholly uncommon with patients in her condition, especially those who, rather than staying in bed, were spending hours and hours each day traveling every which way across Long Island, speaking to everyone from mayors to selectmen to her local congressman to get the fundraiser changed. Everyone echoed the same pass-the-buck refrain, "Well, if the FBI feels it's a potential hazard, I'd be more than happy to do something about it but until then…" So Esme, finally, got through to and scheduled an appointment with the FBI. She had been unaware of Pamela's promotion. Had she known she would be facing her old rival from the Academy, would she still have come? Either way, she had less than fifteen minutes to make her case before it would be time to pick Sophie up from school, and all because Lester purposely had dragged his feet leaving the house.

"So I see you still like sailing," said Esme.

"It's a hobby."

"Does your husband sail too?"

"I never married."

"That's a shame."

"Not really," Pamela replied. "I never saw myself as the marrying type."

"And what's the marrying type?"

"Oh, you know."

Esme politely nodded.

"Congratulations, by the way, Pamela, on your promotion. Your own field office. I'll tell you, when I found out you were here I was a little surprised. I thought you never wanted to leave Washington."

"Some people thought the same about you."

"Well, yes, but I left the Bureau. Being sent to mind the farm in Long Island isn't exactly a step up the bureaucratic food chain, is it?"

"That's true. Actually—" she leaned in confidentially "—sometimes, Esme, I get so bored here. It's hard to fill the day when your jurisdiction's nothing but cookie-cutter suburban housewives."

Esme politely nodded.

"I actually was thinking about you recently, Esme. When I heard about all that poor unfortunate business with Tom Piper. I hear the Bureau may even bring him up on charges of negligence."

"Everyone needs someone to blame."

"I hear you're going around the Island blaming the Unity for a Better Tomorrow."

"Whether you agree with me or not," said Esme, "why take a chance? Ask them to remove themselves from the Kellerman fundraiser and, sure, maybe you'll piss them off. Allow them to remain as sponsors, and what if I'm right, and two months down the line you have dozens of victims right here in your cookie-cutter jurisdiction. And you could have prevented it. Who do you think the Bureau will blame then?"

Pamela politely nodded.

"I definitely will take what you've said under advisement."

"Under advisement?" The clock tallied 1:51 p.m. 11:51 a.m. in the aforementioned Santa Fe. She had ten minutes before she and Lester had to leave this town and return to Oyster Bay to pick up Sophie from school. A pit opened in her stomach. "That's it?"

Pamela Gould's large phone trilled. She held up a finger, as if to shush Esme, and picked up the receiver.

"This is Gould."

Esme wanted the snatch that phone out of her hand and slam it into the special agent's face—and she contemplated doing so—when Pamela Gould suddenly let out a long sad sigh.

"When did this happen?" Gould barked into the receiver.

Whoever was on the other line provided the details. Esme tried to listen in. When did what happen?

"Thank you," murmured the bureau chief, and she let the receiver slide back into its cradle. Her gaze fixed on Esme. There was hatred there, but something else as well… "You need to leave now."

"What happened?"

"That wasn't a request, Mrs. Stuart."

"What happened?"

Pamela Gould pressed down on her intercom. "Jeff? Can you escort Mrs. Stuart out?"

As Jeff, an extraordinarily wide agent, shifted into

the room, Esme felt her gut do a backflip, and she knew—oh God—what had happened. "It's Galileo, isn't it?"

"See Mrs. Stuart out."

"He struck again, didn't he?"

Jeff reached for Esme's arm, but she pulled away. The fact that this gloating woman was refusing to answer her simple question…

"Was it Santa Fe? Jesus Christ, how many did he…?"

Jeff grabbed her now, forcefully. "Don't make this difficult, please."

"Now you have to do something about the fundraiser! Don't you see? Now you have no choice!"

"Please," repeated Jeff, and he tugged. Hard. Her right side exploded in sparks of pain, and she almost buckled to the floor then and there.

"Goodbye, Mrs. Stuart," said Pamela Gould. She'd turned her back.

Esme stood back up, and let Jeff escort her to the stairs. She actually was glad he was there. The past five minutes had left her light-headed, and each step brought a wavering sense of balance. Soon she was gripping Jeff's arm not just to keep from tripping, but to keep from falling over. She finally made it to the bottom of the staircase and out into the parking lot and her wristwatch read 2:04 p.m.—and the Cadillac was gone.

Not only had Tom's phone been confiscated, but he and Norm Petrosky hadn't been allowed to e-mail, fax, or even open a window. It was all for their protection, et cetera, et cetera. They were even restricted on what shows they could watch on the TV. No CNN, no MSNBC, no Fox. The more insulated they were from the world, the more insulated they would be from the world. Tom had to give them credit. The FBI excelled at circular logic. His one comfort was that at least, according to Trumbull, Esme's name had not been on Galileo's list.

Tom had never worked witness protection himself, but his old partner Bobby Fink had spent six years in the "babysitter corps," as he called it, and had many a story to tell. No one wanted to be held under lock and key, essentially grounded, sequestered from everyone you know and subsisting on a diet of frozen food and takeout. According to Bobby, the average witness secluded in a safe house gained ten pounds a month. That didn't include the panic-anorexics ("panorexics," in Fink-speak), those who dealt with their situation through appetite loss.

They also were restricted in wardrobe to what they brought in their suitcases. Tom and Norm had only planned on staying in Omaha overnight. Agents Dwyer and Casey used the tiny stipend they had been given to procure additional shirts, pants, etc. from the neighborhood Salvation Army. On the afternoon of the 18th, Tom sat on the burlap couch, which also had been acquired from the Salvation Army, in an Ivar's Crab Shack T-shirt and a pair of beige shorts. He felt like he was wearing a costume in a play, and he was portraying the character of the idiot nephew.

Norm just wore his briefs all day. He had no shame at all.

Tom and Norm were watching *As the World Turns* when a Breaking News chyron rolled across the bottom third of the screen: *18 confirmed dead at a high school shooting in Santa Fe, New Mexico.*

"Jesus," muttered Norm. "One kid gets picked on so he borrows his dad's Uzi and here comes Columbine Part IX. I got picked on in high school. Who didn't? You didn't see me walking the halls with a—"

Tom shushed him. Santa Fe? It had to be a coincidence, right? Please God, let it be a coincidence....

More information now:

At this time, police are refusing to rule out any connection to similar recent incidents in Atlanta, Georgia and Amarillo, Texas.

Tom moderated his breath. This wasn't some angry kid on a shooting spree. If so, that's what the ticker would have said. No. This was Galileo. Tom had warned them about Santa Fe and they hadn't listened and now eighteen people were dead.

Enough was enough.

Tom walked from the den to the bathroom. Agent Casey had been in there for a while now. Agent Dwyer was out on an errand. Tom pounded on the door.

"Agent Casey?"

"I'll be with you in a few minutes," replied Casey.

Norm joined Tom at the door.

"What's going on?"

"He's on the phone," said Tom. "He doesn't want us to hear the conversation."

"How do you know?"

Tom kicked open the door. Casey stood in the middle of the bathroom. He was in fact on his cell phone.

"What the hell do you think—"

Tom grabbed the phone from his grip.

"Hi, this is Special Agent Tom Piper. Who am I speaking with?"

Click.

Agent Casey went to reach for the phone. Norm shoved his bulk in the way.

"Thanks for the phone," said Tom.

He and Norm exited the bathroom and shoved a chair up to the doorknob, essentially barricading Casey inside.

"Who was on the phone?" asked Norm.

"It's not as important as who's about to be," Tom replied, and after dialing a number held the receiver to his ear.

"AD Trumbull's office. David speaking."

Who was David? Either Trumbull had hired a new assistant or he had some academy cadet screening his calls.

"Yes, hi, David, I'd like to speak with the AD Trumbull. This is Tom Piper."

"I'm sorry, sir, but AD Trumbull is currently in a meeting. If you leave your name and contact information—"

"David, can you give him a message for me?"

"Certainly, sir."

"Tell him that in thirty seconds Tom Piper is going

to tell the *Washington Post* that the FBI knew about Santa Fe and decided to ignore the warnings. Can you do that for me, David?"

"Uh…one moment, sir…"

As Tom waited for David to scamper down the hall and retrieve the officious assistant director, he suddenly found himself ruminating about Lilly Toro. It must have been his threat to go to the press. It was right up Ms. Toro's alley. It was almost identical to the threat she had posited to him when they first met back in Texas.

It seemed so very long ago.

The AD came on the line: "Tom? Is that you?"

"I saw the news."

Trumbull's cancer-cough was worse, and rattled with shards of glass. Tom walked over to the window and peered out at the street. Two boys were playing stickball with a Rottweiler. The boys avoided the puddles. The dog did not. It just scampered to and fro, not a care in the world.

"Tom…"

"What was in the shoe box?"

Another pause. No coughing this time. Just silence.

"Was it another videotape? Was it a message?"

"It was a message."

"What did it say?"

"Tom…"

"I think I've the right to know, don't you?"

Trumbull sighed. "The note said, 'None of this is my fault.' "

"Mmm-hmm. Well, at least he's correct there. None

of this was his fault. Not this time. This time it was the fault of the FBI for fucking up so damn spectacularly."

"Which part pisses you off the most, Tom? That we ignored you or that we threw you under the bus? The fact of the matter is, your names were still on that hit list and—"

"And you fell right into his hands! Don't you see? He knew we were on to him so he had to take us off the playing field. He never was going to hunt us down individually. He goes after crowds. He's had this whole thing planned for months. He only went after Darcy when he ran into her at Walmart, and he didn't go to Amarillo city hall to kill anyone or Esme would be dead. He just needed us off the playing field. And you obliged him."

"He hunted down that journalist in San Francisco."

"But that's not why he was there. He was there to give a message to Bill Kellerman. Just like Darcy, Lilly Toro's death was…circumstantial. She was collateral damage." Tom felt nauseous just speaking the words, despite how truthful they were, but he needed Trumbull to see. So many more lives depended on making this old, dying man see.

Tom could hear Trumbull's labored breathing. The assistant director wasn't a bad guy. And he didn't have blood on his hands any more than Tom had blood on his own. Playing the guilt card was an act of desperation, and Tom was desperate. He wouldn't call the *Post*. They both knew that. And despite Esme's prescience about Santa Fe, Trumbull wasn't obligated to put Tom's task force back on the case. There were other agents in the field, good agents, maybe not as experienced, but certainly qualified. And other than Esme's contributions, what exactly had Tom and his task force done to advance the case anyway? Perhaps the smartest move would be to keep the task force off the radar, just in case Tom was wrong and Galileo did try to track them down.

Finally, the assistant director spoke.

"The next location on the list is Kansas City?"

"Yes."

"Then that's where we'll catch the son of a bitch. In the meantime, I would imagine you'll want to meet up with your team in Santa Fe?"

Tom glanced over at Norm.

Well? gestured Norm.

Yes, smiled Tom.

19

"I need you to pick me up."

Rafe cupped a hand over his free ear so he could better hear his wife's voice. "Where are you?"

She told him.

"Okay," he replied, and hung up.

Melville was a forty-minute drive from the college—but he wasn't at the college. He was at a bar deliberately located in the middle of nowhere. When Esme phoned, he had been flirting semi-harmlessly with a doe-eyed townie named Gladys. As he bid farewell to doe-eyed Gladys and ambled out the door into the glaring accusation of the sun, he calculated the speed he would need to travel to arrive in Melville without garnering suspicion.

A beer buzz at 2:00 p.m. was bound to make anyone a little paranoid.

Rafe slid behind the wheel of his car, popped an Altoid under his tongue, and found his way back onto the main road. At this time of day, he couldn't speed too much—but he could speed a little. He watched the needle climb to 60 mph (15 over the limit) and clicked on the radio for some tunes.

What was she doing in Melville? He hadn't bothered asking, because he knew he wouldn't have liked the answer. Undoubtedly, it was related to her obsession with Galileo, and he wanted that joyful Coors tingle in his brain to last just a little longer before he would have to deal with his wife and her tilting at windmills.

He felt sorry for her, of course, but more than that he felt pity—and a man wasn't supposed to pity his wife, was he? And what did Sophie think? Children were more perceptive than most gave credit. She had to be wondering where her mother had gone to, and who was this woman who had taken her place?

With Tom Piper being eviscerated in the press, Rafe had assumed she would have given up, but instead his public failure had caused her to redouble her crusade to protect Long Island from foul beasties. He knew what his father wanted. His father wanted him to call it a day and send her packing, at least until she stopped trying to save the world and started trying to save her marriage. Sometimes people needed to have their lives jostled in order to gain perspective. Maybe a trial separation would help her see how embarrassing her behavior really—

Police sirens cut off Rafe's train of thought. He heard them before he saw the police cruiser in his rearview. Jesus, how long had the bastard been tailing him? Rafe checked his speed. Seventy-two miles per hour. So much for a casual fifteen over. He eased off the gas pedal and curbed to the side of the forest-lined road. The cruiser had his spotlight on now, despite the fact that the afternoon sun provided more than enough illumination.

"Well," Rafe said to himself, "at least now I'll have a valid excuse for running late."

His valid excuse cost him $300, and he made a point of waving it out the window to Esme the moment he pulled into the parking lot of the federal building. She was sitting on the front steps, took one look at his speeding ticket, and shrugged apathetically.

"I tried to get here as fast as I could," Rafe told her. "The cop just wasn't sympathetic."

She climbed into the passenger seat and fastened her safety belt. Her mascara had smeared a bit around her eyes. Had she been crying? The FBI had shot down her request and now she was crying? This had gone too far….

"I was right," she whispered. Her voice sounded miles away. "I was right and Tom was right and no one listened."

"What are you—"

"He struck again. Galileo. He shot up a school in Santa Fe. A school. Children were there. What could I have done differently? There had to be something I could have done differently. I was right."

But she didn't sound vindicated. She just sounded far, far away.

Rafe drove back to Oyster Bay in silence. He obeyed the speed limit, and occasionally offered Esme a comforting glance. She didn't notice. She just stared out the window at the foliage as it went on by.

When they pulled into the driveway, Sophie raced out of the house to greet them. She must have been sitting by the window.

"Did college get cancelled?" she asked her father.

"I wish," he replied, and scooped her up in his arms.

Inside, Lester was watching a news report about the shootings, with one hand in a bag of mustard-flavored pretzels.

"There she is," he said between bites. "I thought maybe you forgot you had a house."

Esme glared at her father-in-law. "You left early."

"If you say so."

Rafe, sensing an argument brewing, leaned down to his daughter. "If you finish your homework in your bedroom, we can go out tonight to Burger King."

"Yay!" replied Sophie, and she galloped up the stairs.

Lester clicked off the TV, popped one more pretzel in his mouth, and stood up.

"Your wife was so busy gabbing with the feds," he said to Rafe, "that she forgot we had to pick her daughter up from school."

"I was 'gabbing with the feds' to try and protect my daughter, you addle-minded son-of-a—"

Lester returned the pretzels to the pantry. "It's not the first time it's happened. I held my tongue when she was stuck in the couch, but if she's healthy enough to go running off to Melville, I don't see why I have to keep picking up her slack when it comes to Sophie."

"Galileo's killed more people! He's going to come here!"

"Ask her, Rafe. Ask her which she would choose. Ask her which is more important right now. Taking care of her girl or hunting down this Galileo character. Go ahead."

Rafe looked from his father to his wife.

"That's not even a fair choice," she replied. "He's killing dozens of people. He needs to be stopped."

"But where's your duty? Is it there or is it here?"

Esme opened her mouth to reply…but didn't. Couldn't.

Lester wiped clean his hands. "I rest my case." He sauntered toward the bathroom.

Rafe and Esme were alone in the den.

"I was right," she whispered. "I can stop him."

Just as softly, her husband answered her: "You don't belong in that world anymore."

They matched stares. The air became charged with memories, and longing.

"They need my help…."

"Sophie needs her mother. I need my wife. I miss her."

He took a step forward.

"Come back to us," he said. "Please."

Her cell phone rang. It was Tom Piper's ringtone.

Her cell phone rang again.

Her cell phone rang again.

She answered it: "Hi, Tom."

Rafe took a deep breath.

"Yes, Tom, I saw. It's horrible."

He noticed her hands were trembling.

"No, I'm glad they're reinstating the task force, Tom. They never should have mistrusted you."

He watched her listen to her mentor's voice. He'd denied it, perhaps, but he'd known, deep down, that someday it would come to this. He chastised himself for thinking otherwise. How foolish he had been.

"Yes, Tom. I know. And there's another Kellerman fundraiser scheduled next month right here on Long Island. I've been trying to round up support, but…"

His gaze drifted to the floor, and he sat down on the arm of the sofa. How could he hate her? Was it even really a choice? Galileo had murdered dozens of innocent people, and threatened the lives of countless more. They all had families too. How could he and Sophie ever counterbalance that? How could—

"Tom, I need to stop you there."

Rafe looked back up at his wife.

"No, Tom. I can't go to Santa Fe. I'm sorry."

Can't go to Santa Fe? Rafe's fingers dug into a sofa cushion…

"I have every confidence you'll find him, but my place is here now, Tom. I quit, remember?" Esme smiled through tears at her husband. "I made my choice seven years ago. Keep us safe, Tom. Please. Goodbye, Tom."

Darcy Parr's vacant position on the task force as forensics overseer fell to Daryl Hewes. On March 19, Daryl was installed in a small office in the Santa Fe crime lab. By March 20, he was reviewing documentation of hair samples, soil samples, blood spatter analyses, and ballistics analyses. His geek-mind was in a state of bliss, but his poet-heart wished Darcy was still here, beside him, so they could be sifting through the facts and graphs and charts together.

Unlike his task force colleagues, Daryl had enjoyed his protective custody. He viewed it as a vacation, and used the time, isolated in a ramshackle walk-up somewhere in the state of Nevada, to disassemble his laptop. He had always wanted to disassemble his laptop, not so much to study its intricate circuitry but to see if he could reassemble it without the aid of a book. With only a spoon and his fingers as tools, the task took him two days, but he did it. He showed off his accomplishment to his handlers. That night, they all celebrated with three large Hawaiian pizzas and a twelve-pack of Red Bull. Daryl enjoyed his protective custody. It felt like college. So when Tom phoned him up to relay the news about Santa Fe and about the task force's reinstatement, Daryl was a little disappointed. So were his handlers. The drive to the airport was solemn. They exchanged e-mail addresses. They promised to write.

But now the joy was back. Daryl was lost in a forest of data and loving it. He lacked Darcy's scientific acumen, though, so he had the head of the crime lab, Dr. Steve Wu, aid him in parsing the results. Tom already had Anna and Hector Jackson (no relation) shoring up the defenses in Kansas City, and Norm was coordinating activity at the crime scene, so the lab was 100% Daryl's domain.

"These are from the light booth," said Steve, indicating the most recent pile of papers.

Daryl read along with him. The technicians had found footprints in the carpet which were inconsistent with either of the students or the superintendent, so they *may* have come from the perp, or they may have come from anyone else who'd frequented the lighting booth that morning. They had no way of knowing with any certainty if anyone else had visited Gwen while she was setting up the projector, and the trace elements found in the footprints were inconclusive. So Daryl added the results to the Maybe pile. Something was better than nothing.

Next came ballistics. Unsurprisingly, the shell casings matched the ones from Amarillo and Atlanta. If there had been any doubt before that this was the same killer, or at least the same gun, that doubt was eliminated here. Ever since Atlanta, Tom had had Daryl check all available dealers of M107 .50 caliber sniper rifles. It retailed for almost $9,000 and could be purchased from over 9,000 gun shops in forty-three states (seven state legislatures had seen fit to ban it). For those who could afford it, and legally purchase it, the M107 was a popular weapon. The company which manufactured them, Barrett Firearms, boasted that it was their bestselling product.

However, the ability to purchase a sniper rifle did not equal the ability to use a sniper rifle, and this particular sniper, Galileo, was a master sharpshooter. There were no bullet holes in the walls, floor, or ceiling of the auditorium. There were no bullet holes in the stage. There were some bullet holes in the seats, but they were traced back, through blood analysis, to fragments from bullets which had already passed through brain matter. In other words, Galileo had never missed, not once. Yes, there might be thousands of owners of M107s, but how many of them fired with that degree of accuracy?

Now they were wading into Norm's territory—profiling—so Daryl made a note to discuss the matter with his colleague, placed the ballistics reports aside, and moved on to fingerprints. Going on the assumption that Galileo gained entry into the school as a custodian, as he had at that elementary school in Atlanta and at the aquarium in Amarillo, Daryl wasn't surprised to discover that fingerprints on file for Amos Rodman, Peralta High School's recently hired, mysteriously vanished janitor, were nowhere to be found in the lighting booth. Daryl suspected that the fingerprints on file for Amos Rodman would be nowhere to be found anywhere in the school.

"How do you suppose he did it?" asked Dr. Wu.

"Did what?"

"Forged his fingerprints. He did the same in the other cities too, right? I mean, in order to get hired he had to go through a background check. How do you suppose he set it all up?"

Daryl shrugged his shoulders, but knew instinctively that, for a man like Galileo, setting up these false identities couldn't have been difficult. Thinking about it some more, he realized that he too could probably fake his way through a background check. All one needed, really, was someone with a clean record (and no prints already on file) to volunteer (or better yet, be paid) to go through the motions at the local sheriff's office. With advances in color printing and ten minutes on

Adobe Photoshop, forging the documentation (recommendations, IDs) would be the easiest part of all.

If he wanted to, Daryl could drop everything, disappear off the face of the earth, and become someone else. He considered the option. It wasn't wholly unattractive. He liked his job, sure, but there were other jobs. And he had never been to New Zealand. New Zealand looked so appealing in the movies. Did they have good WiFi access in New Zealand? Daryl made a mental note to do some research, after the case was over.

"What's next?" he asked.

"Serology," replied Dr. Wu.

Ah, yes. Blood.

When combined with the ballistics reports, the blood spatter analyses told the story of Ric and Gwen. They each were facing the door when they were shot. Had Galileo surprised them? Ric wasn't even on the A/V squad. Why was he even there? Daryl had been on his high school's A/V squad. Did he ever invite friends into the lighting booth at his high school? Of course not.

Ric and Gwen were facing the door and Galileo shot them each at close range in the forehead. The opening at the back of Ric's skull matched the spatter on the window, while Gwen's matched the spatter on the wall. This made sense. She would have been sitting closest to the lighting board. But according to the crime scene photographs, Ric and Gwen had been found on the floor, side by side, like a pair of sleeping siblings. They couldn't have fallen like that. This meant Galileo had placed them there. Why? It was another psychological question for Norm Petrosky.

The data about Superintendent Longtree was, to Daryl, the most interesting. Unlike every other victim at the crime scene, unlike any other victim at any of the crime scenes save Darcy Parr, the superintendent had been shot with a Beretta. A) Why was the superintendent in the lighting booth? Was he there to evict Ric? B) Why would Galileo shoot the two students with a rifle but then switch to a pistol for Longtree? It didn't make sense…until Daryl read page thirty-eight of the report.

"I need to call Tom," he said, and fumbled for his phone.

"What is it?" asked Dr. Wu.

Daryl handed him page thirty-eight.

Dr. Wu studied it, frowned. "This doesn't necessarily indicate…"

"It does," Daryl replied. Tom's voice mail clicked on. "Tom, it's Daryl Hewes. The two students in the lighting booth were Type O. The superintendent was Type A1. But there's fresh blood on a textbook in the lighting booth that's Type A2. The superintendent was shot with a Beretta at point-blank range. I think there was a struggle. I think the superintendent hit Galileo with the textbook, maybe knocked the rifle out of his hands. I think the blood on the textbook belongs to Galileo. Tom, I think we've got him."

20

They finally got lucky. It was the law of averages, really. How many times could Galileo elude them? He had to make a mistake sometime. He wasn't supernatural. He was just a man, after all, a man who bled.

In the early '90s, the Justice Department launched a pilot program which married the burgeoning fields of computers and genetics. They labeled this program the Combined DNA-Index System, or CODIS, and by the turn of the century it contained records on over 100,000 known felons, just in the United States. In five years, the database passed 500,000. By 2005, though, CODIS had, in the spirit of Big Brother, expanded its jurisdiction to include federal employees. Tom's DNA was in CODIS. The president's DNA was in CODIS.

And Galileo's DNA was there too.

"Or, should we say, Henry Booth."

The technician handed Tom the printout. Twenty-two long hours later, after working the phones, calling in interdepartmental favors, and working every angle he knew, Tom had gotten what he needed and was on a train to Baltimore, home to Booth's last known place of business, a private security company that called itself Bellum Velum. Tom would have taken his bike, but he couldn't ride with his arm, and he wanted to use the time to review all the data extant on Henry Booth. He sat by the window. To his left, the East Coast in bloom. He paid it no attention. His gaze was fixed on the file in his hands, his mind working overtime to compart-mentalize the past, and the future.

Henry Booth was ex-CIA. He'd joined the Agency after completing ROTC at the University of Maryland and got enmeshed in various wetworks activities in the Middle East. All CIA operatives go through rigorous psych screenings, but no amount of Freudian guess-work can predict the effect that combat will have on a person. Henry Booth had a strong religious upbringing. He loved God and his country, in that order. He was in the Middle East for fourteen years. Whatever it is he saw there, whatever it is he did, took its toll. When his handler recommended he return to the states, he didn't argue. He didn't say much of anything. He turned in his letter of resignation and for five years he disappeared off the face of the earth. Eventually, he found his way to Bellum Velum, or they found their way to him, and tax forms were filed and suddenly Henry Booth was back on the grid. Any reservations that the CIA had about Mr. Booth were apparently not shared by Bellum Velum.

"Yes, Henry's been with us for nine years," said the woman on the phone. She said her name was Roberta Watson, and she was the head of PR for the company.

No one else was available. "He's an excellent employee."

"What exactly is it he does for you?"

"We are a private security firm serving North America, Europe and Asia."

"Mmm-hmm. And what exactly is it he does for you?"

"Security."

Tom didn't feel like dancing with this woman, especially not on the phone, especially not with forty people dead. He made an appointment to come up to their main office in Baltimore.

He had a file on them too.

Once the train docked at the city's neo-classicist Penn Station on North Charles Street, Tom flagged down a yellow cab and gave the driver Bellum Velum's address—which turned out to be a skyscraper two blocks away. The private security company occupied the building's top two floors. Mercenary work indeed paid well.

Tom looked both ways down either end of the sidewalk, saw what he wanted to see, then passed through the revolving door into the lobby and obstacle course of construction scaffolding. From the looks of it, the building was being renovated, although islands of burgundy carpeting were scattered throughout the exposed floor. Somewhere in this maze of tarps and orange signs, someone was drilling, by the sound of it, to the center of the earth. The security guard at the desk was wearing earplugs, and had to remove them when Tom approached.

"Tom Piper for Roberta Watson, Bellum Velum."

He didn't bother with his badge. The guard cupped one hand over his left ear, and phoned up. "She'll be right down," he said. But Roberta Watson took her time. Tom lingered in the cacophonous lobby for a good ten minutes before she showed. By then the noise had gifted him with a headache, deposited right behind his eyes.

"Agent Piper, good afternoon."

Roberta Watson held out her hand. Tom shook it. He noticed two things: A) the woman was all smiles B) almost ninety percent of those smiles were genuine. She had a dark complexion that contrasted strikingly with her ice-white pantsuit.

"It's a pleasure to make your acquaintance, Agent Piper," she said. "I hope you haven't come all this way for nothing. I'm afraid that Mr. Yolen, our CEO, is away on business and Mr. Yates, our CFO, is out with the flu. I probably should have told you that on the phone."

Tom was impressed. What an elegant liar she was! He almost complimented her, right then and there. Truly excellent fabricators, like her, were able to believe two contrasting ideas (what they knew to be the truth, and what they knew to be the falsehood) at the same time. They were able to convince themselves, on the spot, that one was just as valid as the other. It was a very difficult skill to master, if only because awareness that one was lying underlined—and undermined—the lie itself. Good for her.

"That's okay, Mrs. Watson."

"Please. Call me Roberta."

"Roberta, can we maybe speak upstairs? The noise…"

She shook her head and grimaced. "It's awful, isn't it? It seems to be never-ending. Some people are never satisfied unless they're making a racket."

"Mmm-hmm."

"Anyway, there really isn't much to see upstairs. The nature of our business being what it is, our non-administrative employees, like Mr. Booth, don't require offices. And, the nature of our business being what it is, the space we do have is, I'm afraid, restricted."

"That's too bad," replied Tom.

"I don't make policy, I'm afraid. If only I did, right?"

"If only."

"Now I know you inquired specifically about Mr. Booth. Perhaps if you told me the nature of your investigation, I might be able to pass that information to either Mr. Yolen or Mr. Yates when they return and they could get back to you?"

"Well, do you know where Booth might be?"

Roberta pretended to think for a moment, and then she shook her head. "No. I'm sorry, I don't. If he's not currently on assignment, he might be at his home address. Have you checked there?"

"His home address. That's good thinking." It was time. Tom took out his cell phone and dialed a number. "Hi, Norm. Are you in place?"

Twenty miles away, in the Baltimore suburb of Severna Park, Norm Petrosky and a squad of armed (and armored) FBI agents stood outside 1114 Charleston Court, an old split-level on a long row of old split-levels on a long, old residential street.

"We're in place, Tom."

Roberta cocked her head. She seemed confused. Her confusion was about to get quite a whole lot murkier.

Tom then dialed another number, and set up a three-way call.

"Agent Cofer, I saw your team outside the building. Are you ready?"

"Affirmative, sir."

"All teams," said Tom, "it's a go."

Twenty miles away, Norm and his squad smashed into Henry Booth's house. Twenty yards away, Agent Cofer and his squad rushed into the lobby, submachine guns at the ready.

The security guard slowly removed his earplugs.

The drilling ceased.

Tom slid a folded warrant out of the inside pocket of his black leather jacket and handed it to Roberta. Her brown eyes went from the barrels of the guns, some pointed at her, to the paper.

"So," said Tom, offering a friendly grin, "how about we go upstairs?"

Henry Booth had a bird. It was an orange-yellow parakeet and it was very happy to have visitors. It squawked and squawked all throughout the FBI's search of the house. After about thirty minutes of it, Norm grabbed the bedsheet off of Booth's bed, dragged it into the living room, and draped it over the parakeet's cage. Convinced that it was night, the parakeet soon went to sleep.

The parakeet turned out to be the only interesting

find in Henry Booth's house. Norm and his company of nine field-trained agents searched every room. It was a typical suburban domicile, albeit abandoned. Four navel oranges in the crisper drawer of the refrigerator had about a month's worth of mold on them.

Madmen tended to collect esoteric books, but Galileo's selection was far from exotic. He had only a few shelves, and they were only half-filled. Norm browsed through the selection, trying to glean whatever insights he could into the mind of their owner. There was a well-thumbed physician's desk reference, but what household these days didn't have one of these for self-diagnoses and first aid? Most of the books were a hodgepodge of used paperback fiction which ran the gamut in both genre and quality. There was no artwork on the walls. There was a stereo, but no CDs.

Aside from the parakeet, the house lacked any semblance of personality.

Norm pondered the discovery. Absence of affectation could, after all, itself be an affectation. But this felt different.

This felt wrong.

Galileo had quoted Mencken. Galileo had dubbed "God Bless America" over footage of the Atlanta massacre. But there were no literary texts here, and the computer in the bedroom was so antiquated that it ran DOS. There was no camcorder. Certainly he might have taken some of these with him on the road, but that didn't fully account for the absolute banality left in this house.

"I'm glad you shut that thing up." The field agent, a

horse-faced woman named Pamela Starkey, indicated the birdcage with a thumb. "If you hadn't, I might've shot it."

Norm was about to offer a reply when he realized exactly what was wrong here. He rushed past Agent Starkey and lifted the sheet off the birdcage. The orange-yellow parakeet bobbed its head at Norm and squawked.

Norm stared at the food and water bins latched to the side of the cage.

They were both full.

"Freeze!" Starkey suddenly bellowed, and Norm turned in her direction toward the front door. Cowering there, arms full of groceries, was a small man, maybe five-four, his brown hair slicked over his bald spot, his brown eyes magnified behind a clunky pair of glasses. His jacket was 100% polyester.

Now this, this was the type of man who lived here.

The groceries tumbled out of his hands. TV dinners, mostly. Two boxes of Twinkies. The latest issue of *People*.

"On the floor!" demanded Starkey.

The man pressed his face against the issue of *People*. The parakeet squawked. As one of the other agents on scene took out a pair of handcuffs, Norm sauntered over and reached into the back pocket of the man's chinos, where a wallet noticeably bulged. Norm opened the wallet, took out the man's license, sighed, and dialed Tom.

"We got a problem."

From the top floor of Bellum Velum, Tom listened patiently to Norm's bad news.

"It would have been easy enough to do," concluded Norm. "Our guy finds someone in the metro area who has the same name as him, and that's the address he gives."

"While his real home could be anywhere." Tom leaned back against the wall. All around him, Agent Cofer's squad was inventorying the contents of Bellum Velum. Much of this inventory was computer-based, so Agent Cofer was being walked through the firm's many pass codes by the CFO, Mr. Yates, who Roberta had seen fit to call into the office despite his "flu." Yates was in his sixties, but had the physique of a monster truck, barely concealed by his brown U.S. Army sweats.

"Thanks, Norm. Do a full sweep anyway. Maybe this patsy knows something. I doubt it, but at this point we've got nothing to lose."

Tom hung up. He hadn't expected all the cards to fall into place, but surely some of them would. Surely they'd be able to find something of value here, wouldn't they? Galileo worked for a mercenary company. There had to be some link between his job and his current activities.

"Tell me about Booth," Tom said to Roberta. She was supervising the agents, instructing them where everything was, the tricks to opening certain file cabinets, etc. Bellum Velum probably looked like every other office in downtown Baltimore, only Tom doubted that the other offices had vaults packed with automatic weapons, body armor, and C-4 (all obtained legally, of course—Roberta had documentation).

She smiled toward him. Her rosy, calm disposition hadn't faded, not one bit. True, she had been momentarily fazed downstairs when the agents had swept into the lobby, but she had quickly regained her composure and her confidence. Perhaps it wasn't a veneer after all. Perhaps Roberta Watson was just that secure in her own skin.

"I wish I could say I knew each of our employees well, Agent Piper, but I just don't. I remember seeing Henry Booth at our Christmas parties, but that's about it. As I've said, when they're not in the field, they tend to keep to themselves."

"The nature of your business being what it is."

"Exactly."

Tom wandered over to Yates. His office was austere. Apparently he tended to keep to himself too, although he undoubtedly had other offices in other countries.

"Do you know Henry Booth?"

"Of course I do," growled Yates, pointing at something on the screen for Agent Cofer's benefit. "He works for me, doesn't he?"

"Well, you're just the chief financial officer. I don't know what kind of relationship—"

"I own forty percent of the fucking company."

"Mmm-hmm."

"Roberta tells me you called first. Why was that? Did the judge stipulate you try to get this information from us peaceably before he'd issue your warrant? It's good to know some jurists in this country still actually read the Bill of Rights before using it as toilet paper."

"Where is Henry Booth?"

"Check his house."

"We did."

Yates shrugged his boulder-shoulders.

"That was real clever of you by the way, Piper, what you did."

"What's that?"

"Waiting until you were *here* before you invaded *there*. A two-pronged assault. Didn't give him much of an opportunity to go to ground or for us to shred any incriminating documents."

"Are there incriminating documents to shred?"

"There are always incriminating documents to shred. If our roles were reversed, I'll bet I could find a thing or two in your office. Of course, no judge is ever going to offer me a warrant to search your workspace. The street doesn't go both ways."

"Mmm-hmm."

"What is it exactly you think Henry did?"

Yates presented himself like a dumb jock, but he was the CFO of a multimillion-dollar company. Tom knew better than to underestimate the man.

"As you implied," said Tom, "we all have skeletons in our closets."

"I'll show you mine if you show me yours."

"But Mr. Yates, I get to see yours for free."

Yates glared at the warrant, lying placidly on his desk. Like a dead albatross.

"You don't think we couldn't dig up your dirt, Piper? How long have you been a government employee? Twenty-five years? You don't think with the resources we got we couldn't unearth some nastiness about you?"

"Are you threatening me, Mr. Yates?"

Yates smirked. "I know better than to threaten a big,

powerful member of the FBI. I open my mouth and words just seem to come out. I can't be held responsible for their interpretation."

Tom resisted the urge to smack that smirk off his face.

Agent Cofer continued plowing through files on the company server.

On the other hand, Yates didn't take his eyes off Tom. The CFO was probably envisioning the many ways he could shape Tom into bloody pulp. They eyeballed each other, lions on the Serengeti, circling, each without moving a muscle.

"You've been with the Bureau, what, twenty-five years?"

Tom nodded. "Mmm-hmm."

"You know a guy named Bobby Fink?"

Tom gritted his teeth at this toad's mention of his beloved ex-partner. "We used to work together."

"Nice guy, Bobby Fink. From what I hear. Runs a surf shop down in Miami now, right?"

"Mmm-hmm."

All Tom had to do was ask Agent Cofer to step outside for a minute. It wouldn't be a clean fight, and he'd probably lose, especially with his arm in a sling, but he'd get in a few good kicks to Yates's groin and that would satisfy his Id.

"I know where Henry Booth is." This came from Agent Cofer, who was reading the information from Yates's computer terminal.

Tom moved to behind the desk and peered over Cofer's shoulder at the screen.

"He's on assignment?"

Cofer clicked on a key, and the assignment was revealed.

"Son of a bitch," said Tom.

Sometimes he hated it when he was right.

21

"I'm so thrilled! I want to give you a big, big hug! Can I give you a big, big hug? I don't want to hurt you."

"Go ahead," replied Esme, and Amy Lieb wrapped her arms around her and gave a big, big hug. They were in the mini-foyer of Amy's mini-mansion.

The Liebs' house was all about space and light. Massive bay windows filled the walls of every room and allowed the maximum amount of sunlight to wash across the soft grass-green carpeting, creating the illusion that one was outdoors and in union with nature, when in fact one was inside and in union with fiberglass. It always felt a few degrees too warm here. Esme removed her coat and a servant, patiently waiting in the corner, whisked it away to wherever the coats got whisked.

Amy led Esme into the study, where six of Oyster Bay's civic-minded adolescents were hard at work on the Kellerman campaign.

"Ladies and gentlemen, this is Mrs. Stuart. She's a great friend of mine and she's going to be helping us out."

They welcomed her with the usual hello's, hi's, etc., then got back to working the phones and labeling the postcards.

"Can I get you anything, Esme?"

"No. I'm good."

Amy brought Esme to a table. On the table was a blue binder.

"Our big event is in three weeks and Billy had to pull out. Something about a niece's graduation."

"Billy…?"

"Joel."

"Right."

"Anyway, but I know you're a huge music fan so how would you like to choose the band for the fundraiser?"

"Uh…"

Amy opened up the blue binder. "In here are the listings for every band that's contributed to the Democratic Party in the past six years. I didn't know how to arrange them so they're arranged alphabetically. Bands that begin with the word *the* are listed under "The" but artists are listed last name first. Each page also has contact information, vitals, all that jazz. If you have any questions, I'll be in the den. I have a three o'clock phone conference with the candidate."

"You have a three o'clock phone conference with Bob Kellerman?"

"And his campaign manager. We're the governor's first stop after his vacation next week. If you'd like to say hi, come on in around 3:10. He's so approachable."

"Even on the phone, huh?"

"Especially on the phone! Oh, and Esme, I'm so

glad your mind got turned around about this benefit. I know how skittish you were about it. Word travels around, after all. But it wouldn't be the same without you."

Amy waved goodbye to her troops and sashayed off to her three o'clock with the probable future president of the United States.

This is my world, thought Esme. She sat down at the table and flipped through the binder. Personal phone numbers for John Mellencamp, Bruce Springsteen, each member of R.E.M. (even Bill Berry). This is my world. Of course, it had been her world for the past seven years really, this planet of prestige and accessibility. She just had kept it at arm's length. And was it so bad? Amy Lieb was using her power and status not to buy the latest Ferrari or to traipse off to the hippest Mediterranean villa but to help elevate by-all-accounts a decent man to leader of the free world. If anything, it was commendable, wasn't it?

"You're that woman, aren't you?"

This from one of the teeny-boppers, a pert redhead with braces.

"That woman?"

"You know, from the news."

"Rachel…" Her friend, a bottle-blonde, punched her in the shoulder. "I want to apologize for Rachel. She got dropped on her head when she was a baby. Repeatedly. From great heights."

"Shut up, Cassie. I'm just asking."

"And I'm just asking you to mind your own business," replied Cassie.

"It's okay," said Esme.

They both turned to her.

"Yeah, I'm the woman from the news."

The room fell silent. Obviously the others had been listening, and waiting.

"So you, like, met him?"

Most of the girls, and a few of the guys, sat effortlessly cross-legged on the floor. Esme remembered when she was that flexible. Now she could barely tie her sneakers without her back spitting hellfire. But she was getting better.

"What was he like?" Cassie asked.

"Well…" Esme saw she had an audience. They were young. She wondered if she should water down her account, or perhaps avoid it entirely. She didn't need late-night phone calls from angry mothers.

"Were you scared?"

"Yes," Esme answered, without hesitation. "I was terrified."

"My uncle's an EMT in the city," chimed one of the boys. "I overheard him talking to my parents. Last week, in the middle of the night shift, they got a call. Someone found the body of a homeless person just lying in the street. What my uncle said was, nobody wanted to take the call. Nobody wanted to go out to the scene and pick up this poor guy who probably died from alcohol poisoning or a drug overdose. They left the body out there in the street until the morning."

"Why?"

"Galileo," replied Rachel. "They thought it might be like what happened in Atlanta."

"I bet that kind of thing is happening a lot now. Cops and firefighters and teachers all scared to do, you know, go to work and do their jobs. No one's talking about it, but remember what school was like the day after Santa Fe? I don't think anyone got detention for a week. No one wanted to stay after school."

"I heard Mrs. Phillips moved rehearsal of *My Fair Lady* from the auditorium to one of the music class-rooms."

"That was so they could work on the songs, genius."

"Maybe."

"Everyone's just overreacting," Cassie said, then looked at Esme. "Right?"

Esme didn't know what to say. Fortunately, she didn't have to reply. Rachel replied for her:

"I'll bet when Galileo was a kid, he used to torture animals," the redhead suggested. "I'll bet he used to strangle rabbits and gerbils and people would wonder where their pets were and I'll bet he enjoyed it."

"Do you think his parents knew?"

"How could they not?"

"Then all this is just as much their fault as his."

"So, what, Rachel, it's your parents' fault you're such a spaz?"

Now it was Rachel who punched Cassie in the shoulder. Hard.

Then silence. Had the conversation run its course?

Leave it to Rachel.

"So, Mrs. Stuart, are you still scared?"

Esme cocked her head. "Still?"

"That he'll come after you and, you know…finish the job?"

This time no one chastised Rachel with a punch to the shoulder. Everyone was too stunned to move.

"Um…" replied Esme, which showed just how coherent her thoughts were at that moment. Had she thought about Galileo coming after her? Of course she had. Every day she had. She refused to live in fear, but she also had remained indoors 24/7 and on the sofa, far from any window, until very recently. But now all that had changed. Now she was back in the world, where Galileo could end you from a mile away.

"If he wanted her dead, he would have done it in Texas," the boy whose uncle was an EMT softly spoke.

"Well, why didn't he?"

Esme wanted to punch Rachel, just not in the shoulder.

"Rachel," added Cassie, "why don't you get us another pitcher of water?"

"But the pitcher's not empty."

"Why put off the inevitable?"

Rachel grimaced, rose to her feet, and carried the pitcher out of the room.

"I'm sorry," said Cassie.

"It's okay," lied Esme. "Why don't we get back to work?"

The circus was in town. It always showed the first weekend of April, with the crowning of the chokecherries. Donald Chappell had attended it when he was a boy, marveling at the caged lions in the big top. The lions had been his favorite part. He had only read about lions before, in the Narnia books, and here they were, alive and beautiful, just as he had imagined. When he had a son of his own, he passed down his love of the April circus, and his collection of Narnia books. Now Donald was here with his boy's boy, his grandson, little Joey, Joey who couldn't stand still, Joey who had never heard of C. S. Lewis and didn't much care when Donald tried to explain who Aslan was. Joey was more interested in his cotton candy than in the show.

When Donald was a boy, the circus seemed to come out of nowhere, like magic, and that felt right. Then one day, shortly after the Unity for a Better Tomorrow began to become successful, the managers of the circus paid Donald and his wife a call. As prominent local business owners, would they be interested in helping to subsidize the circus? It could be tax deductible, they boasted. It could provide great PR, they exclaimed.

That night, in bed, Donald almost cried.

The Unity for a Better Tomorrow did end up subsidizing the circus, and by the time Joey was born, the Unity was the circus's primary sponsor. The cotton candy Joey enjoyed so much was "on the house." So were today's tickets. So would be any tickets, if Joey wanted to return, and Donald would have been more than happy to bring him.

"I'm bored," the boy said.

The audience cheered as a lithe brunette, fifty feet in the air, walked across a line of wire while reading a book. Maybe she was reading *The Lion, the Witch and the Wardrobe.* Donald could barely see the girl, much less her book cover. He needed new glasses. Again. Damn cataracts. He rubbed his hazel eyes and tried to make out the brunette as she made her return stroll, pausing briefly in her journey to turn the page in her book.

Joey yawned. Loudly.

After the grand finale, after the bows and the standing ovation, after Joey begged for another cotton candy, Donald led him with the crowd out of the tent. The circus had a carnival fairway set up between the tent and the parking lot. Children tugged their parents toward shooting galleries, where giant teddy bears hung from poles and longed for ownership. Lines had already formed at the Ferris wheel and the Tilt-a-Whirl. To the left, middle schoolers took turns dunking their heads in a barrel of black water, bobbing for hidden prizes. To the right, high schoolers poured into the Haunted Hall of Mirrors, eager to shriek in terror. The moon looked over them all with a watchful eye, wide and unblinking, on springtime Nebraska.

"I want a white bear!"

Joey pointed and pointed at a row of plush polar bears hanging in a nearby booth. Donald acquiesced, and they approached the barker behind the counter.

"One gets you five, two gets you fifteen," the barker announced.

Donald handed him a dollar bill, and the barker traded it for a BB-rifle.

"I want to shoot! I want to shoot!"

"Of course you do," mumbled Donald, and he

handed the gun to his child's child. The target was a pyramid of seven milk bottles stacked ten feet away. Joey tried to aim the rifle, but it weighed almost as much as he did. Donald supported the underside of the barrel with a finger.

"Okay, now take a deep breath," he said.

Joey took a deep breath.

"Close one eye."

Joey closed one eye.

"And pull the trigger."

Joey pulled the trigger. POP! The top milk bottle tumbled to the netting below.

"I got one, I got one!"

"Four more shots, Joey."

Joey took a deep breath and closed one eye. Donald's attention drifted off to his left. Someone was standing close by. Did they have an audience?

"Hello, Mr. Chappell."

POP! Another milk bottle toppled.

"Tom Piper, isn't it? What a pleasant surprise."

Donald let go of the gun to shake Tom's hand, and the rifle barrel smacked against the booth countertop.

"Grandpa!"

"Oh. Sorry, Joey," Donald said. He returned his hand to its place.

Joey took a deep breath and closed one eye.

"The trick is to aim for the bottom row," said Tom. "You knock out the foundation, and the whole house comes tumbling down."

Donald felt Joey lower the rifle a few inches, and compensated with his steadying hand. POP! One of the bottom milk bottles spun out of place, and the remaining four joined it in the netting.

"We have a winner!" cried the barker.

While he handed Joey a polar bear, the two grown-ups exchanged sentences with a few glances.

"Joey," said Donald, "we're going to go to the car now so this nice man and I can discuss business. Is that okay?"

"Can I have another cotton candy?"

Donald bought his grandson another cotton candy. They strolled out to the parking lot and Joey plopped in the backseat of the black Buick. The bear occupied his lap. Donald closed the door. The boy wouldn't be able to hear them from inside the car, and even if he could, he wouldn't understand, and even if he could, he had his cotton candy and he had his polar bear.

"So, Tom, how can I help you? I assume you're not here for the circus."

"No, sir."

"That's a shame. Everyone loves a circus. Or should." A light breeze mussed Donald's cowlick, which was as white as his grandson's polar bear, and he absently corrected the errant hair. "What can I do for you?"

"Henry Booth."

"Henry Booth? Who's that?"

Tom nodded. "I'll tell you. Because it's an interesting story, and everyone loves an interesting story. Or should. Henry Booth's a God-fearing man. Grew up in rural Maryland. Got a job with the CIA, a good job, too, but eventually the work got to him, and he left for the private sector. He went to work for a security company out of Baltimore called Bellum Velum."

Donald stared into space. "Bellum Velum is an interesting name."

"Oh?"

"It's Latin. It means 'War for Sale.'"

Donald's hazel gaze caught Tom's. He'd taken the agent off-guard. Good.

"Please continue your tale. I'm most interested to hear how it all turns out."

Above, the nighttime clouds were picking up speed. It would rain soon. The circus would have to shutter its doors.

"Henry Booth did a lot of heavy lifting for this security company. They sent him all over the world, doing this and that. Bosnia. Afghanistan. He didn't want to be back in these places, though, so he begged for reassignment. And he got it. Turns out someone had recently hired Bellum Velum to do some small intelligence work. Bellum Velum specializes in all sorts of activities."

"You don't say."

"You see, there was a presidential campaign coming up, and the client was looking to invest a great deal of time and money in some of the candidates. But they needed to vet them first to determine which candidates were worthy. They needed it done low-key and professionally. After all, they had a reputation to maintain. And wouldn't you know it? Henry Booth found some dirt on one of the candidates."

Donald turned away from the wind. It was beginning to irritate his eyes. He glanced into the car.

"What did he find out, Mr. Chappell?"

Joey had fallen asleep. What was left of the cotton candy was stuck to the bear's fur. The boy had his index finger in his mouth.

"Mr. Chappell, what did Henry learn about Bob Kellerman?"

"You don't know?" Donald let slip a small smile. "No, you wouldn't. You know why out of all the private investigators at my disposal I chose Bellum Velum for this job?"

"No, I don't."

"It's because I'm tired of saints. Sanctimony has gotten stale for me. There comes a point when preaching to the choir loses its appeal. After my wife passed, may she rest in peace, I made a decision to use my resources in a different way. I've been doing it subtly, but surely. I've been funding the sinners, Tom."

"Why?"

Donald chuckled at Tom's confusion. "I get in a room with someone like the owners of Bellum Velum, now there's men who need to hear the Good Word, and don't you think with me paying them what I'm paying them they're going to have to listen?"

"And that's why you continued to fund Kellerman, even after finding out whatever it is you found out."

Donald shrugged: exactly.

"Mr. Chappell, Henry Booth has been doing what he's been doing and you've just stood by. All those people are dead and you just stood by."

This raised a sudden fury out of Donald. "I didn't know it was him! I swear! I suspected, but I didn't know! What was I supposed to do? There is a man whose soul is in agony. There is a man who has been betrayed all of his life. By his country. By his faith. Which I thought I could restore! I was being selfish. I thought... I..."

"Do you know where he is?"

Donald shook his head.

"I need to know what he found out about Kellerman. It may help us find him."

"What do you think he found out, Tom? I can see it in your face. You have your suspicions. What is it you're thinking? That Henry found out Bob Kellerman is gay? You think it's something as mundane as homosexuality? Bob Kellerman's not gay. I'm sorry to disappoint you. No, the secret he's hiding—the secret that's driven Henry to commit these unspeakable acts—has much larger ramifications than mere sexual orientation."

22

After his conversation with Donald Chappell, Tom flew back to Washington. He holed up in an office with Norm Petrosky and the Bureau's top profilers. Tom presented them with the facts. They churned them into speculation. For confirmation, they needed to talk with Bob Kellerman. But the candidate had just begun a vacation.

"The day he's back on the clock, we blitz him. What's his first event after his vacation is over?"

"A fundraiser in Long Island."

"What day?"

"April 12."

Like millions of Americans, the Kellermans wanted to vacation in Orlando, Florida. Few of those other hardworking Americans, though, had the media shadowing them 24/7. In order to achieve some semblance of privacy, the Kellerman campaign struck a deal with the major networks: leave the family in peace for one week, and upon his return to civilization the governor's first public speech, at a fundraiser in Long Island, of all places, would be the announcement of his running mate. April was extraordinarily early in the calendar for such an announcement to be made, but it was the highest card Bob Kellerman had that he was willing to play. The media accepted the deal. No one, of course, could keep the unregulated at bay—the bloggers, the paparazzi— but Kellerman's campaign manager came up with a solution for that problem, as well, a solution as old as public fame. Look-alikes of Bob, his wife Betsy, their two children, even their golden retriever were hired, given a paid vacation to Disney World, and sent on their way.

The real family spent the week in Southern California. They went on Space Mountain four times. They shared a chicken dinner at Knott's Berry Farm. They spent a day at Catalina Island. On the ferry ride back to the mainland, they saw dolphins. Everyone on the ferry rushed to the rail and pointed at the sea mammals and whipped out their digital cameras and no one—no one—gave a second's glance to Bob, his wife Betsy, their two children and their golden retriever.

Esme spent the week in nerves. By day two, her fingernails had been gnawed to stubs. By day three, her pacing had inlaid a path on the living room carpet. She looked forward to her daily trips out to Amy Lieb's mansion, if only for the distraction that party-planning provided. April 12 would be her official reintroduction into Long Island society, the return of the old Esme. But was she the same? Could she be the same? Her neighbors had watched the news. They knew what had happened to her. When she walked into the fundraiser, dolled up in a $2000 evening gown, who would they really see?

And did she really care?

That didn't matter. Her actions affected her family, reflected on her family. They affected Sophie. If Esme wasn't looked upon as an everyday mom, the parents wouldn't allow their children to play with hers. It was that simple. And so April 12 was, more than anything else, for her.

Esme hid her anxiety well. At night, when Rafe came home, when the four of them sat at the dinner table (because Lester just refused her kind offer of getting the fuck out of Dodge), she pretended that everything was pre-Amarillo. Everything was copacetic. Pass the broccoli? Sure. Lean forward, lift the plate, ignore the fist knuckle-punching your spine, here you go. When it came time for bed, she would slide into her spot beside her husband. They would kiss and say good-night. He would tell her he loved her. He would tell her he was proud of her. She would spend the next three hours trying to get comfortable, trying to go to sleep. Some nights it helped to tuck a small pillow under her lower back. April 12 approached.

And then there were the phone calls from Tom.

She didn't listen to his messages. She couldn't listen to his messages. He called at least once a day, and she deleted whatever voice mail he left. She deleted his e-mails. She felt awful treating him like this, but she'd made it clear to him how she felt. Sometimes bridges needed to be burned. She knew she was making the rational choice. But logic was a poor salve for a broken heart. If you answered the phone when he called, if they got into another discussion, she didn't trust herself enough to resist whatever he had to say. Maybe after the fundraiser, if she was able to make it through April 12 without a catastrophe, maybe then she would have the fortitude but not now. No way. Not to mention the fact that his messages just served to remind her of the extant, deadly connection between the fundraiser and Galileo.

As days piled on days, as she indoctrinated herself deeper and deeper into her old life, a curious transformation began to happen to Esme's feelings about Tom. She began to resent him. Her therapist played a part in this, as did Rafe, but some of the resentment had to have come from her own psyche. Here she was, trying to do what was best for the people she loved, and he kept tempting her away from them and he had no right. She had been perfectly clear to him on the phone. Did he want her family to crumble?

Tom, for his part, also suffered, each time he picked up his phone to call. Of course he knew how she felt. Of course he remembered their last conversation. He could replay it, word for word, in his mind, like a bad song. He didn't want to be a burden to her. But the April 12 fundraiser was practically in her backyard! Despite the preponderance of facts, the federal judge had deemed the evidence too circumstantial to issue a warrant to investigate the Kellerman campaign, and so Tom needed Esme, once again. He needed her to help him get to the governor. He wasn't even sure she would be at the event, but she was his only hope. He wanted to fly to Long Island in advance and talk with her in person, but the judge kept calling him back into chambers to justify his warrant application and the operation in Kansas City—probable site of Galileo's next attack—kept requiring his presence and so it wasn't until the afternoon of the day itself, April 12, that Tom was able to finally catch a flight to Oyster Bay.

He flew into LaGuardia. Traffic in the airport was ridiculous, probably because the Kellerman campaign had also just arrived, and with them the national press. Baggage claim was a zoo of grabby tourists, and by the time Tom made it to his motorcycle, which he'd had the foresight to have shipped in advance, it was already six o'clock. He motored east through blue-tinged dusk, and to battle.

Rafe was already in his tuxedo. Once he'd showered, shaved and deodorized, it took him a full ten minutes to get dressed. This included his silk-smooth black boxers, his silk-smooth black socks, his corrugated white shirt, his pleated black slacks, his pressed black jacket, and his red bow tie. The bow tie was a clip-on.

In the ten minutes it took Rafe to go from naked to James Bond, Esme had put on an earring. It was a pearl earring, one of a set that he'd given her one anniversary. It felt heavy on her lobe, as if the clam were still attached. Everything felt heavy tonight, lugubrious. She knew it was mental. She was mental. She spent another ten minutes forcing the other pearl earring into her other earlobe.

She was wearing a red evening gown. It made her cheeks look rosy, her breasts look full and her waist look slim. It was a 3:00 a.m. infomercial made out of satin and silk. It was Rafe's favorite outfit of hers. He had specifically requested she wear it.

It was backless.

She wasn't wearing her bandage. She hadn't worn it all day. She couldn't turn around to look at herself in the mirror because the very act of swiveling her head roused the spike-fisted pain from its dormancy. She had to assume she looked okay. She had to assume there wasn't a giant scar, like a tongue, where the wood had pierced her, where her kidney used to be, where the surgeon had sliced her open. She had to assume a lot, if she wanted to muster the courage to leave her bathroom and join her husband downstairs…

Where Sophie was drawing a picture of her dad, all dressed up, on half a sheet of construction paper. She was using colored pencils. Colored pencils were more grown-up, and this was to be a grown-up picture. This was one for the refrigerator. The other half of the paper was reserved for her mom. She was taking a long time.

Finally, she appeared! She looked nervous. She looked beautiful. Her lipstick matched her dress. Sophie tried to duplicate the color with her pencils, but it just wasn't the same, it just wasn't as *lively*. Oh, well.

Rafe held out his arm. It was time for them to go. Lester ambled out of his bedroom and wished them a good time. He already had a deck of cards in his hand. He and Sophie were destined for a marathon of gin rummy. Sophie walked up to the window and watched the car pull out of the driveway, angle onto the road, and drive off, Princess Cinderella and Prince Charming away to the ball.

Since a particularly trenchant winter had done a number on their lawn, the Liebs had an acre of fresh sod imported and implanted days prior to the event. The result was a success. By the time guests began to arrive, their backyard was a verdant wonderland, something out of *The Great Gatsby*. It stretched over six hundred feet from the house's rear patio to a long jagged cliff that overlooked the north shore. A tan fence lined the cliff to deter wayward children from falling to the eroded rocks and the lapping sea. Each of the fence's twenty posts had been carved by a local woodworker to resemble one of the Liebs' dear departed ancestors. Amy was fond of telling her children that someday they'd be a post on the fence.

The media arrived at 6:30 and promptly trampled the backyard to the root. They weren't allowed in the house, so they spent the party here, chowing down on the hot dogs and hamburgers the Liebs had been thoughtful enough to provide for them. But each and every one wished they were inside. That was where the action was. Someone in that house was the man—or woman— that Bob Kellerman was going to announce to be his running mate. Errant speculation bounced from conversation to conversation. Could it be the mayor of New York? They knew he was here in attendance. Every local Democratic politician was here in attendance and some of the Republicans, too. Their nominee, the vice president, was polling in the low thirties. The party had begged the old man not to run. The nation saw him as doddering and patrician. But primary season hadn't awakened any sleeping giants to stomp him down, and so the vice president, unfortunately, was their man in November. And so the governor of New Jersey, a lifelong member of the Grand Old Party, was here, at a Democratic fundraiser, all to cozy up to the presumptive future president of the United States: Bob Kellerman.

"What do you suppose he's like?" asked Rafe.

Esme shrugged her shoulders, stared out the window of their car. They had been sitting in their Prius for an hour now and were twenty-fifth in line for the valet parking up the Mississippi River of a driveway.

"George Washington had bad breath."

Esme glanced at her husband. "What?"

"It was from his dentures. Legend has it that when he was giving the oath of office, the chief justice at the time, John Jay, held his breath for fear of smelling Washington's odor and passing out right there in front of all the dignitaries. That would have been an inauspicious way to start a country, huh?"

Esme smiled at Rafe. He was trying to cheer her up. He knew how nervous she was. She slid her hand along his. Their wedding rings touched.

"Although I don't think Bob Kellerman has wooden teeth," Rafe added.

"Maybe he has a wooden leg."

"Now why do you suppose it is we always associate wooden legs with pirates?"

They moved up in the line. They were now twenty-four cars away from the party.

"This reminds me of the junior prom," said Rafe. "Did I ever tell you about that?"

"I don't know." He had. She wanted to hear the story again. "What happened?"

"It was at this old hotel in downtown. I went with this girl named Carly McGuiness. We went as friends, because the girl I wanted to ask, Hannah Draper, was already taken."

"Poor baby."

"Yeah, thanks." Only twenty-three cars now. "Anyway, so I got all dressed up. It was the first time I ever wore a tuxedo. I was so nervous I had to get my mom to help me put in the cufflinks. My palms were like a dog's tongue."

"Ew."

"Sorry, but they were! Man, I looked like such a dork."

"I've seen the photo album."

"Ugh. I forgot."

"How convenient."

"Anyway, I borrowed the truck and drove out to pick Carly up. When she came to the door…this was not a girl I had ever thought twice about—I mean, we were friends—but when she came to the door in that dress…"

"Let me guess. It was a red dress like the one I'm wearing."

"You know what, Esme? I think you just saved me a year's worth of therapy."

She raspberried him. They were inching closer to the house.

"So after I picked my jaw up off the floor and Carly and I posed for our requisite photographs, we piled back into the truck and headed to the old hotel downtown for the prom. A lot of our friends were sharing a limo but Dad had refused to let me do that because he felt limousines to be juvenile."

"Oh, yeah. Conspicuous consumption is so elementary school."

Rafe snickered. "My dad is my dad."

"Yes, he is."

"It is nice of him to come here, Esme, and take care of Sophie and all that."

Esme had other opinions, but she let it slide. There was no need to spoil this moment with something as jejune as the truth. And besides, they were ten cars away now from the end.

"We pulled up to the front of the hotel and it was a lot like this. A whole row of cars. So we had to wait. Me in the driver's seat, my sweaty palms making a mess of the steering wheel, and Carly to my right, fiddling with the radio. It was May and it was hot and she insisted we keep the windows open. I thought I was going to perspire through my brand-new tux. I really did. But there was a breeze, at least, so I could smell Carly's perfume, and that helped."

"What did she smell like?"

"Apples."

The three-story house was coming into view. Immaculate men and women emerged from their hybrids and their Hummers and strolled up the short brick path to the front portico. Thousands of tiny white lights snaked around the marble columns. It was Christmas in April. Esme rubbed her moist palms on the car seat. She thought of dog's tongues.

"Go on," she said to her husband.

"Okay, so, finally we pull up to the valet. Now I'm sixteen, and I don't know a valet from a hole in the ground but I'm a bright guy, so I quickly figure out the situation. However, I'm also a gentleman, and this is the junior prom, and Carly McGuiness is smelling like apples, so the valet comes over to my door and says hello and I hand him the keys and I open the door to get out and I walk in front of the truck to go open Carly's door but the truck is still moving—"

"It's still moving?"

"It's rolling forward. Not fast, but enough to be noticeable when it bumps me in the ass."

Esme knew the story, so she also knew her cue: "Oh God, Rafe, did you not shift the truck into Park?"

She laughed and he laughed and they pulled up another car length toward the Liebs. They were fourth in line now. Overhead the moon-sliver glowed like cat's eye.

"Well, anyway, so, like a doofus I pretended I'd planned the whole thing and I walked over to Carly's door and said, 'The boat's still moving. Would you like me to carry you across the threshold, madam?'"

"Oh, you didn't."

Rafe put up his hand in an oath. "I swear. Fortunately, we were friends, so, after grinding the gearshift into Park, she poked me in the ribs and let herself out of the truck. The valet stared at me like I was from Mars. And that was just the start of the evening."

"Did you get laid, stud?" asked Esme. That part of the story Rafe had never shared, nor had she ever asked. But she was curious. And right now her husband was so adorable she could have eaten him up with a fork and spoon.

"No." Rafe's smile faltered a bit. "Just as I had set my sights on Hannah Draper, Carly had her sights set on Dale Dougherty. The only part of Carly that went to bed with me that night was whatever apple perfume had rubbed off on my cheek."

Esme caressed the back of his hand. "I'm sorry." And she was. She made a mental note to buy some apple-scented perfume next time she was at the mall. Someone had a fantasy that needed to be exorcised.

"Good evening," said the valet, "and welcome."

There were three valets working tonight. They were professional valets. Esme hadn't realized such a profession still existed, but they did, and she had helped Amy book them for the fundraiser. They wore matching black-and-gold uniforms that were so starch-stiff they might as well have been made of plastic.

Esme tapped Rafe's hand and pointed at the gear-shift.

"Don't forget," she teased.

"Har-har-har." He clicked off the Prius's ignition, grandly (for her benefit) shifted into Park, and handed the keys to the valet. Then he climbed out of the vehicle and before Esme could reach for the handle, he was at her door.

"Would you like me to carry you across the threshold, madam?"

She replied with a wink. "Later."

"Ooh."

She stepped out of the car and joined her husband on the brick walkway. Rafe unsheathed the invitation from his pocket. Without it, they wouldn't be getting in. In fact, some gate-crasher appeared to be creating some commotion ahead of them at the front door. A small crowd of rubberneckers had formed, blocking Esme's view of the action. Suddenly, a cell phone went flying through the crowd and crash-landed right at her feet. The crowd parted for the gate-crasher, as he went to retrieve his broken phone. He stopped, though, mid-reach, and matched stares with her.

"Hello, Esmeralda," Tom said.

23

Tom fucking Piper.

The very sight of the man, here, in his hometown, made Rafe want to spit fire. His groin still recalled (with soreness) their last encounter, back in Amarillo, and now he was here, not five feet away, still wearing that dingy black leather jacket—which he probably slept in. As a sociologist, Rafe understood "motorcycle culture." He didn't appreciate it, but he understood it. Folks still wanted to be cowboys, but the prairies had all been paved so instead of palominos they had Harleys. It was the fantasy of a child made real by the bank account of an adult. How could Esme ever have admired this fool?

And what the hell was he doing in Long Island?

"What the hell are you doing in Long Island?" he asked.

"Hello, Rafe."

Tom pocketed his ruined phone and held out his hand. Rafe stared at it.

Tom turned to Esme. "I called you."

Rafe turned to Esme. He called her?

"And when I didn't call you back any of the sixteen thousand times," replied Esme, "did you think maybe I was trying to say something?"

"How could I know what you were trying to say if you didn't call me back?"

"We had this conversation. I told you how I felt. I told you what my priorities were."

"Believe it or not, the reason I'm here is the same reason everyone else is here. I need to speak with the governor."

"If you need to speak with the governor, why don't you try calling him sixteen thousand times? It's your effective M.O.!"

Esme glared at Tom. Tom glared at Esme. Rafe looked around and saw that everyone else on the front lawn—colleagues, neighbors, executives—was ogling the three of them as if they were a zoo exhibit.

Tom must have noticed them too, because he leaned in to Esme's ear. "Please, dear," he whispered, "let's not bicker in front of the snobs."

He led her to the less populated east lawn. Rafe was torn between wanting to explain the situation to his friends and wanting to follow his wife and her ex-boss. He followed his wife and ex-boss, all the while squeezing the elegant invitation tighter and tighter in his right hand. By the time he reached them, standing in the shadow of the manse, they had already recommenced:

"—don't care if I'm disappointing you, Tom—"

"I never said you were disappointing me. When something's obvious, it doesn't need to be said."

"You have no right to be judgmental. I nearly died for you!"

"See, and here I thought it was for your country. I like your dress, by the way. I think it costs more than my house."

"How badly do you want to get into the party?" asked Rafe.

Esme and Tom both glanced at him.

So Rafe continued:

"You said you need to speak with Governor Kellerman. Well, he's inside that house. Esme and I can get into that house. We're on the list. We might even be able to get you in the house. How badly do you want us to help you?"

"Lives are in danger," replied Tom.

"Lives are always in danger. When that bouncer threw your cell phone, it could've cracked someone in the skull, given them an aneurysm, and killed them. You'd think the Secret Service would be more hospitable to a distinguished member of the FBI, or was it personal?"

Tom shook his head in disgust. "They're not Secret Service. Are you kidding? The Kellerman campaign turned down the Treasury Department's offer of protection. They don't trust anyone from Washington. They think we're all in the pocket of the vice president. That's why they've been impeding our investigation. And the higher-ups are too concerned about appearances of impropriety in an election year to do their jobs. So I'm here on my own time. No backup. No warrant. Knowing the one man who can stop Galileo is here. And I just need five minutes of his time."

"Galileo and Kellerman," echoed Esme.

"And that brings us back to my question, Tom. How badly do you want to get in?"

Rafe felt his wife's curious gaze. She had no idea what was going on inside his mind. Sometimes she underestimated him. That was fine. That made moments like this all the richer.

"What do you have in mind?" asked Tom.

"It's a simple concept. I talk about it in my freshman lectures. It's called 'relative value.' What's priceless to you may be worthless to me. We got invitations because we belong here. We didn't have to beg anyone or wash dishes or do anything, really. This party is our reward for being ourselves. You get to travel the country and fight bad guys and feel righteous. That's your reward. So I guess what I'm asking, Tom, is this—what do you hold dear that you're willing to give up in order to get what you want?"

Esme opened her mouth, but didn't say anything. Was she shocked? Confused? This was about her, in its own way, and Rafe was dying to hear her thoughts. But he kept himself in check. He couldn't show any weakness now. He had to remain in control.

Tom slipped his wallet out of his pocket, but Rafe just knocked it to the ground.

"I'm not asking for money, Tom. Don't be silly. I have money. What is something you hold dear that I don't have? What are you willing to sacrifice?"

"I didn't sacrifice your wife."

"Didn't you?" Esme suddenly inquired.

Tom blinked. "What?"

And all of the resentment that had been building inside of her these past weeks just poured out.

"I'm not criticizing you, Tom, but, I mean, let's be realistic. When you flew me down to Texas, you knew there was an element of risk involved. Don't get me wrong—I knew it, too. The choice was as much mine as yours. But you were in charge. I was your responsibility. Darcy Parr was your responsibility."

"Don't—"

"I'm not blaming you," she added quickly. "Galileo pulled the trigger. Galileo is the villain. You're just… the negligent parent who let it happen."

In that moment, Rafe wanted to kiss his wife so badly, but he just slipped his hands into his pockets. Later. They would celebrate later. "What are you willing to sacrifice, Tom?"

Tom didn't respond. Esme's words had knocked the breath from his body. His mind whirred, but his eyes simply gazed into the dark night air.

Finally, he spoke: "Name your price."

Rafe did. Tom nodded. They left Esme by the side of the house and strolled down the driveway to the street, where the valets were parallel-parking the high-end cars end-to-end. They were running out of room. Rafe and Tom found what they were looking for halfway down the hill.

"Do you have a pen?" asked Tom.

Rafe reached into his pocket. His father had trained him well to always be prepared. Tom unlocked the rear compartment on his motorcycle, fished out a blue piece of paper, and signed along a line on the back. He returned it to the compartment and almost habitually slid his keys back into the left pocket of his leather coat. But he stopped himself, and instead held the keys out to Rafe.

"What are you going to do with it?"

Rafe pocketed the keys. "Does it matter?"

"Yes."

"Maybe I'll sell it. I'm sure there's some Hells Angel who'd love to get his greasy hands on this piece of shit. Or maybe I'll just keep it in my garage, untouched, unused. Collecting dust. I haven't decided yet."

Rafe offered a small grin. He couldn't restrain himself anymore. Victory—vengeance—was too sweet.

"So," he said, "let's get you into this party."

For expediency's sake, they decided to avoid the front door. They probably could have talked their way past the bodyguards, but it would have been a long talk, especially given Tom's recent violent encounter with them. So they decided to try the back.

The back lawn was littered with the nation's top media reporters and cameramen, noshing on their complimentary burgers. A few gave Esme, Rafe and Tom a passing glance, then returned to their gossiping. The servants were setting up the last of the tables for the speech. Governor Kellerman was scheduled to deliver the momentous address from the Liebs' back porch at 7:30 p.m. so the cable anchors could provide analysis during their 8:00 p.m. broadcasts. The musical guest— Tom Petty—would be performing shortly thereafter.

Esme, Rafe and Tom ascended the steps of the back porch, passed the podium and flag stands that Kellerman's advance team had set up, and approached the guard standing by the kitchen door. He was a Nordic fellow—buzz-cut blond hair, frozen blue eyes—and he flashed them the world's tiniest smile.

"The guest entrance is around front," he said. His accent was very streets-of-Chicago. So was the C-shaped scar across his left cheekbone. "Have a delightful evening."

"Actually," replied Rafe, "my wife here, Esme, is with the planning committee. We just wanted to, you know, avoid the line."

"I'm afraid this door is closed to guests. Have a delightful evening."

"Right, but we're not guests. Like I said, my wife Esme—"

And right on cue, the back door opened and Amy Lieb popped out.

"Esme! Rafe!" She wrapped her arms around them both and planted kisses on their cheeks. "You both look so wonderful!" Amy, for her part, looked wonderful too. She wore a narrow gold dress, and looked very much like a flute of champagne. "Did you just arrive? Everything is going so well!"

"We actually are having trouble getting in," Rafe answered.

"What do you mean? Your names are on the list." She turned to the bodyguard. "Their names are on the list. This is Rafe and Esme Stuart. They're among my closest and dearest friends."

"Ma'am, we were instructed not to let any guests in through the rear entrance."

"But they're not guests. I just told you. They're friends. Who's this?" She eyed Tom, who had taken off his leather coat. Underneath he had the common sense to wear a suit, albeit with a tie made out of leather string.

"Tom Piper," he said, oozing Kentucky charm, and kissed Amy's hand. "It's a pleasure."

"Tom's an old pal from Washington," added Rafe.

"Well, come on in! The more the merrier!"

Amy held open the door, wide enough for all to enter. The bodyguard frowned and stepped aside and Rafe, Tom and Esme strode into the kitchen, where a platoon of hyperactive chefs were putting the final touches on the evening's gourmet appetizers.

"It smells a little bit like heaven, doesn't it?" Amy observed. She looked to Esme for confirmation. Esme nodded and smiled. She didn't say anything. She hadn't said a word since Rafe had sprung his scheme.

Did she think what he did was right? No. Yes. Maybe. He was her husband. She had chosen him. She had said as much to Tom on the phone. She had made her choice and now she was standing by it. And if that meant Tom got hurt, well, at the end of the day, Tom wasn't family. Rafe was. For better or worse, as the vows went. Her marriage had been teetering on the brink of something dark and she had rescued it! To be critical of Rafe now would have invalidated all that progress. Even if he deserved her criticism. Even if his treatment of Tom had been nothing more than petty adolescent—

Enough. What's done was done. Rafe got what he wanted and now Tom would get what he wanted. Everyone would be happy.

"Where's the governor?" she asked.

"Oh, he's upstairs with his Special Guest." Amy let out a sly chuckle. "Even I don't know who he is. I think it's going to be General Phillips. But the world's going to find out in less than an hour, and the news will come from here. From my house. I'm so giddy I could burst! Oh, crap, that reminds me. I was heading outside for a reason. I have an interview with MSNBC. Let me introduce you to Paul Ridgely and then I'm gone."

Paul Ridgely was the governor's ubiquitous campaign manager. He was the favorite media surrogate for the campaign, always present with a sound bite. At thirty-one, he was astonishingly young for such responsibility, but in his short career he had already orchestrated three successful senate runs for the Democrats. Plus he was a native-born Ohioan, and that appealed to Kellerman's loyalists. Amy brought Esme, Tom and Rafe with her through a flurry of chatter and exchanged business cards and into the study, where Paul was entertaining an audience of tipsy businessmen on the art of on-the-road cuisine.

"The secret," he said, "is starch. Starchy foods fill you up quickly and they absorb alcohol, which allows you to go shot for shot with the town selectman at the local bar. At the end of the night, he's wasted and you can still walk in a straight line and he's impressed and there's another five hundred votes. It's hard for anyone to accuse you of being an elitist when you've drunk the town selectman under the table!"

The businessmen laughed.

"Paul, these are my dear friends Rafe and Esme Stuart. Rafe is a professor at our college and Esme helped me organize this event."

"Then I am in your debt," replied Paul, shaking hands with each of them.

Amy whisked off to her interview just as Paul turned to Esme and Rafe's un-introduced companion. "And you are?"

Tom held out his hand. "Tom Piper."

Paul's grin wavered slightly. "I believe we've spoken on the phone."

"I believe we have."

The temperature in the room dropped twenty degrees.

"Ladies and gentlemen," proclaimed Paul Ridgely, "we have with us tonight a special guest! Mr. Piper here is a very special agent with our own Federal Bureau of Investigation. Give him a round of applause!"

The guests clapped their hands. Esme watched Tom shift his balance. He knew where this was going and was not happy. Neither was she.

Rafe, on the other hand, clapped along with the rest. The smirk on his face could have been made of platinum.

"Tell me, Mr. Piper, how does it feel to be a member of such an historically important organization?"

Tom chewed the inside of his cheek. "Let's talk privately."

"Ah, see, there you go! With our FBI, everything must be private. Everything must remain opaque. Why is that, Mr. Piper?"

"You know why."

"I know what you think the reason is," Paul retorted. "You think the reason is 'national security.' That's why our Federal Bureau of Investigation has spent millions of our tax dollars tracking down enemies of the state like Martin Luther King and John Lennon. That's why you exerted your authority to extradite terrorists like Charlie Chaplin. It's too bad you didn't see fit to use our funding to stop Osama bin-Laden, but I'm sure you have your reasons. You just can't tell us what they are. 'National security.'"

"Are you finished?"

"Are you? When Bob Kellerman gets elected, ladies and gentlemen, the answer will be a resounding yes. Our intelligence community is an embarrassment and Bob Kellerman intends to dismantle the bureaucracy and rebuild a transparent cooperative nonpartisan apparatus. Pay attention to that word 'nonpartisan.' Currently our FBI is beholden to the executive branch. The director of our FBI is a political appointee. Bob Kellerman aims to change that, ladies and gentlemen. No more will we have lackeys controlling our intelligence. Leadership will be based not on party affiliation but on merit. Imagine that. We will have people in Washington actually qualified for the jobs they hold."

This last comment was pointed directly at Tom. Esme watched him breathe deeply. Then, finally, he spoke:

"You're the one who's been impeding our investigation."

"Here we go again, ladies and gentlemen! The 'blame game'!"

Tom glanced at the small crowd, then back at Paul Ridgely and his smug twinkle-eyed grin. "Kellerman doesn't even know, does he? You've been intercepting all my messages. This maniac is running around murdering people and the one man who can stop him doesn't even know he's connected. Why haven't you told him?"

Now it was Paul's turn to appear uneasy. "I don't know what you're talking about."

"Sure you do. As you admitted, we've spoken on the phone. Since you're all about transparency and access, why don't you tell the nice people here what we've talked about?"

"No one needs their time wasted with conspiracy theories."

"I think you're underestimating the public's curiosity. They do have a right to know, don't they?"

Paul sipped at his brandy.

Tom turned to the crowd. "I'm sorry, ladies and gentlemen, but it appears Mr. Ridgely actually does value his privacy. I'm sure he'd appreciate it if you left us alone for a few minutes. Wouldn't you, Mr. Ridgely?"

Paul sipped at his brandy.

The ladies and gentlemen got the hint, and slowly exited the room, all the while murmuring innuendoes amongst themselves: *conspiracy theory, what conspiracy theory, do you think it's about who he's going to nominate to be his vice president, yes but why would the FBI be involved, I'll bet it's a sex scandal, et cetera.*

"Well, Tom," said Esme, "you sure can clear a room."

Tom replied with a light salute.

Paul cleared his throat, indicated Rafe and Esme. "If you'll excuse us."

"Oh, they can stay," said Tom. "Esme was instrumental in connecting Galileo with your boss. And her husband…well, like you, he needs this lesson in responsibility."

Rafe took a menacing step forward, but Tom stopped him, and leaned in until they were face-to-face. But then the door to the room opened, and the schoolyard boys backed away from each other. Esme backed away from the door. Paul, in deference, put down his glass of brandy on a side table.

"So here's the party," Bob Kellerman said, twirling a cigar between his fingers. "May I join in?"

24

"Hi," he said, hand outstretched, "I'm Bob."

His tuxedo wasn't the flashiest. His brown hair wasn't the most neatly combed. But when he walked into the room, there was no question he was a man of calm authority, and everyone wanted to step up their game just to impress him.

"Esme Stuart." She shook his hand. "Pleasure to meet you, Governor."

"Rafe Stuart." He shook his hand. "Thank you for coming to Long Island."

"Tom Piper." He shook his hand. "Hello."

"Tom Piper," added Paul, "is a special agent with our Federal Bureau of Investigation. He crashed the party armed with some wild accusations."

Bob wasn't fazed a bit. "How may we help you, Special Agent Piper?"

"Well, sir, it's about Galileo."

The governor folded his arms and leaned in slightly, intent on giving Tom every ounce of his attention. The grave expression on his face said it all: yes, he had heard about the tragic events of Atlanta, Amarillo, and Santa Fe. By now, every American had heard about—and feared—Galileo.

"We have reason to believe—we have evidence, actually—that Galileo is committing these murders because of you, Governor."

Bob frowned—his frown seemed to fill his entire malleable face—and he looked to Paul for an explanation.

"This," Paul pointed, "this is what I mean by 'wild accusation,'"

"His real name is Henry Booth. He served a stint in the Middle East as a sniper for the CIA but eventually all that violence committed in the name of God got to him and he quit. He was hired by the Unity for a Better Tomorrow to vet you, Governor. In the course of his investigations, Henry Booth discovered something about you that rocked him to the core. That's when he contacted your organization, begging you to go public with your secret."

Paul snorted. "I assure you, Mr. Piper, Governor Kellerman received no such contact."

"No, because you intercepted it and never showed it to him. Just like you intercepted Galileo's second message back in San Francisco. Maybe you were trying to protect your boss, Mr. Ridgely, but in doing so you endangered lives."

"What secret?" asked Bob. "What skeleton in my closet drove this madman to kill all these people?"

To that, Tom reached into his pocket and took out a tiny voice recorder.

"Henry played this for the head of the Unity for a Better Tomorrow, Donald Chappell. How Henry got it...well...he did his job."

Tom pressed Play.

"—right on through November with a strategy which underlines our positive difference. Let the other guy take all the pot shots he wants. He'll just look desperate."

Everyone in the room recognized that voice as belonging to Paul Ridgely. Paul, at the sound of his own voice, reached again for his glass of brandy. Perhaps he knew what was coming next.

"But what about the other thing?"

This was a female voice, strident, with a Bostonian lilt.

"Kathryn Hightower," said Bob, doling out an explanation. "She's my communications director." He remained nonplussed, and contemplative.

"Kathryn, I assure you—the religion problem has been sewn up. The only people in the know, other than Bob's immediate family, are in this room."

Esme's jaw dropped open in astonishment, as her mind jumped ahead to the solution. Christ, the answer had been right there all along! She looked to Tom for confirmation. He nodded.

"What if they do enough digging, Paul? We need to be prepared with a response."

"We prepare a response and I guarantee you it'll be the response that gets leaked before the actual story and then we're fucked, Kathryn, you and me and Bob and the whole campaign, because the American public

in their puritanical wisdom want their president to be
a man of faith. They love him now—he's a hero to them
now, he's John fucking Kennedy—but this country will
never elect an atheist to the Oval Office."

Rafe cocked his head. "Wait, what?"

Tom clicked the recorder off.

"That's a private conversation," muttered Paul. "It's
obtained illegally and has no standing whatsoever."

The governor sighed. "Paul, shut up."

Paul sat down in the closest available armchair and
shut up.

"So Donald Chappell knows?" asked Bob. "And
he's still supporting my run?"

"He's trying to save your soul," Tom replied.

"So to speak," added Esme.

Bob nodded, taking it all in.

It was Rafe who broke the silence.

"So Galileo or Henry Booth or whatever his name
is, why is he killing all these people? If he's pissed off
at Kellerman for not believing in God, why isn't he
targeting him?"

"That's the thing," said Esme. "He's not pissed off
at Kellerman at all."

"No," Tom agreed, "he's not."

"You said he's been contacting me?" asked the
governor.

"Yes, sir. We believe the first message was probably
delivered late last year. Well before Atlanta. Henry was
so disenchanted by religion and suddenly here you
were, a nonbeliever like him, and you were popular,
and you were on your way to the presidency. His first

messages were probably friendly. But when you didn't respond, when you went ahead and let religious organizations like the Unity for a Better Tomorrow support your campaign, that's probably when he sent you the quid pro quo. Come out, publicly, proudly, as an atheist…or else."

"But I never received any…"

All eyes turned to Paul, whose brandy glass was empty.

"I was protecting you!" he explained. "Half of what we get are crazies with their pipe dreams. How was I to know?"

"You knew after Atlanta," Tom replied. "Because I'm sure Henry was very specific, wasn't he? As soon as you'd heard what had happened in Atlanta, you knew it was him."

"And you did nothing," added Esme.

"If it was in my power to bring those people back to life, I would, but—"

"Paul," Bob said, suddenly, "I believe you're talking again. I thought I asked you not to do that."

The campaign director sank in his armchair and looked very much like a wounded child.

Bob took a deep breath. The weight suddenly on his shoulders seemed to anchor the whole room. "All this time, all those people, and I could have stopped it with a word."

"You didn't know," said Tom.

Bob shrugged. Tom's words were irrelevant. Because of him, people were dead. Children were dead.

"What can I do?" His voice had diminished to a hoarse whisper. "How can I fix this?"

"At this point, sir, I don't know if you can."

Bob nodded thoughtfully. He'd expected that answer.

Once more, it was Rafe who broke the silence:

"For whatever it's worth, Governor, Mr. Ridgely is right. The people want their president to be a God-fearing, churchgoing man. In our country, in many countries, patriotism is synonymous with piety. I'm not telling you anything you don't already know. That's why you've kept this secret all this time. You come out now, and they'll hate you. You'll throw away everything you've worked toward and someone else will get elected. Mediocrity will inhabit the White House. Do you want to be responsible for that?"

The door to the study opened. It was, of all people, Kathryn Hightower.

"Governor, it's time for the speech," she said.

Bob paused for a moment, still deep in thought, and then he turned to Kathryn and nodded. "Thank you, Kathryn. I'll be right there."

The world was watching.

Forty-seven cameras were fixed and focused on the podium. Forty-seven cameras, not counting the chic handhelds the guests wielded. By the end of the night, this speech would be available to anyone on the planet with a computer and an Internet connection.

The fascination was understandable. Bob Kellerman was not only the presumptive nominee of his party, but also, based on the latest polls, the all-but-anointed next president of the United States, and although the

popularity of America waxed and waned with each administration, the power remained constant and
demanded—if not always earned—respect. And the
worldwide prognosis of a Kellerman presidency was
one of optimism. He was a populist, but he wasn't an
isolationist. He favored liberalism, true, but he also
possessed a Red State inclination toward self-suffi-
ciency. In June, he was scheduled to fly abroad, to
Israel and Pakistan and Russia and Egypt, to England
and to France, even to long-neglected Venezuela and
Brazil. Already, the signs were being painted, in a
hundred different languages: We Love Bob.

Not everyone loved Bob. As the governor approached the podium, amidst the customary cheers and
applause, he reflected on his enemies. He knew their
signs too. "Pro-choice = pro-death." "Free trade = no
jobs." He read the editorials criticizing his folksy
approach to politics. He lacked the Washington experience necessary to deal with a bipartisan Congress. He
lacked the international experience necessary to deal
with a war. That was why his choice of a vice president
was so vital. That was why forty-seven plus cameras
were focused and fixed on his face on this night in this
place.

They all expected an announcement.

"My friends," he said, "it gives me great pleasure to
see you all here tonight on this beautiful evening by the
sea."

His speech was prepared. It scrolled in large white
letters down teleprompters, paired to either side of the
crowd. His staff had worked all week on this speech.

They knew how important it was. Consecutive drafts were e-mailed every night to his hotel room in Anaheim, and every night he'd given his notes and made his changes. It was the only communication he'd allowed that week. His cell phone was off. He'd wanted it to be a true vacation. He knew it was the last true vacation his family would be able to enjoy in a long, long time. And he knew that was his fault.

"We come here tonight on the eve of great change. We are on the verge of fulfilling our potential as American citizens and you can see it in the faces of the elderly. You can see it in the faces of the children. They say pride is a sin, but I am here to tell you tonight that I am proud of what the future holds for our country. I am proud of what we can do for our fellow man. I am proud that for the first time in history, freedom has become as vast and limitless as the ocean just beyond that shore."

It was the empty rhetoric expected of an introduction. If he didn't offer the platitudes, his critics assailed him. "Well, he only mentioned the word 'America' fifty-nine times, so he must be losing his patriotism." All part of the process.

His kids were back home in Ohio. About now, they would be sitting down for dinner. Maybe they'd have the TV on, but probably not. Daddy was just giving another speech.

"I come to you tonight as a…"

Kathryn Hightower stood off to his left. He could see her out of his peripheral vision. She had been with him since his first mayoral race so many lifetimes ago.

"I come to you tonight as a…"

This was the paragraph where he would segue into his bit about partnership. It was the build-up to the body of the speech. It was the beginning of his announcement of General Archie Phillips to be his running mate. General Phillips was waiting inside the house, just on the other side of the curtained French doors. He was in full dress uniform. He was a good man. He'd been a benevolent, erudite debater during the primaries. But the people hadn't wanted erudition. They'd wanted homespun. They'd wanted Bob.

The kind of man they could take to church on Sundays.

"I…"

He felt a sideward glance from Kathryn. Loyal, hardworking Kathryn. He wanted to hold her close and kiss her on the forehead and apologize. But that would have to wait. Somewhere in this country, in his country, a man was committing horrific acts of violence in his name. It had to stop.

"Two hundred years ago, when Thomas Jefferson ran for president, there was a great deal of opposition to his campaign. It was the first true bipartisan election, and his opponents realized that since they couldn't attack his thoughtful policies or his impeccable reputation, they had to resort to different tactics."

The large white words on the teleprompters scrolled up, then down, then back up again, as the operator tried to locate this part of the speech.

"This was one of the architects of our democracy. This was the man who wrote the Declaration of Independence. How do you defeat a man like that? You go after his character. And they did. Thomas Jefferson, you see, was a skeptic. He was a scientist, and the scientific pursuit of truth demands evidence, and he looked at the universe and he didn't believe we had it all figured out. So the muckrakers called him an atheist. The label dogged him all through the campaign, but when the time came to vote for the president of the United States, the American people in their wisdom overwhelmingly chose Jefferson. They put into office a man whose ambitious curiosity helped shape our beloved country."

Bob could see it now, past the lights, in the faces of the crowd. He had gone off script and they knew it. He could feel the awkward tension vibrating in the air. This wasn't what they'd expected, and so they weren't prepared with an appropriate response.

So he rolled the boulder farther down the hill.

"You would think, after that tumultuous election, political operatives would have learned their lesson. A man did not have to be pious to be a patriot. Patriotism is itself a religion, isn't it? Our country is one grand cathedral and our Constitution is our hymnal. Our sacred commandments come numbered one through ten, only we call them the Bill of Rights. You would think after that tumultuous election, political operatives would have learned their lesson, but they didn't. Several decades later, they saw another man rise up, a man of ferocious intellect and boundless compassion, and they had no way to stop him so they attacked his personal beliefs. Once again the labels were bandied about.

'Agnostic.' One muckraker even called him 'godless.' But once again, the wisdom of the American people had been underestimated, and in 1860, they voted this 'godless agnostic' to the highest office in the land. Can you imagine what our country would have been like had those small-minded muckrakers won? Can you imagine what our country would have been like had Abraham Lincoln not been elected?"

The awkwardness passed into murmuring. Bob was always amazed how little people knew of their own history. But he wasn't here for a history lesson, not really. This was about the future.

"What makes our country unique is its plurality. We are the United States of America. Not one state, but many. Not one race, not one religion, not one lifestyle but many. It is our greatest strength and those that try to undermine our diversity insult the very fabric of our identity. I am not the same as you, nor should I be. Do you want a president who agrees with everything you say and do and think? What about when you're wrong? What about when he's wrong? Like Mr. Jefferson, I am a skeptic. Like Mr. Lincoln, I place my faith not in an infinite God, but in the infinite potential of mankind."

Bob took a breath. Now it was time for the closer.

"There are those who will look upon my words as an insult toward their personal beliefs. That is emphatically false. Our churches and synagogues are priceless, and I have nothing but the utmost respect for our great religions. As you know, my wife is Catholic. Do we disagree sometimes? Yes, we do. But disagreement is healthy. In a democracy, it is often our solemn duty to disagree. There will be debate and I encourage it. Just be careful of those muckrakers and their tactic of shrinking a candidate to a label. As if any person could be minimized to a word. As if any country could be. I am a man of ambitious curiosity. Stay with me on this journey. There are no limits on what we can do together."

He let out a breath. His hands were shaking. No one could see them but him. He waited.

Silence.

Silence.

Then the noise, erupting all at once. A cymbal-crash of applause. Those seated, stood. Those standing, raised their clapping hands as if reaching for the stars.

Bob smiled out at the crowd, waved, and made his way down the porch steps to greet his people.

Not everyone was outside, though. Many remained inside, enjoying the comfort of soft furniture and watching the speech on closed-circuit TVs. Rafe, Esme and Tom watched it from the study. Paul Ridgely had left for parts unknown, but their encounter with the governor had left them rooted to the carpet, and that was how they remained during the speech, eyes glued to the screen. When the applause erupted, they felt the thunderous noise shake through the room, and that seemed to break their spell.

Rafe sat down in a chair.

"Well," said Tom.

"Yeah," agreed Esme. Then: "Do you think he was watching?"

Tom glanced at her. "I don't know."

"He got what he wanted," she said. "Until that end bit about religion *not* being the root of all evil."

"Yeah, that probably ticked him off. Can I borrow your cell phone? Mine's, well, non-functional."

She reached into her purse and handed him her LG. He stepped out of the room for some privacy.

Esme sat on the arm of Rafe's chair.

"You okay?" she asked.

"I've never seen anything like that."

"I know."

"Do you think it was because of what I said?" He looked at her, eyes wide. "Did that just happen because of what I said?"

She grinned. He was like a little boy. "Just because you were completely and totally wrong doesn't mean I don't still love you."

"There's a lot of double negatives in that sentence."

"I'll give you a double negative."

She leaned in to kiss him. The door opened. It was Tom.

"Galileo didn't hear the speech," he said.

"How do you know?" asked Rafe.

"Because," Tom replied, "we've got him in custody. We caught him thirty minutes ago at a ballpark. We caught him."

25

The ballpark was Kauffman Stadium, home of the Kansas City Royals. On April 12, the Royals were scheduled for a home game against their arch-rivals, the Oakland A's. It would be blue vs. green (the Royals players in the blue and the A's players in the green) at 7:30 p.m. CST.

The stadium had recently undergone a major renovation—new HD scoreboard, beautified concourses, etc.—but the big fountain remained untouched. Located by right field, the fountain geysered thousands of gallons of water per game over 300 feet into air and provided a lovely, frothy backdrop. A small amusement park was set up behind it, and kids could almost always be found running to and fro (although seldom into) the tall white water. Expectedly, some of the priciest skyboxes were located at right field, with a perfect view of the manmade attraction. One of these skyboxes still remained closed, though, due to an architectural problem exposed during the renovation, and it was here that Galileo sat in wait.

He'd gained access the way he always did. "Mark Kenney" was the newest member of the Royals' janitorial staff. As the low man on the totem pole, he didn't have keys to most of the park, but he made friends with some of the veteran custodians, took them out to drinks, excused himself to the men's room, hustled across the street to a locksmith, made duplicates of their keys he'd just lifted, and had the originals replaced before anyone was the wiser.

The windows of the closed skybox remained sheeted over with black plastic, but this made it that much easier for Galileo to hide. No one in the stands would be able to see him. And all he required was a tiny rip in the plastic, and he could see them.

It was Sanitation Engineer Appreciation Night at Kauffman Stadium, and with the promise of discounted tickets, the city's hardworking trash collectors had come out in droves to enjoy a crisp cool night watching the national pastime with their families. They were the most overlooked, least appreciated of Kansas City's civil servants, but tonight the city's superstars had deemed fit to reward them. How good life could sometimes be.

"Mark Kenney" had finished his shift at five and was here now as a fan, wearing a yellow Polo shirt and dark tan khakis. The custodial staff received complimentary bleacher tickets, and as far as anyone knew, that's where he would be. And so no one thought twice as he trotted through the corridor behind right field, passing the snack shops and Royals memorabilia. A few of his coworkers waved, and he waved back. And they were used to seeing him with his long black suitcase, which he usually stored in his work locker. It contained his prized trombone. No one else had seen the trombone, not yet, but "Mark Kenney" was shy about his hobbies. Soon, though, he promised them. Soon.

The skybox was cluttered with tools and sawdust. Thick muslin tarp was draped over what Galileo assumed were tables and chairs. Earlier today, he'd placed his shoe box here, at the base of one of the amorphous covered shapes, waiting to be found later by the authorities. Now he propped up his suitcase and flipped open its latches. His M107 lay unassembled in the felt casing. He'd cleaned it last night.

It took him twenty seconds to assemble. Each part made a reassuring click as it snapped into place. He hefted the rifle in his arms and ejected the ten-round magazine. One final check before—

The magazine was empty.

Galileo frowned, shook it to be sure, then lifted a hidden flap inside the suitcase, where he stored his spare ammo…but that compartment was empty too. What the hell…?

The door to the skybox whipped open and six flak-jacketed FBI agents stomped into the room. Each wielded a pistol and each aimed directly at Galileo's rapidly beating heart. Unlike the M107, their weapons were armed.

Then a seventh FBI agent sauntered in. Galileo recognized the roly-poly man from the database he'd pilfered. This was Norm Petrosky, and he was chomping on about ten ounces of bubblegum.

"See, we would have got you a couple hours ago," he said, casually, "but we wanted to wait until you were in a secure location. You know, where you couldn't run."

As Norm spoke, one of the other agents patted Galileo down, found his ankle Beretta, and removed both it and its holster. Galileo, for his part, didn't raise his hand or flinch or even scowl. He just stared back at Norm, and watched the fat man take a few steps closer.

"You know what trips you guys up every time, don't you? You're creatures of habit. Which is really fucking stupid, but it makes our jobs a whole lot easier. Because we know you like pretending to be janitors and we know where you're going to be. We were here before you ever showed up."

Norm winked at him, then indicated to the other agents. The shackles came out, clanging not unlike the earlier sounds of the rifle being assembled. There was one pair of shackles for the wrists and one for the ankles, and they were yoked together with a third lock to allow for easy towing.

They waited until the second inning to bring Galileo out. There were still people in the corridors, but by now most had found their seats and weren't yet ready for a refill of beer. Still, it was impossible to avoid the gaping looks as the FBI escorted their catch down the ramps, past snack shops and memorabilia, to the exit.

They already had a van in the parking lot. Anna and Hector Jackson (no relation) were waiting there, arms crossed, smiles stretching from ear to ear to ear to ear. Even Daryl Hewes was there. He didn't look as giddy, though. He was just relieved.

"Henry, you ever been to a supermax? You are in for a treat. In two hours, we will be transferring you to one of our nation's finest homes for the criminally fucked. While awaiting your hearing, you'll get a terrific view of, well, nothing, because your room won't have a window. Oh, by the way, you have the right to remain silent."

Norm shoved Galileo into the rear of the van and rounded to the front seat with Anna Jackson. Hector and Daryl joined Galileo in the back. Galileo sat on one bench. The FBI agents sat across from him on the other. While Hector linked Galileo's chains to a hook in the floor, Hector yanked shut the rear doors.

An hour into the drive, Daryl finally asked the question:

"Why didn't you kill Esme Stuart?"

Galileo looked up from his chains. Hector looked over from his magazine.

"You murdered a friend of mine. Her name was Darcy Parr. You murdered dozens of innocent people. But you let Esme live. Why?"

Although the radio was on in the front cab, at the moment no one was listening to the Royals game. Norm, who was riding shotgun, swiveled his head to get a better view of the response.

Galileo responded, "I didn't set out to kill anyone."

"That doesn't answer my question."

"All of this could have been prevented."

"Why did you let her live?"

"Would you rather I'd let her die?"

Without warning, Daryl jumped forward and clasped his left hand around Galileo's throat.

"Would you rather I let you die?" snarled Daryl. "Huh?! How would you like that?!"

They were inches from each other. Although restrained, Galileo had easy access to the technician's gun, exposed at his hip. He didn't go for it.

Hector, for his part, was ignoring the act of brutality until a glare from Norm changed his mind. He separated Daryl from his victim. Galileo gasped for breath. His throat had pale smears where Daryl had dug in his thumbs.

"Daryl," said Norm, "apologize to the psychopath."

Daryl scowled from across the aisle. "I'm sorry."

"So am I," replied Galileo, softly. "I meant what I said. I didn't want any of this to happen. That's why I let Esme live. She was supposed to stop me. I needed to be stopped. I knew God wasn't going to step in. You all brought her in. She was supposed to be your expert, so I chose her to be my wall. But she failed."

That was when Tom called from Long Island, and Norm told him about Galileo's capture. Shortly thereafter, the van crossed the Missouri-Kansas border. They were now ninety minutes from their destination.

By the seventh inning, the A's had climbed up to a 5-2 lead, and Anna Jackson switched the station to talk radio. Unsurprisingly, the main subject of discussion was Governor Kellerman's speech in Long Island:

"—and he couldn't have picked a better place to deliver this address, insulated among his staunchest supporters, preaching to the choir, which I suppose is an inappropriate metaphor now, eh, Charlie?"

"You said it, Mitch. Why don't we replay some of the choicest portions for our listeners?"

Daryl was lost in his own thoughts about Darby Parr and what might have been. Galileo, however, stirred from his stupor. His muscles tensed in his neck, and underneath his yellow Polo shirt. Preaching to the choir as an inappropriate metaphor? Was it possible after all this time that the governor had finally come clean? Was it possible these murders had not been in vain?

As he listened to the broadcast of the speech, Galileo felt warmth spread out from his chest and surfeit his muscles, tendons, and bones. The Jefferson analogy made him smile. The Lincoln analogy made him beam. He was like a kid on Christmas morning and everything he wanted was waiting there underneath the—

"—churches and synagogues are priceless, and I have nothing but the utmost respect for our great religions. As you know, my wife is Catholic. Do we disagree sometimes? Yes, we do. But disagreement is healthy. In a democracy, it is often our solemn duty to disagree."

The warmth inside of him froze, became ice, tipped and jagged. His fingers curled like rotting fruit. Nothing but the utmost respect for our great religions? What was that? How could a true atheist bear anything but contempt for groups that invested their entire purpose in worshiping an imaginary super-being? "Great religion" was an oxymoron. Religion created dependency, encouraged infantilism, and fostered an us vs. them mentality and for that man to stand there, knowing better, and to pander to these dangerous, delusional miscreants…

No. This would not do.

Hector turned a page in his magazine. Daryl, though, noticed the look of disgust painted across Galileo's face. Galileo raised his gaze to match Daryl's.

"Do you know how to dislocate your thumbs?" inquired Galileo, gently.

"What?"

Galileo smashed his thumbs against the hard cartilage of his kneecaps; the digits made soft popping sounds as they separated from their joints. Before Daryl could react, Galileo slipped his now-rubbery hands out of their shackles and launched across the aisle. His left hand went for Daryl's Glock and his right hand went for Hector's and he hoisted their handguns out of their holsters as smoothly as he'd freed his hands only seconds before. The barrels tapped simultaneously against their foreheads. The gunshots were simultaneous too. The backs of their skulls splashed amoeba-like splashes of reddish-gray brain matter against the wall of the van.

Four seconds had passed since he'd dislocated his thumbs.

Norm Petrosky barely had time to reach for his own weapon when Galileo spun around—as dexterously as his leg chains allowed—and fired off two more rounds, one into the cranium of Norm and one into the cranium of Anna. Anything could have happened, then. The van could have spun out of control. It could have swerved into oncoming traffic. But Anna's death throes took her foot off the gas and instead of a violent end, the van just rolled to a stop, angled toward the breakdown lane. All the better, for Galileo had things to do. And people to see.

Tom and Esme were alone in the study. Rafe had gone out to find Governor Kellerman, as if they were old friends. He said he owed him an apology. Esme didn't argue.

"So," said Tom.

Esme nodded.

"How's Sophie?"

"Good."

Tom nodded.

"I'm sorry," she said, quickly adding, "About your motorcycle. I'll try to get it back to you."

"It's okay. I took it for granted, anyway. I didn't realize how important it was to me until I lost it."

Esme cocked an eyebrow. "You're laying the subtext on a bit thick, Tom."

"It's been that kind of night."

"So, do you think Kellerman will be annoyed that he gave that speech for nothing?"

Tom laughed. Esme joined him.

"And after all this," she mused, "they catch him in at a ball game."

"Don't you know? Baseball is full of catchers."

"Ugh."

Their laughter dwindled. So did their smiles, as heavier thoughts moved in.

"Do you really think I'm reckless?" asked Tom.

"You know you are," Esme replied. "It's not necessarily a bad thing."

"It is when the ends don't justify the means."

"In certain jobs, the ends always justify the means."

"Mmm-hmm." Tom flashed her another grin. "Does housewife qualify as one of those jobs?"

"You try raising a precocious little girl while having the absentminded professor for a husband."

"No, thanks," said Tom. "That's not for me."

Esme shrugged: but it is for me.

And that was that.

"I should find Rafe before, well, you never know."

"I never do," answered Tom.

He walked her to the door of the study and watched her disappear into a sea of suburban glamour. He remained in the doorway, and was mostly content. A waiter offered him a flute of champagne, but he declined. It was time to go.

At the very least, it was time to call a cab (although certainly not on the cracked plastic remains of his cell).

He searched the ground floor of the house for a landline, milling through pockets of heightened gossip, but couldn't even find a wall jack. As he passed from room to room, the crowds seemed to expand in size and volume, and a reasonable sense of claustrophobia began to creep into his nerves. Gradually he maneuvered toward—and then out—the front door.

His pal, the bald-pated gorilla who'd wrecked his cell phone, remained stationed there, and gave him a dirty look.

"Hi there," demurred Tom.

"Sorry about before," the gorilla replied. "Just doing what I get paid for."

"Me, too."

Tom ambled down toward the valet station. Surely one of them had to have a phone he could—

"Hey!" called the gorilla. "Is your name Tom Piper?"

Tom stopped, pivoted.

"Yes…"

The gorilla pointed at the earpiece. "The governor's been looking for you."

And so, before long, Tom was back in the study. Bob Kellerman was there. So was his communications director Kathryn Hightower. She looked as if she'd lived a year in the past two hours. Bob, though, remained in high spirits.

"I wanted to thank you, Special Agent Piper, for coming here tonight. And I wanted to apologize for the misconduct of some of my staff. And I wanted to tell you, here and now, that I will offer any support I can to help you find the man who is killing these innocent men and women. I hope what I said out there in that speech encourages him to stop. I bet all my political capital on the line for you just now."

"Mmm-hmm." Tom coughed into his fist. "Well, sir, about that…"

Bob suddenly let out a bellowing laugh.

Tom was confused.

Then he wasn't.

"You heard we caught him."

"About two minutes ago. It's all over the wires." Bob smirked. "Sorry, I couldn't help myself. I've just been on a high for the past half hour. I've wanted to give that speech my entire adult life, Tom. May I call you Tom?"

Bob offered him a gold-rimmed cigar. At first Tom shook his head, but the look of undistilled charisma in the governor's eyes—how could anyone say no to that? Cult of personality indeed. Kathryn excused herself to take a call, and the men sat back and enjoyed some world-class smokes.

"I can't fire Paul," said Bob. "He deserves it, but after the announcement I just made, any shift in my campaign staff would be seen as a sign of weakness and vulnerability. Now if you boys want to go after him with obstruction charges, I won't stand in your way. But I wanted to let you know where I stood. Integrity is important to me, Tom."

"Me, too, sir."

Bob exhaled gray. "What are you doing tomorrow, Tom?"

"Well…"

"Paul told you about my plan to overhaul the intelligence community. With the FBI and the CIA and the NSA and what have you, every agency tripping over the other for jurisdiction, it's alphabet soup in Washington and I want to get rid of the redundancy. How would you like to spend the morning with me and convince me otherwise? I have a scheduled stop on my way to New York City. Very low-key. I promise to keep an open mind. What do you say?"

What else was there to say? Tom said yes.

26

The campaign's scheduled stop on the way to New York City was at a two-story hunting shop called Nassau Firearms, located several miles outside Port Washington. The store was owned and operated by one Will Clay, age sixty-two. Will Clay wasn't a major contributor. He wasn't even a registered Democrat. Ostensibly the purpose of the visit was to demonstrate the governor's connection with all Americans, regardless of who they were, but the truth was…

"I just love guns," he said to Tom and they ascended the stairs to the shop's second floor. It was on the second floor of Nassau Firearms that Will Clay kept his renowned firing range, which was said to be the largest indoor range on Long Island. This was the shop's main attraction, and the real reason why Kellerman had insisted on stopping here on the way to New York City.

A padded door met them at the top of the stairs. Tom used the key the governor had rented to open it, and they trotted into the massive soundproofed room.

Targets—which varied in portrait from deer and elk and buffalo to a wide selection of featureless human shapes—could be flown back as far as 100 yards. Bob had rented them a pair of classic Smith & Wessons and each carried his steel-engraved weapon by its barrel.

As they set up at their stations and donned their protective goggles and plastic earmuffs, Bob elaborated.

"I was raised on guns. In the wintertime, we would drive up to Canada and hunt white-tailed deer. It's a magnificent animal. We shared a cabin with our cousins, who lived over in Windsor. They had a daughter about my age. Her name was Margaret. That's where I learned the essentials of healthy competition. Which is the topic of our discussion today, isn't it, Tom—the unhealthy, downright juvenile competition that exists between our country's intelligence communities."

Bob loaded his pistol. He would have preferred to have a rifle, like a Browning A-Bolt, but shoulder-arms were strictly forbidden at indoor shooting ranges. *C'est la guerre.*

"Like you said," replied Tom, loading his own pistol, "some competition is healthy. It inspires you to reach higher."

"It also inspires you to cripple the other guy."

They attached their deer targets to mechanical clips and with the slap of a button sent them back fifty yards. The back wall of the range, although solid cinder block, was mottled with erosion, reflecting years and years of missed shots.

Tom didn't intend to miss. He also didn't intend to

win his debate with Governor Kellerman. In truth, he agreed—for the most part—with the governor's diagnosis. The intelligence community *was* a sprawling bureaucratic mess. There were simply too many cooks in the kitchen.

After last night's invitation from the governor, Tom had wandered the party in search of Esme and Rafe, but they were nowhere to be found. He did finally find a landline, though, and secure a taxi to drop him off at his hotel.

It was around then that authorities had found the abandoned van, well past the Missouri-Kansas border. The FBI on scene contacted AD Trumbull, who immediately put a clamp on the operation. As far as the media knew, Henry Booth had been delivered to Leavenworth as scheduled.

AD Trumbull then put in a call to Tom's cell to relay the news about his team and about Galileo's disappearance, but the call went straight to voice mail. He tried several more times throughout the evening, but never reached him. Couldn't reach him. Broken cell phones didn't ring.

Tom woke up, showered, watched with amusement as a pop psychologist offered her insights on the nation's newest captured serial killer to the reporters of Fox News, and then at 9:00 a.m. he headed downstairs to meet the governor's entourage of stretched Lincolns for the trip to Nassau Firearms.

All in all, his life had taken a turn for the strange. He made a mental note to get his cell phone replaced as soon as they reached NYC, at the scheduled time of

1:00 p.m. He also needed to replace his dear motorcycle, but that would have to wait until he returned to the D.C. metro area. First, he had some alone time with the governor from Ohio…

Who turned out to be an excellent shot. Different areas on the targets were brocaded into circles, displaying scores for accuracy. When Bob tapped his retrieval button and his mock-deer flew back to greet him, five of his six shots had landed in the highest circle, and the sixth missed the bull's-eye by less than an inch, giving him a point total of a whopping ninety-one out of a hundred points.

Tom managed a sixty-three. He could almost hear his marksmanship instructor now, cackling off-color epithets in his honor.

"Tell you what," said Bob, with a wink. "First person to reach 500 gets to be president of the United States."

Down below, on the first floor, lurked Bob's contingent of security personnel. Additionally, Kathryn Hightower and Paul Ridgely had stuck around, as per the governor's request, rather than join the rest of the staff in New York.

He had matters to discuss with both.

Governor Kellerman had arrived at the store around 10:00 a.m. There he was greeted by Bill Clay; all sixteen of Bill Clay's relatives who lived in the area; every regular customer (who was still alive) who shopped at Bill Clay's store; and several locals who had never set foot in any gun shop, much less the giant one in their township, but were there to meet the famous man. Bill Clay minded these folk the least. They were the ones most likely to buy something useless and expensive, just to show off to Bob Kellerman. By 11:00 a.m., though, Bob had ascended the steps with that FBI agent, and the crowd had mostly dispersed, save for his sixty-nine-year-old wife, who was in the back totaling receipts. At the request of the governor's five bodyguards, Nassau Firearms was now officially closed. That was fine with Bill Clay. They had done a month's worth of sales in an hour.

Kathryn and Paul stood in the corner, near the orange vests.

"You would have done the same thing," he muttered to her.

They had been having the same conversation now for an hour.

"Withheld vital information? No, Paul, I wouldn't."

The bodyguards were stationed at various points through the floor. One actually remained outside, by the entrance. This was an ex-marine named Lisa Penny. The two chauffeurs had tried flirting with her, but she'd deflected their advances with nothing more than a raised eyebrow and a shake of the head. It was her responsibility to mind the door. She was the governor's first line of defense, and she took her job very seriously. So when an orange Chevy pickup dusted into the parking lot and a light-haired man in sunglasses ambled out, Lisa stood at the ready.

"Hey, there," he said. He spoke with a bit of a country drawl. His black T-shirt was untucked from his jeans. "I'm here to buy some ammo." He angled his head toward the two stretch Lincolns. "Is there a movie star or something in town?"

"I'm afraid the store is closed until 1:00 p.m." Lisa tried to catch his gaze, but he kept looking around at everything in sight but her. "If you would like, I've been given a list of similar stores in the area that may be able to help you out."

"Closed until one? Lady, this is America. You can't just pick and choose when you sell just because some big shot's needing an adjustment on his .30-.06. Next you'll be telling me which drinking fountain to use."

That last sentence he punctuated with a finger in her face.

"Sir, if you'll please—"

"No, I won't please." He punctuated again. "I know my rights." And again. "I came here to buy my ammunition and God damn it, I'm going to buy my ammunition." And again.

She stared down at his index finger. It would be so easy to break it in three places. She could say he tripped and fell. There were no witnesses. The chauffeurs had wandered down the road for some fried lunch.

But then another car pulled up, this time a white sedan, and her window of opportunity had passed. Out of the sedan emerged another man, in a polo shirt and khakis.

"Hope you're not wanting to buy anything here, fella," declared the finger-fiend.

The man in the khakis approached. He looked exhausted, but friendly.

"I'm sorry, sir, but the store is closed," Lisa said.

But he just continued on smiling.

* * *

For their fourth targets, Bob and Tom switched to the human shapes. The bull's-eyes here were, obviously, the foreheads and the upper left quadrant of the chest. They pounded their buttons and watched their paper men fly a hundred yards away.

In score, Bob was ahead 292-201.

"Did you always want to be president?" Tom asked casually. He was really warming up to the guy. Getting creamed at target practice had that kind of effect.

"I always wanted to be a fireman," replied Bob, loading his rifle.

"You are a fireman, aren't you?"

"I was a volunteer fireman for twelve years, but once I got elected governor, it was decided to be in the 'best interest of the state of Ohio' that I 'discontinue all risky activities.' There was even a motion on the floor of the state legislature, if you can believe it."

"Do you miss it?"

"Firefighting?" Bob took a long pause, then answered, "Every day, Tom."

They fired off their rounds at the paper men, which fluttered harmlessly with each bullet strike. Tom could see through his slightly foggy goggles that he'd done much better shooting at a human shape than he had with the deer. His score looked to be a respectable eighty-eight. Conversely, Bob only scored a seventy-five, and had aimed solely for his target's heart, not once trying for the head. There was meaning to be found in this, but Tom let it slide.

"How about you, Tom? Does a lawman like yourself have any regrets?"

"Mmm-hmm."

They unclipped their bullet-ridden paper targets and replaced them with a pair of unwounded twins.

"You going to tell me what they are?" prodded Bob.

Tom flashed him a mischievous grin. "Nope."

"Okay." The fresh targets made their hundred-yard journey. "But just for that, this round, I'm so going to kick your ass."

They raised their Smith & Wessons with near synchronicity and began shooting.

"Truth be told, I don't really care about guns. I just came by to meet Governor Kellerman." The sun was in his eyes, and his squinting bunched up his cheeks, making his sanguine grin even broader. "I read he was going to be here on his campaign Web site. Guess I got here too late, huh?"

Lisa smiled back at the tired man in the khakis. "I'm sorry."

"Story of my life," he replied.

They were about the same height, two attractive, athletic folk sharing a moment in the middle of April.

He turned to go, but then stopped. "Say, listen, can presidential candidates accept cash donations? It would really mean a lot if I knew I helped contribute, you know? I'm not a wealthy man, but I believe in a good cause when I see one. You don't have to tell him who I am. It's even better if you don't. Just make sure he knows there's one American out there who thinks he's doing a good job."

"A good job?" The man from the orange Chevy rolled his eyes. "He's closing off a legitimate place of business in our allegedly 'free country' just so he can get his elitist jollies."

"It's for security purposes, sir," answered Lisa curtly. "Perhaps you should leave. I hear the local authorities take trespassing charges very seriously."

The tired man in the khakis ignored their bickering, reached into his pocket, and took out his plump calfskin wallet, which was old and bent out of shape.

"How much do you think I should give?" he asked. "What's the right amount? A hundred dollars?"

He slipped a well-seasoned hundred-dollar bill out of his creaky wallet—and it fell almost immediately out of his hands to the grassy earth by Lisa's feet.

"Nice coordination, buddy," quipped the asshole behind him.

Lisa knelt down to pick up the hundred-dollar bill for him, and the man in the khakis brought his wallet down on top of her scalp with the full force of his weight. The wallet was thick and bent out of shape because it was stuffed with coins, and when it struck her scalp some of the coins spilled out and to the ground. Her blood soon joined them.

Still crouched, she gazed up at him, confused, even a little sad, and he brought the wallet down again against her face. It took two more blows before she was unconscious, and three more blows before he'd cracked her skull.

Then Galileo glanced over at the other guy, the guy in the hat, the guy who'd given Lisa such a hard time.

Finishing him off was a lot easier.

Galileo wasn't especially fond of such guerilla tactics. They were messy, and bordered on barbaric, but he naturally hadn't been allowed to bring a gun on the plane, so this method had to suffice for now. Also, this way created little noise, and didn't alert the guards inside the store, not just yet. He also wasn't concerned about the Lincolns' chauffeurs because they had gone down the road to get a bite to eat. In fact, he had waited for them to walk off before he'd parked his rental.

He removed Lisa Penny's sidearm from her shoulder holster. It was a Heckler & Koch USP. This was a good weapon, well-balanced, large trigger, rubber grip, short recoil. He would have preferred to have his M107 instead, but he would have preferred a lot of things to be different.

In no time at all, he had the two bodies in the trunk of his car. Their eyes stared up at him, but not accusingly. In fact, there was no emotion in them at all. These were pieces of meat.

He tugged on Lisa Penny's white earpiece and followed its cord to its power pack, tucked in a back pocket, and then followed a second cord to the small communication mic attached to her left wrist. With the apparatus in hand, Galileo slid the receiver into his own ear and listened for a few minutes, hoping the guards had left the frequency open and were idly chatting. From this he would have been able to estimate how many guards there were—but all he heard was silence.

No matter. He'd get them talking. He activated the

mic and rubbed it against his pant leg. The swishing sound echoed through his earpiece, magnified, almost resembling the crash of an ocean wave, and then came a voice:

"Lisa? Is that you? Over."

Galileo answered the request with another wipe of the mic along his khakis.

"What the hell is that?" asked a second guard. His question wasn't directed into the mic but was instead picked up as ambient noise. He must have been standing near the first guard. Galileo made a mental note: at least two guards inside the gun shop.

"Lisa?" This, again, from the first guard. Probably the leader. "Answer me. Over."

Fifteen seconds passed.

Finally: "I'm going to check it out," decided the leader.

Galileo cocked the H&K, left the trunk open, and waited for his quarry to emerge.

The final tally was this: Bob, 502 and Tom, 453.

Ever the sportsman, Bob offered his hand, which Tom gladly shook.

"Looks like your FBI is going to be getting a makeover," Bob said.

Tom shrugged. "I'm not sure if that's something I'll regret."

Bob smiled, then guffawed.

"I had a feeling," he said.

They both stared down that hundred-yard alley of their large soundproofed room. Just two men and their guns.

"One more?" offered Tom.

"You didn't even have to ask."

They mounted the paper men onto their clips and sent them to their places. They each only had five bullets left, so this round would be abbreviated, but some fun was better than no fun.

Bob glanced at Tom. "Ready?"

Tom donned his earmuffs. Bob donned his, and they took aim at their targets. Feet apart, hips at an angle, dominant hand forward. The proper stance for firing a handgun created a triangle. These were men who knew what they were doing.

Bob, who was closest to the door, thought he felt a breeze between shots one and two, but ignored it. The floor was ventilated, of course, to handle the discharges from the firearms, but there were no windows or cracks in the walls. The idea of a breeze was preposterous—and distracting. Bob intended to get a perfect score, and his first shot had been dead-center. If only his cousin Margaret could see him now.

He fired off two more rounds. One actually passed through the bullet hole left by another! He felt like Robin Hood. Let his pre-judgmental liberal base disapprove of his gun-love. He was about to get a perfect score, damn it. He was in the zone. So much so that he angled his barrel up and instead of the easier target of the chest, he aimed for the head. Because my platform will reach the American people in their hearts and their brains, he mused. The goofy thought stretched his lips in a smirk. He fingered the trigger and felt something hot touch the back of his head and he paused and he frowned and then the bullet from the H&K ripped through his skull and Bob died.

Tom, for his part, noticed Galileo approach out of his peripheral vision about half a second before the assassination occurred. He swung his Smith & Wesson around toward the sandy-haired man. Galileo glanced over at him and appeared confused. After all, what was Tom Piper doing here?

That confusion was all the opportunity Tom required. He shuttled past the obligatory demand of "Freeze!" and just fired away, two shots, to the killer's chest.

Click, click.

His Smith & Wesson was empty.

He'd fired his last bullet at the paper target.

Fuck.

Galileo raised his own pistol and Tom lunged forward, tackling the man to the soft floor. First step: disarm. Tom slapped the H&K out of Galileo's hands. It scuttled away, harmless. Galileo raised his left knee toward Tom's groin, but the FBI agent was well-accustomed to wrestling thugs and he used the weight of his own knee to keep Galileo's pinned to the ground. Second step: disable. Here, an amateur might resort to a fist-pummeling, but that risked at best bloody knuckles and at worst a broken hand so Tom chose to go a different route. He pressed his right elbow into Galileo's windpipe and waited for the son of a bitch to black out.

Meanwhile, Tom caught a glimpse of Bob Kellerman's body, crumpled in an undignified mess several feet away. Tom's heart keened for the man. He returned his attention to Galileo. This man who had killed Darcy

Parr, who had slaughtered countless men and women and even children, who had—

Wait. What the hell was Galileo doing here? Wasn't he supposed to be in custody? In that moment, Tom knew. He knew that Norm and Daryl and everyone else were dead. He knew that someone had probably tried to contact him on his cell phone.

He pressed harder onto Galileo's windpipe. If it snapped and the fucker died of asphyxiation, well, these things happened, didn't they? Tom poured his grief and wrath into his violence. He could hear Galileo's vague gasps of breath, but he didn't care. Someone needed to end him. And he was so intent on doing so that he failed to notice the heavy wallet in Galileo's hand until it smashed him in the left shoulder. His bad shoulder. The shoulder that had been shot back in February, at Baptist St. Anthony's in Amarillo. It had mended, sure, but it was still sensitive and when Galileo struck it with the full might of a desperate man, the pain resounded through him like sound waves from a tuning fork. He flinched—and Galileo squirmed out of his grip. Tom reached for the man's ankle, but Galileo was like a chased rabbit, too fast, too fast. Galileo went for his Heckler & Koch and Tom finally caught up with him and felt the bullets enter his chest and ignored them—he had a job to do, damn it—but then the world got so dark so quick, and cold, and quiet.

27

When they returned from the fundraiser, after they made sure Sophie was asleep and made sure Lester was preoccupied with the TV, Esme and Rafe retired to their bedroom and fucked like teenagers. Sheets were entangled. Alarm clocks were knocked to the carpet. Headboards were rattled.

The following morning, when Esme awoke, she was on the floor beside the alarm clock. Rafe was nearby, cocooned in their olive-colored comforter. She traced an index finger across the outline of his face. When she reached his lips, she could feel his breath exhale against her fingertip.

She brought her finger back, leaned across the carpet, and kissed him. His lips still tasted like Dom Perignon. She slid her left hand inside his comforter cocoon and against his smooth belly—and he awoke.

"Morning," she said.

He smiled, then grimaced, then frowned. "Where…?"

Befuddled, Rafe sat up and looked around.

"How did we get on the floor?"

"Gravity," Esme replied.

"Ah." He reached for the alarm clock and checked its results. "We've got five minutes."

Five minutes later, Esme wiped the fresh sweat from her forehead and watched her husband wobble into the shower. Between her still-mutinous backbone and her upsy-daisy equilibrium, she required the leverage of the bed to help stand up, but once vertical she quickly donned her pink bathrobe and went about her day. Her first stop was Sophie's bedroom. Unsurprisingly, her daughter was already awake, although still in bed, and was playing with a few of her dolls.

"Morning, peanut."

"Morning, Mommy!"

Esme climbed into her daughter's bed, and they spent the next ten minutes selecting the proper ensemble for Skipper to wear on her big date with SpongeBob SquarePants. Sophie herself was wearing her Bugs Bunny nightgown in honor of Easter, which was next week.

Soon they could smell the sweet aroma of Grandpa Lester's flapjacks, and Sophie scooted out of bed and down the stairs. Esme tried to keep up as fast as her back would allow, but by the time she reached the kitchen, her daughter was already sitting down beside a steaming plate of sugar-sprinkled fried batter.

"Need some tomato juice?" Lester asked Esme, which was his oh-so-clever way of asking if she had a hangover, but she just shook her head and sat beside her flapjack-inhaling daughter.

"Don't forget to breathe," recommended Esme.

Sophie took a deep breath, then launched back into some more.

By the time she was on her second plate, Rafe joined them, dressed for work. He had his specs on, and the blue of his irises appeared misty behind the glass lenses.

"Top of the morning to you, squirt," he said, and dove down to give his daughter a bear hug. He made his way to the fridge and poured himself a glass of tomato juice. Lester, still flapping those jacks, took note of his son's beverage and let loose a rubbery smirk.

It was Rafe's turn to drive Sophie to school, so while she scampered to her bedroom to change into her "daytime clothes," he took the time to click on the TV and catch up on the latest hoopla. Unsurprisingly, the top stories were Governor Kellerman's speech and the capture of Galileo in Kansas City. Few knew the two were related, but Rafe was one of those few. He glanced back at Esme, who was stuffing her face with Lester's cooking.

How had he forgotten how special his wife was? Never again.

He chugged down the remainder of his tomato juice, kissed his wife, shook hands with his old man (because that's what men do), and escorted his little blue-eyed angel out to the car. She was wearing her polka-dot dress today. He complimented her on it. He told her it looked resplendent. She complimented him on his tie. She told him it looked shiny.

Esme stood by the kitchen window and watched them leave. She felt like a wife again, and a mother....

"You going to get dressed today?" murmured Lester.
…and a daughter-in-law.

She wanted to remain in her bathrobe just to spite her
father-in-law, but mindful of the impression that sloth
might imprint on the old man, she wandered back to her
bedroom, enjoyed the massage of a very long shower, and
slipped into a casual white blouse and brown slacks. By
now it was almost 9:00 a.m. She absently wondered what
Tom was up to, how he'd made it home from the fundraiser (home for a field agent being a relative term). His
motorcycle was still parked wherever the valets had put
it. She and Rafe, in their impatient desire to rip each
other's clothes off, had forgotten it at Amy's mansion.
Esme made a mental note to ask Amy about it when she
showed up.

In the meanwhile, it was puzzle time. She booted up
the desktop and navigated to a Web site she'd recently
discovered which offered user-created Sudoku puzzles
which were sorted by difficulty level and, best of all,
timed. The clock factor turned a regular game into a
suspenseful race. Once completed, she could compare
her time with others who had worked the same puzzle.

As she surfed through the day's newest offerings,
her news feed application loaded along the bottom of
the browser window. Just as with the TV, all the online
folk seemed to concentrate on was, as they so suc-
cinctly put it, "the serial killer" or "the atheist
nominee." There was also, it appeared, a genocide oc-
curring in one of the former Soviet republics, but hardly
anyone was blogging about *that*. She loaded up the
Beta Band on her iPod and attacked one of the puzzles

labeled Impossible. Nothing like starting the day with a challenge.

By noontime, after a few coffee breaks, a long argument with Lester about the merits of having Sophie attend sleep-away camp this summer, and a therapeutic walk up and down the street to strengthen her leg muscles, she was on her sixth puzzle. Her iPod growled out Irish punk rock courtesy of the Stiff Little Fingers. Her best time so far on an "impossible" puzzle had been eight minutes, forty-eight seconds. She aimed to beat that. She popped the joints in her neck, stretched her fingers, and, while the puzzle was loading, glanced down halfheartedly at the news ticker.

BREAKING NEWS….Democratic nominee Bob Kellerman shot at firing range in LI…

Esme blinked. Shot at a firing range? It sounded like the punch line to a bad joke. She clicked on the ticker and the full article sprang to life and the bad joke transmogrified into a horrific nightmare.

…one bullet to the head…

…survived by a wife, Betsy, and two children…

…scheduled stop at a local business called Nassau Firearms…

Esme wiped at her eyes. Was she crying? Yes. She hardly knew the man, but had invested so much time in the past month into his campaign, and upon meeting him had been so impressed by his dignity and his integrity, and now, some religious extremist offended by his speech had gunned the man down. She shook her head in disgust, and read the rest of the article.

Other confirmed casualties in the attack include the

owner of the store, Will Clay, 62; his wife Emily, 69; Kathryn Hightower, 40, who served as Governor Kellerman's communications director; several members of the governor's security detail: Devon Smith, 32; Lisa Penny, 28...

She jumped to the next paragraph.

Two victims remain in critical condition and were rushed to nearby Glen Cove Hospital. These are Paul Ridgely, 31, campaign manager for Governor Keller- man, and Tom Piper, 56, a special agent with the Federal Bureau of—

Esme didn't remember reading the rest of the article. She didn't remember going on Google to find the address of Glen Cove Hospital or putting on her shoes or telling Lester she was leaving or even getting into her Prius. One moment she was at her computer and the next she was on the Long Island Expressway, heading west, at ninety miles per hour.

No one pulled her over. All local law enforcement was gathered outside Port Washington, at a local business called Nassau Firearms. She cruised to the hospital in silence. The stereo remained off.

What was Tom doing there? He didn't have a mo- torcycle so he hitched a ride with the future president of the United States? How had anyone been able to get past an entire security detail and Tom? Her mind briefly flitted to Galileo, but no, he was locked away in Middle America. So it found solace in Tom. She would get to the hospital and he would be in surgery and it would be hours and hours but then the doctor would come out and tell her he wasn't out of the woods and that he couldn't see any visitors so she would have to sneak in to see him, as he had come to see her, and he would be lying there in his bed as she had been lying in hers and she would sit beside him and he would look terrible but alive and they would trade quips, because that was how they dealt with tragedy, they would trade quips, and embedded in the quips would be granules of wisdom, and they would have a heart-to-heart, a real heart-to-heart, and she would tell him what he meant to her, and he would tell her what she meant to him, and they would work together to find this assassin, whoever he may be, and Esme careened into the hospital parking lot and sprinted into an entanglement of policemen and someone recognized her, that asshole Pamela Gould from the Long Island bureau, but she let her through the entanglement and into an alcove full of chairs and magazines and it was there and then that Esme knew that Tom was not going to make it.

"It was Galileo," rasped Trumbull.

Esme sipped at her cold coffee.

To his credit, Trumbull came to the hospital first, before heading out to the crime scene. He actually was about to board a government plane to the crime scene in Kansas when he got the news about the massacre on Long Island. He instructed the pilot to alter his flight plan, and soon they were airborne, flying not over the Great Plains but over the great Atlantic. When he arrived at Glen Cove Hospital, the media hubbub had barely subsided; after all, it was here that the governor's body had been brought. Trumbull took a hit from his oxygen tank, which he carried now with him wherever he went, and gruffed his way through the mob. None of the reporters harassed him. To them, he was just another dying old man going in for a checkup.

He found Esme in that same alcove. Pamela Gould was coordinating the efforts at Nassau Firearms. Esme was alone, and near catatonic. He sat beside her. They exchanged pleasantries (or a tragic facsimile thereof). And then Trumbull hit her with his bombshell about Galileo. He told her about the van, and the cover-up. He told her about his efforts to contact Tom. He told her what he knew—so he could tell her what he now wanted.

But she wasn't emotionally ready for that. Not yet.

"I saw Tom," she said.

Trumbull raised a liver-mottled hand to his lip to wipe away some loose saliva. "Oh?"

"Galileo shot him in the chest."

Trumbull nodded. He'd read the report.

"Not in the head," Esme added, pointedly.

"Our boy put up a fight. Galileo got desperate, and took the easier shot." He coughed wetly into his fist. "Yes, he did."

"He didn't have his motorcycle," muttered Esme. "Rafe took it from him last night in a…"

"I don't know if I follow what…"

She gazed up at him. Her eyes were glassy, as if her soul had gone far, far away. "If he had his motorcycle, he wouldn't have needed a ride with Bob Kellerman. He wouldn't have been there at the scene…."

"We don't know yet why he was there," Trumbull

replied. "But we'll piece it all together." Which provided the perfect segue to his request. He opened his mouth to speak and—

"Esme!"

Her overweight professor husband bounded into the alcove and into her embrace. Trumbull shifted in his seat and watched her cry onto his shoulder. He was never one for public displays of affection, even when appropriate.

So he decided to make their public display a private one. "I'll be right back," he muttered, and lolled toward the restroom. Halfway there, he stopped, and turned. "Don't go anywhere, please, Special Agent—forgive me—Mrs. Stuart. I need to talk to you about something."

Once he was gone, Rafe took his seat.

"I'm so sorry," he said. Her hands were in his. "I've been in class and in meetings, but as soon as I heard, I swear, I got in my car and hightailed it as fast as I could, except traffic was insane. I mean, I've never seen traffic like this, not even on the Taconic. The police had set up barricades and were searching every car on the highway in either direction. By the time I got to the house, Dad told me you were here. I should've called, but in all the chaos I must have left my cell in my office. He picked up Sophie from school."

"Sophie…oh, God…"

"She knows something's wrong, but he didn't tell her what it was, and he's not letting her watch the TV. She's too young to be exposed to anything like this. We're all too young to be exposed to anything like this."

He held her again. He could feel the right shoulder of his shirt becoming moist with her tears. He let her cry. He didn't know what else he could do—what could he possibly do at a time like this but be with her—so that's what he did. For his own part, his feelings were definitely muddled. There was shock, of course, and bewilderment, and anger, anger at whoever committed this horrible crime. And yet…deep down…though perhaps not that deep…some part of him had learned that Tom Piper was in critical condition and was…not happy but…relieved. Did that make him a bad person? Did that make him selfish? These were questions best ignored, for the time being.

"Rafe…" she said, and caressed his adorably soft cheekbones.

"Come on. Let's go home."

He got up.

She didn't.

"What is it?" he asked. And maybe he knew what was coming. Maybe he knew what she was going to say. He wasn't a fool. "What is it, Esme?"

"Trumbull's going to ask me to help. He thinks I don't know what he's thinking, but I do. I always did. That's what he needs to talk to me about."

"Help? With what?"

"Rafe…"

He sat back down. "We've had this argument already. You lost, Esme, remember?"

"Things are different now…."

"Yes, you said that too. You said that to me a few weeks ago. When you finally were able to get off the couch. After almost dying. 'Things will be different now,' you said. Things were falling apart between us but you made everything right. You did it. And now you want to, what, throw all of that away?"

"It's not that simple."

"It's always been that simple! Jesus Christ, even with one foot in the grave, I'm still battling Tom Piper for your attention."

And she slapped him across those adorable soft cheekbones she had caressed only minutes earlier. He winced, but didn't apologize.

"You're either one thing or you're something else. Black or white. You want to make your choice? Make your choice. Right here. Because I can't keep doing this, Esme. It's not fair to us and it's not fair to Sophie."

She shook her head. She wasn't upset with him. She was, simply, sad.

Finally, she asked: "Do you love me?"

"What kind of question is that?"

"It's your favorite kind. It's black or white. Do you love me?"

"Of course," he replied.

"Why?"

"What is this? Esme, if I didn't love you…"

"When we met, what was I doing for a living?"

"Is this a test?"

"Sure. It's a test. What was my job when we met?"

"You worked for the FBI."

"Did I enjoy my job?"

"I don't know…."

"Yes, you do."

Rafe shrugged. "Yeah, I guess you enjoyed your job."

"Yes, I did. And then we met and I fell head-over-heels in love with you. I think if you'd asked me to fly to the moon, if you told me that would make you happy, I would have done it. But you didn't ask me to fly to the moon. You just asked me to quit my job."

"So we could start a family—which you said you wanted."

"But here's what I'm getting at, I guess, Rafe. Here's what's bothering me. You knew I loved my job. You knew I was good at it and that it was important. If you care for someone, why would you ask them to give up something like that?"

"Esme, we both made sacrifices…."

"Oh? What have you sacrificed?"

She looked him square in the face. Her brown irises had regained their intimidating potency. His jaw un-latched. Words tumbled down the tip of his tongue—and stayed there.

What had he sacrificed?

"Just because…I mean…it's not necessary for…"

She cocked an eyebrow, waited.

"You quit your job so we could start a family."

"There are families in Washington D.C. Good neigh-borhoods. Dozens of colleges. You could have gotten a teaching job at any of them, but you didn't even apply. I quit my job because you asked me to. We both know that's true. So when I tell you, now, that I need to do this, I'm making that decision as a wife, a mother, and an adult, and you need to swallow your pride and shut the fuck up."

28

Henry Booth had gone to ground. That much was obvious.

Twelve hours after the murders at Nassau Firearms, police checkpoints set up along all major highways and bridges across Long Island and New York City had only resulted in a nervous and/or irate civilian population. There was no sign of the killer, but anyone who had followed the case this far wasn't particularly surprised by this latest lack of development, and a cursory glance at Nassau Firearms' inventory confirmed their worst suspicions. No weapon was missing, not a rifle, not a shotgun, not even a box of shells, and the Heckler & Koch used to perpetrate these acts had been left on the countertop. Henry Booth didn't need it anymore. He was finished with his spree, and now, like any good operative at the end of an assignment, he had disappeared into the ether. Henry Booth. Esme insisted on referring to him by that name, not Galileo. Henry Booth was the name of a man, and men were fallible. Men got caught.

Esme dialed up the Clash's apocalyptic *London Calling* on her iPod and walked the crime scene. Will Clay's two-story store was made mostly of shaved maple. This created a homey rustic ambience, but it also made the invasion of police tape and chalk outlines that much more disconcerting and garish. Despite the gun paraphernalia on the walls, the magazines, despite everything in the store that pointed innately toward violence, what had happened here felt like a violation.

Esme and the forensics experts had pieced together a chronology, and it went something like this:

1. The chauffeurs paid their bill at the Shoney's down the road at, according to their receipts, 11:31 a.m. They then sat down to eat, and walked back to the store, arriving there at 12:01 p.m. This was confirmed by the 911 phone records. It was Bella McDeere, one of the chauffeurs, who called it in. The other chauffeur, Gary Swingole, had a thing about blood and had passed out.

2. As the chauffeurs claimed in their statements that, on their walk back to Nassau Firearms, they didn't see anyone drive off, Henry Booth must have shown up around 11:30 a.m., committed the killings, and driven away by 11:55 a.m. at the latest. In the span of twenty-five minutes, he murdered ten people. Aside from Tom, Paul Ridgely was the sole survivor, and he was being kept alive only by a combination of a ventilator,

a defibrillator and his wife's philosophical opposition to euthanasia.

3. The bodies of Lisa Penny, one of Kellerman's
bodyguards, and Kyle Gooden, a ne'er-do-
well passerby who was apparently in the
wrong place at the wrong time, were discovered in the back of the store. They appeared to
have been carried there, and preliminary lab
work showed the presence of fibers on them
consistent with the interior of a car. This contrasted with the bodies of two of the other
guards, which were found in the parking lot,
and the blood spatter was consistent where
they were found. Another glaring inconsis-
tency: both Lisa and Kyle were bludgeoned to
death, while the two bodyguards in the parking lot and the one inside the store had been
shot.

4. This suggested to Esme that Lisa and Kyle
were struck first and hidden in a car, perhaps
the backseat or the trunk. Henry probably used
some kind of homemade club to take them out
quietly. But why not just pick them off from
afar? After all, that was his modus operandi.
Why? Because to get from Kansas to New
York overnight, he must have flown, and he
wouldn't have been allowed to bring anything
even resembling a rifle on the plane.

Esme stopped, frowned. Henry had flown. Something was niggling her about that. She filed away her

unfocused suspicions and walked up to the front counter.

5. But why stuff their bodies in the car if he was just going to dump them behind the store? The answer stared her in the face. Henry was a control freak. He would want his targets to be exactly where he wanted them when he took aim. He lured them out to the car. Maybe he deliberately left the trunk open to make it look suspicious. The guards approached the car. They found the bodies. And Henry took advantage of their momentary shock to nail them. With one guard left inside, he proceeded into Nassau Firearms, took out the guard, then Will Clay, then his wife, whose body was found by the door to the back room. The wife must have heard the gunshots and come out to investigate. Then Henry had ascended the stairs to the second floor.

Esme, too, ascended the stairs to the second floor. The maplewood creaked so loudly underneath her feet that she could hear it over her rock music. But Bob Kellerman and Tom Piper hadn't heard the gunshots or the creaking stairs. Why? She flicked on the light switch and revealed the obvious. The firing range was soundproofed. She felt the punctuated padding on the walls. Then she saw the two outlines on the floor. The white tape had caked over with dried blood. One of these outlines belonged to Tom. Her eyes flitted from the outlines to the targets dangling 100 yards away, then back again. The similarities sent a chill down her spine.

6. Henry shot Kellerman first. Not only was he closest to the door, but his body didn't show signs of struggle. Tom's did. Henry shot Kellerman first, then Tom reacted and the struggle commenced. According to the hospital reports, Tom sustained severe contusions to his left shoulder. He also had some burst capillaries in his hand, but no bruising on his knuckles or his palm. Tom didn't punch Henry, although he may have kicked him. The burst capillaries suggested that Tom had slapped something hard, perhaps a gun or a wall or even maybe Henry's skull. Then came the two shots to the chest. One nicked his right coronary artery and the other lodged itself in his aorta. The doctors treated the artery first. When she left the hospital, they had moved on to the aorta. But he wasn't a young man….

Esme sat down on the mat, beside the outline of his body. She pressed Pause on her iPod, and traced the tape with her fingertips. So many victims over so many years. Tom spoke for those who had been silenced and avenged their untimely deaths, and now he'd become one of them. If there was a Heaven, surely he would go there….

But Esme's own conclusions about the existence of an afterlife were at best mixed. Did she believe in God?

Yes. Some power must have created the universe. Science and math were too beautiful to be an accident. But the existence of, for lack of a better word, God, did not necessitate the existence of an afterlife. The wellspring of Heaven was hope, and hoping, as Esme sorely knew, rarely made anything so.

Plus she had her own abandonment issues to work out, and oh, my, were they in full force today. There were her own parents, of course, but now on top of that there was the probable departure of her surrogate father, Tom Piper, not to mention whatever was going on between her and Rafe. Maybe they needed a vacation, just the two of them. When all this was over, she would use the money the FBI was paying her to surprise him with a trip to Spain or Costa Rica or Easter Island. Anywhere but here, just the two of them. They would get away from it all and talk—really talk. No more barbs or soliloquies but actual conversation. She had her own credit card, so she could book everything online and it would be a surprise and—

Wait.

Her spider-sense, niggling before, went into overdrive. She got up off the floor and bounded down the stairs. Her file was still on the countertop. She flipped through the timeline, then flipped through it again.

There it was.

She took out her cell and placed a call to AD Trumbull and relayed to him the mistake Henry Booth had made—the mistake she'd just now discovered, hidden in plain sight—and how they were going to use it to ensnare him.

* * *

It's not that he had had a choice. Carelessness out of necessity isn't really carelessness at all. He had been in Kansas and needed to get to New York. He needed to board the next flight into Islip or LaGuardia or wherever and he needed to do it now.

"In the past he probably traveled by car," said Esme, "but now he had no choice. And airlines only accept credit cards."

She was making her pitch before Karl Ziegler, bureau chief for the Manhattan field office of the FBI and de facto foreman in charge of the new shootings; despite the fact they occurred in Nassau County, the resident office in Nassau was technically a substation to the Manhattan field office—and Karl Ziegler wasn't one for acquiescence. And although AD Trumbull had the higher pay grade, this was Ziegler's jurisdiction, and Esme required his approval before any new operation was employed. Ziegler, however, was busy with the mayor (who was a second cousin) at an evening function, and so she had to schedule an appointment for later that night. This gave Esme time to increase the document density of her file. After paying twenty dollars for a parking spot on Broadway, she carried the now-thick folder close to her chest and met him and the assistant director on the eleventh floor of Jacob Javits Federal Office Building, a skyscraper which resembled nothing less than a giant cheese grater.

Ziegler offered her an egg roll. It was 10:12 p.m., which from the looks of it meant dinnertime to the swarthy man behind the desk.

She handed him the manifest for Midwest Flight 28 out of MCI, the medium-sized airport which served the greater Kansas City region. According to the manifest, Flight 28 had departed MCI on April 12 at 11:11 p.m. and had landed at LGA at 2:23 a.m.

"This was the only flight Henry Booth could have been on for this morning's chronology to make any sense."

"How can you be sure?" asked Ziegler, between forkfuls of soy-soaked noodles.

"MCI was the closest airport to where the police found the van, and by the time Henry Booth would have arrived there, Flight 28 was the only available plane left to make the trip to New York City."

"But how could he have known that? Are you implying that Henry Booth had every flight schedule in the country committed to memory?"

"Among the personal possessions found on him during his arrest in Kansas City was a BlackBerry. None of these possessions were found when the police searched the van last night."

"So he used the BlackBerry to book the flight."

Esme brought up page two of the manifest. This was a list of the flight's eighty-two passengers.

"Henry Booth's name isn't there," the bureau chief chided.

"He's not a moron," answered Esme, implying with her tone that the bureau chief was. "Henry Booth wouldn't use a credit card in his own name. But I promise you—one of these passengers is Henry Booth."

"Mrs. Stuart," Ziegler's voice filled his office, as did the fried tang of his Cantonese cuisine. "While I'll agree with your hypothesis, I don't grasp its relevance. Plainly, how can we use this information after the fact?"

Esme glanced over at AD Trumbull, but the old man had retreated to his oxygen. He was here as a courtesy. It was obvious he longed to be anywhere but. Not too long ago he had been a robust, intimidating figure… however, not too long ago she had been a brazen young thing and Trumbull had almost fired her on the spot for, among other things, insubordination had Tom not backed her up and saved her ass.

Tom.

She brought her attention back to her file, and handed Ziegler another page. This was a list of twenty-one names.

"These are the passengers on Flight 28 who rented a car once arriving at the airport. We know because of the fibers found on both Lisa Penny and Kyle Gooden that Henry rented a GM vehicle manufactured after 2001."

She loaded up another page. Now there were four names, two men and two women. All had rented a GM vehicle the previous night.

"We contacted, verified their stories. All except one." She pointed to the last name on the list: Daniel Wise. "The phone number he gave when he booked his flight went straight to anonymous voice mail. The phone number attached to his credit card application went straight to anonymous voice mail. Daniel Wise is Henry Booth."

"That doesn't answer my question." Ziegler wiped his chin with a moist towelette. "How is any of this useful?"

"Because," said Esme, "at 6:12 p.m., about, oh, four hours ago now, 'Daniel Wise' bought an SRO ticket for tonight's performance of *The Phantom of the Opera,* which I believe is in its second act right about now. It's been a while since I saw it."

Ziegler's mouth fell open. So did Trumbull's—in a triumphant grin. Esme watched them both with granite satisfaction. It felt so good to be right.

"Jesus Christ," the bureau chief muttered, then turned to the wizened assistant director. "You knew this?"

Trumbull shrugged. "You called turf."

"You son of a bitch…."

Ziegler went for his phone.

"Nevertheless," continued Trumbull, "I've already taken the liberty of stationing several of our people in the lobby and outside every exit. They're low profile but they're there."

"Do we have a confirmed sighting of Booth himself?"

"It's SRO, so he could be anywhere in the theater. And he's more than likely disguised. But he's there."

"So he kills almost a dozen people and goes to see a Broadway show?"

"It's called 'hiding in plain sight.' And besides…it's a very good show."

She traded glances with Trumbull. She couldn't tell if he was wheezing or giggling. Possibly both.

Ziegler turned to the AD. "Who's the agent in charge at the scene?"

"Pamela Gould," replied Trumbull. "And if you take any of this out on her, Karl, I'll bury you. She did the right thing following this directive."

"It should've come out of this office."

"You were busy schmoozing, Karl. Make this right. Do your job."

Ziegler glared bloody daggers at Trumbull, then picked up the phone and took control of the operation. Soon they were out the door and heading uptown in the back of a Cadillac. Ziegler's driver was an attractive young agent with platinum-blond hair. Esme wondered if she had lobbied to be the field director's chauffeur or if this was some kind of punishment she had to endure as a woman in the boys' club of the FBI.

Nevertheless, it was exciting to be here again, part of the chase, close to the end. If only she'd been able to convey to Rafe the thrill of it all. No, that probably would have backfired. He would have chided her that if it was thrills she was after, Coney Island was just a train ride away. How could she possibly tell him that this wasn't merely an adrenaline rush? This was emotional and mental and even perhaps spiritual. It was that extraordinary, extraordinarily rare feeling of knowing you're in the right place at the right time and—

Her phone vibrated. She glanced at Caller ID. Speak of the devil. Ziegler gave her a nasty look, so she turned her back to him, faced the tinted window, and pressed TALK.

"Hi, Rafe," she said.

"This isn't Rafe," replied Galileo.

29

After their verbal fracas at the hospital, Rafe drove back to Oyster Bay—by way of Laney's Pub. It was a small dive, equal parts dingy bar and second-rate coffeehouse, and was frequented mostly by upperclassmen from his college. He ordered a Coors from the mustachioed bartender (who may or may not have taken one of Rafe's cultural studies seminars) and sipped his way past the rayon divans to the pool tables in the back. As he expected, Hal Kingston was there, just back from his sabbatical and currently hustling coeds for their tuition money (and, often, their virginity). Hal spotted Rafe and raised his own tall-neck bottle in welcome.

"Professor Stuart," he announced, "what a treat!"

Hal Kingston was the epitome of an intellectual Casanova. He used his considerable IQ for the dual masters of charm and woo, and it was only his talent in the former that kept him from being kicked off the faculty due to the latter. Sooner or later, though—and probably sooner—he would run afoul of some administrator he couldn't dazzle, and his good time would cease. And Hal Kingston behaved as if each night was that last night.

Here was a man for whom the word *sacrifice* had no meaning whatsoever. Rafe smiled, gave his colleague a warm embrace, and waited out the rest of his current game until they could be alone.

Hal slipped the phone number of his latest conquest into the back pocket of his Levi's and racked up the billiard balls.

"Haven't seen you here in a while," he said.

"A month," replied Rafe. He chalked the tip of his cue stick.

"So what brings you back? Got thirsty for some action? Or just got thirsty?"

They went head-to-head. Hal got solids and Rafe got stripes. It was a close game, but in the end, it was Hal who sank the 8-ball for the victory. They discussed women and cocktails and the Mets' repugnant pitching staff, and through it all Hal made no mention, nor even a casual allusion, to slain governors, no mention of serial killers on the loose.

Rafe wanted to hug him again, just for that. Instead, he bought him another round. They were on their fourth beers by the time they got to their third game.

"Do you ever think about responsibility?" Rafe asked him, as he knelt beside the table to judge the angles on a particular bank shot.

"Not if I can help it!"

Rafe smiled, nodded. "No, I'm serious. I don't mean responsibility to your job or to your students. I mean, just, you know, your responsibilities as an adult man in this society."

"Well," Hal answered, "that's implying society has a sense of responsibility. And it doesn't. It has a sense of entitlement, but responsibility went out the window with the advent of the hippies. Thank God. What's on your mind, buddy?"

Rafe shrugged. He didn't want to break the mood by getting too serious. Instead, he leaned down, aimed his stick, and shot the blue-chalked cue ball against the wall of the table. It bounced away at a right angle and headed straight toward the 3-ball…and struck it…and Newtonian physics sent the 3-ball rolling toward the corner pocket.

"Nice," said Hal.

Rafe walked around the table to find his next shot.

"But responsibility's a funny thing," Hal added. "We rely on other people—our parents, our civil servants, our leaders—to do the right thing so we won't have to, and when they don't, we get all crazy and start pointing fingers. I'm a lush and a libertine and a bit of a prick, but I know who I am. The world needs people like me so there can be people like you."

Rafe raised an eyebrow. "People like me?"

"The 'upstanding citizens.' You all make me want to spit blue vomit, but I love you just the same. Unless you get this next shot. Then so help me I'll stuff this cue stick so far up your ass…"

Rafe got the shot, and won the game.

"Another?" he asked, after emptying his bottle.

Hal slipped the piece of paper from his back pocket

and waved it. They hugged goodbye, and Rafe paid his tab, still not certain if the bartender was a former student or just resembled a former student. At a certain age, and Rafe was chagrined to discover that age to be thirty-eight, the people whose names and faces he actually remembered became catalogued into Family (always remembered), Friends (sometimes remembered), and Everyone else (rarely remembered). Eventually, if he lived to be old enough, he'd forget everybody, even Sophie and Esme.

His heart lurched at the thought. Maybe it was the combination of beer and frivolity. Maybe it was an aftershock from his argument with his wife. But he suddenly needed, very badly, to hear her voice. He patted himself for his cell phone, but then remembered that in his haste to get to the hospital, he'd left it in his office. Already his mind was going. He crawled into his car and motored home. By the time he pulled into the garage, it was almost ten o'clock.

Esme's car wasn't there.

No, he told himself, it wouldn't be. She was out saving the world. He was here.

Had she been right? Surely what she was doing now served a good purpose. Galileo needed to be stopped. He knew that. And just because his mind prioritized his memory by family, friends, and everyone else, that didn't disqualify everyone else from significance. Civic duty existed. If anything, in specifically targeting policemen and firemen and teachers, Galileo had highlighted the unappreciated importance of civil service. How could he fault his own wife for this? There had to be a point where your community outweighed your family. Soldiers went off to war. Was this a negligent choice? Was it selfish? No.

He opened the driver's side door and his cell phone tumbled out to the cement floor. It had been in his car all along. It must have fallen out of his pocket. It wasn't the first time that had happened, nor would it be the last. Shaking his head at his own foolishness, he picked the phone back up and slipped it back into his pocket. His balance was a little wobbly, but his head was clear. He would kiss his daughter good-night, and then he would call his wife. And apologize.

His father was sitting on the living room sofa, asleep in front of a Discovery Channel program on shark attacks. The narrator's enthusiasm intermingled with Lester's throaty snores. A half-empty bowl of popcorn lay on the cushion next to him. Rafe grabbed a handful and quietly loped up the stairs to the second floor. He relied on the banister to steady his balance, but made it to the top without stumbling.

Sophie was soundlessly asleep in her bed, Bugs Bunny clutched to her chin. Rafe gently removed Bugs, lest the stuffed animal upset her breathing, and instead placed him beside her cheek.

"Good night, angel," he whispered, and kissed his daughter on her scalp. She didn't stir. He paused, then kissed Bugs good-night too. The things we take for granted, he mused, and padded down the corridor to his bedroom. He flicked on the light switch and removed his cell phone from his pocket. Before dialing his wife, though, he needed some fresh air. He turned to unlatch the window—but it was already open. A cool April breeze cavorted through what was left of his hair.

"Hello," said a middle-aged man in a yellow Polo shirt. He was standing by the bedroom door, and he was holding a large revolver.

Instinctively, Rafe tried to rush past him, but Galileo easily blocked his path and smacked him in the chin with a quick jab of his palm. Rafe wobbled back. He tasted copper. He had bit down on his tongue and his mouth was filling with blood.

"Please," said Galileo, "may I have your phone?"

Rafe spat out a tablespoon of blood.

"I had to kill a cop to get this gun. I didn't want to do that. I wanted to fade away, but your wife forced my hand. But I'm confident she'll be able to help me out. Now give me your phone or I'll have to wake up your daughter."

Rafe gave him the cell phone.

Galileo searched it for Esme's number, and dialed. He held the phone to his ear.

"This isn't Rafe," he said.

"It's time for you to come home," he said.

"Tell anyone what you're doing or why and in several days you'll be attending your family's funeral," he said.

He handed the phone back to Rafe.

"Thank you," he said.

Esme came in through the garage door. The first thing she noticed was how dim the living room was. All the blinds and shades were drawn, blocking out the moonlight, and only the one kitchen light—in all its sixty-watt glory—was on. Lester, Rafe and Sophie were seated, hand in hand in hand, on the couch. Sophie's cheeks were red. She had been crying.

"Hello, Esmeralda," said Galileo. He stood behind the couch, in the center of the floor. He held a .44 Colt revolver, and had the barrel aimed in perfect alignment with her right-now-overactive frontal lobe.

"How did you know where I lived? My name wasn't on the list they found in San Francisco."

"Just because I didn't include it, that doesn't mean I didn't have it. From what I can gather, your address and social security number were uploaded about five hours before I accessed the database back in Amarillo. So you could get paid, I would imagine."

Esme felt her veins freeze over. She remained near the door, but her gaze darted back to her family. Rafe broke their daisy chain and hand-holding to dab a white wash towel to his mouth. There was blood on the towel. Their eyes met. She saw so much conflicting emotion in his stare—so much that she couldn't discern most of it.

Sophie appeared uninjured. Thank heaven for small miracles. She sat with her legs folded under her, with her Bugs Bunny nightgown draped over her knees.

She was terrified.

Lester, on the other hand, blamed her. That much was obvious from the hostility he projected at her through his lined face and dark eyes. Esme wondered if he had the choice, who would he take down first, the man with the loaded revolver or the meddling wife of his only son.

Then she looked to Galileo.

"While we were waiting for you to arrive," he said, "I was schooling your daughter about the man whose name I took as my symbol. She had never heard of him."

"She's six years old."

"Is six too young to know the truth? Is four? Why do we teach children illusions at all? Believing in Santa Claus never helped anyone grow up to be great. Believing in Santa Claus only helps people grow up to be disillusioned, wishing the world were the fairy tale they once thought it was. It's bad parenting."

"Have many kids do you have, Henry?"

"Galileo Galilei knew how unpopular the truth was. He knew the dangers involved, but he spoke it anyway because he knew that the truth was the only God worth worshipping. And his truth helped dismantle a thousand years of clerical tyranny."

"Actually," said Rafe, "that's not what happened…."

Galileo cocked his head. "Excuse me?"

"It's a little-known fact, but, well, those are my favorite kind." He offered a quick glance to his wife. Did she have something up her sleeve? Yes, she did. Good. He returned his attention to the carpet. "Galileo Galilei was actually very religious. When he saw the rings of Saturn through his telescope, when he became the first man in history to truly understand how the solar system moved, it confirmed his faith in God."

"That's ridiculous."

"Well, no, not really. Because the universe he beheld was beautiful and perfect. That just underlined for him the idea that a Supreme Maker must have had a hand in its crafting. The Earth may not have revolved around the sun, as Church dogma believed, as Aristotle and Ptolemy believed, but there was no doubt in his mind that everything in its infinite wonder was a product of God."

"And for all that his beloved Church tortured him, forced him to publicly recant, and then locked him under house arrest for the rest of his life. Religion is the enemy of progress. Genetic engineers are hampered in our country from curing cancer because of ignorance preached from the pulpit, and our place in the twenty-first-century will become more and more irrelevant. Do *you* believe in God, Mr. Stuart?"

"Yes. I do."

"Then I think you're about to be disappointed."

He placed the revolver barrel against the back of Rafe's head and cocked the hammer.

"Wait!" cried Esme.

Galileo looked up at her.

"If you wanted to kill them, Henry, they'd already be dead. Tell me why you're here."

"I'm here because you forced me to come here. I'm here because you had the FBI run a check on my credit card. You don't think I know how to check incoming calls? I'm here because I've run out of options and need some assistance in avoiding capture. It's time for you to use your commendable skills to help me."

Esme took a deep breath. She still hadn't moved from the welcome mat by the door to the garage. She still had her coat on.

"Time is a bit of an issue," added Galileo. "So what do you say?"

She took off her coat—slowly, so as not to startle the man with the gun—and hung it up on its hook.

"I don't know what you expect me to do," she said. "I'm not a magician."

"Don't underestimate your talents." He moved the gun barrel to Sophie's head. "And don't underestimate mine. I've shot children before."

"Mommy…"

Esme locked eyes with her daughter. "Everything's going to be okay. I promise."

"Right," said Galileo. "Now keep your promise."

Esme hesitated, then nodded. "There's a hole in our security. It occurred to me this afternoon. I thought you'd exploited it, but it's really only something you'd know if you worked for the FBI." She indicated her computer, asleep as it was on her desk, hidden in deep shadows imbued by its nearest window's closed curtains. "May I?"

"What do you need from that?"

"What I need is to check to make sure the hole still exists. I'll just need to access a traffic report. It's right on the home page for the *New York Times*. You can stand over my shoulder and watch me if you want."

He considered her offer, then, with the brush of a hand, indicated his acquiescence. She quickly made her way across the carpet to her computer. He followed her, all the while keeping his gun trained on Sophie. Esme had no doubt this man could look at the computer screen and kill her daughter simultaneously and without breaking a sweat.

Esme swallowed some saliva and touched the power

button on the machine. Nothing happened. She touched it again. And again.

All eyes were on her now. Galileo's. Lester's. Rafe's. Sophie's.

"The plug must be loose," she said.

Galileo sighed. "Then plug it in."

She nodded and climbed behind the desk. Her left hand casually brushed against the curtains. She knelt down to the outlet. The plug wasn't loose. But she already knew that. She'd touched the power button, but she hadn't pressed it. Her left hand just as casually closed around the curtain fabric.

Galileo frowned.

Esme yanked down on the curtain. The heavy fabric popped off its rod and bunched onto the floor. Galileo, confused, arced the gun from the little girl to her, and in doing so caught a glimpse of the FBI sniper positioned on the roof across the street just moments before he fired his rifle and sent several ounces of copper and lead into Galileo's lower right ventricle. His yellow Polo shirt turned red, and he fell to his knees, then to the floor.

The dozens of agents outside the house scurried out of hiding and toward the house. Esme scurried to her family on the couch, and embraced them all, even Lester. Sophie was crying again.

"It's over," her mother said. "It's over."

30

The rain fell down in soupy buckets against the grassy Eastern countryside. Esme didn't mind. A funeral without rain was like a wedding without sunshine. Everyone stood around the fresh, muddy grave and under a makeshift tent. The rain pitter-pattered a Gene Krupa rhythm against the canvas top. Their black sunglasses concealed their wet eyes, although occasionally an errant tear would slip past the protection of the lens and appear on a cheek or lip.

A good man was in a pine box.

His body, at least, was there. That much Esme was sure of. As to questions of the soul…those were best left to scholars and poets, weren't they? There were some puzzles even she chose to avoid.

Right now, in Ohio, thousands were gathered at a megachurch in Columbus to mourn the passing of Bob Kellerman. His funeral would be private, but his memorial service was open to the public. The fact that the country's most famous atheist was being memorialized in a church, of all places, stirred a small grin inside Esme's heart. She had a feeling the populist governor wouldn't have minded, and she *knew* it would have just infuriated Galileo.

As to this far smaller affair in the Virginia country-side…

"He loved to eat," eulogized the old pastor, and the dozens in attendance nodded in agreement. Esme couldn't help but smile a little. Tom, sitting beside her, smiled a little, too. A horse-faced nurse, who went by the name of Imelda and lacked all mirth whatsoever, shadowed them both. The hospital had only agreed to allow Tom to attend Norm's funeral on the condition that he be accompanied at all times by a medical professional. On the helicopter ride down here, Tom had done his Kentucky best to charm Imelda, but she just shook her head disapprovingly and checked his pulse. He had a fresh-out-of-the-box pace-maker embedded in his chest, and these first forty-eight hours were, quite literally, critical.

The old pastor intoned his eulogy, and it was obvious he knew Norm very well. He spoke of a reckless adolescent who had notoriously egged the mayor's house one Halloween. The mayor had launched a full-scale investigation into the matter. The sneakiest junior criminals often grew up to be the wiliest detectives. Eventually it came time to bury the box. There would be no one else stepping to the podium to share their memories of Norm. He had wanted a simple service, and a simple service was what he was going to get. The service concluded, two well-dressed cemetery workers began to wheel a well-oiled winch and Norm's coffin slowly drifted into the earth.

Tom took out a notepad from the pocket of his black leather jacket and with a shaky hand scribbled a brief message. He indicated for Imelda to roll him forward, and she did, and he let the piece of paper fall down into the hole to be with his lost pal.

Esme placed a hand on Tom's shoulder. He clasped it with his own, and looked up at her. They shared a lifetime in a moment, and then the crowd began to disperse.

Tom jotted a note on his pad and handed it to her:

Come with me to my car.

Esme followed Tom to the black sedan that the government had provided to transport him from the helipad to the cemetery. Imelda helped him into the backseat. It pained Esme to watch her mentor so weak, but she took comfort in the fact that this was temporary. In a week, Tom would be speaking again. In a month, he'd be up and about without the need of a wheelchair. She had recovered, and so would he, but never fully. Her kidney, his heart…such was but a fraction of Galileo's legacy.

But they were alive.

As soon as the car door shut, Tom picked up the car phone and dialed a number. Before Esme could ask anything, he pushed the speaker button.

The phone rang once, twice, and then someone picked up: "Yes?"

That unmistakable croak could only have belonged to AD Trumbull. Why was Tom calling him? What was going on here? Why did—

"Hello?" Trumbull coughed. "For fuck's sake, is anyone there?"

"Yes, sir," Esme quickly replied. "I'm sorry, sir. It's Esme Stuart. I'm here with Tom Piper."

Silence, then: "You did good with the Galileo case, Mrs. Stuart."

Trumbull didn't sound surprised to hear from her. Esme looked to Tom for an explanation but he just replied with a mischievous grin and scratched at his day-old gray stubble.

"Tom's task force was a valuable asset and the Bureau won't find its replacement in my lifetime. Probably not even yours. We lost a lot of good people over the past few months. I don't need to tell you this."

The assistant director took a deep breath. Esme couldn't tell if it was his illness or simply the weight of the deaths on his soul.

"Regardless," he continued, "time keeps on ticking and people keep on committing acts of madness and lunacy and we need smart capable folk on our team to beat back the tide."

Esme couldn't help herself: "Sir, are you asking me out on a date?"

Tom laughed—or tried to laugh, but the pain in his chest quickly put an end to that. But despite it all, that silly smile remained plastered on his lips. Around them, the rain had tapered off into drizzle. What had been a steady knocking on the roof of the car became gentler tapping.

"Tom has made a recommendation to me and I'm going to follow it. Quite simply, Mrs. Stuart, we want you back in the fold."

Esme blinked.

Tom wrote something on his pad. He showed it to her.
Ask him for perks.

Perks?

Ah. Perks. Her face lit up. Tom nodded.

"Mrs. Stuart, are you still there?"

"If you want me back, sir, you're going to have to give me some assurances in return."

Trumbull coughed. "Go on."

"I get to stay in Long Island. I'm not uprooting my family."

"That would put you under Karl Ziegler's jurisdiction, you know. Not to mention your old friend Pamela Gould."

"Not if I'm hired as a consultant instead of a field agent."

"What's the difference?"

Esme paused. It had sounded good when she said it but what was the difference?

Leave it to Tom to provide the answer with a simple drawing:

$$$

"Consultants get paid more."

Trumbull coughed. "Go on."

"I don't work a regular shift. I can do most of the work out of my home, provided the Bureau sees fit to give my computer a major upgrade."

"Is that all?"

"I don't miss a school play. I don't miss one of my husband's lectures. I don't miss Thanksgiving or Christmas or even Earth Day. I'll close cases no one else can close—that's what you get to keep—but my family comes first. That's what I get to keep, and it's a deal-breaker."

Silence.

Had she asked for too much?

"You've always been a pain in the ass. You know that, Mrs. Stuart?"

Esme grinned. Yep. She knew that.

"I'll get the paperwork in order."

"Thank you, sir."

"You said Tom Piper's there?"

"Yes, sir. He's sitting right across from me."

"Tell him he's always been a pain in the ass too."

Click.

Tom leaned in toward her, almost romantically.

"Thank you," he whispered.

Her first case came a week after Easter Sunday. The phone rang at 5:33 a.m. It rang four times, before Esme cracked open an eyelid. It was on her night table. She watched it ring a fifth time and then it went to voice mail. And then it rang again, briefly, to let her know someone had left a voice mail. She let her eyelid shut and tried to recall her dream so as to best slip back into it. Rafe shifted in his spot on the bed. His elbow absently brushed against her lip.

Then her phone rang again, at 5:35. This time she kept her eyelid shut. She nudged Rafe's elbow away from her face, grabbed the device in the abject darkness, and brought it to an ear.

"What?" she mumbled.

"There's been a murder in Albany," said Karl

Ziegler. Despite her requests—or perhaps because of them, as one final ha-ha before he shuffled off this mortal coil—Trumbull had assigned the bureau chief to be her handler until Tom returned to active duty. "We need you to come in."

"Aunt Harriet, is that you?"

"This isn't funny, Mrs. Stuart. A young woman was stabbed forty-six times on her way home from work. Her wounds are consistent with three other victims in the Albany metro area."

"Albany has a metro area?"

"When can you be here? 6:00? 6:15?"

Now she had to open an eyelid. Damn you, Ziegler. She checked the glowing digits on her alarm clock.

"6:30," she replied. "Going, going, gone."

She hung up, was tempted to go back to sleep, but mustered her wherewithal and crawled out of bed. After the world's quickest shower, she poked Rafe until he woke up.

"I need to go to work," she said.

Ever since the incident with Galileo, things had been pleasant between them. Not good, not healthy, but pleasant. They had a lot of issues that needed resolving, but like every other suburban couple they were keeping their issues shut away, for now. Someday soon, though, they would need to have a serious talk. She had no idea what would happen after that. She hoped for the best. It was all she could do. For now, she had to settle with poking him in his cute paunch, even after he heard her, nodded and went back to sleep.

"I love you," she added, and planted a kiss on his lips.

"Love you, too," he echoed.

She slipped into a T-shirt and jeans and headed out into the hall, stopping for a minute to check in on Sophie. There was no reason to wake her, but it was nice just the same to stand and watch her daughter while she slept. Few sights in this world provided her with such complete…optimism. She took a mental photograph of her daughter, curled up with Bugs Bunny, quietly adrift in dreamland. She knew she would need that image to counter whatever horrors Karl Ziegler had waiting for her at the Federal Building in NYC.

Downstairs, Lester was already awake, and watching TV. The old man didn't sleep like other human beings. He napped on and off, sure, but more often than not he was awake and in front of that TV. His temporary visit was becoming more and more permanent. Esme hadn't objected. She needed someone to babysit Sophie while Rafe was at work and she was…well, doing whatever she was doing. This was her first case as a "special consultant." She wasn't quite sure how things were going to work. But she was hopeful.

"Where are you off to?" asked Lester, glancing away from a news report about Macao. "Jogging?"

"Work," she answered, and grabbed a strawberry Pop-Tart from the cupboard and her iPod from her computer desk.

The curtain rod, almost defiantly, had still not been replaced.

"'Work?'" Lester offered a judgmental grunt. She gave him the middle finger as she passed and entered the garage. Tom's motorcycle greeted her from the corner. They had finally managed to retrieve it from Amy Lieb's property. Esme was tempted to ride it into the city, but Tom had only given her a few lessons and that had been years ago. She looked forward to the day that Tom would show up to ride it again. She hoped that day would be soon.

She backed her Prius out of the garage and hooked her iPod into the car stereo. Perhaps it would be a warm and sunny end-of-April day, but right now the sky was dark, and starless, and cool. Esme reflected for a moment on the metaphor, then cranked up the Rolling Stones and let Mick Jagger croon her troubles away. *"Ti-i-i-ime is on my side...."*

Yes it was.

* * * * *

Acknowledgments

This time, I've decided to divide my thank-yous into three categories.

People whose last name is Corin: Alan (my dad), Sharon (my mom), Shiela (my stepmom), Heather (my sister), Seth (my brother), Noah (my other brother), Kelly (Noah's wife), and Michele (Seth's wife). Thank you all for your love, your kindness and your leftovers.

People whose last name isn't Corin: Amber Hutchison, Jordan White, Meghan McAsey, John Russo, Kristy Hamer, Jud Laghi, David Cromer and Ted Wadley. Thank you all for your friendship, your support, and your patience.

Organizations: MIRA Books (esp. Linda McFall), Georgia Perimeter College (esp. Alan Jackson), the Mystery Writers of America (esp. Margery Flax) and the International Thriller Writers (esp. the 2008-2009 Debut Authors). Thank you all for taking into your arms an insecure writer and making him feel welcome.

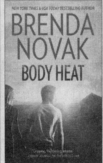

AWARD-WINNING AUTHOR

JOSEPH TELLER

Harrison J. Walker—Jaywalker, to the world—is a frayed-at-the-edges defense attorney with a ninety-percent acquittal rate, thanks to an obsessive streak a mile wide. But winning this case will take more than just dedication.

Seventeen-year-old Jeremy Estrada killed another boy after a fight over a girl. This kid is jammed up big-time, but almost unable to help himself. He's got the face of an angel but can hardly string together three words to explain what happened that day...yet he's determined to go to trial.

Jaywalker is accustomed to bending the rules—and this case will stretch the law to the breaking point and beyond.

OVERKILL

Available wherever books are sold.

MIRA®

www.MIRABooks.com

MJT2776

REQUEST YOUR FREE BOOKS!

2 FREE NOVELS
FROM THE SUSPENSE COLLECTION
PLUS 2 FREE GIFTS!

YES! Please send me 2 FREE novels from the Suspense Collection and my 2 FREE gifts (gifts are worth about $10). After receiving them, if I don't wish to receive any more books, I can return the shipping statement marked "cancel." If I don't cancel, I will receive 3 brand-new novels every month and be billed just $5.74 per book in the U.S. or $6.24 per book in Canada. That's a saving of at least 28% off the cover price. It's quite a bargain! Shipping and handling is just 50¢ per book.* I understand that accepting the 2 free books and gifts places me under no obligation to buy anything. I can always return a shipment and cancel at any time. Even if I never buy another book, the two free books and gifts are mine to keep forever.

192/392 MDN E7PD

Name _____ (PLEASE PRINT) _____

Address _____ Apt. # _____

City _____ State/Prov. _____ Zip/Postal Code _____

Signature (if under 18, a parent or guardian must sign)

Mail to **The Reader Service:**
IN U.S.A.: P.O. Box 1867, Buffalo, NY 14240-1867
IN CANADA: P.O. Box 609, Fort Erie, Ontario L2A 5X3

Not valid for current subscribers to the Suspense Collection
or the Romance/Suspense Collection.

Want to try two free books from another line?
Call 1-800-873-8635 or visit www.morefreebooks.com.

* Terms and prices subject to change without notice. Prices do not include applicable taxes. N.Y. residents add applicable sales tax. Canadian residents will be charged applicable provincial taxes and GST. Offer not valid in Quebec. This offer is limited to one order per household. All orders subject to approval. Credit or debit balances in a customer's account(s) may be offset by any other outstanding balance owed by or to the customer. Please allow 4 to 6 weeks for delivery. Offer available while quantities last.

Your Privacy: Harlequin Books is committed to protecting your privacy. Our Privacy Policy is available online at www.eHarlequin.com or upon request from the Reader Service. From time to time we make our lists of customers available to reputable third parties who may have a product or service of interest to you. If you would prefer we not share your name and address, please check here. ☐

Help us get it right—We strive for accurate, respectful and relevant communications. To clarify or modify your communication preferences, visit us at www.ReaderService.com/consumerschoice.

MSUS10R

RICK MOFINA

A young mother, thrown clear of a devastating car crash, is convinced she sees a figure pull her infant son from the flames.

In a Rio de Janeiro café, a bomb kills ten people, including two World Press Alliance journalists. Jack Gannon must find out whether his colleagues were victims or targets who got too close to a huge story.

With millions of lives at stake, experts work frantically against time. And as an anguished mother searches for her child and Jack Gannon pursues the truth, an unstoppable force hurls them all into the panic zone.

THE
PANIC
ZONE

Available wherever books are sold.

MIRA®

www.MIRABooks.com

MRM2794